TOMB OF EMPIRES

by
Rehan Khan

www.uhibbook.com

www.uhibbook.com

Published by Uhibbook Publishing
UAE
www.uhibbook.com

Cover design: Fatima Mejbil
Map illustration: Asya Leztizia

ISBN: 978-9948-738-33-6
First Edition

Ordering Information
For details contact: info@uhibbook.com

*For Fadi, without whom this book
would not have seen the light of day.*

AUTHOR'S NOTE

This novel is set in the year 90 BC, which from the prism of the 21st century does feel a long time ago. Yet many things remain the same. In Tomb of Empires, two western powers are vying for control of resources in the Middle East - it is a time of intrigue and machination, a time of imperial stratagem and subterfuge, a time of broken promises and broken hearts.

Thematically this is a novel of heroic deeds and ferocious battles, of compassion in the face of cruelty, of moderation in a time of excess, of love earned and love lost. These are perennial human conditions. What I suppose is unique, is that the empires written about in this work of fiction are not particularly well-known today.

When I ask friends, acquaintances or school teachers if they've heard of the Roman Empire, they normally affirm they have. Yet, when I ask whether they've come across the Seleucid empire, or the Ptolemaic empire, it's generally a shake of the head. Some have heard of the Nabataeans because of their close association with Petra in Jordan.

Yet the Seleucids ruled for nearly two hundred and fifty years (312BC-63BC), covering territory as vast as: Anatolia, Persia, the Levant, Mesopotamia, Kuwait, Afghanistan, and parts of Turkmenistan. The Ptolemaic empire lasted a little longer and controlled much of North Africa. Both these empires were founded by Macedonian generals who served Alexander the Great (356BC-323BC).

Yet the Seleucids, Ptolemy and the Nabataeans are lost to the collective memory, entombed. I'd like to prise open the tomb a little and narrate a fictional tale from the period, which I hope you'll agree has a contemporary feel to it.

Let us then begin our journey into this forgotten world by turning our attention to a small island off the coast of Kuwait and let us begin with the best of beginnings: In the Name of God, Most Gracious, Most Merciful.

Rehan Khan
October 2024

CONTENTS

CAST OF CHARACTERS

Aegeans

Andreas	Commander of the Aegean vessel, the Chloe
Pelagios	King of Mithymna, part of the Aegean Islands
Theron	Navigator of the Aegean vessel, the Chloe

Han Chinese

Chao Zhang	Explorer and representative of the Han Emperor
Fu Youde	Lieutenant of the Han Royal Guard
Ganfu	Cartographer to Chao Zhang
Jin Guliang	Scribe to Chao Zhang
Zhu Di	Captain of the Han Royal Guard

Hasmoneans

Alexander Jannaeus	King of the Hasmonean Dynasty
Anan Ben Jacob	Rabbi of the Sadducees sect

Nabataeans

Asylaion	Prince of Nabataea, known as the Shrewd
Fahad	Captain of the Nabataean Falcons
Fastiq	Prince of Nabataea, known as the Grim
Fazluna	Queen of Nabataea
Ghassan	General of Nabataea

Haddad	Nabataean treasury official
Hesham	Strategos of Nabataea
Luay	Nabataean quartermaster
Luja	Princess of Nabataea
Obodos III	King of Nabataea
Stylian	Prince of Nabataea, known as the Opulent
Taimur	Lieutenant of the Nabataean Falcons
Zaim	Prince of Nabataea, youngest son of Obodos

Ptolemy

Apollonia	Princess of Ptolemy
Cleopatra IV	Queen of the Ptolemaic Empire, mother of Apollonia
Corrina	Aunt of Apollonia
Ptolemy Soter IX	Ptolemaic Emperor, father of Apollonia
Zoe	Handmaiden to Apollonia

Seleucids

Achaeus	Former General of the Seleucid Empire
Antiochus	XIISeleucid Emperor
Pharnuches	General of the Seleucid Empire
Spitamenes	Commander of the Seleucid elephant legions
Tigranous	General of the Seleucid Empire
Tryphanea	Mother to Antiochus XII

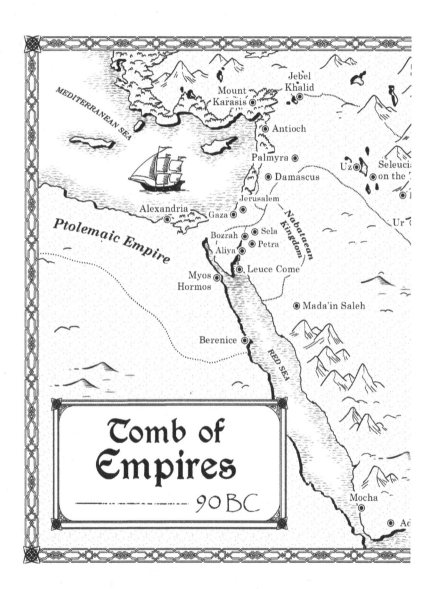

MEDITERRANEAN SEA

Mount
Karasis

Jebel
Khalid

Antioch

Palmyra

Uz

Seleuci
on the

Damascus

Alexandria

Jerusalem

Gaza

Ur

Ptolemaic Empire

Bozrah

Sela

Nabataean Kingdom

Aliya

Petra

Leuce Come

Myos
Hormos

Mada'in Saleh

Berenice

RED SEA

Tomb of Empires

90 BC

Mocha

Ad

Empires rise and fall. Some become legend, others myth, but most are lost to time.

PROLOGUE

The First Century BCE

A storm rumbled over the Seleucid Empire, from the mountain fortress of Aï Khanoun in the east, to the gardens of Antioch in the west. The storm thundered across the razor-edged crags of the Hindu Kush, where only the reaper of souls roamed freely amidst snowy peaks. Death patrolled the roof of the world, yet the storm did not stop its thrashing: it licked the high passes and roared on. Onward the tempest snarled, twisting along the foothills of the Zagros, shattering its mighty oaks and scarring ancient trails, till the wind and rain fell upon the Persian Gulf and the stone temple of the Oracle on the Failaka Island. The storm blanketed the isle, smothering it with sleet and rain. Yet as it did so, seven men remained motionless as statues. Flame-light shimmered on their metal breastplates; their cloaks flapped in the gale, the heraldic emblem of an elephant etched into the helmet of each man.

These were Seleucids, elephant lords, inheritors of Alexander the Great.

Their leader, Emperor Antiochus, stood in the centre of the seven, he was of middling height, clean-shaven, his golden breastplate and greaves catching the light of the cressets. His helmet also carried the mark of the elephant, but was inlaid with gold, with two blood-red rubies inserted into the elephant's eyes.

A reed of a man, dressed all in white, bent by the pressure of the wind, approached from the temple of Dioscuri, a one-storey square building with three columns at the front. Raising his head, the man motioned the party to enter.

'About time,' Antiochus growled.

He led the six towards the temple.

Oud-scented smoke filled the narrow entrance, as the warriors followed their sovereign in single file, removing their helmets as they entered. Once inside, Antiochus was directed to sit on the floor and his followers behind him, their armour clattering as they took up positions on the stone surface. A fire crackled before them.

Both emperor and adherents stared through the flames at the Oracle partly veiled in the shadows. A nasal voice rasped like sand rustling across shingle. 'The son seizes the mantle of the father.'

'I am honoured to be in your presence,' said Antiochus, his voice straining for self-control as he looked up at the Oracle. *She chides me before my generals,* he thought.

Wearing a brown robe, her hair matted like dried twigs, the Oracle had piercing cat-like eyes shimmering in the flame-light. She sat cross-legged upon a raised dais. Her age was indeterminate; a fossil with blood flowing through her knotty veins. Many emperors had visited her and she had outlived them all.

Stones were placed in a ring around the fire. Two priestesses of the temple, dressed in white, veiled, stood either side of the shrine. A smile creased the Oracle's lips. 'Aspirations you have, Antiochus Emperor, yet defeat you have tasted.'

Antiochus shuffled, suddenly feeling the weight of his armour. He pressed the palms of his hands to his thighs, steadying himself. He would need to wash his hands of blame, deflect the loss to Ptolemy to another. As the scent of oud filled his lungs, he thought of the perfect scapegoat – an honourable dignified man, a warrior with an outstanding reputation, a man who would not refuse any imperial command. He smiled silently to himself. That man sat faithfully behind him.

The old crone's eyes sparkled as the flames licked the air between them.

'The road to glory is paved with defeat. Such is the way of the world, so I am told,' Antiochus replied.

A grin flashed across the Oracle's face. 'So proclaims one whose ambition is thwarted.'

The emperor glared across the russet flames at the Oracle of Failaka Island, noticing her tongue for the first time, black upon black, and forked like a serpent.

'Do not be so tetchy, Antiochus Emperor; even an emperor must kneel before a higher authority.'

The Oracle continued to stare down at him, her vexing smirk ever present. Her tongue moved, sliding over her lips, with serpentine precision.

'Ask your questions, Antiochus Emperor,' she said, her feline eyes glittering behind the flame.

'What will become of my empire?'

Placing her hand inside a coal-black pot, the Oracle withdrew a handful of ash, and gently blew it from the tips of her fingers. The ash hung momentarily in the air, mixing with the scents permeating the temple, before sinking to the ground before her. She repeated this twice, before turning to gaze at the pattern forming on the ground. She wiped the ash with the tips of her fingers and sat back to stare at it.

Outside, a clap of thunder shook the building. The men stirred behind him. It was not a good omen, but Antiochus kept his gaze firmly upon the Oracle. The crone's eyes seemed to twinkle at first, but then the emperor read uncertainty in them, followed by doubt.

'What do you see, Oracle?' he asked.

'Battles will be fought, with old enemies and … new. Treaties will be broken, others forged.'

'Yes,' Antiochus enquired.

The Oracle continued. 'Ptolemy and Nabataea, an alliance forged from a marriage…'

'Marriage?' Antiochus said in disgust.

'The daughter of Ptolemy and the son of Obodos…'

The Oracle tilted her head to one side, as though contemplating what to say next from her reading of the ash marks.

'Yet the downfall of Ptolemy is close …'

He leant forward. *This was more like it*, he thought.

'The Eagle of Rome will rise …'

That is unwelcome news, Antiochus considered.

'For the time of the Elephant Lords … nears its end.'

The emperor clenched his fists.

The wizened witch shielded her sight with her hands as though about to cry out. 'A light, shining so bright, rising from the desert, relentless! It will leave behind a tomb of empires.'

The Oracle screamed.

Silence descended on the temple, only the crackling flames making a sound. The Oracle sat motionless before reaching for a bowl of water, throwing it over the ash marks.

This was nonsense. Antiochus had not travelled so far to be ridiculed. 'Tell me something of substance, woman,' he ordered.

'I have relayed the reading,' the crone rasped, as though a hefty weight pinned her shoulders down.

Antiochus struggled to control his rage. He stood abruptly, his adherents following suit, armour rattling on stone. The emperor's hand moved to the hilt of his weapon. *I cannot*, he told himself.

This was a ridiculous custom; he would not return.

Awkwardly the Oracle peered again at the ash marks. Her tongue, black on black, slithered across her lips.

'Antiochus Emperor …'

'Yes,' he spat.

'Beware the day the Dragon enters the Falcon,' the Oracle declared in a solemn voice.

He halted, turning to stare at her, before leading his followers out into the pelting rain and placing his helmet upon his head.

Once outside the emperor turned to stare at his six generals.

'Tigranous,' Antiochus addressed the tallest warrior, broad as an ox. 'Find out which Princess of Ptolemy is being wedded to the Nabataean Arabs. Have her kidnapped and bring her to Damascus. If she is pleasing in appearance, I will take her as a bride, otherwise I will keep her captive.'

'Yes, my Emperor,' Tigranous replied.

'Achaeus,' the emperor tuned to his most accomplished general.

'You will travel to Alexandria, negotiate a truce with Ptolemy. I will provide you the terms.'

Achaeus hesitated, before saying. 'Yes, my Emperor.'

And Antiochus thought, *since you Achaeus are the most honourable man amongst us, the most decent Seleucid, you can also be sacrificed, for these are indecent times, which call for indecent men.*

'Pharnuches,' Antiochus said.

'Yes, my Emperor.'

'Romans! Squeeze their spy networks, unearth them, then bury them. Be sure nothing can be traced back to any Seleucid. Use mercenaries if you must.'

'I will, my Emperor,' Pharnuches replied.

The emperor glanced back at the temple. Shaking his head. He addressed his generals again. 'What of this Falcon?'

'Elite Nabataean soldiers are known as *Falcons*,' said Tigranous. 'Their commander is Prince Zaim. We could …'

'Have him killed. We will not let the seeds of our destruction sprout in the desert.'

'Yes, my Emperor,' Tigranous replied.

'In fact,' said Antiochus. 'The Nabataean's have for too long profited from the spice routes. It's about time we relieved them of their duties. Tigranous, make sure it happens. Seize the spice.'

'It will be done,' said Tigranous.

'What of this "Dragon"?' asked Antiochus.

All the generals shook their heads.

'Send pigeons to all cities. I want to know what this Dragon is. Is it a person, a weapon, something else?'

Lightning lit up the sky overhead, highlighting a group of decrepit figures huddled by a ghaf tree.

'Who are they?' Antiochus asked.

'Local villagers,' Tigranous said. 'They've come to seek the emperor's mercy.'

Antiochus snarled. He was not having a good day. 'Put them to the sword.'

Chapter 1

ALEXANDRIA

Three months later

———————

Having lived a life of luxury in the palace of Alexandria, tall brunette Apollonia knew from overhearing conversations between servants in her household that these men and women subsisted in poor conditions. Yet despite their impoverishment they were cheerful and content with their place in the world, whereas her own family, the ruling dynasty of the Ptolemaic Empire, governing lands across North Africa, in possession of incredible wealth, were miserable and melancholy. Even as a sixteen-year-old princess with little experience outside the palace, she knew something was amiss.

Her family members spent hours bemoaning what might have been and calculating where they went wrong. Or they would be fussing over what might be and how they could position themselves for influence in the royal court. Her two older brothers were contending for who would succeed her father, Ptolemy Soter, as monarch of the empire. As were her two older sisters, whose furious hunger for power rivalled that of her brothers. She would not be surprised if one of them were to succeed her father as sovereign.

Apollonia herself desired neither power nor influence.

It was most likely for this reason she was being married off to a prince of a faraway desert kingdom.

From the balcony outside her chambers, Apollonia contemplated the blue waters of the Mediterranean embracing the coast of Alexandria. Water and lots of it, full of aquatic life. When the cool sea breeze of early winter touched her skin Apollonia felt alive and she thought: *What is the desert like? Will I miss the fresh gusts of the sea, hearing the spray of waves, seeing the fishermen bring in their daily catch?* She sighed deeply, her hands in her lap, feeling the silk on her skin. *What does the desert feel like? Not like this, but most likely coarse and gritty.*

Her mood was sombre and reflective, but in the palace, others were celebrating the recent victory over the Seleucid empire. It had been a humiliating defeat for Emperor Antiochus and he had sent an envoy, the legendary warrior and Seleucid General Achaeus, to agree terms with her father's court. The task Achaeus had been given was an unenviable one and the man was, according to servants' gossip, humiliated by her father's courtiers.

To deter the Seleucids from launching another campaign soon, her father had reached out to the desert Arabs, the Nabataeans, who controlled a kingdom extending from their mountain stronghold of Petra down to the desert of Hegra in northern Arabia, as well as along trade routes up from Aden and Mocha in the south, routes which carried spice and silks from India, the Han empire, and Indonesia. The Nabataeans were traders who had begun to influence the politics of the region. They were also a thorn in the side of the Seleucids. Forming an alliance through marriage between Ptolemy and Nabataea would position the Arabs as a prickly ally right under the belly of the Seleucids. That would give Emperor Antiochus something to think about, her father said.

Apollonia was only a piece on the board in the game of empires and she knew it. Her hand reached out to the recurve bow she always kept close, and which she found solace in during times of stress. She had little practical use for it, neither did she need to hunt nor fight, but nonetheless had become quite adept at using it under the guidance of her mother's bodyguards. She pulled the bowstring back and imagined firing an arrow up and out into the blue sky, out into the heavens and further still. What would the arrow come across? *A God out on the sea watching the fishermen? A God up in the sky watching the city? A God watching over me?* she doubted the last part.

The princess felt the warm fur of Javairea, her cat, against her ankles. Putting the bow down she lifted Javairea onto her lap. The cat, well attuned to what was going to happen next, curled into a comfortable position, as Apollonia rubbed it from the crown of its head down through the back of its neck. Javairea purred in pleasure, eyes closing, all but asleep as her mistress continued to stroke her.

'I know you won't like it, all that sand under your paws, but you are going to have to get used to it, Javairea. Just as I am. You and I, we have no choice.'

The princess heard sandalled feet crossing her chambers, then the familiar voice of her handmaiden Zoe.

'Your Highness?' enquired Zoe. 'The wedding dress has arrived back from the dressmaker.'

A girl should be joyful to see the ensemble she will be wearing on the most important day of her life, but Apollonia struggled to feel any enthusiasm, and continued to sit in silence.

'Your Highness?' Zoe called.

Taking a deep breath, she replied. 'I am on the balcony Zoe.'

Stout, mousy-haired Zoe, only a few years older than the princess, appeared through the curtains. 'Don't you want to see the dress, your Highness?'

'Come on Javairea, let us delight in the dress.'

'It's magnificent, your Highness,' Zoe said, clearly having noticed her forlorn expression.

'I am sure it is,' said Apollonia, parting the netted curtains as she followed her handmaiden into her labyrinthine chambers, Javairea tucked close to her feet, criss-crossing her path as she liked to. 'One day I am going to trip over you,' Apollonia chided her pet, which dashed out of sight.

A mahogany bed with nets around it stood against the southern wall, before which was a Persian rug with deep rustic red print. Two large cupboards adorned with mosaics were placed against the northern end of the room. Between them was a set of rugs and cushions. Closest to her was a sturdy table on which were stained glasses and jars, containing sherbets topped with slices of lemon. Oud burned in holders, filling the room with the scent of white jasmine.

Zoe had laid the dress on the bed; when Apollonia looked at it there was no denying it, it was magnificent. The green gown for her wedding day was embroidered with flowers and geometric designs and a cream-coloured belt separated the upper and lower parts of the dress. Emeralds were stitched into the neckline as well as the cuffs. The skill of the seamstress was displayed in the finished garment.

'What do you think, your Highness?' enquired Zoe eagerly.

'Matchless, I have never seen such fine embroidery.'

'I knew you'd like it,' continued Zoe. 'The Queen will be up shortly; would you like me to pack this away in the meantime?'

Mother. She sulked at the thought of speaking to her. Throughout Apollonia's young life her parents had had little time for her, particularly as she showed no desire to participate in the politics of the royal court.

'You can leave it.'

'Isn't it exciting? We'll be departing for the desert kingdom within the week. Who knows what we might see along the way?'

'I can't imagine there is much to enjoy in the desert.'

'The journey, your Highness, the journey! I have never been outside Alexandria, and to think that I will now be travelling so far by sea, then caravan!'

'But it's a desert kingdom we are journeying to.'

'Oh but the emptiness – there is divine majesty in that. The stars forming a canopy overhead, a serene stillness amongst the dunes. I'd take that any time, rather than the bustling overcrowded lanes of Alexandria. Any time.'

How strange, thought Apollonia, studying Zoe. *She means it. She would rather live in a wilderness than a city. Am I missing something? No, surely not: the comforts and delights of an urban existence will always surpass those of a desolate tract of land.*

'Queen Cleopatra!' a female voice announced from the doorway.

The queen's female guard always announced the arrival of the monarch just moments before she made her entrance.

'I'll be on my way then, your Highness,' Zoe said, tucking up her long hemp skirt, before making for the servants' exit, at the rear of the chamber.

The next moment, Apollonia's glamorous mother, Cleopatra IV, swanned into the room, her long neck bedecked with a necklace of pearls from the island of Tylos. Her soft skin was a tone of olive and the waves of her brunette hair like those of the sea, folding one into another. She stood as tall as Apollonia and was still immensely handsome, despite being mother to five children. Her figure was striking, as was the dress she wore, with its low neckline.

Apollonia observed the firmness of her mother's figure, her graceful movements, noticed the piqued expression on her face. Others might have missed that trifling look of tetchiness but not a daughter of Cleopatra, who had been schooled at court to read the intricacies of facial and bodily movements.

She prefers red rubies and green emeralds but today she wears pearls from the Persian Gulf. She is telling me something.

'My daughter,' Cleopatra said with the formality reserved for court – but then, both her parents spoke to their children in the same manner.

'Mother,' said Apollonia, taking her mother's hand and kissing it.

Javairea was back by Apollonia's ankles, moving about in the hem of her dress. Cleopatra detested cats and Javairea seemed to sense this, always being present when Apollonia's mother visited, which was rare.

Cleopatra exclaimed at the sight of the cat, 'Remove it before I have it taken away.'

'Yes, Mother,' replied Apollonia, lifting Javairea into her arms and taking the cat to the servants' exit. Javairea would soon return, but she was out of the way for now.

Cleopatra turned, studied the wedding dress, walked over to it. 'Your outfit?' she said. Cleopatra rubbed the fabric and eyed the stitching. 'They should have cut it a bit tighter around the bust.'

'I like it loose, Mother,' replied Apollonia.

'Humph,' scoffed the queen. 'You are supposed to look desirable on your wedding night, not like a sack stuffed with half-rotten onions. Have you tried it on?'

'I have, Mother, and it fits well.' She would try it on at some point, she thought to herself.

Cleopatra threw back her head. 'I don't want a daughter of mine giving a poor first impression of who her parents are.'

'I won't, Mother.'

'Make sure you don't,' said the queen, spinning on her heel. 'Come, sit,' she motioned towards two high-backed chairs close to the nets leading onto the balcony.

Once seated, Cleopatra glanced around the room, as though taking in her daughter's chambers for the first time.

'Daughter, you should know that this journey you are about to take, is vitally important to your father and me.'

And Apollonia thought: *Straight to matters of statecraft. No concern about how I am feeling before this journey.* 'I do, Mother.'

'Excellent. The Arabs, these Nabataeans, are a nomadic people who have finally settled and inhabited cities – Petra and Hegra being the most prominent. Though there are others, such as Bozrah and Aela. However, they have not discarded their nomadic roots; they still like to stay in tents most of the time. You will need to tread carefully, learn their ways, understand their politics. A century before we would not have entertained even talking to them, but they have potential, and most importantly they can be an annoyance for the Seleucids.'

The breeze picked up, the nets billowing out, momentarily obscuring her mother from view, before the wind settled.

Cleopatra continued, 'The Nabataeans control the spice routes from Aden to Gaza, after which the spice is sent across the Mediterranean and further afield. This trade is lucrative. The Nabataeans have learned to maximise their profits and conceal their wealth, building monuments within mountains and cave systems, rarely displaying opulence, but our spies know they hoard their treasures. Spice is critical to their wealth. The Seleucids also know this and, having emptied their own treasury fighting us, they need to replenish their wealth, and the fastest way to do this is to take control of the spice trade.'

So, this is it. I am being sent to a land where war is imminent. For the Seleucids to take the spice, they will need to seize Petra. I am even more dispensable than I thought.

'What would you have me do, Mother?'

Cleopatra smiled. 'Charm the Nabataeans. You are after all a daughter of Cleopatra. Win them over, captivate and mesmerise them, enrapture and fascinate them as a princess of Ptolemy. War will be upon them soon, so give them something to fight for, as in times of conflict people need a beacon to rally around. You are Ptolemaic royalty, and these desert Arabs will never have seen someone like you. Make them proud of their newly formed alliance with Ptolemy because life for the Nabataeans is about to get gruelling. Antiochus will marshal his forces to capture their spice routes. He will come at them from every angle. They will need to remain strong, firm in their conviction, confident in their alliance with Ptolemy. We need them to keep the Seleucids busy. You, daughter, are the key to that, for you will represent all of us by your presence amongst them. Seeing you in their ranks will embolden them to fight harder.'

'And will Father send them reinforcements?'

The queen opened her mouth to say something but paused. 'It will be for them to ask.'

'But will Father answer?'

'It depends on how they ask,' Cleopatra retorted. 'Now enough of this talk. Are we clear on what you must do?'

Apollonia let out a long breath. 'We are, Mother.'

'Good child. Your Aunt Corrina will accompany you on the journey, along with Zoe. Corrina will represent the royal family, attend your wedding and then return. All three of you will sail to Gaza with Pelagios, King of Mithymna, friend to all, enemy to none. He will hand you safely over to the Nabataeans in Bozrah, from whence you will travel to Petra for your wedding to Prince Fastiq, eldest son of King Obodos and Queen Fazluna. Is this clear?'

'Yes, Mother.'

'Good,' said Cleopatra gripping the armrests of her chair and standing. Apollonia also rose. 'We are done.' She held out her hand and Apollonia kissed it.

As the queen turned to leave, Apollonia called out to her. 'Mother!'

Cleopatra paused. 'Yes.'

'I dreamt of the desert.'

'What did you see?'

'A great city built into the mountains, surrounded by sand, and high above a falcon soaring, watching me … as a protector would.'

As God would, if I knew where to find Him? she thought.

'It is a good omen. The Nabataean elite guard are known as the Falcons.'

The Falcons, pondered Apollonia, before asking, 'Mother, do you … do you think I will ever see Alexandria again?'

Cleopatra turned slightly towards her daughter. 'Do not have such high expectations, daughter, for you are now of the desert, and the desert does not give back what it takes.'

Chapter 2
AELA

It is said that trade is the handmaiden of cultural exchange, a tributary along which commerce flows, facilitating the meeting of nations and the interchange of goods and services. The port of Aela, known as the bride of the Red Sea, was once one such brook in the stream of commerce carrying spice and silks from east to west. Vessels with bulky square sails and nimbler triangular ones docked in its harbour, where port hands busied themselves with the unenviable task of loading and unloading holds under the steady watch of stern port masters.

One such vessel, the *Falcon*, a Nabataean ship laden with spices, softly swayed in the harbour, as the aloes, frankincense, myrrh, musk, pepper, cinnamon, cloves and ginger it had taken on board in Aden were offloaded. During the process, the Nabataean prince under whose command the *Falcon* sailed, let out a sigh of relief. The voyage up from Aden had been a success, both in terms of profit and absence of incident.

He knew these were unsettled times with Nabataea's larger imperial neighbours – the Ptolemys and the Seleucids – waging war against one another. The twenty-year-old Prince Zaim of Nabataea found himself wondering *What does this mean for us? Will war spill over into Arabia? Thank God our land has been spared bloodshed so far.*

Tall and broad, with a close-cropped beard, and a thick head of black hair which curled at the nape, the Nabataean lord surveyed the horizon, gazing intently out to sea. Where the water met the sky, a crimson haze had settled: a storm, he supposed, or something more menacing, as though a reddish sore erupted from the bowels of the earth. Unusual for early winter.

He swung his gaze back to his vessel. Haddad, an experienced Nabataean treasury official, was handling the unloading of the *Falcon*. Haddad was a balding middle-aged man, with thick bushy eyebrows conveying a demeanour of seriousness – always useful in a negotiation, as far as Zaim was concerned.

'Do we have buyers?' Zaim asked.

'Yes, my lord,' Haddad responded, checking over the manifest.

'At the price we want?'

'More than what we asked for, my lord. Conflict between the Seleucids and Ptolemy has driven prices up. We are to make quite a profit.'

'Haddad,' Zaim said, 'we must maintain our margin but let us not take advantage of the situation and overcharge our buyers.'

Haddad shook his head. 'No, my lord, we will not.'

The prince was pleased to have Haddad on the *Falcon*: he was the most honest treasury official in the empire. A scrupulous official would always find work as part of his crew and a fair price charged to customers was eternally appreciated when others were raking in the profits.

The crew were singing: Winds from the east. Storms from the north. The *Falcon* rises above it all.

A man with short spiky hair and a forked beard hung on the rigging of the *Falcon*. Zaim called out to him, 'Taimur.'

'Your Highness,' answered his lieutenant, the finest bowman in Nabataea, as well as one of the most accomplished musicians to play the *rababa*, a single stringed instrument which soothed the soul on cold desert nights.

'Fahad and I will be in town. Come find us if you need anything,' instructed Zaim.

'Yes, Sire.'

Joined by the long-haired Captain Fahad, the prince set off from the pier, striding into Aela. Fahad's curved blade fitted elegantly in its scabbard, and his sword belt was bedecked with an array of knives. Soon the two of them had left the port and entered the noisy colourful souk with its spice and silk merchants, carpenters and metalsmiths, jewellers and embroiderers. A mixture of locals and those coming off the pier were packed tight along its narrow lanes.

'What did you learn from your informants in Aela?' Zaim asked.

'Ptolemy gloats in victory. The Seleucids fume and the Romans spin a web across the region, transparent for now, but in time they will tug the web closed.'

The prince pursed his lips. 'You think the Romans have it in them to confront the Emperors Ptolemy and Antiochus?'

'They have already subdued the remnants of Alexander's Greek empire; is it not inevitable they will move east against the Seleucids in Anatolia and Ptolemy in Africa?'

'What of our region?' Zaim demanded.

Fahad shook his head. 'I do not know, your Highness.'

As he walked up the partly paved path into town, Zaim could not help thinking about what he had seen on the horizon: the sky a fuming bruising volcanic red. *Is it a sign of what is to come*, he wondered.

'Does the Roman net reach Gaza and Jerusalem?' Zaim asked.

'I believe it does, Sire; reputedly they have informants across this region. Many were in the pay of the Seleucids, but have changed allegiances, though of course they are still being paid by the Seleucids who have not comprehended this switch in loyalty.'

'And in Arabia?'

'I do not think so, but I believe they will send agents into Nabataean territory to assess our strengths and our weaknesses.'

Disunity: this is our greatest weakness, easy to spot and even easier to exploit, reflected the prince.

'And the Hasmonaean king, Alexander Jannaeus, in Jerusalem?' asked Zaim.

Fahad shrugged. 'He goads the Seleucids, but then the Seleucids are not what they used to be, and we do not know what the Romans will become. The Jewish king treads a fine line. It would be a shame to see the holy city sacked once more.'

The Temple of Solomon, the wise prophet of the Israelites, was a sacred site for all *hunafa*, monotheists, such as Zaim who held to the Abrahamic teachings and awaited the coming of the Messiah.

'We do not want to get caught between the Seleucids and Romans over Jerusalem, Sire,' added Fahad.

The prince thought: *No, indeed we do not, but Jerusalem is worth protecting, for it is holy. Nabataeans have always been traders, but our success is now drawing the attention of imperial powers. This is a dangerous time for us. We must not get caught in their war.*

'I want the guidance of my father in these matters. When will we be ready to leave for Petra?'

'Tomorrow, my lord,' Fahad replied.

'Let us pray for an easy passage. I want to get there as early as possible. My brother Fastiq is to be married to the Ptolemaic Princess, Apollonia, and there will be matters related to the wedding to prepare for. I do not know what this alliance with Ptolemy will bring to our people but it is already bringing unwanted attention from the Seleucids.'

'Yes, my lord, but to think a princess of the Ptolemaic empire will be marrying a Nabataean prince. Quite something, Sire.'

'No doubt the Seleucids and Romans have also noticed,' Zaim said, rubbing his forehead. *Does my brother Fastiq appreciate the risk we are taking by agreeing to this union? But then he is not known as "The Grim" without reason.*

'Sire, is there anything else you would have me do?'

'No, you are free to do as you please; you and the men have worked hard.'

'Then I will take my leave of you, as I have an old aunt in town, who I must pay my respects to.'

'And send my best wishes to her, Fahad.'

'Thank you, my prince, for it is said *the stars in the heavens above are not enough to explain my love for you. You are like my mother and my best friend all in one. Oh, dear aunt, in my heart and in my thoughts you always remain.*'

The prince smiled as he watched the captain depart and thought, *Fahad has a poem for every occasion. One day I will catch him lost for words, but then again, I hope not to.*

He decided to pass along the main thoroughfare in Aela, with its merchants' guilds and port masters' offices. Ahead of him was a hill which he strode towards. A crude pathway had been made up one side. The walk was hazardous, with loose pebbles and crumbling crevices; the drop to his left was sheer. Reaching the apex, Zaim eyed the pier beneath, his heart warming as he saw the *Falcon* docked below and its crew. Fine men they were, and he was privileged to serve them.

Behind him Zaim heard boots scuffing the earth. He turned to see two armed men approaching, their faces veiled, only their eyes visible. Then two more, coming up the path he had just taken. Similarly equipped with swords.

'You are Prince Zaim, son of Obodos?' the short stocky one said.

The prince regarded the four men, thinking *Who sent them?* 'I am.'

'Then you are a dead man,' came the reply.

Swords raised, the two who had come from behind lunged with vicious intent. The prince's sword was out in a single swift movement, and he blocked the first blow, before ducking and swivelling past the second attacker.

'I want no trouble,' Zaim said. 'If it is money you need, I can spare it.'

'We've already been paid,' replied the stocky assailant.

Assassins. Someone wants me dead.

'Who sent you?' asked Zaim.

Silence.

'I said, who sent you?'

The stocky assassin leapt forward, sword swinging for his chest. Zaim took a step back, then caught the man's wrist with this own sword, causing the assassin to drop his weapon. Zaim rolled forwards and drove his blade through the belly of the man standing beside the stocky one. Instinctively, Zaim leapt out of the way as the third attacker thrust his steel into the ground where he'd been moments before. The prince's weapon slashed the man's Achilles tendon, forcing him down, before he opened his windpipe. The fourth assassin brought his blade down, causing Zaim to drop to his knee to parry the blow, before he kicked away the man's legs and plunged his blade into the assailant's chest. Finally, he turned back to the stocky attacker who was nursing his wrist.

'I asked you a question, who sent you?'

'You've troubled the Elephant Lords for the last time,' the stocky man said, as he whipped out a concealed knife and threw it at the prince. The Nabataean lord shifted his weight, moving his chest out of the way of the blade which missed him by an inch, before he leapt into the air and brought his weapon down on the man's neck.

Silence.

Pools of crimson stained the ground. His hands shook as he eyed the corpses. *What madness is this?* Zaim thought. *I have taken the lives of four men, four souls. I have sent them back to the Creator, but who am I to have done such a thing?* He hated fighting, detested it, for it always ended in bloodshed.

The Nabataean prince took a calming breath, noticing a bead of sweat falling from the bridge of his nose. He cleaned his weapon and sheathed it.

Out before him a bleeding horizon with a purple sea and ochre sky told of worse to come.

Chapter 3
ROME'S AGENT

Apollonia watched the Ptolemaic legislators in the foyer below, from her position one floor up on the balcony of the legislature in Alexandria. The politicians spoke belligerently about humiliating the Seleucid envoy. Magnanimity in victory was a virtue, so Apollonia had been taught by her tutors, but perhaps these administrators had not learned such from their teachers.

Behind Apollonia the arched doors to the emperor's private visiting chamber swung open and the humbled Seleucid envoy, legendary warrior and Seleucid general, Achaeus, strode out, red in the face. He was alone. Achaeus clenched his fists, looking left and right, before spotting Apollonia and her mother Cleopatra by her side. The illustrious Achaeus composed himself, straightened his posture and bowed to them, then marched away.

'A decent man by all accounts, a widower as well,' Cleopatra said, more to herself before turning to Apollonia. 'Come child, your father awaits.'

Cleopatra guided her daughter towards the colossal terrace, where Apollonia halted momentarily, her breath was always taken away by the stunning view of the Mediterranean below.

'Ah daughter, come! Sit,' said Emperor Ptolemy Soter, rising and giving Apollonia a fatherly hug before smiling serenely at his wife. Apollonia sat opposite her father in a chestnut-coloured chair, with a gold leaf finished wooden frame, cabriole feet and several plush cushions. Cleopatra took up a seat beside the emperor.

'Apollonia my dear...' her father was saying, when his attention was caught by an official at the door.

Ptolemy instructed the man: 'Send him in.'

Moments later an announcer at the door declared: 'Pelagios, King of Mithymna.'

Apollonia had learned from her mother Cleopatra, shortly before arriving for this appointment that Mithymna, was an island in the Aegean, nestled amongst the imperial powers of Greece, Ptolemy, and Rome. Each empire sought to control the island as a strategic outpost from which to launch offensive moves against the others, as well as cherishing the vines grown on it. King Pelagios of Mithymna had somehow throughout his reign managed to be a friend to all, enemy to none and it enabled him to trade lucratively anywhere in the Mediterranean and further afield.

As he entered Apollonia observed that he had some grey in his golden-brown hair and beard and was of medium height, with a solid frame. His arms and fingers were thickened by years of seafaring, and his skin deeply tanned. He donned a disarming, almost boyish smile as the emperor rose to greet him with an embrace.

'My dear friend,' Ptolemy declared.

Pelagios turned to Cleopatra and bowed politely, then took in Apollonia for the first time, and unsure who she was, bowed once more.

'You already know my lovely wife Cleopatra, and this is my delightful daughter, Apollonia, our youngest,' Ptolemy said before directing Pelagios to a seat.

'A pleasure to also meet you Princess Apollonia,' Pelagios said.

Glasses of lemon sherbet were served by a male servant who then departed, leaving the four alone.

'How is your dear wife, the Lady Cassandra?' enquired Ptolemy.

'As well as can be but awaiting my imminent arrival as the sailing season nears its end. And I too am looking forward to returning home.'

'Home, yes. We all crave the embrace of what we hold most dear.' The emperor chuckled, turning towards Cleopatra, who merely sat in a regal posture.

Apollonia wondered if there was a concealed meaning in her

father's words.

'Your children, how old are they now?' the emperor enquired.

The Aegean king shifted in his seat. 'In their eighth and sixth years.'

'Boy and girl, if I remember rightly?'

'Yes,' Pelagios replied sipping his sherbet.

'Good, good to have children. I have so many that I have lost count,' Ptolemy said, waving his arms about as though it were nothing to do with him.

Even Apollonia at her delicate age knew her father had five children with her mother, Cleopatra, but then there were rumours of other children with concubines. Apollonia brushed the thought from her mind.

Ptolemy rubbed his chin. 'Our youngest jewel here, Apollonia has been betrothed to one of the Nabataean princes. I know, it's certainly unconventional sending a child of such beauty to live with the Arabs in the desert, but the Nabataeans have proven to be useful allies: they have commercial acumen, they make a tidy profit from their control of the spice route from Aden to Gaza.'

'My congratulations to the Princess and to you as parents on the forthcoming wedding,' Pelagious said. 'But…'

'Yes,' Ptolemy said.

Pelagios leant forward in his seat. 'Do you mean to fight a war with the Seleucids by proxy in Arabia?'

'Ah, this is what I like about you, Pelagios, you see straight through to the heart of the matter. Yes.'

He is very frank, pondered Apollonia. *Other rulers I have met speak with double meaning.*

The emperor smiled, leaning forward in his chair, hands still gripping the armrests. 'I summoned you here today, as there is something very important, I want you to attend to. I need you to take Apollonia to Gaza, then Bozrah, where you will be met by the Nabataeans, who will take her south to Petra.'

'But I am sailing west, home to Mithymna, before the weather turns,' Pelagios replied.

So, he does not know that he is taking me to the Nabataeans as mother indicated, thought Apollonia. *Is that why father and mother asked me to attend today, the Aegean king needed some convincing.*

'You will be sailing east, Pelagios,' Ptolemy said as though it were a matter of fact.

'I do not want to see out the winter stranded in some godforsaken port far from home.'

'You will be handsomely rewarded for this one task, Pelagios. More gold for one short sea voyage from Alexandria to Gaza, than in an entire season's earnings.'

Pelagious appeared uncomfortable at the mention of payment, his cheeks becoming redder than they already were.

'Why me? Surely you have your own fleet, capable captains and crew for such a voyage?'

'My vessels are needed for … let us just say the Romans are rooting about the north coast of Africa a little too much these days. Besides, I need someone who is seen as a neutral to take Apollonia to Gaza, in a vessel that will not be attacked by Seleucids nor anyone else. The *Chloe* and its crew are the perfect choice.'

Is father planning a pre-emptive strike on Roman positions along the coast? The palace officials are certainly jubilant following victory over the Seleucids, considered Apollonia.

The Aegean king took a deep breath, staring out to the coast where the azure waters of the Mediterranean washed against the coastline of Alexandria. 'I will take the Princess Apollonia, but you should know I earn a considerable amount from a season of trade.'

The emperor smiled. 'I know exactly what you earn from a season, Pelagios. Exactly.'

Once more the Aegean king shifted uncertainly in his seat.

'Then if there is nothing else, I will return to my crew and inform them of our new destination,' declared Pelagios. 'There will be groans so you had best ensure the gold is ready for when we depart.'

'I have already had it sent to your vessel. It will be there when you arrive.'

A flush of anger heated Pelagios face. *My,* thought Apollonia, *father has the measure of the man.*

The Aegean rose from his seat but the emperor held up a hand. 'One more thing, Pelagios. The Seleucid envoy and warrior Achaeus requires passage to Gaza. His own emperor Antiochus seems to have abandoned him, recalling all other diplomats and vessels. I have told Achaeus he is to voyage with you and that his trip is paid for by my court. Do the man a favour – he has already been disgraced by many of my legislators – drop him off in Gaza.'

'You know my history with Seleucids; though I do not take sides against them, I do not let them sail upon the *Chloe*.'

'He is not that scoundrel Tigranous, the beast of Antiochus who pillages at his pleasure. I know what happened to your sister and her children at his hands and offer you my deepest sympathy. But Achaeus is an honourable man, if such a one can exist amongst the Seleucids.'

Pelagios bit his lip.

Even Apollonia had heard of the legendary Achaeus, a man of heroic virtue, even if he was a Seleucid.

Letting out a long sigh, Pelagious said, 'I will take him.'

****

The visit to Ptolemy weighing heavy on his mind, Pelagios did not return to the *Chloe* yet as he had one more errand to run. After shaking off the spies the Alexandrians had clearly ordered to follow him, he was finally able to double back past the Library of Alexandria.

The Aegean ruler took the path he had been instructed to take – right at the wellhouse, left at the lemon tree, then past the stonemasons, and under the arches on the right. He swiftly moved through a wooden doorway, the top of which brushed his head, after which he found the tailor in his shop. He was an old man, with a crooked nose and deep wrinkles over his ancient brow. But his gaze was penetrating, taking in Pelagios in one clean sweep.

'Vine leaves are best harvested in the early summer sun,' Pelagios declared.

'And what of grapes?' enquired the tailor.

'Pluck them when they are at their prime, and the wine will

be divine.'

The old man chuckled, then indicated to Pelagios he should go through the curtain at the back of the shop. 'Down the stairs. He is expecting you.'

'Thank you.'

The Aegean followed the tailor's instructions, walking down wooden stairs into the basement. The interior was sparse, but for a table with two seats, one of which was occupied by a man in a white toga embroidered in black. Clean-shaven, with a high forehead and sharp nose, he gave Pelagios a terse smile, motioning him to the seat opposite.

He was never told the names of the Roman spies and informants, for their own protection, but they all knew him and who he was – an agent of Rome. *Damn the Romans*, thought Pelagios. *They have snared me in their web, and as much as I try, there is no way to get free. Damn them.*

'What does Ptolemy Soter ask of you?'

'He wants me to take his daughter Apollonia to Gaza, then Bozrah, where the Nabataeans will collect her. I will then sail for home.'

The Roman agent nodded. 'Predictable. The crew of the *Chloe* are regarded as neutrals. It makes sense in this time of conflict.'

The Aegean ruler rubbed the tips of his fingers together. They always had some tasks for him: to undertake some surveillance and keep their spy networks fresh with information. *I might as well ask and get this over with*, he thought.

'You have any requests?' asked Pelagios.

The Roman agent raised an eyebrow. 'Why so hasty, King Pelagios?'

'Let's say I don't like sitting in underground cellars: it reminds me too much of the grave.'

'Well then, let me get straight to the matter at hand. Did Ptolemy speak of any plans for action against Roman positions?'

Pelagios did not know Ptolemy well enough to make a considered decision as to whether he should disclose what he had heard. The Ptolemaic emperor might have fed him with intelligence on attacking Roman positions in north Africa deliberately, to see whether he would disclose it to another. Ptolemy might have suspected that the Romans had got to him, threatened his island, his people and family with extinction. It's the type of pressure Ptolemy would exert on a neighbouring kingdom. It wasn't worth parroting what he had learnt to the Romans. *Damn them instead.*

'He was more concerned about his daughter's wedding to an Arab prince. He didn't speak about any moves against Rome.'

'Really?' replied the agent. 'Curious – for I have learnt from other informants, that Ptolemy plans to move against Roman positions in north Africa.'

'Then if I were you, that is what I would relay to Rome,' replied Pelagios.

'I will,' the agent said with a sardonic smile. 'Though it is a shame you did not tell me yourself. Clearly your usefulness as an informant diminishes. Anyway, how well do you know the Nabataeans?'

Pelagios kept perfectly still. He knew them well enough; King Obodos was a self-centred ruler much like Ptolemy and Antiochus, and the Nabataean royal family loved flattery, apart from the young Zaim, with whom Pelagios had developed an avuncular relationship over the years. The lad had a good heart and a sense of virtue. His courage would no doubt get him killed one day.

'I have had some dealings with them.'

'Have you made an assessment of their military strength?'

Pelagios didn't like this line of questioning.

'Can't say I have.'

The agent adjusted the belt on his toga. 'We want you to get closer to the Nabataeans. They see you as a neutral. Use your well-earned position to discover the size of their navy, as well as their ground forces. The intelligence we have to date is sketchy, but they have a reputation, well-earned it would seem, for their control of spices in Arabia. As they've thrown their lot in with Ptolemy, we need to know the extent of their power.'

'Is Rome going to move against Ptolemy?'

The agent gave him a questioning look. 'That is for Rome to determine. We are but humble servants, doing her bidding.'

'I will do what I can,' replied Pelagios.

'You will do more than that, King Pelagios. I hear Mithymna is beautiful this time of year. We wouldn't want to see it visited by Roman legions.'

Pelagios leant forward, palms flat on the table, fingers going white with the strain. 'Little man, know your position, and what you can say to a king.'

The agent went red in the face. 'Rome wants you to go to Petra and make a proper assessment of Nabataean forces.'

'No. I sail for home once I have dropped the princess off in Bozrah. My men have worked hard this season and long to be reunited with their families.'

'Petra is your next destination after Bozrah. Make some excuse. Tell the Nabataeans that Ptolemy insisted you take his precious daughter safely into the desert and leave her with her new family.'

Pelagios' chair tilted and fell as he stood up. 'This meeting is over, nameless spy. I sail for Gaza, then journey down to Bozrah but no further.' The Aegean king whirled on his heel and made his way back up the ladder, past the frail tailor and out onto the street above. 'Damn bloody Romans,' he said under his breath, stomping away.

Chapter 4

PETRA

'When you become king, you stop thinking about yourself,'
Obodos said as he pounded a fist on the table. 'This is the advice my
father gave me. Yet when it comes to the lives of one's own children
how can one do this? It cannot be done.'

Obodos, King of the Nabataeans, did not take well the news of an
attempt on the life of his beloved son, Zaim, and this was apparent to
the young prince as he observed his father rise, move away from the
cushioned seating on the floor and march up and down the room.
He rarely displays his anger, thought Zaim. *This has rattled him more
than I thought. Perhaps I was rash, conveying the news of it before I had
undertaken my own enquiries.*

Father and son, along with the battle-hardened General Ghassan,
occupied an antechamber in the upper portion of the armoury, opposite the open-air theatre. The king's hawkish face with its angular
nose was creased in a menacing scowl. 'How dare they!' he spat,
whirling on his heels, hands clasped behind his back. 'Attempt to
kill a Nabataean Prince?'

The monarch had smooth black hair and beard; he was of medium
height, but tall enough to stand out in a crowd.

'Ghassan,' Obodos declared, turning to his old confidant and general. 'How can such an attack have occurred in our own city, in Aela,
a port we control?'

Like Zaim, the general sat in one of the cushioned chairs close
to the ground. Ghassan was older than his king, and his beard and
close-cropped hair contained strands of grey. He had a thick sunburnt

neck, a square face and piercing brown eyes.

'This is my failing, Sire; I have been too lax with port security. We have allowed assassins to enter freely into a city we control. Maybe I am just getting too old to play this game.'

Obodos pointed a finger at him. 'Old, you? Rubbish! You could beat half the soldiers in my army.'

After a moment's hesitation, Ghassan smiled wryly and said: 'Only half?'

'Ah yes, that's the spirit old friend! You aren't going anywhere so long as I am king. No, we need to think about establishing more security along trade routes, and entrances to the cities we control. Have the patrols actively watch for Seleucid agents; our alliance with Ptolemy has them lashing out. The success of the spice trade is our life blood, and Zaim, you more than your brothers are the tributary through which this river flows. They must know this, because they sent assassins after you and not your brothers. Trade routes cannot be blocked.'

'The Seleucids,' said Zaim, though he had suspected after the assassin had mentioned the Elephant Lords.

'Indubitably,' replied Obodos. 'And with the Ptolemaic alliance, matters are likely to get worse, much worse.' Turning to his general, he said, 'Ghassan, have plans drawn up showing what options the Seleucids have. Include scenarios which involve their elephant legions. I doubt they will mobilise the beasts, but they are a devious lot and I want to understand what alternatives they might have.'

'I will, my King.'

'Father,' said Zaim. 'I cannot seal myself within the walls of Petra. I must be on board the *Falcon*, sailing to ports, ensuring the spice is moving up the coast.'

'I know, son, but from now on, you don't go anywhere by yourself, anywhere. At all times you will have at least two – no, make it three guards with you.'

Obodos saw the look of consternation on his son's face. 'Do it, Zaim, or I will personally speak with Fahad and have it announced before all your men.'

'I will, Father.'

'Right,' said Obodos. 'Let's keep this news between the three of us for now. I don't want the others calling the Ptolemaic alliance into question at the first sign of aggression from the Seleucids. Zaim, I trust your men will remain silent on the matter.'

'Yes, Father. Only Fahad is aware, and he will not tell another.'

'Good,' said Obodos, releasing the tension in his shoulders as he took his seat once more. 'Ghassan, have the others come in.'

The general nodded and went out into the corridor. Soon a small group was led in by the strategos. Hesham, a man who in Zaim's estimation was incredibly smart, cunning, and ruthless: a double-edged sword Zaim had never taken into his confidence. Beside him was trusted treasury official Haddad, a regular crew member on the *Falcon*, and a reliable administrator Zaim was pleased to see. Behind him was the most handsome man in the party, Asylaion, Zaim's older brother. Despite his outward splendour, Zaim knew Asylaion was possessed of a merciless heart, for his outlook on life centred on his own needs. Zaim's uncle, Ahwas, who was the king's first minister and also brother to his mother Fazluna, trailed in at the back, with Zaim's other brother Stylian, also known as the Opulent. Stylian waddled duck-like, his enormous girth hidden by swishing robes as he finished chewing on some leftover morsel of meat before collapsing onto a cushion, which sank flat to the floor.

Servants followed behind the king's advisors, serving spiced tea and leaving trays filled with dates and figs before each person. Their task performed, the servants departed and Ghassan took his seat again beside the king. They were sitting in a small circle, and Zaim allowed his two brothers to sit closer to their father.

'Let us convene our council, the first since returning to Petra, in the month my son Fastiq is set to marry Princess Apollonia,' Obodos declared, beaming with delight. 'And where is Fastiq? He should be here.'

'Sire,' said Ahwas, who had a squint. 'Prince Fastiq was indisposed this morning. He had, it would seem, a long night.'

'Has he been drinking again?' Obodos asked.

Ahwas winced before replying. 'It would seem so.'

Why does Fastiq display such indifference? thought Zaim. *Mother must speak to him. His heavy drinking dulls his ability and mood. It will affect the relationship with his wife. What woman, let alone a Ptolemaic princess, will tolerate a drunkard as a husband? This marriage alliance is too important for it to be ruined by my brother's vices.*

'With the bride due to arrive soon,' Obodos declared, 'we cannot have such behaviour upsetting this new relationship. I will – no, his *mother* will speak to him.'

There was an uncomfortable silence in the room, before Obodos cleared this throat. 'Haddad, I think it best we first turn to the state of the treasury. How are our finances?'

'Never been better, your Highness,' said Haddad in the serious tone which Zaim was used to hearing. 'Profits are nearly double what we have taken in the best seasons.'

'We maintain a fair price?' Obodos questioned.

Haddad exchanged a look with Zaim. 'Yes, your Highness, we have not taken advantage of the turmoil caused by the wars between Ptolemy and the Seleucids.'

'Good. That is the only way. Buyers always remember the fair and just trader and return to buy from them.'

'But Father,' Asylaion interjected. 'With imperial conflicts taking place around us, it would be prudent to raise our prices. We now have additional costs related to security – and why should these eat into our profits? We are not the ones causing the insecurity.'

'You are right to raise the point,' Obodos replied. 'However, we have already built in a buffer for the security and safety of supply lines, as well as improving the margins of our best buyers so they remain indifferent to any counter-offers from the Seleucids.'

'If I may add, your Highness,' said Ghassan, before addressing Asylaion. 'My Prince would also be pleased to know we are reinforcing the defences around key cities in the coming weeks.'

Asylaion smiled, lips pursed. 'That is excellent news. Have the plans for new reinforcements sent over to me for examination.'

Ghassan exchanged a glance with the king, then said. 'Of course, my Prince.'

Why is Asylaion displaying such an interest in the reinforcement work around our cities? wondered Zaim. *His vocation has never been military and to imply that Ghassan cannot do his job is deeply insulting.*

'Haddad,' Obodos motioned for the treasury official to continue.

'Our profits are healthy,' declared Haddad, 'as the volume of orders has doubled at little additional cost to us. Buyers who would source from the Seleucids are now directly approaching us, as Seleucid supply lines have been affected by their war with Ptolemy. In previous years our excess stock was returned to suppliers, but this year the excess has found immediate currency with those taking flight from the Seleucids supply lines.'

Stylian was cleaning his tooth with a stick, before emitting a low belch. 'Good,' he said, turning to Zaim. 'Profits are healthy, aren't they, little brother.'

Zaim smiled politely.

Stylian has the mind of a child, Zaim thought. *His inability to control his consumption of worldly pleasures is rendering him ineffectual. I pray, dear brother, you one day realise this is not your purpose– to consume is the tradition of the trickster who was cast out from the Magisterial realm of the Most Bountiful. It is not the path of the ennobled who seek to return to the presence of the most Merciful.*

'The Seleucids will have noticed the surge in our profits,' Hesham the strategos declared, 'Though they have run back to lick their wounds after defeat by Ptolemy, their assessment of how to replenish their own finances will lead them to one clear conclusion: control the spice trade of the Nabataeans. I would, as Prince Asylaion suggested, focus our reserves on militarisation of supply lines.'

Asylaion nodded vigorously.

Zaim glanced at General Ghassan.

The strategos had long whispered into the ear of the king that it was time to replace the old general with a younger man and had suggested a few names to the effect. By probing like this, Hesham was once more questioning the general's ability to do his job effectively. *Is this a deliberate ploy between Hesham and Asylaion to undermine Ghassan?*

'Ghassan,' the king said, turning to his general.

'Sire.'

'Please share with Hesham the details of the military plans you have already drawn up for reinforcing supply lines.'

'I will, my king,' replied Ghassan.

Hesham nodded before Asylaion added, 'I would also care to see such plans, general.'

'Your Highness will be most welcome to study the design,' Ghassan replied calmly.

Zaim had been consulted and advised on the defences for each city as well as the supply lines, weeks ago, when they had first had these conversations. As he was the only one of his brothers who spent most of his time away from the luxury of the royal court, the king had been keen to obtain his input before they finalised budgets to undertake the work. His brothers did not know this, nor was it appropriate for him to mention it, as Asylaion's jealousy of him was well-known.

'We must also address the matter of the Romans, your Highness,' said Hesham.

'Go on,' Obodos said.

'My intelligence has confirmed Roman spy networks in all the major regional cities, including Gaza and Jerusalem. The Romans, it would seem, are actively collecting intelligence.'

'Have they professed any preference towards Ptolemy or the Seleucids?' Obodos enquired.

'Neither,' Hesham stated.

The room went quiet. Rome was the rising power, it was plain. It was only a matter of time before it showed its military muscle in the region. Zaim thought, *we need to make alliances with one of the great powers. We cannot survive alone; we have chosen Ptolemy, but what if the Romans defeat Ptolemy? What then?*

'They too await the outcome of the great imperial war of our time,' Obodos declared.

'As do I,' Asylaion whispered, half to himself.

Zaim studied his brother. *He says 'I' not 'we': an odd expression even for an egoist such as Asylaion.* The comment was not picked up by the others, and Zaim pretended not to notice.

'What of the Jewish king, Alexander Jannaeus? Where do his loyalties lie?' Obodos asked.

Ghassan cleared his throat. 'The Hasmoneans have been playing the Seleucids off against Ptolemy. Jannaeus has not declared for either side, but his expansionist intent is clear. I fear he also has designs on our territories.'

'Hesham,' Obodos said. 'Deploy additional informants to Jerusalem, I want to know how the Hasmoneans will play the board.'

'I will, your Highness,' Hesham replied, before adding, 'On the subject of the Hasmoneans, I must also inform you that information is coming in about the arrival of the much-awaited Messiah amongst the Jews. It would seem they expect him any day.'

Zaim leant forward. *The Messiah! A Prophet in our time, to follow the Abrahamic line.* This was welcome news to the prince, for he was of the *hunafa*, those who had remained monotheists, despite the openly-practised polytheism around them.

Obodos paused, a faraway look in his eyes. 'The Messiah? Let him arrive, then we will decide what to do.'

'Yes, your Highness,' said Hesham.

It will change everything, thought Zaim. *Should there be a Prophet in our time, I will be one of the first to go to him, to pledge my allegiance. Would my family follow?* He looked around at his brothers, then his father. *I cannot be sure.*

'Fastiq's bride will soon be in Gaza, before Pelagios brings her to Bozrah,' said Obodos. 'We must send a delegation to receive them.'

The king regarded his sons, before his kindly eyes settled on Zaim.

'I will go, Father,' Zaim replied, before he was asked.

The meeting continued with more procedural matters, then concluded. Zaim found himself alone after the others had left, staring out from a balcony at the curved theatre carved from solid rock, which could seat at least eight thousand Nabataeans. To the east, beyond the treasury, was the narrow pass between the mountains, which no army could penetrate. It was barely wide enough for two or three soldiers at a time. It was the perfect shield against invaders and had kept the Nabataeans secure behind the natural defences around Petra.

The prince slowly turned his gaze towards the southern city wall. He noted a lone figure, barely able to stand up, staggering towards the outer city defences. Zaim collected his weapon and raced down the staircase of the armoury and out into the main thoroughfare, before approaching the outer guard post on the southern wall.

'Soldiers,' said Zaim. 'There is an injured man beyond the wall. You three, arm yourselves and join me.'

The postern was opened and Zaim led them out towards the man, who had now collapsed. He was lying flat on his back when Zaim reached him. The man was an easterner: his slanted eyes told the prince that.

'Lift him,' said Zaim to his men. 'We will see to his needs within the walls.'

As the soldiers supported the newcomer, Zaim happened to glance down at the symbol on the easterner's scabbard.

A dragon – the image was unmistakable.

Chapter 5

SICKLY VOYAGE

———

Soon after the voyage on the *Chloe* commenced, Apollonia's Aunt Corrina discovered she did not have sea legs. Sickness gripped her, forcing her to stay confined to her cabin. The princess stayed with her for several hours but sensing the girl was quite stable at sea, the aunt encouraged her niece to get some air on deck. Apollonia left her aunt in the care of her handmaiden Zoe and ventured above. On deck Apollonia was met by a cool breeze and she headed to the portside rail. Gripping it, she stared out at the waves. She had been raised by the sea, but had never seen only water, with no land in sight. *There must be a God*, she thought. *Who else could have created all this? How can I know Him?* Suddenly she felt very small, abandoned, and desolate; she yearned for Pelagios, captain of this vessel and King of Mithymna, to take her home.

The sails of the *Chloe* caught the western wind, as the vessel moved east, towards Gaza. Her parents had waved her off with all the formality of a departing ambassador and most likely they did not expect to see her again. *You are now of the desert, and the desert does not give back what it takes*, her mother had said. She was to become the wife of Fastiq, a Nabataean prince, in a loveless marriage. Very little was known about her husband-to-be, other than he was the eldest son of King Obodos. By all accounts he was twice her age and her primary function in the marriage would be to produce children to strengthen the alliance between Ptolemy and Nabataea.

A chill winter wind blew across the ship's bows and Apollonia tightened her cloak about her. The vessel cut through the spray; she stared at the foamy white water until she lost track of time.

'You have strong sea legs, your Highness,' said a man's voice.

She glanced over her shoulder. Pelagios. In the sunlight his plain features had a handsome charm to them.

'Thank you, your Majesty,' replied Apollonia.

'Please, call me Pelagios when it is only the two of us.'

She smiled. He had a kindly avuncular air to him. 'And you may call me Apollonia.'

He nodded. Coming to stand beside her, he gazed out at the horizon.

'I'm sorry father asked you to take me to Gaza when you were on your way home.'

The Aegean looked embarrassed. *No doubt father paid him handsomely for the voyage*, thought Apollonia.

'I consider it a duty; you are always welcome to sail upon the *Chloe*.'

'Your home, Mithymna, it is an island?' Apollonia asked.

'Surrounded by the deepest blue sea you could imagine,' Pelagios said.

'I would like to hear more about it.'

Pelagios replied, 'It has the finest vines and most ancient forests adorned with lupins, poppies, clover, orchids and rock roses. Most of all, it is home to my beloved wife Cassandra. and she waits for me there, for the sailing season nears its end.'

'Then you are a fortunate man, more fortunate than most in the world, to love and be loved,' replied Apollonia.

'I suppose I am,' said the king, scratching his beard. He turned to look at her once more.

'Many a young woman dreams of finding love,' Apollonia said.

'And what of princesses?'

'We are women after all, we have the same desires.'

'Indeed.'

'Yet we are subject to matters of statecraft, objects to be used in marriage alliances, in a game of empires. I recognise this and do not expect I will find love in this life.'

The Aegean monarch turned back to look out to sea, resting his elbows on the rail. 'Love can grow on you.'

She shrugged. Hers would be a marriage of political convenience, and she did not expect anything more from it. 'Is that how it was for you and the Lady Cassandra?' she enquired.

Pelagios smiled, leaning forward, his fingers interlocked, staring out at the odd magenta horizon. 'When we first met, it wasn't love at first sight, but we both felt there was something between us that could grow. And so it has proven. The longer we have been together the stronger our love has grown, like the roots of a healthy tree; when it finds good soil, it anchors itself to watch its fruits grow.'

'You are blessed Pelagios, I for one consider love too highly valued.'

'When someone earnestly loves you, it makes you determined, when you earnestly love someone, it makes you brave,' said Pelagios.

Apollonia observed him anew. There was a sincere honesty in what he said, unusual in a ruler, she thought. He was making every effort to make her predicament sound better than it was, so she decided to press him. 'What do you know of these Nabataeans, these desert Arabs?'

Pelagios sucked in the chill air between his teeth. 'They were once nomads roaming the desert, moving their herds to wherever they could find pasture and water. Over the centuries they survived in a waterless wilderness, vanquishing enemies by hiding in the desert, digging deep underground cisterns where they collected the annual rainwater, and which were only known to them. They are a proud people with a fierce sense of freedom and most of all of honour. From wanderers they became traders, maintaining favourable relationships with all whom they encountered, so much so that today all of the spice arriving in Arabia from the east is in their custody and trust, as it is brought safely north to be loaded onto vessels in the Mediterranean. Now,' the Aegean turned to look at her once more. 'They occupy cities such as Petra and Hegra, Bozrah, Aela, Sela, Mampis and others. And they institute ties of marriage with the great empire of Ptolemy. I would say these nomadic Arabs are coming up in the world.'

'I see.'

Pelagios continued, 'But this brings with it unwanted attention, from the likes of the Seleucids and the Romans. Not empires you want to make enemies of.'

She stood up a little straighter, suddenly feeling more assured of herself. Perhaps she was not going to a glorified tent in the desert after all.

'What of the royal family? Do you know them?'

His smile waned for a moment.

'King Obodos is much like your father, an ambitious man. His wife Fazluna is a lover all of things Greek and would get on well with your own mother. I don't think you will have any difficulty becoming acquainted with them, as they will remind you of your own parents.'

Too bad. I had hoped they would not be like my own distant parents, reflected Apollonia.

'As for the rest of the family, Fastiq is the eldest. I cannot say I know him, nor have I met him. The second son is known as Stylian the Opulent, and I fear his love of food and earthly pleasures dulls his mental abilities. Next there is Asylaion, the most ambitious of the brothers; he has a cunning mind. I would steer clear of him if I were you. Zaim is the youngest son, a fine lad with a sanguine temperament, a few years your senior.' Pelagios paused. She sensed he wanted to say something more about Zaim, but he did not. 'Then there is young Luja, the only daughter. She is a lovely child, but strange, strange indeed. So much so that her parents have entered her into the priesthood.'

'How do you mean strange?'

'She sees things others do not, speaks to people who are not present, babbles to herself when alone in a room. She is unlike any princess you will ever meet.'

'Is she … dangerous?'

'Oh no,' said Pelagios. 'Not at all. Luja has a gentle temperament; she would not hurt a beetle in the desert. But she is peculiar.'

A curious sister-in-law, a complicated set of brothers-in-law, and in-laws who reminded her of her own parents. *I must be strong*, Apollonia counselled herself. *I must be strong, for now I too am of the desert.*

****

Achaeus, envoy of the Seleucid empire, a man others referred to as legend, gripped the rigging in the stern of the vessel *Chloe*, as the square-sailed ship ploughed through the Mediterranean on its eastward course towards a blood-red horizon. He was of medium height and with a wiry frame. His eyes were deep-set, black and penetrating. His black hair and beard remained in immaculate condition, despite the sea winds. Achaeus glanced over at Andreas, the barrel-chested first mate on board, whose arms and legs were thick as tree stumps. He was known to have served under Pelagios for decades and had lost his left eyeball when rigging struck him during a storm. The story went that it barely affected him; he'd had a black eye patch made and carried on as though only a stray eyelash had troubled him.

Truly Andreas is a devoted servant to his captain and king, thought Achaeus. He too had been loyal to his people, the Seleucids, and now as the final year of his third decade approached, for the first time he was reflecting where it had got him. Sent to negotiate a one-sided agreement by the emperor he'd obtained far better terms than anyone thought possible. Yet the court officials who accompanied him as well as the Seleucid vessel he journeyed on to Alexandria, had been recalled partway through the negotiations, leaving him alone and without transport. This hurt more than the humiliation he suffered at the hands of Ptolemy's administrators.

Since boarding, no one had spoken with Achaeus, instead giving him a wide berth. He did not blame them. There was an unpleasant history between the Seleucids and King Pelagios. The beast Tigranous had dishonoured the king's sister. It was a shameful thing to have done; there was no virtue in attacking women and children, yet in response Antiochus had promoted Tigranous.

Since the start of the voyage Achaeus had occupied the stern of the *Chloe,* which had been empty, but now other passengers were trickling back. He pulled his cloak about him, taking up a position between two barrels. The Aegean king had taken some last-minute passengers on board when it was announced he was sailing for Gaza.

There had been a few merchants, who could afford the cost of the voyage, as well as a metalsmith and his apprentice, and there were three men Achaeus could not place.

The trio had boarded individually, but he soon picked up on the subtle eye and hand exchanges between them. The tall shaven-headed brute stood a head taller than him. The other two were both of middling height. Their movements gave them away as soldiers of some sort, either regimented or mercenary. They were also armed, with at least two weapons apiece. The tall fellow might even be hiding a knife in his boot by the way he walked. What concerned him most was how, over the past hour, they had steadily been drawing closer to him, so that all three now sat at points within five metres of his position.

Under cover of his cloak his hand went to the hilt of his blade.

Two merchants, deep in conversation about the price of Ptolemaic wheat came to the stern section of the *Chloe*, taking seats on a set of crates, followed by the metalsmith and his apprentice who took up similar positions opposite them.

The trio exchanged furtive glances, clearly deciding to make their move.

On Achaeus' right was the fellow with a spiked beard and he now approached. The Seleucid tightened his grip around the hilt of his weapon.

'You Achaeus?' Spiky Beard demanded, causing all the other passengers around them to stare and wait for the answer.

Achaeus looked up. 'I am he.'

'People call you a legend, toughest man around,' the provocateur continued.

'People are wont to say many things, most of which I would not believe,' Achaeus replied.

'If you're the toughest man around and I defeat you, that would make me the toughest, wouldn't it?'

The two merchants exchanged glances with one another and decided to relocate their conversation to the port side of the vessel, tucking in their togas as they departed. The smiths remained.

Spiky Beard halved the distance between them, his arms swinging.

'I suppose it would,' said Achaeus coolly.

'Hey, hey, calm down friend,' the second provocateur, clean-shaven with blond hair down to his shoulders, now moved into play. 'This is Achaeus – he is a legend. Don't bother him.'

Long Hair placed himself between Achaeus and Spiky Beard, as though he were protecting the Seleucid envoy.

'Keep out of it,' Spiky Beard said, as Long Hair placed his hand on his chest to slow him down.

With everyone's attention diverted, the tall shaven-headed fellow struck. Short sword drawn, he lunged at Achaeus from the left, but the Seleucid was expecting it and immediately rolled forwards and away from the trio. He parted his cloak, exhibiting his own range of weapons.

The three gave up the ruse and now formed a single line of attack against him, the ship swaying from side to side, as the wind picked up.

'Who are you?' Achaeus demanded.

Shaven Head withdrew a vicious-looking knife from its sheath, the steel glistening. Spiky Beard and Long Hair did the same.

The metalsmith and his apprentice, realising what was unfolding, quickly made their way from the stern, leaving him alone with the assailants.

The attackers advanced.

Achaeus did not draw his weapons.

Long Hair skipped forward, plunging his weapon towards the unarmed Seleucid. Achaeus watched the blade, side-stepping at the last moment, then gripping Long Hair's wrist and forearm in a vice-like manoeuvre, before snapping it the wrong way. *Crunch.* The bone cracked and the man dropped his blade, writhing in agony. Spiky Beard thrust his dagger from the right, but when the blow failed to connect, he swept his sword at the Seleucid. Achaeus moved back, but realised he was up against the base of the wooden panelling leading to the upper deck. He placed his heel flat against the wood, then launched himself forward, using his hands to spread the arms of his attacker wide, thrusting his knee into the man's midriff. Winded, his assailant fell to his knees. Achaeus swung back and kicked his first attacker in the head, then dug his thumbs into the wrists of Spiky Beard, so that both his weapons clattered to the ground. Achaeus twisted the man's right arm full circle, causing the fellow to land flat on his back, before a boot to the attacker's head knocked him senseless.

'Useless,' snarled the shaven-headed brute, burying one of his blades in the heart of Long Hair, and driving the other through the stomach of Spiky Beard.

Weaponless, he crunched his bare knuckles and rolled his neck. 'I much prefer the old-fashioned way of killing a man by snapping his neck.'

Achaeus eyed the man carefully. His rippling forearms demonstrated he possessed considerable upper body strength, but his feet were unsteady on the swaying deck, and he kept adjusting them to maintain his balance.

The blood from the wounds of the dead men seeped across the deck, mixing with seawater, as red turned pink, diluted into the clear wash of the sea.

Achaeus remained motionless. The shaven-headed assailant lost patience and swung a meaty fist at the Seleucid. Ducking to avoid the blow, he moved aside, tucking in his cloak as he did.

'Will you state the name of your patron?' Achaeus asked.

For a moment the thug was uncertain what was being asked, then he cottoned on to it, smiling, showing a full set of white teeth, which glinted in the sunlight.

'The Elephant Lord sends his best wishes,' Shaven Head replied. He jumped forward, lunging for Achaeus, attempting to slam into him like a wrestler. Achaeus moved fast, leaping forward to clasp the bigger man's windpipe. He squeezed, forcing the fellow to his knees, before he took the man's head and slammed it into the deck. The brute tried to get up, so he repeated his action, then a third time. The man was out cold.

The Seleucid envoy straightened up.

'My, that is a mess,' said a man's voice.

Achaeus spun around to find Pelagios eyeing the bodies littered around the stern. The young Ptolemaic princess, Apollonia, stood open-mouthed beside him.

'I am sorry, your Highness, that you should witness such a thing,' Achaeus said bowing to Apollonia.

'Who were these men?' the young woman asked, her voice cracking.

The one-eyed stout Andreas now joined his captain as did other members of the crew, taking in the scene of violence.

Achaeus looked at Pelagios. 'Assassins, I believe.'

'Did they say who sent them?' Apollonia asked, tearing her gaze away from the bodies.

'They did not give a name,' Achaeus replied.

And he watched Pelagios carefully, thinking: *Did the King of Mithymna know this attack was going to take place?*

'Tie him up, Andreas, then put him in the brig. When he wakes, see if you can get some sense from him,' said Pelagios. 'The other two, give coin to their eyes, then throw them overboard, they are fish food now. And get this deck cleaned. We're a trading vessel: we have standards to maintain.'

The Aegean's voice did not give anything away, but then in Achaeus' experience, rulers were trained to speak with forked tongues, as he knew too well from his own dealings with Emperor Antiochus. The shaven-headed attacker mentioned the 'General'. There were many around Antiochus. Which one? He needed time to think, to reflect on the past few days and try and piece it all together.

'My apologies, King Pelagios, for this incident,' he said, motioning towards the bodies. 'I think it best if I confine myself to my cabin for the remainder of the voyage.'

The Aegean nodded. 'Wouldn't be a bad idea,' he said.

'Your Highness,' Achaeus bowed once more to Apollonia, before making his way from the stern.

Chapter 6

AWAKENING

The traveller from the east whom Zaim had discovered outside the gates of Petra opened his eyes. He was laid on a bedroll, fresh linen over him. He had been changed into clean clothes, and his own garments had been washed and pressed. His sword belt and other possessions were placed neatly on top of his other belongings. Zaim observed the man, in the guest quarters that were carved from the inside of a mountain, the temperature cool.

Zaim recalled the words of a religious mendicant he met in the deep desert: 'The path of the sun traverses east to west; travel it but do not go solely where it leads, rather wander to the places that have no path, leaving behind a trail for others to follow.' *Which path did this wanderer take and where is he headed?*

The traveller wanted to rise, but his tired limbs refused to move, so he shut his eyes, drifting back into a light sleep. Zaim remained sitting on a cushioned chair, young Faaris who was tasked to look after the man was close by on a stool. When the easterner next opened his eyes, he seemed to take them in.

'Faaris, looks like our guest is waking up. Now pour him some water.'

A beaker was pressed to the man's lips, and he drank, slowly at first, then in gulps.

Once he had drunk his fill, Zaim said. 'We found you outside the gates of our city. What is your name, friend? Where have you come from?'

The man's hoarse voice was difficult to understand. He asked for some more water; sipping it, he seemed to let it settle on his throat before continuing. 'I am Zhang.'

'Zhang,' Zaim tried out the unfamiliar name.

The easterner nodded. 'This is the name of my family. You may call me Chao.'

'Chao,' Zaim repeated.

Chao Zhang continued, 'My men and I are explorers dispatched by Emperor Wu, lord of the east. We have been sent to explore the lands of the west and build alliances of mutual benefit. We seek to journey to the Middle Sea, charting the course and the people we encounter, before returning.'

'I am Zaim, son of King Obodos. This,' he pointed at the young lad, 'is Faaris, son of Khalid.'

'I thank you, for showing me such kindness your highness.'

'You are a traveller, and our customs prescribe that a traveller must feel welcome in our home and receive what provisions they need.'

'I honour your customs and hope to return this benevolence,' Chao replied.

The prince smiled, turning to Faaris. 'Lad, tell the cook our guest has woken. Bring him some soup and bread.'

Faaris dashed off.

'You mentioned your men,' Zaim enquired.

Chao raised himself up on his elbows, then sat back against the wall. He felt his strength returning to his joints. 'We were five, who set off from the lands of the Han. Captain Zhu Di, Lieutenant Fu Youde, Ganfu our Cartographer and Jin Guliang our Scribe. Five comrades who left the imperial capital, Chang'an but it seems I am the only one who remains.'

The prince nodded, glancing across at his sword belt momentarily before returning his gaze to him. 'What happened to your party?' he asked.

Chao let out a deep breath.

'At Aï Khanoun, when we crossed into the west, we were warned the Seleucid empire was collapsing. It had lost control of all territories in Bactria, and its grip was loosening even in western lands.'

Zaim nodded. *It is true then,* he thought. *The Seleucids are losing control of their territories. It is clear why Ptolemy wishes to ally with us in Arabia. Now is the time for him to strike at his mortal enemy.*

Chao continued. 'For much of our journey we evaded detection, sticking to the high passes where we could observe and document the terrain, or we travelled during the night to avoid exposure where there was a large population. It was not till we crossed the Euphrates that matters took a turn for the worse. Our party came across a village where a terrible slaughter had taken place. The bodies still smouldered and …' Chao paused, shutting his eyes for a moment before he continued, looking straight at the Nabataean prince, 'many were women, children, the elderly. None had been spared'

Zaim pursed his lips and shook his head.

'Our mission instructed us not to interfere with the lives of the people we encounter, but such was the massacre, we felt compelled to do something should there be any survivors amongst the carnage. And there were – two, a mother and child, who had hidden themselves under the piles of bodies. We could not take them with us, so we led them to the closest caravanserai and left them with a small purse of coins and some silver for the keeper of the caravanserai to look after them till they were fit to leave.'

'An honourable act,' said Zaim.

'Yes, but more dishonour was to follow. When the warlord who had committed the massacre in the village, a brutal thug named Yazdeg, heard of the survivors, he sent his militia after us. We fought them on a mountain pass, and in a wadi. Eventually they lost too many men and gave up the chase.'

'You and your companions are warriors?' Zaim enquired.

'We have fought in some wars for our Emperor and have some training in the martial ways of my people, the Han.'

'I see,' the prince eyed him curiously. 'Please continue.'

'The toll of fighting the bandits over three days left us less vigilant, and we let our guard slip. The very next day a party of slave catchers snared us whilst we slept. The shame of it. One of my men, who I will not name, had been on guard duty. He did what all people do when they are exhausted from the exertions of fighting: he fell asleep and issued no warning.

We were chained and taken to a market to be sold. One thing led to another, but we managed to get away. During the escape I was separated from my men when I was pushed into a river and dragged downstream miles from where they were. I tried to find them but could not. I feared the slave traders might have captured them once more.'

'What did you do then?' Zaim asked, leaning forwards.

'We had agreed, that should the party be split up, we would journey west to the Middle Sea. There we would wait for two months, allowing time for any others to arrive, after which we would make our way back east, via a more northern route. So I decided to continue westwards, till I unfortunately fell into the hands of a group of bandits. I managed to escape but was only able to take the one possession I could not do without.' Chao looked towards the sword. 'The Dragon Blade.'

'I see,' Zaim contemplated the weapon with renewed interest but did not enquire further.

'Tired, hungry and lacking provisions, I lost my bearings, and instead of keeping west, I inadvertently turned south-west and ended up here.'

'You already have quite a tale to tell your people when you return,' Zaim said.

'I pray I live to tell it.'

'God willing you will, my friend.'

'As you have been so kind to me, offering me shelter and provision, may I enquire about your people and this place?'

'We are Nabataeans, descendants of Nabjot, second son of the Prophet Ismail, son of the great Prophet Abraham, who was a believer in the one true God and a messenger sent to the people by Him to remind them that we came from God and to God we will return. The Nabataeans are an itinerant people, who have recently begun to occupy cities, such as this one, called Petra, and establish a fixed abode, yet in our hearts we prefer the confines of a nomadic tent than the stone walls of a palace.' The prince smiled before continuing. 'We trade along the Arabian coast, buying goods and spices that arrive from the east into the ports of Aden and Mocha from whence we transport them north to Gaza, after which what is not already sold is shipped to western markets. This income has, by the grace of God, provided us with some stability and offered us a means of livelihood.'

'You buy from the Han?'

'Silks and spices arrive from China regularly and are much sought after items amongst our buyers.'

'I am pleased to hear this.'

Faaris returned with the steaming soup and bread, placing it on a tray beside Chao, who thanked him for it.

'I will leave you to eat and rest, Chao Zhang, but before I go, I wish to ask something of your traditions. Share with me some wisdom from your ancients?'

Chao was silent for a moment, before proclaiming: 'The *Way* teaches us: *In a home it is the site that matters. In quality of mind it is depth that matters. In an ally it is benevolence that matters. In speech it is good faith that matters. In government it is order that matters. In affairs it is ability that matters. In action it is timeliness that matters.*'

Zaim listened attentively, nodding as he considered the words.

Yet as Chao spoke Zaim also knew that every home would crumble at some point, every mind grow forgetful, every ally unreliable, every speech disloyal, every government disorganised, every ability curbed, every action untimely. When it did the cycle would restart. Perhaps this was the *Way* that Chao referred to. All things were cyclical. The weak became strong, the strong became weak. The endless cycle of expansion and contraction continued and only God who created all remained ever-present, omniscient and omnipresent, above creation but also around it.

'Your *Way* is wise, and I will take counsel from the words you have spoken. I would like to learn more about your traditions, and can, if you are interested, share some of ours.'

'I would welcome that, Prince Zaim, for I am an explorer, and that means searching for new places and knowledge.'

'We will speak further, explorer Chao, but I must journey to one of our other cities tomorrow. My men will be here and can look after your needs till I return in a few days.' The prince got up to leave.

'Prince Zaim, if I may,' Chao said.

'Yes.'

'I feel my strength returning every moment I am awake, and the wanderer within me is restless to discover. May I venture to ask, whether I can accompany you? I do not ask for any special privileges, only that I have an opportunity to experience your lands and learn.'

Zaim smiled.

'I like you, Chao, there is a strong spirit within you. We leave tomorrow, as the dawn breaks.'

Chapter 7

NEEDING A FIXER

Notwithstanding the late hour, many families of Bozrah still occupied the public places across the high mountain plateau, sitting, laughing, and eating around cooking fires. There were bursts of laughter that sank into murmurs. To the east of the plateau was a plot of land, the site of bungalows for imperial dignitaries and royal visitors. In one such dwelling, outside which stood two armed sentries, Apollonia observed Aunt Corrina pacing between a set of lamps illuminating the dim interior. Her aunt, slender of build with what seemed to Apollonia a permanent expression of anxiety, had a habit of walking when she grew troubled.

For her part Apollonia was curled up on a chair, a shawl around her shoulders, her cat Javairea in her lap, purring as she rubbed its neck. The journey from Alexandria to Gaza had been an eventful one, with her conversations with King Pelagios and the attempt on the life of Achaeus the Seleucid envoy. Upon landing in Gaza, the Seleucid had quickly left the port, not disclosing where he was headed next. Not that it was any of her business, but he did strike her as a decent man, and by all accounts, even those of his enemies such as her father's court, Achaeus was a living legend and man of honour.

'What is taking Zoe so long?' Corrina said.

'I am sure she is doing her best. This is a new place for her,' Apollonia replied.

'Why, in Alexandria, you would merely snap your fingers, and three smiths would be at hand.'

'We are in Bozrah dear Aunt; this is not Alexandria.'

'Humph, you would have thought they'd have smiths in this city in case people needed them.'

Sighing, Apollonia said, 'We had best get used to not being in Alexandria, Auntie, for we soon travel into the desert.'

Corrina stopped pacing and looked at her niece. Nodding, she said. 'Yes, you are right, you are correct my niece, patience. This entire journey requires a degree of endurance in the face of hardship. And you are truthful, for greater hardships will soon be upon us as we journey to Petra.'

'They will,' Apollonia replied.

Pouting, Corrina added, 'For you, the desert will become your way of life. I, thank Zeus, will be returning to Alexandria as soon as you are married, and the formalities of the wedding are over. Though the terrible sea voyage awaits me, it is a small price to pay for being back in civilisation.'

Corrina put her hand on her heart, as though consoling herself, before resuming her pacing up and down.

'It may be better for you on the return, now that you have experienced being at sea.'

'Perhaps Poseidon will choose to be less exacting on me the next time I venture into his realm, but I expect not,' replied Corrina. 'Now, where is that girl?'

Apollonia's heart did ache for home, the palatial comforts and most of all, the gentle sea breezes and lapping blue waters of Alexandria. When she closed her eyes she could smell the sea air and hear the waves.

The oak trunks containing her wedding dress and other attire were in the centre of the room. They had been unable to open them as the locks had jammed during the sea crossing. The two Ptolemaic guards accompanying them had also tried, but when one of them said he could smash one open with an axe, her aunt dismissed the pair, asking Zoe to fetch a nimble-fingered smith who could pick the lock open, without destroying it.

The languid Javairea opened an eye, stretched her paws, then bounced off Apollonia's lap, making for a spot she had seen on a terracotta-coloured rug in the corner, to which she applied her claws before slipping into a meditative posture, staring out across the plateau. Cats were creatures of such precise habit, thought Apollonia. When they prayed, as Javairea did now, they always assumed such a regal pose.

Her recurve bow was never far from her, she stood up, reached for it, feeling the familiar weight, she pulled on the string, whilst focussing on the pitch-black horizon. *I will practise tomorrow*, she told herself. *Early in the morning before breakfast.*

The sound of sandalled feet on stone heralded Zoe's return. With her was a young lad, who could not have been more than twelve.

'I found a smith,' Zoe announced.

Corrina looked past the newcomer. 'Where?' she said, expecting another to arrive.

'This lad,' Zoe pointed to the young man.

The youngster had very light brown hair and his eyes were of a similar colour. He bounced around on his heels as though eager to get on with the work. Rolled up at his side was a piece of sackcloth with a set of tools inside.

'We need a smith, not an apprentice,' snapped Corrina.

'Begging your pardon my lady, but at this late hour, this boy is all I could find.'

'Lad,' Corrina spoke firmly. 'You have a name?'

'Yes, my lady, it is Faaris,' he bowed, unsure of the correct convention, then repeated the bow when he noticed Apollonia.

'You have experience of working as a smith?' Corrina continued.

'Yes and ... no my lady, but I ... well, I am really good at fixing things. Why, just recently I managed to repair the strap on the saddle belonging to Jamil, the cooking stove for Umm Ayan, and even the *rababa* for Captain Fahad. People say I can fix most things, my lady.'

'All right Faaris. Look at this trunk. See if you can get it open,' Corrina commanded, as she strode off to another part of the bungalow.

The young lad set to work. He unrolled his tools from the sackcloth, set them out neatly on the ground, placing each item alongside another in straight lines all pointing north. Each one shone as though brand new. He went over to the trunk and began to move his fingers over it, examining it in more detail.

Apollonia looked back at the mountain plateau of Bozrah. The voices from the residents provided a steady background rhythm, as the curtains gently billowed in the breeze. Love can be cultivated, Pelagios had said, but the ground must be fertile and well-watered with light and shade for it to become lasting. *Will I find the opportunity to love in Petra? What is my husband-to-be like? Will he share my desires and hopes?*

Javairea was up from her meditations, taking an interest in the newcomer, as she swished about him. Faaris for his part kept his attention on the work, picking through his tools carefully to select the right one. He chose a pick and wrench, then applied it to the lock. *Click.* The lock opened.

'He did it!' Zoe exclaimed joyfully.

The sound of her exclamation brought Corrina back into the room. 'My, that was quick! What did you do, lad?'

'I just choose the right tool. Lucky, I suppose,' Faaris said.

'Pay the lad well, Zoe, and give him something to eat,' Corrina said.

'Thank you, my lady, thank you, but I am due to eat at a feast with my prince this evening, and I had better get going.'

'Prince,' Corrina asked. 'What prince is this?'

'Prince Zaim of Nabatea, son of King Obodos.'

The name roused Apollonia from her seat. 'Prince Zaim, you say, brother of Prince Fastiq? You serve him?'

The lad bowed. 'Yes, my lady.'

'In what capacity?' Apollonia asked.

'I am ... well I will be ... I suppose I am already a ship hand on the *Falcon*, the vessel belonging to Prince Zaim.'

'I see,' Apollonia said, remembering her dream of a falcon soaring overhead.

The lad was eager to go, appearing not sure whether he had said something which would get him into trouble. Noting his dilemma, Apollonia added. 'It is good to have met you, Faaris, and I am certain we will see you again. You may go now.'

The youngster bowed once more to her, then Corrina, before Zoe led him out, Javairea following them.

'Zaim, yes, he is the youngest of the sons. Prefers the sea to the desert I hear and is quite … dashing if the accounts of the serving girls are to be believed. If he is anything like his brother Fastiq, then you are very fortunate to be marrying the elder brother, Apollonia.'

Apollonia returned to her chair, curled back on it, considering the encounter with the lad. *If Zaim is like his brother, Auntie? But according to Pelagios, he is not.*

Chapter 8

JAMMED BETWEEN ROCKS

High up on the plateau of the mountain stronghold of Bozrah, a cool wind blew east across the Nabataean city. Mushroom-shaped clouds filled the sky as the sun set. Across the mesa, families huddled around cooking fires, laughing and narrating stories. Some whispered about changing times, foretold by a blood-red horizon they had seen and rumours of ash rain in the east.

The tapering city streets were quiet. By the western edge of the city, removed from the family gatherings, was the solitary figure of Zaim, who sat on a boulder observing the dying remnants of the setting sun. *Somewhere to the west the Seleucids plan our downfall,* he considered. Usually, he would be with his men, but not tonight as he felt the growing sense of responsibility falling on his young shoulders.

'Zaim,' the voice startled him.

He turned to see the beaming face of his adopted Uncle, Pelagios King of Mithymna.

'You look far too troubled for one so young,' Pelagios exclaimed before embracing the younger man, as they both sat back down, gazing out to the west.

Zaim recalled the first time he had come on board Pelagios' vessel the *Chloe*, at the request of his father Obodos, who knew he had an inclination for life at sea and had asked the Aegean monarch to take him under his wing for a few sailing seasons and train him, so that one day he could command the Nabataean fleet. Zaim remembered taking well to life on a ship and the crew had been patient with him.

'How are the men?' asked Zaim.

'They miss your good humour, Zaim, but I hear you now have your own command.'

'The *Falcon*, she's a fine vessel. Not quite as magnificent as the *Chloe*, but fine nonetheless.'

'Your first command is the most special. You always remember your first ship, like the first time you fall in love.'

Zaim smiled.

'And what of my Aunt Cassandra? I miss her cooking.'

'And I miss her warm embrace, but it will not be long now,' Pelagios sighed. 'The sailing season nears an end and this is our last assignment.' He winced and Zaim thought. *My Uncle wishes not to offend me, as I am sure he was paid handsomely for bringing the Ptolemaic Princess to Bozrah.*

'How was the season?' Zaim enquired.

'Slow to begin with, but a few jobs turned a tidy profit, enough to keep the men and their families happy till next season. Pay your men a wage, but share your profits with them, that is what I say. Keeps the crew loyal and hard-working.'

'I will heed the advice, though my father may disagree about sharing profits.'

His father maintained a tight rein on commerce. Zaim put it down to the need to survive successfully in the desert where every resource was used and nothing wasted. The wilderness of Arabia was an unforgiving environment where maintaining reserves was essential for the survival of the tribe.

'I'm sure you'll find a way,' Pelagios said.

'What was the mood like in Alexandria?'

'Euphoric,' Pelagios scoffed. 'It was as though it were their first victory over an old enemy. Ptolemy's administrators were brutal in their negotiations for terms with the sulking Seleucids and particularly callous in their treatment of the Seleucid envoy Achaeus.'

'*The* Achaeus, the legend?' enquired Zaim.

'Indeed, I must say I felt sorry for him. The fellow was even attacked by a group of assassins on the *Chloe*, but he made short work of those brutes.'

Zaim thought back to the assassins sent to slay him in Sela. He suspected this was also the handiwork of the Seleucids.

'Who would want Achaeus dead?' Zaim asked.

'When you are a public figure, such as the legendary Achaeus, there are always others who believe they would benefit from your demise. Even if you were a hermit living by yourself up in the mountain, you would still have enemies, people who thought you were up to no good. They would find some way to turn others against you. As to who it could have been in the case of Achaeus, I have enough concerns of my own than to worry about a Seleucid.'

The last word was uttered with menace and Zaim grimaced when he remembered what the Seleucid General, Tigranous had done to Pelagios' sister and nephew.

'Anyhow,' Pelagios declared in a cheery tone, 'we have also brought with us the charming Princess Apollonia, daughter of Ptolemy and Cleopatra.'

'What is my sister-in-law like?'

'You will like her,' is all he said.

Zaim studied his face, but did not probe, instead adding, 'When she is rested, I will visit her tomorrow, and if she is willing to see me, it would warm my heart to be of service to her.'

'I think she will enjoy your company; you are after all of a similar age.'

The prince smiled then looked right and left and continued in a quieter tone. 'Pelagios, there is a matter which troubles me. May I seek your counsel?'

'Of course, lad, go ahead.'

The prince lifted two rocks from the ground. 'The Seleucids and Ptolemy,' Zaim said, indicating the rocks, 'have been at each other's throats since the death of Alexander the Great which is now several hundred years ago. This is not going to change. It is a never-ending war over land and influence going back to the rivalry between the two generals themselves, Ptolemy and Seleucius. A Ptolemaic princess, Apollonia, marrying into Nabataean royalty I fear ... will compel us to support Ptolemy in all matters of statecraft, whether diplomacy or military action. Through this marriage alliance we will become a satellite of the Ptolemaic kingdom, whereas to date we have retained our independence, much like you. We are not aligned to any party, but choose to trade with all and make war with none. What do you think this means for us Nabataeans?'

Zaim sensed that the current situation would drastically alter the geopolitical dynamic for the Nabataeans. They were going to be dragged into alliances, conflicts, trade pacts, and other imperial games which did not suit their own domestic needs, but instead served Ptolemaic ambitions, and there was going to be little they could do about it.

'You will be forced into making decisions when you would have preferred to remain out of the decision-making process.' Pelagios grimaced as though remembering something. 'You will be asked to form alliances with people you consider dishonourable, you will be asked to undertake wars you do not subscribe to, you will be asked to spy on those who are your friends.' He stopped abruptly, as though he had said too much.

'I would never do that, Pelagios, spy on my friends for Ptolemy. That is shameful. My word is my bond, and my bond cannot be broken, even if it means death.'

Zaim had been schooled in keeping his word and to break it was to dishonour the tribe, and that was worse than death.

'If only more men were like you Arabs. Alas they are not, and a man's word is easily bought when delights are dangled before his eyes or pressure is placed on what he treasures most in the world.'

My Uncle appears conflicted when he speaks with me today. I have never asked him what pressures his Kingdom is under, but perhaps even the Aegean is under strain from the empires surrounding it, thought Zaim.

'As for the other things you mention – wars, alliances and other such matters,' Zaim said. 'Well, I will follow my father. He is wise in these matters and serves the interest of our kingdom.'

Pelagios nodded.

What did the future hold for the Nabataeans who were just coming into the orbit of the greater powers of Ptolemy, Seleucid and Rome?

A wise man puts his trust in ideas, not in situations. Zaim had heard someone utter once. *What will I do?*

'Well said, young Prince,' Pelagios said, slapping Zaim on the back.

Chapter 9

SHEATHED DRAGON

———

Up on the high mountain plateau of Bozrah, a garrison town north of Petra, cold gusts shook the young olive trees growing in the semi-arid terrain. Sparse shrubs and bushes pockmarked the hills. Clumps of white saxaul and white broom ran down the mountain to the wadis saturated with seasonal rain. Foxes, rabbits and a deer darted through the acacias whilst a predatory falcon circled overhead. A single road, choked with men shouting at mules pulling carts laden with spices, wound its way up the mountain side.

A tang of dust hung in the air; the horizon oozed red at the edges, the sun veiled by a swell of clouds. The plateau offered expansive views of the surrounding land, providing Bozrah with natural protection from an invading army. A single track with hairpin bends could be defended by a small regiment of soldiers. Boulders placed in pivotal positions could strike down an ascending aggressor, and hidden crevices within rock formations provided bowmen with many shooting positions. By daylight a well-equipped army might attempt an ascent, but dusk would bring with it the added fear of the razor-edged drops at each turn.

This morning the wind snarled its way up the mountain and despite its pitiful resonance, a peculiar sense of anticipation filled the Han explorer Chao Zhang, for the first time in weeks. He perched cross-legged on a flat rock, eyes scanning the eastern horizon. Rhythmically he inhaled and exhaled, his breath broken into seven constituent parts. His Chi grew stronger by the day, his meridians clear for the first time in weeks. Breath and energy flowed. He remembered his father saying stress will shorten your life by one-third, so do not swim against the current; rather be one with it, then the river will take you to where you are meant to be. *Where has it taken me? I am deprived of my men, who perished under my command. Men with families, responsibilities to their spouses and children, and duties to their elders.*

Even now he clearly remembered the conversation he had with his men outside the walls of Aï Khanoun.

'Beyond those walls lies the west,' Chao had proclaimed.

'It does, Lord Chao,' chubby-faced Captain Zhu had replied.

'If any of you wish to turn back, you may do so now. You will not lose honour, for we know not what lies on the other side nor what reception we will receive. Explorers sent by our kingdom beyond this point have never returned,' announced Chao Zhang.

The round-faced companion glanced at the others, who nodded. 'We will stay with you till the end, till the Middle Sea, my Lord Chao.'

Like him, they had been told by the imperial court at Weiyang Palace in Chang'an they *were* undertaking this mission and should not expect to return. Some of the men in his company had families, young children. They had not said so, but they were not present by choice. In his own case, initial excitement – for what explorer would not want to venture to new lands – soon gave way to uncertainty, then fear

'You honour me, Captain Zhu, and I pray the Jade Emperor in Heaven will repay the trust you show in me. For my part, I will endeavour to demonstrate virtue, to show though my words and deeds wisdom, courage, justice and temperance, in good times and bad.'

Chao himself no longer had a wife and son.

And Chao recalled that at the time he thought: *I have led these men on military campaigns, with armies under my command, I have fought in sieges and now as I approach my thirty-fifth year, is it because of my advanced age that I am sent on this mission? Or is it because I am the grandson of the legendary explorer Zhang Qian?*

In one swift movement Chao rose, settling into a steady stroll along the edge of the plateau. Following the perimeter of Bozrah, the town to his left, he eventually came upon a group of men training with wooden weapons. He recognised them as Prince Zaim's company, having been introduced when he arrived in Bozrah.

Noticing him approach, one of the group waved him over. They practised with staff and sword, going through well worked-out sequences. There were nine hearty-looking fellows who halted their drills when he joined them. A man with long brown hair, the one he remembered as Captain Fahad, spoke first.

'Greetings, explorer Chao Zhang, a good morning to you,' Fahad said.

'Good morning to you, Captain Fahad, and your comrades,' replied Chao, bowing his respects.

The men smiled. Chao noted their easy manner, a reflection of their commanding officer. For one cruel moment he was reminded of his own troop – the jovial Captain Zhu Di, the hawk-eyed Lieutenant Fu Youde, the adept cartographer Ganfu, and the meticulous scribe Jin Guliang.

Captain Fahad had been informed by his Prince of Chao's story, and the Han explorer noted how the captain's interest had been piqued by the mention of the Dragon Blade.

'Would you join us?' Fahad asked, turning to seek the approval of the other men, who nodded, before adding. 'That is, if you are familiar with the martial disciplines.'

Chao inspected the men. Each viewed him expectantly, Fahad more so as he tried to suppress an eagerness which broke through at the edges of his mouth. *If I decline,* Chao thought, *and feign tiredness, it will not go down well amongst these hardened men, yet if I accept, I will reveal more than I wish to about my abilities.* His recalled his grandfather saying, *appearing less than you are will serve you well by keeping you out of harm's way in foreign lands.*

'Explorer Chao?' Fahad asked.

'I have some familiarity with the martial arts,' Chao replied.

The spiky-haired Taimur, who Chao recollected as having the rank of lieutenant, stroked his forked beard. 'It would honour us if you would impart some of your martial knowledge. We are always keen to learn. The world has become, for us at least, a much larger place after meeting such a man as yourself.'

There was an all-round murmur of agreement, the men eager to watch him fight.

Taimur continued. 'What fighting form do your people adopt?'

Chao addressed the troop. 'There are many armed and unarmed fighting techniques, equally effective. We call this martial system *wushu*.' He paused. Their faces and their expressions told him they were unfamiliar with the martial art of his ancestors. 'There are various forms and hundreds of styles of *wushu;* mostly these involve palm, elbow, leg and foot strikes, pressure point attacks, throws and the like. Balance and the flow of breath through the body are key to success and practitioners spend decades perfecting forms and movements. There are few genuine *Sifus*, masters, some disciples and many more students, such as I, who are mere beginners on the path.'

One of the group asked. 'Surely an unarmed fighter cannot overcome an armed opponent who carries a sword or spear?'

'A skilled *wushu* practitioner who has a good grasp of hard and soft fighting systems such as *Jiao Di* or *shoubo* can overpower an opponent with a weapon or several opponents each wielding weapons.'

This drew a murmur from the men, and Chao checked himself, for his manner was boastful. His masters would not be pleased with his lack of modesty. He quickly added, 'What I mean to say is that an experienced *wushu* exponent can shift the odds in his favour during a fight with a larger group. He is supple and malleable like water, which can wear down the hardest of things.'

'I see,' said Taimur. 'And would you say you are such an exponent?'

'I am a beginner,' Chao repeated, not wanting to get drawn in further.

'I see,' said Taimur again, adding, 'It would be good to see what a beginner of *wushu* is capable of, so we are able to gauge what a master could do. Would you show us?'

Chao hesitated.

The Nabataeans were curious. He had talked himself into this position quite unintentionally, but now that he had he would need to go through with this demonstration.

Fahad added, 'But only if you are fully recovered from your recent adventures.'

Truth was Chao's joints still ached, but these men were keen.

'I will,' he replied.

Chao moved to the clearing where the men had been practising and took up a position. Feet firmly planted, legs in a wide fighting position, arms slightly crossed before him – Dragon takes flight over frozen lake. He motioned for the men to fan out around him.

'You may use your weapons,' Chao announced.

The Nabataeans hesitated.

'You are our guest, we wish you no harm,' Fahad declared, to general agreement from the company.

'We are practising, are we not? And you are using wooden weapons, are you not?' Chao replied.

'Hardly seems a fair fight,' one of the men mumbled.

Chao centred himself. Deep breaths rose from the pit of his stomach as Chi pulsed to the tips of his fingers and revigorated his muscles. 'Begin,' he instructed.

Hesitantly at first, two men approached in a languid manner, before they lunged at him with raised staffs, their footsteps heavy. He let the first blow glide past him, before he gripped the staff and launched a flat boot into the stomach of the man, sending him back, as he circled the staff in a quick motion and knocked the attacking weapon clear from the second fellow, who stopped and was in such shock, that he missed Chao's round kick taking out his heels, which left him flat on his back.

The group around froze, gaping. Chao held both staffs in his hands. The two men got back on their feet and Chao threw their weapons to them; as they plucked them from the air before they sat out on some boulders to watch.

'Impressive,' said Fahad.

Taimur and four others came at him with smoother movements, wooden practice swords raised. The first strike came down faster than expected. Chao skipped sideways and the attacker's momentum carried him low, whereupon Chao kicked the pommel from the man's hand, then rolled over his flat back. Landing crouched, he swept under the next strike, before back-heeling the attacker in the rear of the knee, dropping him down, then kicking the blade from his hand. As Taimur and the remaining opponent watched, Chao cartwheeled at them and knocked their swords from their hands. The four Nabataean swordsmen, empty-handed, stared at one another, before they erupted in wild fits of laughter.

'Incredible!' said one man.

'Never seen anything like it,' another bellowed.

The one remaining man standing with Fahad turned to look at the captain and shrugged, before he too sat down with the others.

'Aha!' Fahad laughed and recited:

Here where the warriors strode out,

I followed behind them,

Chastened, they withdrew.

I fought, using my war tested skills,

Refined and honed,

Till I declared, victory, it was never in doubt.

Fahad hefted two wooden swords, throwing one to Chao, who plucked it from the air before swishing it around, feeling its weight. He gripped the handle, blade pointed upwards, knees bent in a wide stance – Dragon fire.

'Right, let's see how good you are with the sword,' Fahad declared, turning the wooden blade about in his left hand.

Chao took in the poetic captain's movements. Light on his feet, strong back and posture; his sword danced about in Fahad's grip. The Nabataean circled Chao, who remained rooted. When the attack came it was from the right. Chao's wooden blade collided with his opponent's, high and low the blades struck in a criss-cross of strikes. Faster and faster the weapons moved, before each man drew back. Fahad smiled and Chao wore a thin grin.

One of the men said: 'Captain Fahad, best swordsman in Nabataea, has met his match.'

He is a skilled swordsman, thought Chao. *Finest I have encountered in the west. His movements are lightning fast and his motion is like*

Crane on a Bamboo Tree.

Across the plateau edge they fought – strike and block, parry and counter, feign and retreat. Chips of wood split from the blades, yet the flurry of blows did not cease. With each new movement and counter the men watching gasped in wonder.

Sweat trickled from Chao's brow. This dance could last the whole morning, as neither was willing to give an inch nor possessed the skill to break through the other's defence. Chao spotted a gap in Fahad's defence. Whenever the Nabataean drew back from an exchange, he left an opening on his left side. Chao attacked, the swords striking each other. As they separated, Chao spotted the opening and launched himself at it, then realised it was a trap. Fahad swivelled, using Chao's momentum to swing around him, before Fahad swung a reverse blade at the easterner's chest. Chao had no choice but drop flat to the ground to avoid the strike, before back-flipping and rolling away.

'Almost,' Fahad declared. 'I had planted that trap for you after our first exchange, when it occurred to me I had met a swordsman worth fighting.'

Before they could launch themselves at one another once more, a voice called out. 'I would declare it a draw.'

The group turned to see Prince Zaim making his way towards them.

'An explorer!' Zaim asked Chao quizzically. 'Who can defeat a group of armed men with his hands and feet as well as match the best swordsman in Arabia?'

Fahad bowed respectfully to his prince, before smiling and doing the same to Chao, who returned the gesture.

'An explorer must know how to defend himself, should the need arise,' Chao replied.

'I would say you have mastery of your art.'

'I am but a beginner,' Chao bowed respectfully.

'Then I would love to see the prowess of your master,' said Zaim. 'But since we have only you, explorer Chao, I will ask if you can teach us some of what you have learned as a *beginner.*'

The men concurred with their prince and Chao considered once more whether he had revealed more than he should have about *wushu*. It was a sacred martial art, handed down through a line of masters. *I am no teacher of wushu, yet these Arabs now look to me to impart some knowledge to them when I am not worthy of such a designation.*

'I will share what may be useful,' Chao replied.

Zaim clapped him on the back and turned to Fahad. 'I knew you would meet your match one day, Captain.'

Fahad bowed low, sweeping his arms in a majestic manoeuvre, before rising and declaring:

With my sword thrust I pressed him,

Unwavering fought we,

Till the Dragon and Falcon declared solidarity.

The men laughed and Chao felt himself truly at ease for the first time in weeks. These were good men. Honourable and dignified, though they could not replace the company he lost due to his recklessness. To honour the men and their families he would strive harder to reach the Middle Sea and complete his imperial mission. He did not want to be remembered as a footnote in a Mandarin's report as a voyager who never returned from the west. *No*, he counselled himself, he would venerate the name of his family and return home to Chang'an in the footsteps of his illustrious grandfather Zhang Qian.

Chapter 10

HEARTS TURN

—————

The prospect of encountering a royal of the Ptolemaic line, a princess no less, brought out sweat on Zaim's forehead. The notion of such an imperial personage becoming part of his family gave him a stomach-ache. Zaim thought an encounter with a group of assassins would be a simpler ordeal than this, as he made his way to the appointed meeting with Apollonia. The Nabataean prince's mood was lightened that morning by the lad Faaris walking beside him, his incessant babbling bringing with it a certain rhythmic calm.

'It was simple, Prince Zaim, they had forgotten to tie the ends together through a grip. Once I pointed it out, the whole system got working once more.'

He thought the lad was referring to the rudder of the *Falcon*, but not having listened attentively to the opening explanation he was unsure what Faaris was talking about. The young lad, apparently a distant cousin of his, tended to talk till he ran out of his energy. Faaris also had a habit of relaying entire conversations word for word. Zaim was unsure whether the lad had ever heard of the concept of brevity. Still, he was good-natured trustworthy and no one was perfect.

The prince opened his mouth to say something but forgot what it was and shut it again. *Don't be such a fool*, he told himself. *Calm yourself, she is only a young woman. No, not any woman, a Princess of Ptolemy!* Irritated by the dryness in his throat he coughed.

'My Lord,' Faaris broke off from his jabbering. 'Shall I bring you water? If you have something caught in your throat, I can fetch it and be back before you know it. You cannot meet the Princess Apollonia coughing.' The lad was about to dart off, when Zaim raised a hand to stop him.

'It's all right Faaris, thank you.' The lad was far too eager to please, in fact his eagerness sometimes bordered on the bothersome. Yet he was young and would learn. *I was probably the same onboard the Chloe, but Pelagios and his crew were patient with me, as I will be with this lad.*

'If you say so, my Lord.'

'I do.'

'As I was saying, the axle on the …' The lad continued with his explanation about some repair he'd undertaken as Zaim searched the path ahead for Pelagios. The prince spotted the King of Mithymna leaning against a ghaf tree.

Seeing them approach, Pelagios pushed off from the trunk.

'Peace to you,' said Zaim.

'And you,' Pelagios replied as they clutched arms before embracing.

Faaris stopped talking, bowed to the Aegean monarch.

'This is Faaris, an able hand on the *Falcon*, with a talent for making repairs. Quite handy to have around,' Zaim said.

'Fixer, eh?' Pelagios ruffled the boy's hair. 'You'll always find work, if you're good at mending things, boy.'

'Thank you, my Lord, why just last week, I managed to repair the – '

'Faaris,' Zaim cut him off. 'Perhaps you can save the explanation till later.'

The lad looked from one man to the other, then nodded. 'I will remain silent, my Lord.'

'Thank you,' Zaim said, taking Pelagios by the elbow and guiding him down the path.

The boy trailed some paces behind. And Pelagios thought, *he resembles Zaim in his eagerness when he first came to us on board the Chloe, willing to please and engage himself with the crew. He will do all right.*

'Pelagios, you have conveyed to the Princess Apollonia that she should expect a Nabataean delegation this morning?' Zaim asked.

'Delegation? No!'

'You haven't?'

'It's just you.'

'Well, yes.'

'I told her to expect you, Zaim, a fine young man, noble and courageous, and without doubt the finest Arab navigator on the sea.'

'You told her that?'

'Something like that. I don't remember exactly.'

'What did she say?'

'She smiled and said she was looking forward to meeting you,' replied Pelagios.

Zaim gulped before saying, 'You set very high expectations, Uncle.'

'I did?'

'What if I disappoint her, what then?'

Pelagios gently punched him on the shoulder. 'Pull yourself together, lad. She's like any other young woman.'

'Which is like what?' asked Zaim.

Pelagios slapped his forehead.

'What?' Zaim said.

'Relax, my young friend. I'll take the lead, you follow, if that makes it any easier.'

'It does, but I still feel like I'm sinking in quicksand.'

Pelagios smiled. 'You do look nervy.' The Aegean put an arm around his shoulder. 'I grant you this, Ptolemaic royalty are known for their arrogance, their haughtiness, their pride and sense of self-importance, but having spent time with Apollonia, I would say she goes against the grain.'

'She does?' asked Zaim.

'You will like her and I am sure she will like you.' The king grinned, but his confident mood did not settle the prince, who puffed out the air from his cheeks.

Zaim loosened his muscles and rolled his neck, but it felt like a rod had stiffened his back. *Relax*, he told himself. No chance of that, when meeting Ptolemaic royalty, no matter what Pelagios said. *I would rather face a Roman legion.* Zaim's stomach churned. *She will take one look at me and tell me to go fetch my father. Why didn't my older brothers Asylaion or even Stylian come to collect Fastiq's bride?*

Why send the youngest?

'But she is the daughter of Ptolemy and Cleopatra, a royal of the highest distinction. And we are desert nomads.'

'You too are royalty,' Pelagios said.

'There is nothing we can do which will impress her. Why, she might even glance at my attire, and decide I am not worthy to accompany her any further.'

Stepping away from him, Ptolemy eyed the prince's breeches and shirt. 'You look hideous. She is bound to mistake you for a servant.'

'Really?'

Pelagios roared with laughter. 'Of course, not Zaim, you are one of the most handsome and well-turned-out men I know. Why...' Pelagios stopped abruptly, catching himself, thinking *Zaim and Apollonia are a perfect match for one another. The poor girl will be wasted, tied to Fastiq the Grim.* The match was made, and the match had to stand. It could only be broken by those who instigated it.

'What?'

'Nothing. Come on, we are almost there.' He took them down a narrow lane towards a bungalow.

Faaris caught up with them, announcing. 'Why my Lord, this is precisely where I came last night.'

As they approached the building, the three sped up.

'What!' exclaimed Zaim.

Outside the entrance, two bodies lay slumped on the ground. The Ptolemaic guards. Both had had their throats slit and had bled to death.

Pelagios took a closer look. 'Recent.'

The prince and the lad rushed inside to inspect the bungalow.

'Empty,' cried Zaim, emerging almost immediately.

Outside, Pelagios inspected the trail leading away from the bungalow. It told him there had been a group of men, at least six. They had dragged away three women – Apollonia, Corrina and the handmaiden Zoe, he assumed. *Blast, I got them this far only to lose them.* He thought about the princess and her retinue then remembered the handsome payment Ptolemy had given him for conveying his daughters to the Nabataeans. He had never failed to deliver on a paid task and he was not going to start now.

Zaim was beside him; the Nabataean's mood had clearly altered. Pelagios recognised that look – *the hunter is out in him. Good, we will need it.*

The prince turned to Faaris. 'Inform the men what has happened. Ensure all roads out of Bozrah are sealed and any other routes we know are guarded.'

Faaris took one last look at the felled bodies then bolted back along the path.

'This way,' Pelagios instructed.

The Aegean and Nabataean proceeded at pace, following the trail of flattened tufts of *nasi* desert grass and broken heads of white broom, proof of a recent struggle. There was blood in the grass, along with a broken arrowhead. The shaft was made of cedar wood, one of Apollonia's. She had put up a struggle. Downward the trail went, away from the plateau, the slope dipping viciously at the western end of the ridge.

Zaim peered over the drop.

Far below a carriage was parked. Approaching it was a group of men dragging three women. Recklessly the party descended along a twisting tortuous path, wire-thin as it zig-zagged downwards. Zaim leapt from his position, landing five metres below on the trail and set off in pursuit.

'I'm too old for that move,' Pelagios grumbled and followed the prince, using an outstretched hand to balance himself against the rock wall as he descended. Pelagios watched Zaim leap from level to level in a bid to catch the assailants. Angry at himself for not posting his own Aegean guards along with those sent by Ptolemy, Pelagios, with a watchful eye on the drop, kept up a steady pace.

Don't look down, Zaim said to himself. *Leap, run, don't stop.*

The Nabataean was halfway down the slope when he noticed one of the women look up at him, before she was bundled into a wagon. It was Apollonia, no doubt about that, radiating regal beauty even at this distance. Clenching his teeth, he leapt clear over two trails, landed, rolled, almost went over the edge, righted himself with an outstretched arm, ran, leapt again, clearing two more, and rolled. He stood, ran, then leapt again, till he was only one path away from the assailants.

Below Zaim the men had bundled the women into the cart. Three captors had gone inside with them, the others sat on a bench behind the four horses pulling the wagon. They whipped the horses into action. The wagon started to move.

Zaim approached a ledge; below him the wagon made a turn. He sped up before launching himself through the air. *Whack!* He landed on the roof of the wagon, before rolling off it and to the side of it. His fingers gripped the edge, and he looked inside. Princess Apollonia's face was pressed against the iron bars of the wagon, only inches from his on the other side.

He felt her breath on his lips, their eyes met, he felt himself drowning. Momentarily he froze.

The carriage jolted. Zaim snapped out of his reverie and hauled himself back onto the roof.

'What!' one of the men sitting at the front called out. Another fellow left his seat and clambered onto the roof, swinging a club at Zaim. The prince ducked, let the man's motion take him past him, then booted the fellow in the rear, sending him tumbling from the wagon, as the horses shot forward.

A second man swung at him with a sword. Zaim moved faster, gripping the man's wrist, then applying pressure to it so that he dropped his weapon, before Zaim shoved him off the roof. The horses sped up.

The final man at the reins turned momentarily, only to have Zaim barrel into him with his legs and knock him from the wagon. The prince took hold of the reins, leant back and started to slow the galloping steeds, till they came to a halt.

Below him the wagon door burst open and the three remaining abductors emerged, holding daggers to the necks of the women.

Zaim leapt down, landing on the rocky ground with a crunch.

'We'll slit their throats, like we gutted the guards,' a brawny man with a predatory look said as he held the princess close to him.

The older woman, Corrina, let out a yelp.

'Shut it,' snapped the man holding her, whose right arm was bleeding.

Zaim stood motionless. 'Who sent you?' he asked. The prince could not help but exchange looks with Apollonia. Those eyes, like deep pools of rose water, glittering within a bed of sapphires.

The brawny man continued, 'Move aside and let us leave with these maidens.'

'I asked you a question,' Zaim said, taking a step forward. From the corner of his eyes he noticed Pelagios carefully making his way down the rocky slope. However, another figure was hurtling down the mountainside, rapidly gaining on the Aegean ruler.

The brawny man pressed his blade closer to the princess' throat. 'I mean it.' The other two kidnappers followed suit, forcing blades to throats.

Zaim took a step back.

'That's more like it,' Brawny declared. 'Now, move away from the wagon. Make it quick!'

The prince noticed the other man shoot past Pelagios who himself was now approaching the stand-off. Zaim shifted his position further back, his eyes firmly on the assailant holding the princess. The three men shuffled toward the wagon; their blades pressed against the women's flesh. The handmaiden was in tears, as she was hauled back inside. The aunt was thrust in, then Apollonia.

Zaim watched the stoutest fellow leap onto the front of the carriage and pick up the reins, whilst the other two made their way inside.

Before they could slam the door behind them, Brawny flew out of the wagon and hit the dirt, followed shortly by the second man, who landed on top of him. Their heads smacked into one another, before they passed out.

The driver turned in shock to see his comrades floored. Before he could whip the horses into action, Zaim leapt up and cuffed him on the side of his head, sending the man cartwheeling off the carriage. Smack! He landed on the ground and lay motionless.

Apollonia, Corrina and the handmaiden Zoe emerged from the

carriage.

Zaim peered inside.

Chao appeared. The easterner bowed to the women, then to Zaim.

'You got them, thank Zeus,' Pelagios declared as he caught up. 'Your Highness,' he said, turning to Apollonia. 'Are you all right?'

'I am fine. A little flustered, but otherwise unhurt.'

The words were crisp and melodious in Zaim's ear, and he realised his eyes lingered longer than they should have on her.

'And you, my ladies,' Pelagios turned to Corrina and Zoe.

'Well I ...' Corrina started, then caught Zaim staring at Apollonia, and smiled. 'And who is this dashing young man?' she asked.

'Zaim son of Obodos,' Pelagios declared.

'Oh, I see,' Corrina purred. 'The younger brother of Fastiq.'

Pelagios observed the continued visual exchange between Zaim and Apollonia, his two young friends. *So*, he pondered, *that is what love at first sight looks like.*

Pelagios turned to Chao, then looked back at Zaim. The prince and the princess were lost in their own world.

'Humph,' Pelagios coughed. 'Zaim.'

'Oh, Uncle,' Zaim said, shaking his head and looking towards the Aegean monarch.

'The easterner,' motioning towards Chao. 'Shot past me like an arrow, I may be getting old, but I've never seen someone move so fast. Friend of yours, Zaim?'

Zaim cleared his throat, desperately trying to avoid looking at Apollonia. He stood up a little straighter and replied, 'This is explorer Chao Zhang of the Han empire, sent on an imperial mission to map out the lands to the Middle Sea.'

Chao politely bowed to Pelagios, who copied the respectful salutation.

'You have any experience on the sea?' Pelagios asked Chao.

Before the explorer could reply, the group's attention was caught by a troop of Nabataeans making their way hurriedly down the rock face. The men ran over to join the party. Pelagios recognised Captain Fahad, who skidded to a halt before his prince.

'Your Highness,' said Fahad. 'We've just received word that Sela was attacked by Seleucid forces.'

'Sela! Less than half a day's ride from our position!' Zaim said.

The Seleucids move faster than I gave them credit for, thought Pelagios. *The impending royal marriage between Ptolemy and Nabataea has irritated Antiochus. Was this attempt to kidnap the three maidens part of the same scheme?*

'We must ride to Sela, assess their intentions. Prepare my horse. We leave immediately,' Zaim declared, before turning to Apollonia. 'My lady,' he said bowing to her, then to Corrina.

The prince walked over to Pelagios and the Aegean monarch knew at that moment, the Romans were going to get precisely what they wanted. With Seleucid forces so close to Bozrah he felt a sinking sensation. He should have been on his way back to his beloved wife Cassandra, along with his crew. He'd taken one last job and was now well and truly caught in a game of empires. *The Roman spider moves ever closer.*

'Uncle,' Zaim said, glancing briefly back at Apollonia. 'I have a favour to ask you.'

'Say it, lad,' said Pelagios. *Though I know what you will ask.*

'Can you and your men accompany the Princess Apollonia and her Aunt Corrina to Petra? Leave them in the safe custody of my father and brothers. After which, make haste and return to the blue waters of Mithymna where my Aunt Cassandra awaits you.'

Pelagios thought, *damn bloody Romans. I am going to Petra after all.*

Chapter 11

EXPECTATIONS

The eastern entryway into the mountain stronghold of Petra took the chariot carrying the royal visitors past the colossal squat Djin blocks before the road sloped down towards the dam and then the cool shaded passageways of Jabal al-Jilf. The rocky track meandered through the mountain passes, surrounded by high rock walls on either side. Statues were carved into the stone at intervals, some demanding devotion, others providing information about where the traveller was within the city. Crystal-clear water ran along the purpose-built channels sculpted into the side of the mountain. As the pathway narrowed, Apollonia caught sight of a magnificent building also cut into the mountain; then it disappeared, as an overhanging rock obscured the view, before the passageway opened and she could see it once more.

The Nabataean soldier navigating the chariot with Apollonia and Pelagios standing behind him announced, 'The treasury, your Highness.'

'Yes, I have heard stories about it,' Pelagios said. 'Truly, it is a magnificent sight.'

Apollonia could only stare silently at the frontage of a many-columned building sculpted from the rock which held a rose tinge as sunlight bathed it. Two large eagles framed its upper section; a goddess, Isis perhaps, stood in the centre. Other figures held axes and there were two imposing lions. Further down, Apollonia recognised Castor and Pollux, the sons of Zeus.

Beside her Pelagios also appeared stunned at the architectural marvel. *Perhaps he has never seen anything like it,* thought Apollonia. *But then neither has anyone from Alexandria. What other marvels does this hidden city hold?*

Apollonia gripped the chariot rail as they trundled past the treasury along a new road sloping downwards. She felt worn out from the over exertions of her trip and a part of her craved to return home, to Alexandria. The chill of winter was beginning to set in, and she tightened the cloak around her. She remembered her dream of a falcon soaring above the desert. Then she remembered her encounter with Prince Zaim and the thought of it made her blush. But the sky overhead was empty but for a mass of clouds, interspaced with blue sky. And Prince Zaim was nowhere to be seen.

I wonder why they call my betrothed Fastiq the Grim, thought Apollonia.

They soon passed the high place of sacrifice and then the semi-circular theatre with seats cut shaped from rock. Apollonia estimated the venue could hold several thousand. Then the chariot made its way towards the great temple.

'There,' Pelagios motioned with his head.

Apollonia's gaze swept up to the left. On a platform carved out of the mountainside a delegation of royals awaited them. Their brilliant white clothes fluttered in the morning breeze.

'Your new family,' Pelagios said softly.

'Yes,' Apollonia replied. 'Which one is Fastiq?'

Pelagios replied. 'Perhaps he waits inside.'

'I see,' whispered Apollonia.

The new faces came into focus for Apollonia. King Obodos' hawk-like features which had been described to Apollonia by Pelagios stood out even at this distance. *He wears military garb; the Seleucids are close.* Her mother-in-law to be Fazluna, who was a lover of all things Greek, was beside him, her arms partly bare and her auburn hair descending like a waterfall across her shoulders. Stylian the Opulent, was distinguishable amongst any group, stooped like a duck. To the other side of the royal couple Apollonia considered must be Prince Asylaion, a handsome man in anyone's estimation, but she had been told his heart was as cold as stone on a glacier. *One to avoid*, Apollonia reminded herself.

Her betrothed was absent, as was the young princess Luja. *By all accounts a strange girl*, Apollonia recalled.

The horses trotted along the stone and pebbled path and the charioteer drew them to a halt when they reached the platform. Pelagios descended, took Apollonia by the hand and guided her down from the chariot. The Ptolemaic princess was dressed in a brilliant white silk gown, with a saffron-tinged riding cloak, which covered her head. Two earrings of pearls from the Persian Gulf gleamed amongst her ringlets. Behind them she heard the other chariot carrying her aunt, Corrina, draw to a halt.

Apollonia observed that Obodos, Fazluna and the two Princes wore expressions of curious wonder as she ascended the steps of the temple.

When they reached the top, Pelagios turned to Obodos and Fazluna. 'May I present the Princess Apollonia, daughter of Ptolemy Soter and Cleopatra.'

He let go of the princess' hand for the Queen of Petra to warmly embrace her future daughter-n-law.

My duty is done. I have completed the task Ptolemy paid me for and the trust Zaim placed in me, Pelagios sighed to himself. *Now I must prepare myself for the journey home to my beloved Cassandra.* He felt lighter, free of the burden others had placed upon him.

'My dear friend,' Obodos embraced Pelagios warmly. They were old acquaintances and Obodos always reminded the Aegean the great favour he did the Nabataeans by training the young Zaim in seafaring, as he now ran their shipping fleet up and down the coast, carrying vital cargos of spice from the east.

'It is good to see you Obodos – it's been years. Yet you and your charming wife have not changed at all in the intervening years.'

'Ah, he jests! The desert is an inhospitable environment,' Obodos chided.

At this point Pelagios turned to look at the two princes – Stylian and Asylaion – waiting in the wings and shook hands with them both. *Well, they have changed, for the worse. They lack Zaim's warmth and compassion*, thought Pelagios. *Particularly Asylaion, who bears a look of envy. He desires the throne of his father, and it would seem he also has eyes on the young princess.* The lustful gaze Asylaion pinned on Apollonia had not failed to register with the Aegean.

The Lady Corrina now appeared by her niece's side and further introductions were made.

'How was your journey, daughter?' Fazluna enquired of Apollonia.

The words of her mother Cleopatra echoed clearly in her mind. *"You are now of the desert, and the desert does not give back what it takes."* And Apollonia thought: *This is the city in my dream, built into the mountainside.* Automatically she looked up at the sky, expecting to see a falcon flying overhead, but there was none to see.

Apollonia smiled. 'Thank God, I arrived safely in my new home, Mother.'

Fazluna leant across and kissed Apollonia on the forehead. 'And you are most welcome, daughter,' she said. 'Now let us leave the men to talk about what they love to talk about, politics and war, and let us take care of more important matters – home and family.'

The queen slipped her hand into Apollonia's and led the princess away from the men, the Lady Corrina on Apollonia's other side.

'How are you?' Fazluna asked Corrina.

'Tired from the long journey, but it was important to bring my niece safely to Petra, so I have endured many trials along the way. We have had adventures, including witnessing the legendary warrior Achaeus slaughter a man right before our eyes.'

'Oh?' exclaimed Fazluna.

'If he were not a Seleucid, I would declare him the most handsome widower I have met, but alas his being associated with the like of Antiochus disfavours him to most women. I would not consider him a suitable match for myself.'

Fazluna exchanged a quick smile with Apollonia as they entered the building through a square doorway, the height of two horses, a patterned border inlaid into its rocky frame. Inside, the area opened into a large hall, and Apollonia glanced up to see a high ceiling above her. Cressets and lanterns were dotted about in specific locations, but air holes were also carved into the rock to allow light to stream through, bouncing off a shiny glazed surface, which reflected sunlight around the room. Apollonia had never seen such an ingenious method of illuminating an interior.

'I thought it would be darker in here,' Corrina commented.

'The light of Al-Uzza radiates throughout Petra,' replied Fazluna. 'Our engineers have found ingenious methods of carrying the rays of her light to deeper places within the palace.'

'Mother,' Apollonia asked. 'I have not seen my betrothed. Is he in Petra?'

Fazluna smiled. 'Yes, Fastiq is here. You will meet him soon enough. After all, you will be spending your entire life with him. Be patient a little longer, dear child.'

'I will, Mother,' Apollonia said, but all she could think of at the time was her meeting with Zaim. Her heart skipped a beat when she remembered the young prince. Their faces had been so close on either side of the carriage's bars; she could remember his features perfectly. *Did I just imagine it or was there something more? No, I cannot think in this way. I am due to marry his older brother and that is it. I must forget Zaim, for I am Ptolemaic royalty and must fulfil my duty.*

Apollonia bit her lip, clenching her fists, and tried to forget the handsome features of the queen's youngest son, but however hard she tried, his virtuous qualities swam back before her.

****

Pelagios watched the three women leave. He turned to Obodos. 'The situation is grave. Sela has fallen to Seleucid forces.'

'We received word of this,' Obodos replied.

'Zaim rides with his Falcons to assess the size of the enemy forces, before returning to Petra.'

'What of Bozrah?' asked Obodos.

'Your fortress city appears safe from an invading army, for the passes are easily defensible by a small force. However, I would not put it past the Seleucids to attempt to take the city to consolidate their position. Yet I would be more concerned about them attacking Petra.'

'They have the audacity to attack Petra?' Obodos asked.

Pelagios paused, considering the king's question.

'They would not do such a thing,' Asylaion interjected, taking a step towards them. 'Everyone knows Petra's defences cannot be breached. No army can march on the city and the walls in the mountain passes are well guarded and have height advantage. An attacking army would need to scale the mountain to get close to the walls. We should not worry.'

From what Pelagios observed, Asylaion was right. The city appeared impenetrable, but was that not what the defenders of Troy had thought before the attack? Every city has a weakness, he thought. *What is Petra's soft underbelly – a secret passage, an unknown mountain pass, a traitor in their midst?*

Obodos studied his son's face, then turned to Pelagios.

'Pelagios, you have fought the Seleucids on many occasions; we all know about the unfortunate incident with your sister. What does your experience tell you?'

'Your marriage alliance with Ptolemy has drawn the ire of Antiochus,' said Pelagios. 'The emperor is licking his wounds after his loss to Ptolemy and is lashing out at those he considers an easy target. You control the spice routes from Aden and Mocha up to Gaza. Antiochus wants his treasury to be replenished by income from the spice. My sources tell me he has even reached out to the Hasmonean King, Alexander Jannaeus, to form an alliance against the Nabataeans.'

'Jannaeus, that scoundrel!' said Obodos. 'Has he forgotten what the Seleucids did to Jerusalem, to the holy site of the Jews? He cannot be in his right mind if he thinks Antiochus can be trusted. But if they form an alliance, it will leave us exposed, as Gaza will be within easy striking distance of a joint Seleucid-Hasmonean force. If we lose Gaza, we lose the Mediterranean Sea route. It would be a catastrophe.'

'You are worrying unnecessarily, Father,' said Asylaion. 'I grant you the Seleucids are lashing out, but they know Petra cannot be taken. They will tarry for a few days in Sela, possibly march some men in the direction of Petra, but they will do no more. They *can* do no more. There is no need for us to be alarmed by this turn of events. As for the Hasmoneans, the Jews would not ally themselves with the Seleucids after the destruction of Jerusalem. The rabbis would be up in arms against the king, and he needs their support to maintain his position as King and High-Priest.'

Asylaion is confident in his assessment, but I do not see why. What does he know that we do not? Pelagios pondered. *It is not my place to ask, I must leave as soon as I am able, without causing insult to Obodos' hospitality.*

The King of the Nabataeans exchanged a look with Pelagios, which told the Aegean all he needed to know about the relationship between Obodos and Asylaion. *He does not trust his son.*

'We will prepare for the worst. Should the gods wish it, they will protect us,' declared Obodos. 'When will Zaim return, Pelagios? I must consult with him on our preparations to defend the city.'

The name of the young prince drew a momentary scowl from Asylaion, before he regained his composure.

'I expect his return by this evening. We will know more about the extent of the Seleucid forces,' replied Pelagios.

Obodos nodded, lost in thought. He turned to Stylian. 'Son.'

'Yes, Father,' Stylian replied.

'Prepare a messenger to depart within the hour. The fastest man and horse you can find. Send word to Ptolemy that Seleucid forces have taken Sela and we expect them in Petra soon. Tell him his daughter Apollonia is now in Petra.'

'I will, Father,' replied Stylian.

'Let us test this new alliance with Ptolemy and see what reinforcements he sends,' Obodos said.

Pelagios observed the momentary glint of uncertainty in Asylaion's eyes. He thought: *Your son Asylaion is planning something, and I have my doubts that Ptolemy will answer your missive, as he is busy fighting the Romans in Africa.*

Chapter 12

UPON A CLIFF

———————

Sprawling over a mountainside, the Nabataean town of Sela had limited points of entry and those were now guarded by Seleucid troops. Unlike Bozrah it was not garrisoned and its conquerors had faced little resistance. Seleucid forces moved unencumbered through Sela.

Chao watched Zaim study the climb up the cliff into Sela. It was a tricky one in Chao's estimation. Moonlight illuminated the hazardous steep gradient. Zaim turned towards Chao and Fahad.

'I will make the ascent and secure the rope for you to follow,' he said.

The two men nodded.

The prince set off, following his chosen route, anchoring his fingers and finding leverage for his boots. Ascending, he uncoiled the rope by his side. The climb was arduous, and it took some time for him to reach the summit. The prince disappeared from view, then threw back the rope, which only came halfway down. It was a signal for Fahad to follow. The captain set off, choosing the same route as Zaim.

Fahad found it harder to make the climb. At one point he lost his footing, dropped, then caught himself and steadily made his way towards the rope.

Nearby voices drew Chao's attention and he decided to investigate. Swiftly moving through the undergrowth, he peered through some shrubs at a group of Seleucid soldiers standing behind one particularly tall warrior, with long blond hair. Before him was another man, with a wicked scar running down his scowling face. The black armour he wore bore the symbol of a scorpion on it.

Their exchange of words was too distant for Chao to hear, but at the end of the conversation Scarface and the tall warrior shook hands before parting. Scarface walked back to his mount, where Chao noted there were two other men also bearing the scorpion emblem waiting for him. The tall warrior and his entourage also returned to their mounts and steered them towards the path into Sela. The Han warrior did not know the men concerned but it was clear there was some kind of alliance between the two parties.

He returned to the base of the cliff in time to see Fahad disappear over the summit. The rope was tugged once more: the signal for him to start his ascent. Chao took the tried and tested route the other two had laid out. He moved quickly, scaling the cliff at pace.

****

At the summit Zaim let Fahad take a moment's rest after the climb. Peering over the edge, he noted Chao approaching. Zaim thought: *He possesses a superior inner strength making the climb appear effortless. If this is part of his wushu training then we must also learn this martial art.*

The prince had earlier instructed his men to remain at a meeting point on the highway leading back to Bozrah. They were ordered to go back to Petra should Zaim and his party not return by dawn. He doubted the men would leave without finding out what had happened to him, though.

The cliff scaled, Zaim, Fahad and Chao stole forward, gliding low, remaining hidden. Ahead, fires burned in makeshift camps, illuminating a multitude of soldiers stationed on the summit of Sela. Dodging around tents and a pavilion, the three men clung to the darkness like an old friend. The souq to their right was a ramshackle mess, emptied of items, carts overturned. Zaim paused to survey the scene. *It has been stripped bare by the Bedouin. Yet this is not the Bedouin way; there is no honour in a raid such as this. Why would they take what they did not earn?*

Zaim pressed on, guiding his small party over the remaining en-campments and around a cluster of buildings. Silently they advanced till the prince turned right into a narrow alley, then cut left. He approached a door with a bronze knocker. Ignoring it, he tapped the base of the door three times. He waited. The door opened a little.

'Who is it?'

'I am here to see Elder Atiq; this is Zaim son of Obodos.'

The door opened fully; the three men slipped inside.

'Prince Zaim,' said the short shaggy-haired man who had opened the door. 'I am Ghannam, son of Atiq.'

'Peace be with you, Ghannam son of Atiq. Where is your father?' said Zaim.

Ghannam noticed Chao, the Han explorer. He looked at the prince.

'A man of the east: he is with me,' Zaim assured him.

'Welcome to you all,' said Ghannam. 'This way. My father was hurt by Seleucid soldiers when he went to speak with their general.'

Ghannam led them through a narrow corridor, the roof of which was patched with palm fibre, before entering a courtyard and immediately turning right into a square room.

On a bed in one corner lay Ghannam's father.

Zaim rushed over, coming to kneel beside his bedside. 'Elder Atiq,' he said.

Hearing his voice, Atiq perked up, squinting, noticing the newcomers. His old weather-beaten brow was knotted with pain. 'Prince Zaim,' he exclaimed.

Zaim clenched his teeth. Striking an elder was an abominable act only committed by the most abhorrent. He took Atiq's hand. 'How are you?' he spoke softly.

'Looks worse than it is.'

Zaim exchanged a glance with Ghannam whose expression did not match his father's casual tone.

'If you are well enough, can you tell me what happened?' Zaim asked.

Sounds of running sandals and spear tips on stone drew their attention. Zaim turned to Fahad. The Nabataean captain rose to guard the entrance.

'It is dangerous for you to be here, Prince Zaim. Do not tarry long.

I have known you since you were a boy, sitting on your father's knee, I would not want you to come to harm.'

Zaim smiled at the old man, squeezed his hand.

The old man looked to his son, then continued. 'Three days ago, the alarm was raised when the Seleucid army was spotted coming south down the valley. We sent messengers to intercept them but they were repelled without any dialogue. Then we sent our scouts to assess their motives. When it became apparent they were heading towards Sela we fortified the town as best we could and sent a rider to Bozrah, warning them of the approaching army, and another messenger to Petra to notify your father. The Seleucids did not engage in any discourse: they simply arrived, positioned themselves, then attacked. We are not a garrisoned town, so the defences did not hold for long. People fled to their homes and some escaped down the other side of the mountain, hoping to head for Bozrah or maybe even reach Petra. Others fled to caves to the east.'

'The souq has been looted, stripped bare,' Zaim said.

'The Bedouin,' Ghannam announced. 'They met the Seleucid leader. He gave them free rein to loot the souq.'

'Most dishonourable,' said Atiq.

'Which tribe?' asked Zaim.

'The Banu Ghufaan. Their chief is Sakhr,' Ghannam replied.

Zaim nodded. Sakhr was a name known to him. He was ruthless, but then he would need to be, to rise amongst the Bedouin.

'Elder Atiq, how did you get hurt?' Zaim asked.

'I went to seek clemency from their leader, but he would not listen and some of his guards roughed me up,' said Atiq.

'I am sorry to hear this, Elder,' Zaim said, squeezing the old man's hand again. 'Do you know who leads the Seleucids?'

'Tigranous. They called him General Tigranous,' Ghannam replied.

'Tigranous,' Zaim whispered, as memories of his Aegean uncle rushed to mind. *Should Pelagios hear of Tigranous being in Sela he will surely seek revenge. But Pelagios would not be here had I not asked him to escort Apollonia. He should be sailing back to Mithymna and the warm embrace of his beloved. What should I do? Tell him about his nemesis so he can seek revenge for his sister, but possibly get hurt or even die in the process? Or remain silent and let him return home?*

After a few moments of silence Ghannam asked. 'Prince Zaim, you know the man?'

'His reputation,' Zaim replied. 'Have you heard what they plan to do?'

'Some of our young men overhead soldiers talking about marching south tomorrow,' Ghannam said.

'How far south do they intend to go?' Zaim asked aloud.

'They do not have the strength in numbers nor supply lines to lay siege to Petra,' Ghannam assured him.

'But what are they planning with the Bedouin?' pondered the Nabataean prince. 'Bozrah would be a futile target; it is inaccessible by a large army. They must be headed to Petra. But why? We must return quickly and let my father know of their numbers.'

'There is one more thing, Prince Zaim,' Ghannam said, glancing at his father. 'Some of the men in town reported seeing General Tigranous hold a secret meeting with a man.'

'Secret?' Zaim asked.

Ghannam continued. 'Yes. The man silently entered Sela with three bodyguards. He was well dressed and his horse sported the finest livery. They spoke, then the men departed, heading back down the mountain. Our men followed him and his party when they reached the base, and saw them head south, towards Bozrah and Petra maybe.'

'Who was he?' Zaim asked.

'They do not know; his face was hidden all the while within his riding cloak, but he was a person of some standing by his general bearing.'

Zaim noted the information. 'Have they made any further demands?'

Atiq coughed, sat up a little straighter. 'I believe they mean to move on soon. They have done their wicked work here. We will start to rebuild once they leave.'

Zaim admired his fortitude – here was a man thinking about how to move forward, not wallowing in what was lost. *'This was a show of strength,' Zaim thought.*

Fahad returned. 'Your Highness, we should leave, there is something happening close by.'

Elder Atiq squeezed Zaim's hand. 'Go, my Prince, ride to Petra, tell your father the people of Sela will always be with him and I remain his loyal servant. And remember life and death have fixed terms, everything else is providential.'

Zaim leant over the old man and kissed him on the forehead, before clutching his hand one last time. Then he left, Fahad before him, Chao behind him and Ghannam by his side. As they reached the door, Zaim turned to Ghannam. 'Your father is good man – look after him. God willing, we will see you soon in Petra.'

'God willing,' Ghannam replied, then embraced him.

Outside there was quiet, but Zaim heard the unmistakeable shuffling of dozens of boots on the ground. The three men cleared the houses and headed back towards the cliff edge. Moving through the tents and pavilions, they stuck to the shadows. Once through the encampment, they sped up, the cliff ahead of them.

A cresset ignited before them. They skidded to a halt.

The flaming cresset was placed on a spear shaft driven into the ground. Then others were lit ten yards to the right, and left, followed by more.

Zaim's hand went to the hilt of his sword.

Seleucids: a dozen at least, in battle armour.

More boots came up behind them, emerging from close to the pavilion. Zaim swung around. *They must have seen us come over the cliff edge and were waiting for us to descend.*

A tall muscular figure with a billowing cloak cut through the line of troops. The emblem of the elephant lords on the helmet he carried under his arm shone in the light of the cressets. His blond hair fell to his shoulders.

The man's lips curled in a malevolent manner, as his eyes darted between the Nabataeans and the Han explorer.

'An easterner from the Dragon kingdom,' he said. 'So, the witch was right.' He almost spat out the words.

'Who are you?' Zaim asked, though he feared he already knew the answer.

'The question is, who are *you*?' Tigranous replied. 'And what are you doing in Sela? Organising a rescue? Or seeking to take back the city?'

This is the beast, thought Zaim. *A brute and wretch. The nemesis of my uncle Pelagios. I would do my uncle a favour and strike this man down, but now is not the right time. We must return with intelligence to Petra.* 'We are locals. We came to see what had happened to the people of this town, for we were not able to visit them.'

'Locals?' Tigranous grinned. 'He is not local,' the general pointed to Chao.

'A visitor from the east, our friend,' Zaim replied.

'Well armed locals,' Tigranous said. 'Enough of this. State your names, then my men will kill you. Otherwise, we will torture you, then kill you.'

Chao studied the powerfully built man. He was the same man he'd seen at the foot of the mountain, meeting with Scarface. The formation of soldiers before him in a single row was haphazard. Chao considered that some of these soldiers had just woken, others had been eating. They were not ready. He remembered the teachings of his martial masters. *When the odds are overwhelming, escape to fight another day.*

'Your Highness,' Chao whispered as he recalled the formation of *Rooster Pecks the Swine.* 'I can clear a path to the cliff edge, but you must stay behind me, very close behind me, watch our backs.'

'No!' Tigranous roared fixing Zaim with a deadly stare. 'Kill them or capture them – I do not care. Attack!'

Chao drew the Dragon Blade, its red-tinted edge, catching the light of the cressets.

The Han explorer launched himself at the men standing close to the cliff edge, swiping left and right, cutting down the Seleucids with ease. A path was cleared, but other soldiers quickly closed the space. He felt the presence of the Nabataeans behind him, as they defended his rear. A soldier swept a blade at Chao's head. He ducked, then struck the man's wrist, sending the soldier away writhing in agony. He spun as his blade cut down two men in a single stroke, slashing the breastplate of one, and the knees of another. A spear missed the tip of his nose; he caught its shaft with his left hand, snapping it out of the grip of the attacker, before throwing the spear in one movement into the chest of an oncoming soldier, as he whirled and slammed his blade into the midriff of the spearman.

'Now!' Chao shouted. 'Go, I will hold them!'

Zaim ducked past him, diving through the gap in soldiers and over the cliff edge. Fahad followed. Chao repelled two more soldiers, slicing across their arms and legs. The men hesitated, as none were now keen to approach him. They formed a tight ring but did not advance. Two soldiers were shoved aside as Tigranous strode forward.

The general eyed the sword, glittering red in the light of the cressets. 'A Dragon's blade,' he said. 'Bring me that sword and the head of the wielder,' he growled at his men.

Chao took one step back into emptiness, then bent his other knee and somersaulted himself back over the cliff, falling to the ledge below. He crouched, looked up, saw the terrified faces of soldiers peering over the edge, then sped away down the cliff wall, using the rope they had left to support his descent.

Chapter 13
AN ODD ENCOUNTER

Apollonia had been in Petra for two days and still there was no sign of her betrothed. Her new family entertained her with lavish meals, trips to some of their foremost monuments such as the treasury, and told her about their desert kingdom of Hegra, further south. Apollonia marvelled at the ingenuity of the Nabataean engineers who had shaped such striking formations from rock, as well as the multitude of buildings constructed against the side of the mountains. These included government offices, commercial centres and residences. Each used the mountain itself as a store, whether for perishable food stuffs, or items for safe keeping.

This morning her mother-in-law-to-be Queen Fazluna and her Aunt Corrina had taken her to the temple and left her with the High Priestess, who now stood before Apollonia, white hood raised. The fabric shone as beams of sunlight pierced the rocks overhead. The grey milky eyes of the High Priestess above her hollow cheeks bore witness to a lifetime of devotion to the Nabataean gods. Apollonia thought, *I never believed in the pantheon of gods my family worshipped, nor will I prostrate myself to the idols of the Nabataeans.*

She looked past the High Priestess at the display of idols scattered across the chamber. And it dawned upon Apollonia that this edifice of worship, this reverential construction, was all in vain, for these *sacred* statues held no power nor sway, yet she also discerned she had no choice but to make a show of worshipping them. It made her stomach churn, but she hid her feelings.

With no alternative she smiled at the High Priestess and asked:

'What are the gods of the Nabataean pantheon?'

Hands clasped before her the old priestess croaked, 'Imperative for a member of the royal household to know,' ushering Apollonia deeper into the chamber. Overhead the rock ceiling was chiselled into a hollow, reflecting sunlight around the sacred space. Oud burnt close to images of the deities.

Apollonia glanced around the chamber, familiarising herself with its nuances – a holy site, fabricated with the sensual adornments of the world, to create in the worshipper a sense of detachment from daily existence. It was well constructed, equal to the temples in her birthplace, Alexandria.

Approaching the first deity the old woman said: 'This is Al-Qaum, the warrior god of our people. He protects our caravans when they travel in the desert, he guards us during the darkness of the night, and protects our souls as we sleep.'

Apollonia stared at the proud martial effigy. *He sounds like Ares whom the Greeks worship*, she thought. She observed the High Priestess raise her hands and pray, so she followed suit, mumbling some indiscernible words to satisfy her host.

Circling to the left they came upon a second idol, tall and thin. The High Priestess halted by it, announcing. 'Al Kutbay, the god of learning, transactions, and writing.' The High Priestess prayed and Apollonia followed, thinking to herself: *Al-Kutbay is like the Greek Hermes.*

A broad smile appeared on the face of the High Priestess as she approached the third statue. 'This,' she declared with solemn satisfaction. 'Is the goddess Allat; she brings with her spring and fertility. The desert would remain barren were it not for her blessings upon our people. My Princess would do well to pray to her, for she will bless the one who desires to be with child.'

Apollonia's cheeks flushed at the thought of motherhood. Of course, she knew this was what was expected of her, to produce an heir as soon as possible, to unite the two kingdoms, but having someone say it flustered her. The High Priestess declared her solemn devotion to the goddess. *My family worship Aphrodite and Athena.*

They came to the largest effigy in the chamber.

'Al-Uzza is the goddess of power,' said the High Priestess.

Apollonia remembered seeing her inscription carved into the Treasury of Petra.

'She is the supreme goddess,' declared the High Priestess. 'With her coming we receive vegetation, fruits, cereal, and she showers us with love, spreading it like sweet honey on the tongue.'

'In the land of my fathers, we have a goddess called Isis: Al-Uzza reminds me of her,' said Apollonia.

'Isis the supreme goddess of the Pharaohs. I have heard her mentioned by travellers from the Nile delta, who sometimes visit. Think of Al-Uza as Isis then, if this brings comfort to your heart.'

It does not, Apollonia said to herself.

Finally, the High Priestess guided her to the remaining statue.

'The goddess Manawat,' announced the High Priestess. 'Is the goddess of destiny.'

Destiny, like the Moirai worshipped by the Greeks, considered Apollonia. *What fate brings me to the land of the Arabs? Is my life predestined, or is it for me to make?* Standing before the statue, Apollonia said a prayer, not to the goddess herself, but to a God of her imagination who she did not know and doubted He knew her.

The smile on the High Priestess's face told Apollonia she was pleased with her devotions.

'My child, I will leave you in this chamber for a time, so you can pray and meditate on your own. There are cushions to the side, please use these so that you are comfortable. There is fresh water in the urn beside the cushions. I will return later.'

'Thank you,' Apollonia replied. The High Priestess departed, leaving Apollonia with the Nabataean idols.

She let out a deep breath, turned to one of the cushions and promptly sat on it, not paying the idols any further attention.

Time passed. As she waited for the High Priestess to return, she heard a whistle behind her. At first she ignored it, but then a tiny pebble landed beside her feet. It had come from the corridor behind her. She swivelled, to see a girl's head duck out of the way.

'What is this?' Apollonia said, rising to her feet.

A small hand crept around the edge of the wall, and porcelain-coloured fingers motioned for her to come close.

Apollonia glanced about the empty chamber. There was no one else there.

She moved in the direction of the hand. As she drew close to it, she peered around the corner, to see a girl of perhaps nine or ten, skipping away down the corridor. The girl stopped, smiled, then motioned for Apollonia to follow.

How peculiar, she thought. Who was this child?

Curious, Apollonia trailed after her. At the end the corridor she turned left. Along this new corridor were several rooms, and the girl stood by the door of one of them. As the princess headed towards her, the youngster disappeared, diving into another area of the Temple. Moments later Apollonia came up to the door, which led to a cell of sorts, very spartan and empty but for a bed in the corner, a set of chairs, a chest of drawers and a beaker holding what Apollonia took to be water.

'Come in,' the scrawny girl squeaked. The youngster's skin was pasty white: this child had not seen much sun. Her brown hair was unkempt, falling down her back. She was barefoot and wore a long dress, frayed at the hem and sleeves. Only a tiny necklace strung with what looked like a pearl distinguished the girl's appearance.

Staring up and down the corridor to check no one had followed her, Apollonia stepped into the girl's compartment.

'Shut the door,' the girl said.

Apollonia did so. 'Who are you, child?' she asked.

'Guess!' replied the girl, giggling.

'May I sit?' Apollonia asked.

'Oh yes, take this chair, it's the one mama and papa use when they come to see me.'

The girl was not an orphan, then, as Apollonia had first assumed when she caught sight of her. But what kind of parents would leave their daughter in a temple and for what purpose?

'Come on, who do you think I am?' the girl asked.

It was an odd question. How could Apollonia possibly know her identity and her lineage? But then it was a child who was asking it, and children had a tendency to assume adults knew everything. Not too long ago, she remembered becoming exasperated with her older siblings when they didn't understand what she wanted. *If this child expects me to know her, then who is it that I have not met but should have whilst I have been in Petra?* She stared at the girl, whose round face was bursting with a smile from cheek to cheek. *Could it really be the strange sister-in-law?*

'You are Luja!'

'Yes!' the girl leapt from the bed and embraced Apollonia, burying her head against Apollonia's chest. 'My sister, my sister,' said the excited youngster. 'I have been waiting for you to come to see me since the first day you arrived. I was watching you from afar, arriving with Uncle Pelagios. I wanted to visit you but the High Priestess forbade it. I'm so happy you came to see me.'

'Yes, of course, my little sister,' said Apollonia. The princess cleared the strands of hair from Luja's forehead and brushed off the stain on her temple. 'I am pleased to see you, Luja.'

'I knew you would be,' replied Luja.

Why was this child kept in this cell within the temple, under the watch of the High Priestess? She was after all a Nabataean princess. Apollonia wanted to know the truth but thought it best to tread carefully. *Was this girl being kept a prisoner?*

'Tell me Luja, how old are you?'

'I am nine.'

'You are very grown up for a nine-year-old.'

Luja giggled.

Apollonia wanted to ask the girl what she was doing in this place and why her parents allowed it, but she did not know her well enough, so she said, 'I've just arrived in Petra, so what should I see?'

'There is so much. We have buildings made inside mountains, we have the store house where we keep the grain for the whole year, we have secret passageways running across the city but few people, even the grown-ups, know about them. I do,' she said proudly.

'Secret?'

'Oh yes, I crawl around all kinds of tunnels and holes. Sometimes they are filled with insects and snakes, so I avoid those ones, but mostly they are fine and no one bothers me. I can go where I want, see who I want and listen to people talking when they don't even know I am close by.'

'Where do the tunnels go?'

'Most places,' said Luja. 'Have you met him?'

Apollonia stared at the girl. 'Who?'

'My brother!'

'Which one?'

'The one you are supposed to get married to. Fastiq.'

Feeling embarrassed, Apollonia replied. 'I am sure I will meet him soon. He is no doubt busy with the affairs of state and other business he has to attend to.'

'Bah! He is drunk most of the time or spends time with women he should not be with,' said Luja, crossing her arms in disgust.

'Oh,' was all Apollonia could muster.

'You should marry Zaim. He is lovely, Zaim is so kind and brave. He is always trying to help others, especially father, even our brothers, though none deserve his kindness for they're all jealous of him.' Luja's brow was creased in annoyance.

'Zaim ...' Apollonia's voice trailed off.

'Why are you marrying Fastiq?' Luja's annoyance was palpable.

'My father and your father agreed,' Apollonia replied. She had briefly met Zaim and there was no doubting it, she felt something and was sure he did too.

'Well, they shouldn't have, they should have asked me, as I usually know what's going to happen. I'm right most of the time, and I would have told them that Fastiq will be ...' Luja stopped abruptly.

'You can see the future?' asked Apollonia, taking the girl's hands in her own.

Luja was no longer cross with her, and brightness returned to her face.

'Only God knows what will happen and when it will happen,

but I see things, sometimes when I am awake, other times when I am asleep. When I tell others, they believe it, for many things have come true.'

'Like?'

'I had a waking dream showing me that a nest of rats had made a home inside the central granary which kept food for the city for the following year. It was sealed and would not be opened for some time. If I had not told my father, he said the rats would have eaten through the store by the time they'd opened it up.'

'What else?'

'One night whilst I was sleeping I dreamt of an ambush that my father would have fallen into. He avoided the route on his way to Gaza and was told later that an ambush had been planned by some Bedouin.'

'Have you seen anything about … me?'

'I saw you with Uncle Pelagios on a ship at sea; there was another man, a warrior and there was lots of blood on the deck. That was a scary dream and I woke up frightened, looking for Mama but she wasn't here.' Luja stared around the cell.

'Oh sister, I'm sorry,' Apollonia said, clutching Luja in a loving embrace.

They held onto one another, before Luja looked up and asked. 'Are you *really* going to marry Fastiq?'

Chapter 14

BLADES IN A WADI

Grim-faced soldiers from the Nabataean fortress town of Bozrah listened patiently to Prince Zaim's commands, before turning their mules around and riding up the winding path to the summit. The prince considered the position of these men: *The Seleucids may attack Bozrah as they did Sela, but this city will not fall so easily and can hold for weeks. The Seleucids do not have enough supplies for a long-term siege. Do they really have the mettle to attack Petra?*

Once mounted on his steed, Zaim turned to Captain Fahad. 'We ride for Petra.'

'Yes, your Highness,' replied the long-haired swordsman, issuing orders to the dozen men.

The Han explorer Chao Zhang rode beside Zaim who was once more indebted to his deadly poetic martial skills. Zaim had thanked God several times for gifting him the company of such a man.

The small party turned their steeds south, taking a route away from Bozrah. They rode for much of the morning, making camp in an oasis surrounded by date palms, where they drew water from a well and rested before moving on. The winter sun glowed behind a bank of clouds, intermittent streaks of light bursting through. As the afternoon came upon them, they reached the final leg of their journey with the winding road leading into the valley beyond which Petra, the Nabataean stronghold, lay.

It was just then that the distinct beating of hooves sounded.

The men in Zaim's party halted their mounts, as they caught sight of a dust of cloud, on the road behind them.

'What banner do they carry?' Fahad asked.

The men peered into the distance.

'Elephants are on it,' Chao said.

'Seleucids,' Fahad replied. 'They must have our scent and have followed us since Sela.'

'Yah! Let's ride,' said Zaim, spurring his horse into a gallop.

His companions streamed behind him, galloping for safety. They skirted the mountain and came to a downhill stretch leading into a low valley, which once crossed would turn east before swinging back south and becoming the highway which eventually led to Petra.

The horses careered at pace down into the valley, the vegetation sparse on either side. To the east was a wadi and to the west a mountain range unsuitable for horses. The sound of shouts behind them echoed along the pass.

As Zaim led his men his gaze was caught by movement up ahead and he slowed his steed.

'What is it,' Fahad asked, drawing up beside him.

Ahead of them were at least fifty, possibly more, armoured riders, lances raised and the elephant emblem of the Seleucids fluttering on their flags.

'Seleucids,' said Zaim. 'So close to Petra.'

He had underestimated Emperor Antiochus' boldness in taking the battle to the Nabataean stronghold, yet here they were within striking distance of Petra. The horses of the Seleucids started trotting in their direction. Behind him Zaim heard the pursuing riders' voices becoming clearer and soon he could see them. They were boxed in, the road ahead and behind blocked by Seleucids.

'Your Highness?' Fahad asked. 'Do we stand and fight?'

Zaim was not sure whether they could make it against what looked like one hundred mounted soldiers, when he had only a dozen men. There was also no knowing if the Seleucids had further troops close to hand. The west was blocked by the mountain, so he turned his mount east. The wadi was deep, and partly flooded by recent rainfall. He acted, riding his horse into the wadi, the men following. The winding wadi channel closed in on both sides, surrounded as it was by mountains. They were locked into this route, and it was taking them east away from Petra.

'What are you thinking, your Highness?' asked Fahad.

'They want us to go into the wadi,' Zaim said.

An arrow flew past the prince's head. The riders were within range; other arrows started flying past.

They had no choice.

Zaim urged his men forward and soon a dense clump of olive trees obscured the pack behind them. Ahead, the wadi dipped lower, a stream running through it. The horses slipped on some of the rocks.

'Dismount,' ordered Zaim. The cramp in his stomach spread to his chest. *What awaits us here?*

The pathway narrowed, rock walls rising either side, as water gushed around the hooves of their animals, wetting the men's boots. The rushing stream muted other sounds, and Zaim was not sure whether the Seleucid horsemen were pursuing them into the wadi. Nerves on edge, he looked about. The afternoon sun was obscured from much of the wadi, where different levels of shade dominated. Overhanging ghaf and Acacia trees growing on the edge of the plateau above them cast further shadows onto the wadi floor, plunging the route ahead in murk.

Clink.

Zaim heard the sound of metal on metal. He exchanged a worried glance with Fahad, then with Chao who'd also heard it. The edgy steeds strained at the reins, wanting to free themselves from this winding constricted path.

A loose pebble fell from above, splashing into the ankle-deep stream. Zaim froze.

The men cast nervous glances overhead. Still no movement. *Someone else is here. How many and who is going to be revealed soon,* thought Zaim, gripping the hilt of his weapon. If they were going to be attacked they needed room to fight.

'Release the horses,' Zaim said. 'Let them ride on ahead of us.'

The men complied.

Then it began.

'Aieee!'

The wail went up around the wadi, echoing off the rock walls. Dozens of piercing voices, if not hundreds, as the first Bedouin appeared. Robes flowing, face partly-veiled, dagger in hand, the man leaped straight at the closest Nabataean soldier, who to his credit managed to deflect the blow, before being overwhelmed by four other Bedouin who plunged Khanjars into him.

'Together!' Zaim cried at the top of his voice, as the men folded around the prince, their backs against one another.

Bedouin leapt at the men from every angle, and still more came. The fierce fighting was precise, the narrow space making any mistakes lethal.

A spear thrust came at Zaim. He kicked the weapon from the man's hand, before plunging his sword into his attacker's belly. Zaim pushed the slain man away as another Bedouin swung his sword at the prince's head. Zaim blocked, before swivelling and opening the man's jugular vein with the dagger in his left hand.

The Nabataean soldiers were soon overwhelmed by the Bedouin leaping at them, thrusting with daggers and spears, hacked-off broken swords and camel whips. His men retreated, as the onslaught continued with unrelenting ferocity. The Bedouin poured into the wadi from hidden places in the mountainside. *This attack was pre-planned,* thought Zaim. *The Bedouin and the Seleucids are working together.*

Though Bedouin numbers were significant, most were unskilled with weapons, and fell easily to such skilled fighters as Chao, Fahad, Taimur and the prince. The Bedouin soon realised the Han explorer was not to be approached and avoided him, focusing their efforts on the Nabataeans. Chao, now less busy defending himself, plunged into other skirmishes about him, helping the overwhelmed Nabataean soldiers. He saved several, but the onslaught continued and little by little the Nabataean soldiers fell, their numbers dwindling.

Just then Zaim noticed a group of four Bedouin dressed in black with glittering swords enter the fray. These fleet-footed men quickly surrounded Fahad. Close behind was another fighter, with a confident swagger, carrying swords in both hands. He wore a red cummerbund, and immediately made eye contact with Zaim coming in his direction.

These are the elite fighters, the others were sent to tire us out, thought Zaim.

Fahad was pinned against the rock wall, where he defended himself from a dual attack. Sensing the threat, Chao entered the fray, his Dragon Blade drawing blood from one of the black-robed fighters, who immediately turned his attention to the Han explorer and called over two others to assist him. The easterner was now fighting against three Bedouin. His movements a blur, he leapt high and low, ducked and swivelled, his speed impressive as his blade pierced the side of one of his opponents, felling the man.

The Bedouin with the red cummerbund was now before Zaim, his eyes ferocious and intense. There was no mistaking the face of their chief.

'Prince Zaim,' the Bedouin spoke with scorn in his voice amongst the din of battle.

'You break the unspoken alliances we have with the Bedouin,' Zaim replied.

The man twirled his swords in his hands. 'They only benefit the Nabataeans in their towns, leaving us to scavenge in the desert like beetles.'

'What is your name?' Zaim asked.

'Sakhr.'

The name was familiar, and he remembered his father mentioning a Bedouin chief who had risen above the others in the neighbouring desert. *So, this is the man*, thought Zaim. *I can see the leadership qualities in him.*

Sakhr smiled, then leapt at Zaim, his swords aiming for the prince's head. Zaim rolled under the sword strike, then flicked his sword arm back to catch the chieftain by surprise, but the Bedouin read his move and was already out of reach. Instead, he came back with his own flurry of low strikes aimed at the prince's stomach. Zaim blocked, then leapt back to avoid the second sword.

The Bedouin chief dived straight at him, swords circling out then snapping shut in a pincer movement. Zaim ducked once more, then flicked out his daggered hand and cut the Bedouin chief's arm, drawing a red line of blood. Sakhr seemed not to notice and simply spun away before leaping at him once more, swords twirling in a furious whirlwind. Zaim backed away, as a Bedouin lunged at him from behind, hoping to catch the prince off-guard. Zaim dodged the weak thrust, before slicing open the man's stomach.

The distraction allowed Sakhr to catch Zaim on the left wrist as the prince tried to twist away, but in doing so Zaim dropped his dagger. Zaim propelled himself backwards, avoiding the deadly strike swishing through the air, where his neck had been moments before. The prince clattered into a group of Bedouin, who now grabbed both of his arms, as two more helped. Sakhr came at him with his blade. There was a blur of movement from the left and both of Sakhr's blades flew from his hands.

Zaim watched as Chao skidded to a halt. Such speed caught the Bedouin holding Zaim by surprise and they loosened their grip, so Zaim yanked the two men on his right and left, sending them sprawling at the Bedouin chief.

'Run,' instructed Chao, racing past Zaim and cutting a path through the Bedouin. Zaim followed suit. Fahad and Taimur soon joined him, swatting away other attackers beside them. The other Nabataean soldiers did not make it out of the wadi.

They rounded a corner in the wadi, the area cleared, the stream still running through the middle. Zaim spotted their horses up ahead. The Bedouin chased them, screaming at the tops of their voices. The remaining Nabataeans and the Han explorer accelerated. An arrow flew past Zaim's head, as others followed. Reaching his steed he leapt onto it in one swift movement, digging his heels in, kicking the horse into a gallop. The three men by his side, they accelerated out of the wadi, leaving the Bedouin behind them.

Chapter 15

A WRAITH AT NIGHT

The daily evening ritual of having her hair brushed always appealed to Apollonia. The comb untied the knots in her hair, whilst she tried to untie the knots in her soul. She would use these moments to reflect on the day, forgive those who might have offended her and be grateful for what she had. It was a habit instilled by one of her teachers, who had instructed her to go to sleep with a light heart, so she woke feeling refreshed. In her bedchamber her maid applied the brush to her hair, whilst Apollonia turned her attention inward.

The silence was broken when Zoe asked, 'What was she like?'

'Who?' enquired Apollonia.

'The young princess?'

Recalling the odd encounter with Luja, she was once more drawn into thinking about Prince Zaim. *Where was he now? Was he safe? When would he return?* She had not seen Fastiq since arriving and Apollonia grew more anxious with the passing of each day. *Why did Fastiq not show himself? Was there something awful about his appearance that the Nabataeans were hiding till their wedding day?*

'I did meet Luja. She is a delightful child.'

'Why do they keep her in the temple?' asked Zoe.

'I do not know.'

'Is she dangerous?' asked Zoe.

'No, she would not harm a fly.'

'Why keep her in the temple, then?'

It was a question Apollonia had asked herself several times since she met the princess. Certainly, the child was odd, possessing an ability to see visions. Perhaps this gift unnerved her parents, who kept her away from the prying eyes of the court. Either way, they did not know that Luja's curiosity had her crawling about Petra through dangerous tunnels and holes.

'I think they regard her as very special, and want her to be safe,' said Apollonia.

'It's a strange way of keeping your daughter safe,' Zoe mumbled quietly to herself.

Marry Zaim, Luja had implored Apollonia. *For Fastiq is always drunk*. It unnerved her, this foresight the child had.

Javairea was back by her feet, swishing around her legs. The touch of the cat's fur was comforting against her bare ankles. Apollonia bent down and scratched Javairea behind the ear. The cat purred in delight.

In Alexandria, Apollonia had longed to be alone, as the royal court was a vibrant place, and the demands on her time many. She was always being called to events she was expected to attend, though she knew she was invited as an afterthought, as her older brothers and sisters, the ones contending for the throne after her father, were the chief guests at most gatherings. Petra, in contrast, was quiet in the evenings. The city seemed to be swallowed up by the surrounding mountains and people barely went out in the dusk. Apollonia would never have believed she'd say it, but she missed the nightlife of Alexandria.

Zoe plaited her hair, before rubbing her shoulders. 'Your Highness, is there anything else?'

'Thank you, Zoe, you are free to go. See you in the morning.'

The handmaiden packed away the comb and left.

Apollonia removed the shawl from around her shoulders, making her way to bed in her chemise. Javairea padded along beside her. As the princess pulled back her bedsheets, the door to her chamber was thrust open.

A man with bloodshot eyes entered. He was of medium height, thin, with a stern expression, and as he looked at her in her night clothes a lecherous smile appeared on his face. HIs robes were made of fine silk, but he wore them in a dishevelled manner. An ornate dagger hung from the cummerbund round his waist. Swaggering towards Apollonia, he left the door ajar behind him.

'You are a beauty,' he said, eyeing her up and down.

Apollonia felt naked, so penetrating was his gaze.

'Who are you?' she demanded, moving toward where her recurve bow and set of arrows was kept.

'I am the man you travelled to Petra for,' he replied.

Apollonia let out a gasp. 'Fastiq!' she whispered.

He bowed, approaching.

Javairea hissed, the hairs on her body standing up.

'I hate cats. I will bury this one in the desert,' Fastiq said.

Apollonia swept Javairea up and held her close to her bosom. 'No, you will not.'

'Feisty. I like that. Tell me Princess, what else do you know that will keep me happy?'

The sickening looks he gave her repulsed Apollonia as Fastiq licked his lips, unclothing her with his eyes.

'An honourable man would not ask such a question,' replied Apollonia.

Fastiq cackled. Coughing, he wiped the spittle from his mouth with the back of his hand.

'Honourable?' he smirked. 'I am not an honourable man, and never will be. I am known as a debaucher. My parents are displeased by my habits, but what do I care? I was never their favourite son.'

Apollonia's heart sank as she looked upon this cruel man, the man who was her betrothed, the man she had left Alexandria for, the man she had endured the desert journey for. Meeting him, she wanted nothing more than to flee back to Alexandria, back to her parents.

Fastiq approached, now only a few steps from her.

'Don't come closer,' she said, only a step away from her weapon.

'Why not? You are my betrothed. Why shouldn't I have a closer look at you?'

Apollonia tightened her grip on Javairea and moved away.

Fastiq laughed. Hands on his hips, he cocked his head to one side. 'Do not be frightened, I will not touch you tonight. Even I am not so reckless to ruin this marriage alliance that my parents have organised. Besides I have a slew of other women waiting to satisfy my pleasures tonight. I will make love to them and drink till sunrise.'

The immediate convulsing fear subsided, but not the dread of what was coming.

'But know this, on our wedding night, you,' he pointed his finger up and down her body, 'will be mine. All of you. Every single piece of you. I will taste you to see for myself whether a Ptolemaic Princess can entertain me as much as a Nabataean commoner.'

Noting the terror on her face, Fastiq continued, 'Know this, Apollonia. From now on you are a breeding cow with only one purpose. Produce my heirs. We will begin on our wedding night. I suggest you come to bed with all your seductive powers, as I am a man used to bedding many women.'

He let out a cackle, blew her a kiss, then strode from the chamber.

Shaken, Apollonia stared at his departing figure. *If there is a God, now is the time for Him to act. Now!* Her body trembled, then the tears fell, before she collapsed onto her bed, sobbing uncontrollably into the sheets.

Beside her Javairea meowed plaintively.

Chapter 16
A TIMELY FEINT

It was a steel blade, forged in Damascus, resting on a stand, the rubies around its hilt sparkling as the sun caught them. The solitary sword was displayed in the centre of a personal armoury, a square room whose walls housed an assortment of swords, shields, daggers and maces exclusively for Antiochus, Emperor of Seleucid. Sunlight streaked into the armoury through topaz and azure glass. A circular dais wide enough for two was positioned beside the blade.

Antiochus, his eyes brooding, danced his fingers around the hilt of the damascened sword. On a cushioned seat set against a wall, Tryphanea, youthful-looking mother of Antiochus, reclined, legs casually crossed. Ageless, she could be mistaken for the emperor's elder sister. Her faintly elongated eyes with their long lashes, set in a perfect sun-tinted face turned to look admiringly at her son. Closer to the emperor, some paces from the platform, General Pharnuches stood erect, fingers clasped behind his back.

Tryphanea and Pharnuches watched the emperor clasp and release the hilt of the ruby encrusted blade.

'We feint first,' declared Antiochus. 'Distract the Nabataeans with our attack on Sela, force them back to Petra. Then we strike at Gaza, our real target. Seize the spice, all of it.'

'Indeed Sire,' Pharnuches said, his voice gruff from a lifetime of barking orders at subordinates.

Antiochus forced a smile as he studied the muscular military man arms behind his back, chest out. His jet-black hair had begun to grey at the sides, but his square face with its deep-set eyes and chiselled jaw still made for a formidable presence. *He does not show me the deference he exhibited with my father. I could have pinned the loss to Ptolemy on Pharnuches but I found a more honourable man instead, Achaeus. But my dear Pharnuches, next time it will be you. It will be you. But I will need to wait, till I have Gaza in my grip, till I have the port secured, till I have the spice routes in my hands.* He stared at his most senior general, who even in his middle age remained a ferocious fighting man with impressive strength. *A dangerous rival.* Antiochus' eyes flicked back to his mother.

A taut smile crossed the general's chiselled face, as though he had read the thoughts of the young monarch. He said, 'Tigranous will have sacked Sela by now. After he lays siege to Petra there will be few Nabataean forces to face the Seleucid army in Gaza.'

In a melodious voice Tryphanea asked, 'And what of their alliance with Ptolemy? Have you considered this?'

The emperor noticed the subtle exchange of glances between his mother and Pharnuches. *They are joined at the hip, those two. Would my mother really betray me for her lover?*

The general ever so slightly tilted his head back and addressed Tryphanea. 'Oh, we have, my lady. Ptolemy is currently occupied in a campaign against the Romans in north Africa. Of course, neither side wants full scale conflict over the territory, so each is moving its troops, in battle formations, and declaring to the other that they are prepared to fight should they be pushed. It keeps our two greatest rivals occupied with one another whilst we pick off these desert Arabs, secure the spice routes from the south and replenish our treasury with coin.'

For some strange reason the words of the Oracle came to Antiochus' mind: The Eagle of Rome will rise...For the time of the Elephant Lords...nears its end. *Damn haggard old witch. Why put doubt in my mind when glory is so close?*

'I grant you it is a mischievous plan, Pharnuches, but what of the Hasmonean King of Jerusalem?' Tryphanea asked. Antiochus noted how his mother had taken to using the general's first name recently. *I do not like this level of intimacy between them. I will need to split up the lovebirds.*

The general turned to face her. 'Jannaeus is an obstinate fellow with grand designs regarding his own legacy in Jewish folklore. He has not declared whether he is with us or against us.'

Antiochus exchanged a look with his mother. *All rulers are obstinate with an eye on their legacy, Pharnuches.*

'He has a choice?' Tryphanea sounded perplexed. 'Seleucids do not give choices to the likes of the Jews or Arabs. We issue ultimatums, tell them what must be done, by when, and by whom. That is all.'

Pharnuches swung his gaze from mother to son.

Antiochus stroked the hilt of the sword one last time, then strolled across and flung himself into the cushioned armchair beside his mother. He placed his arms on the side rests and looked at her. *They are playing a game with me,* thought Antiochus. *They ask one another such questions, when they know the answer, but they want to gauge my reaction.*

Antiochus cupped his chin and said, 'That is how it should be, Mother, yet these inferior desert dwellers have taken it upon themselves to assume they are worthy of discussing terms with the inheritors of Alexander. It is a sign of decay in our times, the breakdown of all respectable norms in society. Yet, we must deal with it, for we have been destined to live in this moment, and it is for us to restore the glories of the Seleucid past. By the time we have finished with the Jews and the Arabs, they will wish they had never heard the name Seleucid.'

'Well spoken,' Pharnuches said, stealing a lover's look at Tryphanea.

'Son, these are my sentiments precisely, but without action, these are merely words. What are you going to *do* about it?'

So, this is it. They have placed me in a corner and want to see what I will do. It would have been more subtle had you not trained me so well, Mother, for there are games within games within games, and we are playing one at present. Let us then play.

'Should the Hasmonean King reject our advances,' he declared, 'after Gaza we will advance our Elephant Legions and sack Jerusalem. It has been done in the past and we will do it once more. It will silence the Jews and send a firm message to the Arabs to remain within their desert Kingdom of Hegra, or else we'll march our legions into the godforsaken desert if we have to.'

Pharnuches shuffled his feet. 'The desert is a difficult terrain, Sire; our soldiers are not trained for such warfare.'

'I care not whether we destroy the Arabs in their stronghold, General, only that they remain out of the way and do not interfere in our plans to profit from the spice routes.'

'They will resort to guerrilla tactics, and we will need to consider the wisdom of advancing deeper into the desert.'

'Tigranous is mobilising the Bedouin against the Nabataeans. We will pay these scourges with the booty they so crave, and it will keep the Nabataeans busy whilst we secure the route south to Aden and the spice.'

'The Bedouin are ... an unreliable feral ally. They may be a friend today, but a perceived slight to their honour can make them a ferocious vengeful enemy for generations. We must be careful when dealing with such ignorant people,' said Pharnuches.

'Tigranous will make them or break them,' declared Antiochus. 'We know the beast's methods work. Leave it to him, Pharnuches, and do not concern yourself with such matters.'

Tryphanea tucked up her legs onto the chair, taking up a more comfortable position. 'My informants in Jerusalem tell me there is a messianic mood amongst the Jews,' she said. 'They expect the Messiah to appear any day.'

'The Jews have been sent many so-called prophets,' said Antiochus. 'Yet one has not appeared for hundreds of years. Besides, if the stories about King Alexander Jannaeus are correct, he will not want a Messiah usurping his power. He will put an end to the fellow. Of that, I am sure. Enough of this talk of prophets and messengers. Now Pharnuches, where is this Ptolemaic bride you promised me? What was the girl's name again?'

'Apollonia,' replied Tryphanea.

'Yes, when should we expect her in Damascus?'

Pharnuches stood a little straighter. 'A unit has been sent to extract her from the guardianship of the Nabataeans. We expect news any day.'

Antiochus cocked his head to one side. 'I see. Make it soon, for it will offer us options when dealing with Ptolemy. If Ptolemy is engaged with the Romans in north Africa, it keeps them away from supporting the Nabataeans as part of their fledging alliance with the Arabs. But what could be better than to take the girl and hold her hostage in Damascus? Then there is no marriage alliance between Ptolemy and Nabataea, and the Arabs will truly be without imperial partners. We can then do with them as we please.'

'We will, my Lord,' replied Pharnuches.

Now let me test their allegiance to me, thought Antiochus.

'General,' said Antiochus, crossing his legs and sitting up straight. 'I fear the previous campaign against Ptolemy did not bear dividends as I was absent from the field of battle, relying on lesser men to make decisions.' The emperor paused, watching the impact of the words on Pharnuches, who had commanded the Seleucid forces. The general's impassive expression remained the same. *He hides his hatred of me. This makes him more dangerous, for when the senses are guarded so well it is difficult to determine what malevolence lurks in the soul.* 'On this occasion I will personally command my legions to Gaza.'

'Son,' remonstrated Tryphanea. 'Why take the risk when you have fine generals such as Pharnuches and Tigranous who can take to the field? You are far too important to the empire to risk anything happening to you in a fight with desert nomads. There will only be kings on the battlefield, there will be no emperors for you to treat with.'

'Had Alexander taken such an approach we would have no empire today. No, Mother, I will take to the field. Pharnuches, you will take command of the fleet off the shore of Gaza. Have ten vessels each laden with three hundred men ready should we need them. We will not, but it will be a morale breaker for the Nabataeans who, as they engage with our infantry and elephant cavalry, will look out to sea and know there are plenty more Seleucids to fight.'

Pharnuches exchanged a momentary glance with Tryphanea; it told Antiochus everything he needed to know about their little plot to overthrow him.

Chapter 17
A DIFFICULT QUESTION

War edged closer to Petra, but Arab hospitality being what it was meant Pelagios received the full formal hospitality due to a visiting royal. He banqueted and was honoured in every possible way by his hosts, King Obodos and Queen Fazluna. For his part, Pelagios was keen to be on his way and informed Andreas and Theron they would soon go back to Gaza where the *Chloe* was docked. Presently he waited by the Nymphaeum, beside which was a tank collecting water from the other side of the northern valley.

He expected his crew to be fully equipped with supplies and he intended to set sail as soon as he arrived in Gaza. The last thing Pelagios desired was to be caught in a battle between the Seleucids, Nabataeans and the might of Ptolemy. All men must die, he told himself, but to die for another's cause seemed like wasting one's precious life. Far better to die in the arms of one's family in one's home. Despite his swashbuckling seafaring ways, he had no wish to perish in the ocean and end up as fish food. No, Pelagios was a man of the sea who wanted a domestic death.

Pelagios hoped to see Apollonia before his departure in the morning. He had caught sight of her at the banquet the previous evening, but she did not stay long and was surrounded by women of the royal household, making it awkward for him to approach. *A lovely girl, burdened with a deplorable husband to be. I feel for the child*, he thought. *Yet there is nothing I can do.*

His own wife and children were on his mind. They would be expecting him any day now and yet here he was in Arabia. The voyage back would take two weeks and if they were delayed there was the chance of getting caught in one of the early winter storms, when sailing was too dangerous, even for an experienced sea hand.

Gripping the stone wall of the water tank he observed Prince Stylian waddling along the other side of the street. Catching sight of the Aegean ruler, the prince smiled and waved to him, before he continued down the street and disappeared from view. The sound of soft sandalled feet behind Pelagios drew his attention, and he noticed a thin sickly-looking man wearing the gown of the royal household approach him and bow.

'Your Highness, Prince Asylaion will see you now. If you can come with me.'

'Of course,' replied Pelagios in a formal tone.

The Aegean had no desire to meet Asylaion, but the prince had insisted on taking Pelagios on a tour of the city's defences, seeking his assessment of them. Pelagios doubted the prince's sincerity, for King Obodos was an experienced fighting man, as were the generals surrounding him. Their evaluation of desert warfare was superior to any Pelagios could offer, so there must be some other reason the prince sought time with him alone. *I will soon find out his intentions, or at least have a better understanding of what the true purpose of this meeting is.*

Following the messenger, Pelagios crossed the street, climbing two sets of stairs built into the mountainside, before walking through a tunnel. They emerged in the northern part of the city, with the outer defence wall in the distance ahead of them. Here, Asylaion stood waiting. The messenger bowed to the prince, before withdrawing.

'Pelagios, I am pleased you can spare me the time,' Asylaion said.

'It is the least I can do in return for the gracious hospitality your family has shown me.' Pelagios replied.

'We all have a soft spot for you. Even my wayward younger brother Zaim lived for several years under your tutelage.'

Zaim was a good lad when he came to me, pure of heart. We just sharpened his skills, thought Pelagios. *Whereas you, Asylaion, are a cold-hearted wretch.*

'Come Pelagios, I wish to show you our defences and seek your counsel.'

Pelagios thought, *this is precisely what the Romans wanted me to do, and I refused. Yet here I am, being given access to this information. Blast those damn Romans! How am I going to avoid their questioning?*

The prince led the Aegean monarch up another flight of stone stairs, which were wet from the overnight rain, then along a rampart which led to the side of a raised wall. They ascended a steady incline till they reached a small platform. From here, the prince directed Pelagios up a second slope till they arrived at the summit of the northern wall. Lookout towers were built every fifty yards and two soldiers patrolled each of these. On the other side of the wall was a drop of ten metres, leading to an open expanse of land, which was filled with small water pools that had collected from the season's first rains and where one hundred soldiers could stand in formation. Beyond this was the craggy maze of a mountain range.

'This is the highest wall we have built,' said Asylaion. 'As you can see, there is no room here for an army to mass, and none would approach from Jabal al-Mu'aysra ash Shariyya, for crossing it is playing with death.'

The Aegean cast his gaze around the area, then back towards the wall and the lookout towers. 'Better to subdue an army without fighting, I'd say that is the best result. I cannot see how an invading army could mass on this wall. At most they could assemble a hundred soldiers who could be picked off by archers.'

'Precisely,' said Asylaion. 'Yet my father plans to increase the height of the wall, which I see little point in doing.'

Pelagios retained a straight face but knew Asylaion was seeking his opinion on whether Obodos was right or not. *I must guard my tongue for this one is like a serpent and will use my words to hound his father.*

'Your father's judgement in this matter is far weightier than any observation I can make. If I were you, I would pay little attention to my comments and go with those of Obodos.'

'You are being diplomatic, Pelagios,' said Asylaion, casting a wary gaze up and down the outer wall. The nearest guards were well out of earshot, but when Asylaion spoke, his voice was low and for the ears of Pelagios only.

'My father is getting old, he makes … mistakes. These are dangerous times for our people, as several empires vie for influence over the spice routes in Arabia. Yet my father in his wisdom has chosen to build an alliance with the weakest of the empires: Ptolemy.'

This is a dangerous conversation this lad is getting me embroiled in, thought Pelagios.

'Others are better suited as allies for the Nabataeans, but father does not consider them.'

'Others?'

'The Seleucids vie for influence in Arabia and are courting partners in their plans for expansion. Meanwhile the Romans consider their moves in the region; they watch and learn, evaluate potential allies and enemies. It is not a question of *whether* the Romans will enter Arabia, but *when*, for to them the land of spice is promising and they seek to control it,' said Asylaion, stopping to observe Pelagios. 'You are of a region close to Rome, and so I would ask, what say you of an alliance between Nabataea and Rome?'

Does this prince know about my position with the Romans and is not letting on? I must tread cautiously here. He may be bluffing and if I reveal my contacts with Rome, he may hold me captive. If I say I don't have ties to Rome, but he knows that I meet with their spies, then he will have caught me out.

'What interests you about the Romans that the existing alliance with Ptolemy does not offer?' asked Pelagios.

Asylaion smiled. He gripped the edge of the wall, applying his weight to it. 'Solid wall,' he said, pushing away from it. 'Built from rock and sand.'

Pelagios looked at the wall. 'Indeed,' he replied.

Asylaion kicked the lower part of the wall with his sandal and a chunk came away, along with flecks of sand and stone.

'Yet the lower section is weak, not made with such care. Smash this, and the upper part will break. The Ptolemaic and Seleucid imperial dynasties are like the crumbling lower section of this wall. They have

withered over the centuries and have lost their steel. They are riven by
in-fighting. I hear that the daughters of Ptolemy are more suitable for
the throne than his sons, whereas Antiochus is weary of his brothers
trying to usurp his throne. It is a well-known fact that his mother,
Tryphanea, cannot be trusted by any of her sons.'

'These are common problems in several imperial and royal families,'
replied Pelagios. *Your hatred of your brothers is testimony to this.*

'True,' said Asylaion, waving his hand about. 'And we have our
own difficulties as a royal family. But, my dear Pelagios, Rome seems
different, for there is no imperial dynasty which rules it. Is this not
the case?'

'It is, though the Romans have many competing factions and considerable bloodletting goes on amongst the elite governing classes,'
said Pelagios.

Asylaion considered this comment. He nodded thoughtfully.

'Let us consider a theoretical situation for a moment, Pelagios.'

'Very well,' said Pelagios, as the sight of two soldiers changing
positions caught his attention.

'If you ruled Nabataea and had to choose which of the three imperial powers you would form an alliance with – Ptolemy, Seleucid
or Rome – which would you select?'

Pelagios sucked in the air between his teeth. 'I am grateful I do
not rule and so have no opinion on the matter.'

'I know you do not, which is why I said it is hypothetical, but if
you did, which power would you ally with?'

The prince pushes me to an answer, which I will not give.

'When decisions such as this are to be made, rulers like your father
consider several factors. They look to their immediate political and
economic needs, asking whether the alliance will protect the borders
of their kingdom and ensure income continues to flow to the treasury.
They consider the long-term ramifications of such a move, and who
the ally is. I am sure your father addressed all such factors before
choosing Ptolemy.'

'Yes, I understand, but what would you have done, Pelagios?'

The lad does not let up.

'I dare say that if had the information your father had at his disposal, it is quite likely I would have made the same choice. If, however other intelligence came to me, then perhaps my decision would have been different. You can never make the perfect choice, only the best one at the time, but once you make it you must honour the alliance, for one's word is one's bond.'

'Yes, so we Arabs say,' smirked Asylaion.

Pelagios was keen to leave the subject but something inside him would not let it go just yet. He asked, 'And what would Asylaion have done?'

The prince flashed a cold brutal smile. 'As you say, it depends on what intelligence you have.'

This lad is crafty, he holds back, yet asks me to reveal my position. The sooner I depart the better for my health.

'One more matter, if I may, Pelagios?'

'Please.'

'My disreputable brother Fastiq the Grim is to marry Apollonia, a beautiful girl if I ever saw one. With this marriage my father seeks to cement our alliance with Ptolemy. If Nabataea calls on Ptolemy for assistance, will they heed this call?'

'Ptolemy has formed an alliance with Nabataea and with it made a military commitment to come to your assistance. Why do you question such a matter, when it has already been agreed?'

'Let me ask the question another way – would Ptolemy go to war with the Seleucids or the Romans over Nabataea? After all, the Seleucids are presently not far from Petra?'

Pelagios remembered his conversation with Emperor Ptolemy and he had doubts that Ptolemy would honour such a commitment. He was more interested in distracting the Seleucids, and the Nabataeans were a useful distraction.

'Only Ptolemy can answer that.'

The prince nodded and Pelagios was left with the distinct feeling that Asylaion did not want Ptolemy to come to their aid.

Chapter 18

AN UNSTEADY GATHERING

Dawn broke as Prince Zaim led his weary decimated party west towards the mountain passes leading to Petra. Nabataean soldiers placed as field lookouts popped their heads up from concealed watch-holes as the prince passed. He noted the looks of concern on their faces.

'What comes up the road, your Highness?' asked one of the soldiers, calling down from his position above a cliff wall.

'A sizeable Seleucid and Bedouin force. We must prepare ourselves,' replied Zaim.

'Bedouin!' the other lookout exclaimed.

'You will not be safe in your current locations: fall back to the first fortress and tell the captains to pull their sentries back. The Bedouin will not take the straight road: they will come via the mountain and your hiding places will be revealed.'

'Yes, your Highness,' the soldiers replied, collecting up their belongings.

Zaim rode with Fahad by his side and Taimur and Chao trailing behind. *When these troubles are over, and if we survive, I will forever be indebted to Chao Zhang.* The prince allowed his mount to fall back, indicating that Taimur should ride ahead, so that he could speak with Chao.

'I have not thanked you properly for saving my life last night,' Zaim said.

'You saved mine,' Chao replied. 'When you took me in. I was lost and would not have survived another day.'

Zaim nodded.

'With this debt repaid, you are now free to be on your way and there is no need for you to become entangled in this war. Why risk yourself? Take what provisions you need from Petra, then ride west to complete your imperial mission. God willing, your companions will be waiting for you by the Middle Sea.'

'Thank you, Prince Zaim. As you say the debt is cleared, but the *Way* teaches us "One who excels as a warrior does not appear formidable; One who excels in fighting is never roused in anger; One who excels in defeating his enemy does not join issue; One who excels in employing others humbles himself before them. This is known as the virtue of non-contention; This is known as making use of the efforts of others; This is known as matching the sublimity of heaven." So, I wait for now, with your people, by your side, my weapon at your disposal. When the peril to your kingdom is cleared, I will complete my imperial mission.'

Zaim reached out his hand and the Han explorer shook it.

'Till the threat is over,' Zaim said.

Chao nodded.

The two men rode on silently, the narrow eastern entry to Petra coming into view, at the end of which there stood a set of gates. As they approached the fortifications, riders were emerging. Zaim immediately recognised the Aegean islanders, Pelagios, Andreas and Theron. They were accompanied by a small troop of Nabataean soldiers as an honour guard to accompany the guests north.

Zaim sped up, as did the other three men, drawing to a halt before Pelagios.

'Lad,' Pelagios said. 'You look awful. What happened?'

Zaim hadn't considered the state of his shredded clothes, bloodstained tunic, and mud-dried hair. 'The Seleucids led us into an ambush by the Bedouin,' he replied. 'We lost several men, good men, men with families.'

'Damn Seleucids,' said Pelagios. 'Who leads them?'

'It is difficult to say,' Zaim spoke quickly, glancing across at Fahad and Taimur who understood his meaning. *I cannot embroil my uncle any further; he must return to his family, not seeking out Tigranous.*

'Difficult?' Pelagios asked.

'There were several legions, King Pelagios,' Fahad added. 'We barely made it out of Sela alive, before the attack by the Bedouin in the wadi.'

'I see,' said Pelagios glancing at his own men before addressing Fahad. 'Captain, what road should we take to avoid these blasted Seleucids and Bedouin?'

'Take the high northern pass over the mountains.' Fahad indicated a spot behind him. 'The elevation will keep you above the Seleucid army as it marches this way and it is unlikely the Bedouin will roam so high into the mountains when there is little need to do so. They will prefer to stay in the lower valleys where there are streams and vegetation.'

Pelagios nodded. 'The northern high pass it is, then.'

The Aegean monarch leaned towards Zaim. 'Look after yourself, lad.'

'I will, God willing,' Zaim replied.

Pelagios leant even closer, whispering, 'All it takes is for someone on the inside to betray you. Keep a close watch on all, otherwise the wolves and hyenas will be amongst you.'

Zaim remembered being told of a secret meeting taking place in Sela with General Tigranous. *Who is that man? Is he already in Petra? And what does he have to gain in siding with the Seleucids?*

'I will, Uncle. Now, you must return home, it is where you will find light, as the world grows dark' he replied.

Pelagios leant back in his saddle and smiled.

The prince watched the Aegeans depart, before turning his weary mount towards the entrance.

Once inside, Zaim ordered a messenger to go on ahead and notify his parents of his return, as well as asking his brothers to assemble along with General Ghassan. He instructed his companions to take some rest and meet him at midday.

When Zaim entered the king's private assembly room his mother was present, but the others had not yet arrived.

'Son,' Fazluna called out, rising from her seat, crossing the burgundy carpet to take him by the hand. 'How are you?'

Obodos was soon beside them, his hand on Zaim's shoulder.

'I look worse than I feel.'

'Are you hurt?' Fazluna asked.

'No,' Zaim replied. 'Just tired.'

Fazluna placed her hand upon his cheek. 'Promise?'

'Yes, mother, I am fine.' Zaim looked to his father.

'Then he is fine, dear,' Obodos said. 'Come sit.'

Zaim took the cushioned seat opposite his parents, as a servant poured him a glass of cool lemon and mint sherbet before departing.

'Where are the others?' Zaim asked.

'They will be here soon,' Obodos replied.

Zaim nodded, quenching his thirst as the liquid slid down his parched throat.

'There is something I would like to share before the others arrive,' Zaim said.

'Go on, son,' Obodos replied.

'In Sela, I was told about a secret meeting between Tigranous, the Seleucid general and a man who may be Nabataean.'

'Tigranous!' Fazluna exclaimed. 'You did not tell Pelagios, did you?'

'No, I did not, Mother. The only thing I want for my uncle is his safe return home.'

'Good boy,' Fazluna said, reaching over to squeeze his hand.

'Any idea who this man was?' Obodos asked.

'No,' Zaim replied.

'Then how can we be sure it was a Nabataean?' Obodos said.

'We cannot, but if we have a traitor in Petra, we are at risk from this Seleucid raiding party, who are supported by Bedouin.'

The door at the far end of the room opened.

'Brother,' Asylaion said, striding in. Behind him, more slowly. waddled Stylian, brandishing a roasted leg of lamb which he was gamely chewing on.

Seeing the appalled look on his parents' faces, the gluttonous prince declared, 'It seemed a shame to waste it.'

General Ghassan arrived moments later and they took seats in a semicircle. Ghassan gave a reassuring nod to Zaim as he sat down.

Father is fortunate to have such a loyal soldier by his side. God willing, may Fahad and Taimur have a long life and may I be blessed with wise counsellors.

The door swung open, and everyone turned to see the newcomer.

'Fastiq, son!' Fazluna said in surprise.

'Yes, mother, your son is sometimes sober enough to hear the call of the royal messenger.'

Obodos wore a grim expression, motioning for his wayward son to take a seat beside Stylian.

'Explain the situation,' Obodos said to Zaim.

The prince described conditions in Sela, avoiding mention of a possible traitor who'd been seen in the city, and finished with the ambush on the journey back to Petra.

'The Seleucids are crawling all over Nabataean territories,' Ghassan declared. 'How did they team up with the Bedouin? The nomads have no allegiances.'

'Only to their love of booty. The souq of Sela was looted by them,' Zaim said, adding. 'I fear Petra is their true target.'

'Nonsense!' Asylaion interjected. 'No army can breach our walls. Everyone knows this. They would not waste their precious resources on such an endeavour.'

'A siege, maybe?' Fazluna asked.

'Your Highness,' Ghassan said. 'We have provisions and water supplies to last the year and they do not; they will not lay a long siege, for they cannot endure through the winter let alone the summer.'

'We have food, then,' Stylian stated, happy in the knowledge he would not starve. He tore the last piece of meat off the bone, licking his lips as he did so.

'And women,' added Fastiq, leaning over to Stylian as he said it, so that his mother would not hear.

'You have a bride now,' Stylian whispered back.

'A man can never be satisfied with one woman,' Fastiq replied.

Zaim heard the exchange. His cheeks flushed with anger and

embarrassment. Apollonia deserved a loyal husband. *I must not let my feelings for her colour the impression of my brother. He merely jests, but what a filthy quip*, he thought.

'There is no need to worry, Mother,' Asylaion declared. 'The Seleucids are not getting into Petra.'

Obodos exchanged a glance with Zaim, before saying. 'Tell them what you told me and your mother.'

Zaim recounted the news he'd received in Sela concerning Tigranous' clandestine meeting with a man of standing, who may have been Nabataean, adding, 'It begs the question – do we have a traitor within our walls?'

'*If* there is one,' Asylaion said. 'It will be an army man.'

'Ghassan?' Obodos enquired.

'My soldiers are loyal, your Highness, always have been, you know this. I find it hard to believe it could be a military man,' Ghassan said.

'Well, it's not a member of the royal family, is it,' Asylaion retorted. 'That leaves only the military, for the administrators would have neither the knowledge nor the access to let anyone in. I'd suggest, General, you undertake a thorough investigation of your officers. Interview them all, make them sweat a little. Traitors tend to squeal like swine being taken to slaughter.'

Fastiq nudged Stylian in the ribs, whispering. 'Wench or princess, they all squeal when I have my way with them.'

Stylian licked his fingers. 'I'm not very good with women. Perhaps you can pass on some tips,' he said.

'You're too fat, brother,' Fastiq muttered back. 'Women are worried you might crush them.'

'I never thought about that,' Stylian replied, patting his stomach.

The vulgar conversation between his two older brothers made Zaim uneasy, as he tried to focus on the conversation about the traitor. He could see that Asylaion was attempting to shift suspicion to the army and ultimately General Ghassan. *The general has been my father's lifelong advocate: it is beyond question he is loyal. Who else could it be?*

'I will happily question your officers myself,' Asylaion added.

'Your Highness, I don't think you need to spend your time in such an endeavour,' Ghassan said.

'Why not?' Asylaion retorted. 'You aren't hiding something are you?'

Ghassan's face flushed red with anger, and he looked to the king for support.

'Asylaion, you are my son, but Ghassan is my oldest confidant and trusted advisor. I would without hesitation consign my family and our empire to his temporary safekeeping and I know he would not abuse his position.'

'I understand, Father, but we are talking about the future of the kingdom. If there is an iota of suspicion, then we must root it out and expose the traitor.'

'We must,' Obodos said.

'Then I propose,' Asylaion continued. 'Whilst I arrange for these interviews to take place, that I order officers and soldiers from my own Scorpion regiment to take control of the northern and southern defence walls. I trust them implicitly. We cannot afford to have a security failure at this time.'

'Ghassan?' Obodos turned to his general.

'As the prince wishes, your Highness. However, I would recommend that the existing divisions remain in place, but that the guard is doubled with the presence of the Scorpion regiment,' Ghassan said.

'Asylaion?' Obodos asked.

'This is of course a sensible precaution, but all existing officers must stand down. My officers under the leadership of Captain Jahm will take command.'

Listening to the exchange, Zaim thought, *the traitor is not in the army, Ghassan runs a tight ship. Yet my brother insists on questioning Ghassan's officers. Surely, it would be a better use of our time to fortify the defences further.*

'Father,' Zaim said. 'I would ask that we send messengers to Hegra and other Nabataean fortifications, asking them to send as many soldiers as they can to Petra. It will take time for them to send a relief force, but if we are in for a long siege, their numbers will make a difference and force the Seleucids back north.'

'Agreed,' the king said.

'What about Ptolemy's army? When do we expect them to show up?' Fastiq asked.

'Word has been sent,' Obodos replied.

'There has to be some benefit to marrying his daughter,' Fastiq quipped.

Anger flared inside Zaim. Clenching his fists, he remained silent in the presence of his parents.

Chapter 19

SEARCHING FOR ONE

Achaeus, legendary Seleucid warrior and General had chosen to take the road from Gaza to Jerusalem. He was not sure why, nor what he would find, but it was something in his heart. An unusual thing he pondered, to be relying on intuition, but a gnawing in his stomach implored him to follow this path.

As the city of Jerusalem drew closer, he noticed two men pushing a cart laden with figs and lemons up the road in the opposite direction to him. Seeing him, they waved their hands in greeting. Achaeus returned the gesture. The sound of the cart faded and was replaced by the swish and clatter of a merchant's wagon. Two riders steered it and offered salutations to Achaeus, which were returned in kind. The morning wore on in much the same way – there were long periods of silent reflection for the General, broken by short interludes when travellers headed in the direction of Jerusalem or away from it.

Whilst in Gaza Achaeus had been set on returning to Damascus to meet his emperor, Antiochus, but then something happened that changed all of that.

He thought back to it now - the temple of Helios in Gaza had been overcrowded, after the recent arrival of several sailing vessels, their crews and passengers eager to pay homage to the sun god.

After he had said his litanies, he departed. Lost in his musings, Achaeus turned away from the souk and headed towards the sea. He wanted to feel the clean air in his lungs. He remembered pushing the recent humiliation he had suffered at the hands of Ptolemy's administrators out of his mind, as well as the frustrating loss of imperial support from Antiochus. Warehouses stood either side of him, as the gravel path between them narrowed. It was a long stretch leading to an opening beside the beach. It was quiet and he liked it this way.

Three men stepped out from a storehouse ahead of him. Two drew swords, the third a lance. Hearing footsteps behind, he turned to see three more. Scolding himself for his lack of vigilance, Achaeus pushed back the hood of his cloak to reveal his features. A door swung open to his right and three more armed men emerged. *Nine.* He would be very lucky to escape this ambush. Achaeus retreated, the wall of a storehouse against his back.

'I am Achaeus, Seleucid envoy. I am on imperial business.'

'We know,' growled a short man.

'I have no quarrel with you. Allow me to leave,' Achaeus said.

The short man sniggered. 'They say you're the most courageous man in the world.' He turned to his companions. 'Doesn't sound like the words of a brave man.'

'Who sent you?' Achaeus asked.

Shorty rubbed his thumb and forefingers together, indicating they had been paid.

Achaeus unbuckled the pin of his cloak, allowing the garment to fall to the ground. He drew his sword.

The six assailants closed in on either side, as did the one in front of him. There was not much room to manoeuvre and nowhere to run. Taking a deep breath, he settled himself and looked forward to entering the fields of Elysium.

Achaeus leapt forward, catching Shorty by surprise. The man barely had time to raise his weapon, before he fell back trying, to avoid the strike. Achaeus swung right then left, the men momentarily backing away, as he took up a low crouching position.

'Attack him together,' Shorty cried out.

A flurry of weapons came in his direction. Too many at once. He blocked and parried, lashed out with his own sword, which entered one man's belly and another's neck. Some assailants backed off having been cut, whilst more surged forward. Block, parry, thrust. He rolled under one blade, but tripped on the leg of a slain man. He stumbled, hands on the ground balancing himself, as a man kicked away his legs. Another kicked him in the back. He spun away on the ground. *Get up.* By his reckoning there were still six, maybe seven men to fight. His weapon was knocked out of his hand and a boot came for his face. He grabbed it whilst on the ground, twisted the man's ankle, heard it snap, before releasing it. He leapt up, to land back on his heels, but then took the flat of a blade against the back of his head, pushing him to one knee.

The blades around him suddenly stopped.

He heard metal on metal, the cries of men falling. He wiped the blood from his nose, squinting through a bruised eye. Three men were cutting through his attackers, like scythes at a harvest. He watched their impressive swordplay; the assassins fell one by one, till there were none remaining.

Pelagios, King of Mithymna, walked over to him, offering his hand. Behind him were Theron the navigator and Dorian the helmsman.

Achaeus gripped it, rising. He was sore all over and the king's strength was welcome.

'Thank you,' he whispered hoarsely.

'It hardly seemed a fair fight,' Pelagios said.

Through narrow eyes, Achaeus regarded Pelagios. 'Your Highness,' Achaeus offered a bow, 'I thank you. I am indebted to you. If ever you need a sword hand by your side, I pledge mine. Now if you will excuse me, I have some matters to take care of.'

After a moment Pelagios replied, 'I may hold you to that pledge, Achaeus of Seleucid.'

Had his mind been clearer he may not have needed the assistance of Pelagios and his men, though he was grateful for it.

Jerusalem drew closer, it's walls now apparent. It was then Achaeus noticed an old Jewish rabbi nestled between two olive trees. Achaeus instinctively stopped, placed his hand on his heart, then bowed reverentially. He was not sure why he did this but there was something about the man that necessitated it. He then made to continue when the rabbi called him over.

'Sir, please come, sit,' the rabbi said. The priest bore a cheerful disposition and had a beaming smile upon his face.

Achaeus paused, before approaching. 'Rabbi, good morning and peace be with you.'

'Please sit with me, young man,' the jolly rabbi said.

Achaeus swept his cloak back and sat down with his knees pointed towards the elder. He loosened the pack he was carrying, placing it to one side, before adjusting his sword belt.

When the rabbi noticed Achaeus' sword belt, the Seleucid noticed a momentary look of disappointment on the elder's face, but then it was gone and replaced by a jovial disposition.

'I am Anan Ben Jacob, I serve the Jews of this city in whatever manner God sees fit for me. You, my young friend, appear to be a visitor. How was your journey?'

'It is an honour to meet you, rabbi,' Achaeus said, placing his hand over his heart again. 'I am but a traveller.'

'We are all travellers in this world on our journey back to God, where we will be reunited with His divine majesty,' said Anan.

Achaeus nodded but did not say anything.

'Can I be of any service to my young friend?'

Achaeus let out a long deep breath. 'I am not a Jew,' he said.

'That does not matter; we are all creatures of God, each finding a way up the mountain. There are many paths one can take. So long as they head upwards, then we all seek the same destination, to be in the divine presence.'

'I come from a place where there is a pantheon of gods. There are many one can choose from, depending on one's need and profession in life,' Achaeus said.

'We are monotheists. We believe in one God.'

Achaeus rubbed his beard with his fingers, before saying. 'I am searching for a path.'

'Towards?'

'I do not know. Honestly, I cannot even be sure if it will take me to Elysium, to dwell with the heroes of the past or to Hades to rot in the underworld. All I know is that my whole life, there was a path I travelled. It took me to places which I did not desire to be, but it was a well-trodden path for a man in my profession. Now, I am a man in the desert, with only sand dunes before him and clouds overhead, so I am unable to orient myself.'

'Sometimes it is best to let the clouds pass. Then you will see the stars,' said the Anan.

'Sit it out,' mumbled Achaeus, more to himself.

'Son, I have witnessed generations come and go. What family I had, has passed from this world. If I may be of some assistance to you, it would be my honour.'

Achaeus smiled, settling himself comfortably on the ground, placing his scabbard under his thigh.

Achaeus cleared his throat then said. 'Throughout my life I have served the interests of those who aspire to greatness yet use deceitful means to attain their ends.'

The rabbi asked: 'How does that make you feel?'

'Unjust. I care little for my name or reputation, but how can I redress the wrong I have committed?'

Achaeus' voice trembled as he uttered the final word in the sentence. Anan reached out and put his hand on his, squeezing his fingers to give him comfort. Achaeus sighed, as though a weight was lifting off his shoulders.

The rabbi waited for Achaeus to recompose himself then said, 'Truly a wrong has befallen you, son, and though words cannot heal this wound, they can soften the pain, and with time, the hurt may become tolerable, but it will always remain. God tells us that when he gives us blessing, then we must be thankful, and when he sends trials and tribulations, we must be patient. For even the trials are means for a person to turn back to God.'

Achaeus nodded, his head remained lowered, thoughtful. 'My name is Achaeus. I have been a soldier in the Seleucid army, I have led many to death, and sometimes to glory. I have tried to demonstrate valour towards a defeated enemy but cannot say I have succeeded. Yet, despite all the things I have done, I am now in the autumn of my life, left without a home, without a nation, without a purpose.'

Achaeus was unsure why he shared so much with the rabbi. Perhaps it was his pleasant avuncular manner, or the fact that he needed to speak with someone. It was apparent the rabbi did not know him, which only made the warrior warm to him.

The rabbi rocked forward, saying, 'I have little knowledge of the outside world, though of course I know of the Seleucids – which Jew would not?'

Achaeus winced, as he remembered it was Emperor Antiochus Epiphanes who had destroyed the Jewish temple in Jerusalem, two generations previously.

'What you may or may not have done in the past, is now the past. What you do today is what is important. God wants you to be present in the moment, to reflect upon his signs, to marvel at his creation, to ask yourself a question every morning when you awaken – "What does my Lord want of me today?" With this intention, He will present you with opportunities throughout the day which will draw you closer to Him. It may be a kind word you say to someone, a gift of charity you offer, an old relation you visit, the daily litany you perform. Intention is the axiomatic principle here. What is your intention, for you will attain what you intended.'

Intention thought Achaeus. *I have never stopped to consider this. I have served my entire life under a martial system, where I have been told what to do and told others what to do. I was never asked to consider what I intended, only whether I executed orders. What then is my intention?*

'The question of intention is tantalising, now that I am in this hiatus between two worlds, the one which I know, and another one, which I do not.'

'To transcend to a better way of living is also an intention,' the rabbi said.

Achaeus considered this. *Yes, he has a point, to transcend from what I was doing can be my intention. Yet there is still a problem in his logic.*

'Rabbi, how will I know what I must transcend to?' asked Achaeus.

'You will know when the time is right for you to know, for God will reveal it like a secret in your heart. If you make the intention, he will put you in the very place you need to be. Trust in him, but be warned, you may receive blessing or tribulation, as both are sent to the wayfarer on his journey to God. Ponder this and you will remain resolute whether he sends divine breezes or harsh winds. He sends these so you become the man you are destined to be.'

The words of the rabbi echoed in Achaeus' mind. *Now is my time to reflect*, he thought. *I must not miss this opportunity for it may not come again.*

'Rabbi, your words run like a deep chasm in a valley. I would like to ask you a question.'

'Go ahead.'

'You were waiting by the trunk of an olive tree on the road to Jerusalem. Were you waiting for a particular person? I believe you come and sit in this exact position every morning, for the grass and roots around you show some erosion. In addition, the robe you wear has a slight discolouration indicating you have been sitting on soft earth, such as that found in this area. Who are you waiting for?'

The rabbi chuckled. 'Very observant, Achaeus, a military man you are indeed. Though I was not waiting for you, God sent you, and so I was waiting for you.'

Achaeus shook his head. 'I do not understand.'

'Guests are like divine missives sent from beyond. Always welcome them, and God will continue to bless you. It was you God wanted me to meet today, not the one I desired to meet when I set off from my home this morning.'

'Who did you desire to meet?'

'He is one who God has promised will arrive. We call him the Messiah.'

Achaeus remembered hearing about a Jewish saviour who would deliver God's message to his people on earth.

'When will he come?'

'I do not know whether it will happen in my lifetime, but his arrival is imminent. I hope to see him when he comes.'

'I see,' mused Achaeus. 'May I wait with you, so that I too may meet him?'

The rabbi smiled. 'Of course, Achaeus of Seleucid. Perhaps he may come in your lifetime if he does not appear in mine.'

Chapter 20

BREAKING A HEART

Cool breezy air circulated through the Great Temple of Petra where Apollonia silently stood before the goddess of power Al-Uzza. She tried with all her heart to pray but there was something missing. This statue was not God, she knew this all too well. Where was He then? *How can I know you?* she asked herself. *If I cannot see you or feel you? Do you even exist?*

She kept up the pretence of worship yet she knew her actions were devoid of anything other than outward appearance.

Since her encounter with the callous Fastiq, Apollonia had felt herself fall into a whirlpool of despair. Revolted by the thought of such a vile unclean man touching her, Apollonia shuddered, and her eyes welled up. Mustering as much control as was possible she refrained from bursting into tears, but her thundering heart strained her body.

She had not spoken to anyone about the encounter. *What can I say? He is my betrothed. I cannot complain to my mother-in-law, for he is her son. My aunt will think I am weak. I have no one to share my feelings with.*

Apollonia closed her eyes. Time passed. Eventually Apollonia opened her eyes and found everything in the temple was as it had been. It was then she remembered her future sister-in-law, Luja, was most likely still here.

The question prompted her to leave the deities, return to the corridor and follow it down the hall as she had when she first met the young princess. She retraced her steps and came to the room where she had met Luja. She knocked on the door.

Silence.

She knocked again and waited. Nothing. The girl was not here. She pushed at the door and found it open. A look inside confirmed Luja was elsewhere. She wanted to see her, if only to take her mind off her own worries. Apollonia turned when the sound of giggling caught her attention.

Hesitantly, Apollonia followed the sound, to another chamber at the end of the hall. The voice, which she took to be Luja's was joined by a man's voice, one vaguely familiar to her. As she waited outside the closed door, considering what to do, a voice called out.

'You may come in.'

Startled, she looked up and down the corridor.

'Come in, sister,' Luja said. Apollonia heard soft footsteps and a moment later the door swung open. Luja took her hand and pulled her into the chamber.

Unlike the girl's own cell-like room, this one had a large window, through which cool draughts of air entered. Ornate carvings decorated one side of the room, and there was seating laid out in a circle in the middle, along with a set of small tables with unlit candles upon them.

There was a man in the room, who stood up. She realised it was Prince Zaim. Apollonia immediately blushed.

The prince also turned a shade of red, avoiding looking at her directly. 'Your Highness,' he said. 'It is good to see you once more.'

'And you,' Apollonia replied, her cheeks becoming a darker shade of red.

Luja pulled Apollonia to the cushioned seating and sat down beside her. She appeared acutely aware of the embarrassment both were feeling, for she said. 'No need to blush in my presence,' after which she began giggling once more.

Zaim also sat down.

'My brother was just telling me about Chao Zhang, the Han explorer who has been accompanying him on his journeys. Friend Chao is an accomplished martial artist and brother thinks it would take at least ten experienced fighting men to subdue him, so great are his skills.'

'Really?' Apollonia asked.

'Brother says that friend Chao has learned many martial moves, such as *Swallow takes the Goose's Egg*, and *Crane leaps over the Frozen Lake*, and *Tiger claws at the Elephant's Back*. Each technique consists of dozens of moves, palm thrusts, kicks, blocks and feints. Friend Chao says they have a whole martial system which has been collected over thousands of years. According to him, he is just a beginner in *wushu*.'

'*Wushu?*'

'It is the name the Han give to the martial arts. I want to be a *wushu* master one day. *Hiya, whosh!*' Luja imitated a chopping palm thrust, followed by a straight punch, as Zaim had described watching Chao deliver.

Apollonia laughed. 'Oh my, a *wushu* princess. Now that will be a first.' Apollonia noticed the preoccupied smile on Zaim's face. *He must have many worries. I cannot bear to burden him with the ones I carry, for what can he do? Fastiq is his brother, and he will not want to hear anything terrible about him, nor go against the wishes of his parents by intervening.*

'No, I'm sure they have dozens of them already in Han lands. But I would be the first Arabian one, wouldn't I, brother?'

Zaim nodded, smiling at his younger sister and thinking to himself, *my beautiful little sister, how long does she have left in this world? The illness inside her weakens her every year: it will not be long before she will need someone always by her side nursing her till the inevitable end.*

'Can you ask friend Chao to show me some of the moves he has learned? I particularly like the sound of *Monkey Rides the Two-humped Camel*,' Luja enquired.

Zaim leaned over. Ruffling his younger sister's hair, he said, 'How about he teaches you, *Girl stops Crawling down dark Tunnels*.'

'That's not fair! What else can I do? Being stuck in the temple the whole day with little to do is boring, so this way I get out and about and visit many people without them even knowing I am there.'

'I worry you may get yourself stuck inside one of these tiny crevices you crawl into, or worse, be bitten by a scorpion whilst you are crawling through a tunnel. We would not even be able to find you if that happened,' Zaim said.

'Oh Luja, that does sound rather dangerous,' Apollonia added, placing her hand on the girl's.

Luja frowned at them both, pouting, before breaking into a cheeky smile. 'All right, I will only do it in the daytime when there is enough light to see where I'm going.'

'What!' exclaimed Zaim. 'You go out at night as well?'

Placing two fingers over her lips, Luja smiled innocently. 'I should have kept my mouth shut.'

Am I too protective of her? Zaim wondered. *The healer says she does not have long left to live, so wouldn't it be better if she enjoyed the time she has left in this world, before her soul returns to the Creator? Isn't it wrong to keep her confined, despite the best intentions of my parents?*

'I won't tell mother and father, so long as you don't go out again at night-time,' Zaim added.

Luja nodded her consent, beaming at the little victory.

Zaim turned towards Apollonia. 'Your Highness, I am sorry for not having spent time with you while you have been in Petra. I only returned yesterday, and there have been so many matters to deal with, including an approaching army of Seleucids who intend to lay siege to us.'

'I fear I am the cause of this invading force,' Apollonia replied.

Zaim thought to himself: *This must be the reason she appears so glum, for when I saw her in Bozrah, her spirits were up. It is not her fault that we have a Seleucid force waging war against us, but without the marriage alliance with Ptolemy the Seleucids would not have been given a reason to attack. Still, she is innocent of any blame, and now that matters have taken such a course, we must be honourable and protect those we call family.*

'Not at all, your Highness,' said Zaim. 'The Seleucids do not need much of an excuse to wage war. The Jews know this from the destruction of their temple in Jerusalem by an earlier emperor also by the name of Antiochus, as do other peoples who have fallen under their shadow. They have never ventured this far south before, and perhaps this will be their undoing, for this is our land, we know how to defend it.'

'I *pray* this is the case,' Apollonia said.

****

The high northern pass proved a useful avenue of escape from Petra and the oncoming Seleucid forces. Even the Bedouin did not venture so high into the mountain and so the journey back north allowed Pelagios a clear view of the enemy forces making their way south. The two regiments the Seleucids were bringing were, in Pelagios' opinion, insufficient to lay siege to Petra, and their supply lines were negligible. The Bedouin were difficult to assess, their lines slithering through the lower valley like a camouflaged reptile. He suspected more might be massing in the southern desert.

On the afternoon of the following day since leaving Petra, Pelagios and his troop of ten men decided to rest and make camp on a plateau. A clump of ghaf trees made a good spot to build camp. Theron, the navigator of the *Chloe*, suggested they set up their cooking fires to the east, as the westerly wind would carry the smoke across the plateau as opposed to over its edge, thus not revealing their position to anyone passing below. With the meal of stewed rabbit over, the men sat back for a time, each alone with his thoughts and trying to keep warm as winter started to bite.

I should feel pleased to be returning home, thought Pelagios. *I am, yet I am also torn by loyalty to my young friend Zaim. Leaving his people when an army approaches is not what a friend would do. Can I still call myself a friend to any of these people, after the way the Romans have me spying on them on all? What am I to do, for my reputation for neutrality also serves me well commercially and all are willing to trade with me. If it became known that Pelagios of Mithymna had taken sides then it would impact the trade we do around the Mediterranean. It would not be a good legacy for me to leave to my children.*

As the evening approached, a sentry Theron had posted ahead raised an alarm. The man came running back, halting before Pelagios.

Panting, the sentry declared, 'Your Highness, there is a band of fifty or so men, making their way across the plateau in our direction.'

'Fifty!' Pelagios exclaimed, looking at the ten men he had with him. 'Any idea who they might be.'

'They were too distant for me to tell,' the sentry said.

'Put the fire out, pack up camp. We retreat to those boulders. Let's hope they pass by without noticing us,' Pelagios ordered.

Within moments the site was cleared and the men along with their animals had disappeared from view. Theron, who had the sharpest eyes in the group, took up a position a few yards ahead of Pelagios, peering from behind one of the large boulders.

The approaching men were now visible, guiding their animals by their reins over the rocky plateau. It looked like they were planning to take the same route back down as Pelagios and his men had taken coming up.

Pelagios rubbed the tips of his fingers to release the tension. They were heavily outnumbered and if these were Seleucid forces, he doubted they would show mercy. Their best strategy was not to fight, but let the men pass. Then he had a thought. *What if they, spotting the same good location we found, decide to make camp in precisely the same place we were in? We will be done for then, for the recently extinguished campfire will be noticeable. What then? Fight or flee.*

The progress of the soldiers across the rocky terrain was slow, and as they drew closer Pelagios carefully watched Theron. The navigator peered out into the gloom before he turned to Pelagios and whispered that the soldiers were Nabataeans. Pelagios still considered remaining hidden and letting the Nabataeans pass through, but when they drew up to make camp in precisely the same place the Aegeans had chosen, the game was up. Pelagios emerged from his hiding place along with Theron and his men, uttering friendly greetings.

After their initial hesitation at finding another group, albeit a smaller one, at the same site, many of the Nabataean soldiers recognised Pelagios and pleasantries were exchanged. The captain of the group engaged Pelagios in conversation, explaining they were a relief force sent from Bozrah, after Seleucid forces did not stop at the town and made instead for Petra.

'We have another party of one hundred men following us,' explained the captain. 'They will also take the high northern pass, remaining out of sight of the Seleucids and the Bedouin.'

'Do the Seleucids remain at Sela?' Pelagios asked.

'No, your Highness, the Seleucids abandoned Sela entirely.'

It is a strange game Antiochus plays, thought Pelagios. *If he is not trying to acquire Nabataean territory in the south, why is he sending an army here? What possible purpose does it serve?*

'What other troops do you have moving to support Petra?' Pelagios asked.

'We sent messengers north, up to Gaza, asking for any men who can be spared. It will take time, but Petra cannot be breached, no matter how long the siege,' the captain declared confidently.

Pelagios rubbed his chin with his thumb. 'True enough and the Seleucid supply lines do not indicate they intend a long siege. They have some other stratagem they plan to use.'

'Before they know it, we will have reinforcements arriving from the north and south and we will be able to break them against the walls of Petra. They will not return after such a humiliation.'

The Seleucids were more cunning than the Nabataean captain gave them credit for, particularly if that old rascal General Pharnuches was at the head of the army. His devious mind was full of plots within plots and Pelagios would not put it past him to have something up his sleeve which would incapacitate the defenders of Petra entirely.

'Who leads the Seleucid force south?' Pelagios asked.

'It is the beast, General Tigranous,' the captain replied.

The blood in his veins seemed to turn ice cold, before he felt his head erupt in fire and he realised he was clenching his fists.

Truly, the world is not large enough for you to hide, beast.

'Tigranous,' Theron murmured the name softly, turning to look at his king.

Chapter 21

TRAVERSING AN OCEAN

———

Achaeus of Seleucid spent several days in the home of the Rabbi Anan Ben Jacob. The old man had taken in the traveller, who had no clear destination or fixed abode, allowing him to lodge in an annex. Achaeus in turn took to cleaning the temple, making some repairs to the building, and cooking for the rabbi. All in all, it was an amicable arrangement and for the first time in years Achaeus was enjoying life. His daily routine was slow paced, thoughtful and reflective, precisely what he had been missing as a general and diplomat. Now, he woke each morning curious as to what God had in store for him that day; how could he serve those he encountered?

After his morning chores, Achaeus joined the rabbi on the small terrace adjoining his lodging. Anan offered him a plate of dates with mint tea and together they observed the olive trees in the courtyard sway to the melody of the easterly wind.

There was a question which had been on Achaeus' mind since arriving in Jerusalem and he thought it best to ask it now.

'Rabbi, in my land, the gods are manifest in the carvings within the temples. I can pray to Mars, or Apollo, or to any of the gods in the pantheon. The gods are apparent: I can see them and touch them. In this land, God is not manifest before me. If I cannot see Him, how can I worship Him?'

The rabbi chuckled softly.

'Moses asked to see God, who made himself manifest on the mountain, which crumbled to dust. In this world we cannot behold the divine majesty. That, my young friend, is a gift for the next realm when we transcend from the physical to the metaphysical.'

'Yet when I gaze upon the gods of the Greeks my certainty in them increases, for they are apparent. How is it that your God is not present, yet your faith appears stronger than any other man's I have ever met?'

'As to the level of a man's faith, only God can judge that. Outwardly a man may appear pious, but inwardly his character is foul and so he is a wretched man. And of course, the reverse is true. I have met saints who by the measure of the world would be called ugly, yet their faces shine with a celestial light and there is a nobility in their every action. As to the questions of God's apparency – the absence of a thing is not a proof of its non-existence.'

'How so?'

'I cannot see the air, but I know it is there, for I breathe it.'

Achaeus furrowed his brow. 'Then how can I increase my certainty in a God I cannot see?'

'Whatever you imagine God to be He is not, yet He is both immanent and transcendent. He is at all times with you whilst also orchestrating the entire universe. If you want to see Him you cannot do so with the physical eye.'

'How else can I see unless through my eyes?' Achaeus enquired.

The rabbi placed his palm over his heart before saying. 'The only way we can *see* Him is through the heart, but not the physical heart: you must see God through the spiritual heart which is made from His divine light.'

The Seleucid warrior rubbed his chin with his fingers. 'I have seen a man's heart; it is flesh and blood. Drive a sword through it and he will live no more. What is this spiritual heart you speak of Rabbi?'

'Before we came into this world, we were souls. At the time of creation our souls were spread before our father Adam. Before our arrival into this physical world the soul of each person is blown by the angels into our mother's belly. Every human being is first and foremost a soul. And so, every person still retains this connection with the metaphysical, with the previous realm, which will also be our reality when we depart from this world. Therefore, the heart has two aspects: the physical which is flesh and blood and the metaphysical which is light.'

'If a man dies, what happens to this spiritual heart?' Achaeus asked.

'It returns to the metaphysical realm.'

'So, I am to see God through this spiritual heart which is light?'

'As your knowledge of God increases, so your soul is elevated to a higher rank. The ties which bind it to this world are loosened as you ascend higher and higher. We can become blinded to God's presence by two types of veils which cover the spiritual heart. One is a dark veil: this is like a thick wall, when the person is not even aware of what is on the other side, and they cannot even perceive there is another realm, nor do they acknowledge they were a soul before entering this world and so they deny the existence of God. These types of people are unfortunate and may God have mercy upon them. Then there is a translucent veil: the soul of this person recognises this world is like a prison, and as they ascend to a higher station through their remembrance of God, he sends divine sparks through from the other metaphysical world. They still cannot *see* it, but they know there is light on the other side. This reinforces their faith in Him and His divine mercy and so they aspire to greater heights.'

'How can I hope to *see* in this world?' Achaeus asked.

'By remembrance of God and the acquisition of knowledge. These are safest avenues to take if you want to free your heart from the trappings of this world. You must live in this world but not grow attached to it.'

'And is there anything I should avoid?'

'God placed His divine spark within us, but he also made every person susceptible to the vices of the lower soul – such as arrogance, pride and envy. We should not let our lower soul get in the way of our journey back to God. The truly enlightened soul is the one others are safe from. You are a military man, and you know that courage without wisdom can become recklessness and arrogance, but when there is wisdom, courage manifests itself as valour. This is the divine balance God seeks from us. If we appease our lower soul we will err towards recklessness. If we aspire to a higher purpose, we will display valour.'

Achaeus had to blink hard. There was much to take in from what the rabbi said each morning, and he was barely able to grasp the previous day's lesson before his mind was filled with more ideas. *I feel like a man who never learned how to think about thinking. I spent my whole life reacting to the world, but never stopped to ask myself this existential question – where is the journey of this world taking me? What a fool I have been to have wasted so much time It is only now, as the first strands of grey appear in my hair that I remember the One who should always be remembered.*

Noticing the look of concern on the Seleucid warrior's face, Anan added, 'Do not be too hard on yourself, Achaeus. What is past is past. What you do now is what matters. You were like the man on the beach standing with his back to the ocean, admiring a few fish swimming around in a bucket before him, thinking this represented all the water in the world. Yet if only he turned around, he would realise there is an entire ocean filled with whales, sharks, fishes, crabs and every manner of sea creature. You have turned to face the ocean, and its enormity is overwhelming. Yet with time you will learn to swim in it, and one day traverse it.'

The rabbi leaned across and tapped Achaeus' hand, reassuring him.

'I hope so,' Achaeus said.

The two men sat in companionable silence for a time, as Achaeus turned the rabbi's words over in his mind.

Their solitude was broken by the sound of boots approaching.

Achaeus' hand instinctively went to where his weapon would have been, before he realised he had left it inside a trunk in the annex.

'Rabbi Anan,' said a voice at the door.

'Wait a moment,' Anan replied. He gathered up his robes and walked over to the door leading out onto the street.

Two soldiers he recognised from the palace waited for him.

'Rabbi,' said the shorter man. 'King Jannaeus wishes to see you now, as well as your guest.'

'Now? My guest?' Anan asked.

'Please come immediately, the king does not like to be kept waiting,' the soldier said.

'I will be with you in a moment but what has my guest to do with the matter?' the rabbi asked.

The soldier shrugged. 'The king was very clear we should not return unless your guest accompanies you.'

Anan stared at him. 'Very well then, I will return shortly,' he said, closing the door.

The rabbi returned to Achaeus. 'The king wants to see me and … you.'

'Me?' Achaeus asked.

'So it seems, but as to why, forgive me, I do not know the reason.'

'Who else knows of my presence here?' Achaeus asked.

'Some of the younger priests who serve at the Temple.'

Achaeus pondered the request. There was little he could do now to avoid the summons. *I will see what this Jannaeus wants, but if he knows who I am, I already have my suspicions. There is no peace in this world.*

The two collected some belongings and were soon following the soldiers on their way to the palace. Entering they were shepherded to an outer chamber, where they were told to wait. Time passed, before they were guided by more soldiers to a place deeper within the palace grounds. They arrived at a hall, at the end of which was an ornate throne upon which sat King Jannaeus, ruler of the Hasmonean kingdom.

Beside the King was his chamberlain and on his other side two of his generals, decked out in military attire.

'Rabbi Anan,' said Jannaeus. 'It seems like it was only yesterday we last met. Time passes so quickly.'

'Your Highness, it is good to see you once more,' Anan replied.

The king's gaze fell upon Achaeus. He took in the Seleucid, a look of admiration and respect on his face. Jannaeus said, 'Rabbi Anan, you play host to a distinguished guest, a military legend, no less. Yet you did not see it fit to let me know about this.'

'I do? This man is a traveller. His name is Achaeus and he is my guest. He was passing through and needed a place to stay.'

'Seleucid generals do not simply pass through Jewish lands,'

Jannaeus said.

'General?' Anan asked.

Jannaeus continued, 'Yes, it seems you did not know, but believe me when I say Seleucid generals come to conquer our lands or to sow the seeds of discord.' Turning his steely gaze on Achaeus he asked, 'What do you really seek, General Achaeus?'

Achaeus placed a hand on the rabbi's shoulder. 'Rabbi Anan is unaware of my, let us say, prior reputation and it is a good thing too, for there are many things I have done in life that I regret. He is not to blame for not knowing who I am. If I may ask, King Jannaeus, how is it that news of my presence reached your court?'

'Do not shroud yourself in humility, Achaeus. Your name is known throughout the martial world and your deeds are legendary. A man with your lofty reputation can never pass unnoticed wherever he travels. Why have you come to Jerusalem? Conquest or discord?'

Achaeus smiled at Rabbi Anan reassuringly.

'I have no goal nor aim in your kingdom, I am simply a traveller passing through,' he said.

'*Achaeus*,' huffed Jannaeus, 'is not simply a traveller. Do you take me for a fool, Seleucid? Why did Emperor Antiochus send you to Jerusalem? Tell me!'

'I have not spoken with the emperor for months, nor to anyone close to him. In fact, since returning from Ptolemy, I have had no communications with the Seleucid court at all.'

'He has sent you to negotiate with us, hasn't he?' Jannaeus continued, ignoring the explanation Achaeus had just given.

'Your Highness, it is true I was in my time a Seleucid general, but I am no longer that man. My own, or those who were my own soldiers, have tried to assassinate me several times since I left Alexandria. I have come to believe these orders came from the emperor himself.'

Jannaeus opened his mouth to reply, then leaned over to his chamberlain who whispered some words into this ear. Then he listened attentively to the two generals on his other side, who also quietly conveyed their advice.

'So, you are an outcast from the Seleucid empire, cut adrift,' the king declared.

'I am.'

'If I ordered your execution there would be no comeback on us,' Jannaeus continued.

'Your Highness –' Rabbi Anan began.

Achaeus raised his hand and smiled at the Rabbi to calm him. 'If the king so desires, he can take my life.'

'Bah!' scoffed Jannaeus. 'I have no need for you dead. Alive is what makes you useful. Besides Antiochus is far too unpredictable. If he hears of your execution by the Hasmoneans, he may order a larger force against us than he already intends to bring.'

Achaeus noticed one of the general's wince. *Has the King told me something he should not have? What is this news of Antiochus sending a force to Hasmonean lands?*

'Your Highness,' Achaeus said, 'I am not aware of Seleucid designs on your lands.'

Jannaeus turned to the generals. 'There's no point hiding the news from him if he's going to help us.'

Achaeus and Rabbi Anan exchanged glances. And Achaeus thought, *at least he does not intend to execute me. Perhaps I may have time to learn more from this dear rabbi.*

'Antiochus assembles an elephant legion, intending to land at Gaza, to wrestle control of the port from the Nabataeans. He has issued us with an ultimatum, to join him or oppose him. Unfortunately, the Jews do not trust a Seleucid emperor with the name Antiochus, after what the last one did to Jerusalem. We cannot oppose him, but we can remain neutral. Yet your unexpected presence here may tilt matters in our favour.' The king smiled.

Achaeus knew precisely where this conversation was going; reluctantly, he felt himself being sucked back into the imperial game.

Chapter 22

DISRUPTING DINNER

A banquet before a battle was an odd way to prepare for a martial encounter, in Chao Zhang's opinion, but the Nabataean culture held many surprises for him. Living as the Arabs did occasionally within a mountain complex so intricately engineered and sculpted was the first wonder he beheld when stumbling into Petra.

Upon Zaim's insistence, Chao found himself attending a feast to celebrate the upcoming marriage of Prince Fastiq and Princess Apollonia. From his position at the rear of the great banquet hall he observed the gathering of Nabataean luminaries.

The men from the royal household sat at the front upon brass-studded high-backed chairs. In the centre was King Obodos, his sons either side. It was the first time Chao had had the opportunity to see Zaim's brothers. Beside the prince was a portly brother, who looked like a glutton, avidly consuming his meal.

To the other side of the King, sat the eldest son, Chao assumed, the one to be married, Fastiq. Chao noted how Fastiq's head turned whenever an attractive woman walked along the fringes of the hall. He appeared agitated, chewing his fingernails, his eyes darting left and right. To his left was the other son, Asylaion, who was by all accounts a man of clever words and a pleasing countenance, but lacking in humanity.

The monarch himself, Obodos, had a commanding presence, and it was clear that when his eyes turned to Zaim, he felt fatherly pride in his youngest son. *Other than the fat one, the other two have a frostiness in their manner towards Zaim, for they do not even look at him, preferring instead to talk with their gaze directed elsewhere, as though the youngest of the brothers is below them. Jealousy is the obvious reason for their seeming indifference.*

At the left of the hall, tables, carpets, cushions and stools were arranged in floral designs; this was where the women from the royal household sat. None were familiar to Chao, other than Apollonia and her aunt, Corrina. The aunt was involved in a lively conversation with the Nabataean women, whilst the young princess sat silently, head lowered. It could have been bashfulness, for that was befitting for a bride to be, yet in the way in which her shoulders drooped, Chao sensed unease. Looking at Fastiq, then at Apollonia, it became apparent to him what the source of that apprehension was. This poor girl was miserable at the prospect of marrying the eldest prince. In fact, on the few occasions he saw her glance up briefly, her gaze lingered on Zaim.

They are a match, Zaim and Apollonia, thought Chao. *But destiny seems to have conspired against them. This is the way of the world, and there is very little that can be done about it. Royal figures marry not for love but for political purpose.*

'Friend Chao,' Fahad, the Nabataean captain sitting beside him, said.

'Fahad,' Chao replied.

'I wish to challenge you!'

The Falcons seated around them sat forwards. The spiky-haired Taimur interjected, 'Not even with ten men will you defeat Chao in a martial contest, Fahad.'

Fahad turned to Taimur. 'Who said it was a martial challenge?'

'Ah, so it is but a jest,' Taimur said, sinking back into his chair.

'No,' Fahad said.

'What then?' Taimur pressed.

'I wish to lay down a friendly challenge,' Fahad said once more.

'I see,' Chao replied, scanning the faces of the other Nabataeans. 'I am always willing to take part in a friendly challenge.'

'My challenge is poetic.'

Chao felt himself relax. *Fahad is an accomplished poet; the other*

Falcons often quote his sonnets. 'I am no poet, Captain Fahad, but perhaps I can rise to the challenge.'

'Of course!' exclaimed Fahad. 'We expect nothing less.'

Chao noticed Asylaion rise from his chair and leave the podium at the front. As he made for the entrance, he was joined by a man in a leather jerkin.

I have seen this scar-faced man! thought Chao.

At the foot of Sela, he had been meeting with the Seleucid General, Tigranous. *It is him, I am sure. The Scorpion insignia is on his breast-plate and that face with those cold dead eyes is not one I would forget.*

The prince and the commander of his Scorpion legion Captain Jahm strode towards Chao and the assembled Falcons, casting a mistrustful glance at them.

'Your Highness,' someone said.

'Prince Asylaion,' another voice said.

Around Chao the guests rose to their feet as the prince swept by with barely a glance at them. The scar-faced man by his side did not even look in their direction.

'Miserable pair,' one of the men said when the prince was out of earshot.

Once the Falcons were seated again, Fahad turned to Chao and said, 'In honour of the royal wedding, we each will recite a poem, and my comrades will decide whose is more eloquent.'

Chao let out a laugh. 'Fahad, you are an accomplished poet, I am not. I will happily try my best, but do not expect much from me.'

'Let me obtain a fresh round of drinks for the poets,' Taimur declared, getting up to fetch the sherbets.

Whilst the spiky-haired lieutenant was gone, Chao's mind raced – what was Scar-face, a Nabataean officer, doing with the Seleucids? Was he on an imperial mission for the king? Or was it something more sinister?

Taimur soon returned with the sherbets and both men quenched their thirsts before the oral jousting. Word of the duel had spread and other guests who had been sitting close by now crowded around their table, eager to hear each man's lyrics.

Taimur addressed Chao. 'As our guest we will give you the honour of starting.'

In truth he would have preferred a little more time to gather his thoughts, but just then a passage came into his mind.

'This poem is about a husband's longing for his wife and son,' Chao said in a sober tone and continued:

'Onwards the army rolls, forcing us apart.

An endless sky overhead, me at one end you at the other.

Battles rage around me, men shedding their blood.

My trusty steed, my fallen comrades and the steel of my blade keep me alive.

Each day takes me further, from you, and I grow old on the memories.

Days become weeks, and weeks months.

Yet when I stare at the moon, I know you do too.

Do not think I have abandoned you.

Remain strong, till I return.'

The Falcons stared solemnly at him, a tear in the eye of more than one man. 'My,' Taimur announced. 'You have wrenched my heart from my body, friend Chao.'

'I will forever weep for my beloved,' someone said.

Fahad placed his hand upon his heart and said. 'Friend Chao. You honour us with your words. I am humbled and will attempt to rise to this level but fear I will be a poor reflection.'

'Get on with it,' Taimur chided his friend.

Chao smiled, sitting back, relaxing now that he knew he had not made a fool of himself or dishonoured the Han. But the longing for his deceased wife and son burned bright in his heart.

'This poem,' Fahad started. 'Is about losing one's beloved and seeking recompense.' He cleared his throat then began:

'My words have dried up. Why? For these debris are where Nusayma once reclined.

Like Queen Bilkis' gazelle, fawn-coloured, honey eyed, soft and supple.

Oh Nusayma, even the dust from the ruins does not settle where you once walked.

The outline of your footsteps amongst the relics calms my racing heart.

I weep, what more can I do as I abandoned you when you needed me.

Your tribe was decimated by the hounds of war.

You captured my heart, like no other has. Why was I not there?

Now your murderers witness the glint of my blade before I slit their necks.

I take revenge upon many a man in this way.

Will you praise me for what I have done, or scold me for what I have become?'

Fahad stopped and lowered his head. The little crowd cheered.

'What words,' one said.

'Revenge and honour,' another said.

Chao placed his hand over his heart again. 'Fahad, your radiant words touch the heart. I can only consider myself a student in your presence, for the words I spoke were not my own, but those of another. Yours are original. I declare my friend Fahad is victor of this challenge.'

Fahad nodded in acceptance.

'You are both too generous,' said Taimur, clapping both men on the shoulder.

As Fahad was about to reply, two soldiers, fully armed, ran into the hall, making their way towards the head table where the king sat. General Ghassan met the men, who whispered in his ear. Even at this distance, Chao could see the colour drain from the old soldier's face. Ghassan issued an instruction to the soldiers and went straight to the king to convey the message. In turn the king's and his sons' faces turned ashen.

The two soldiers were now running back out of the hall; Fahad stopped one of them. 'What is the matter?' he asked.

'The walls have been breached. Seleucid and Bedouin forces are running wild through the city.'

Chapter 23

SILENT APPROACHES

The area beyond the northern wall could hold a hundred men at most. Not the optimum location in which to assemble an invading army. But it was the location under the watch of the Scorpion regiment and the prince had ensured the postern at the foot of the wall was opened. Tigranous crouched as he passed through the low gate and came out on the inner side of the northern wall. It would take some time for his men as well as the Bedouin to file through this solitary doorway, staying silent and hidden from the defenders. He looked up at the walls and could see some of the men from the Scorpion regiment staring down at him. He waved to them and the fools waved back.

Tigranous smiled.

Once his Seleucid forces had all come through the postern along with the Bedouin he would let the desert nomads run riot in Petra, looting, and distracting the city defenders, whilst his men went to kill the royal family.

The walls were high around him, the passageways leading off from the open area outside the walls dark, but for a few lamps burning in the corners. His men began to spread out in silence. They knew what needed to be done. Responsibilities were clear. Slaughter the royal family and any inhabitants who resist, spare others. He had not wanted to let any live, but there were some practicalities about maintaining a city; it needed people for it to function and the spice routes needed workers for it to operate. He had no intention of sending his men down to Aden to receive the spice from the east, a few overseers perhaps, but the bulk of the effort must fall on the Arabs. The bulk of the profits of course, would be with the Seleucids.

A hooded figure emerged from one of the passages, a soldier beside him. Tigranous was expecting him and strode across to meet him and Captain Jahm of the Scorpion regiment. As Tigranous drew closer to the prince, he noted the look of apprehension at seeing so many Seleucid soldiers within Petra's walls. Tigranous thought, *blades will only return to their sheaths once they are red with the blood of the Arabs.*

Jahm, the scar-faced man, maintained the snarl on his face as Tigranous approached, and the Seleucid thought, *if the prince shows weakness at any point, this man will do – he can run things for me after we have finished.*

The prince said. 'I have kept my side of the bargain. Now I want you to keep your side.'

'Do not fear, Prince, my word is my bond.'

Tigranous smiled.

The prince needed appeasing for he was a fickle one and Tigranous, despite his harsh methods, grasped the import of his words. 'We will devastate the Nabataeans for you to rebuild them in your own image and choose your own alliances.'

'Undeniably,' the prince replied. 'Ensure the deaths of my family are swift. They should not be tortured; a clean death is what we agreed,' he said.

'It will be so,' Tigranous replied.

'And you will personally see to the deaths of my mother and youngest sister. I do not want them touched by any other man.'

'Of course,' Tigranous said. *Though it is highly unlikely my men will recognise your mother, the queen, nor your sister.*

'Good.' The man observed the Seleucid soldiers filing through the portico, before he turned back to Tigranous. 'I will remain beside my father, the king, to avoid any suspicion.'

'As we agreed, so it will be done.'

The prince glanced about nervously as more and more Seleucid soldiers began to fill the open space inside the inner wall. 'In the morning, I will be declared king.'

'Yes, you will be the king of the Arabs and your allegiance will be to Emperor Antiochus.'

'Make sure I am king and you will have my allegiance,' the prince declared.

I could kill this inane princeling at this very moment and my emperor would barely bat an eyelid. Yet even I have some standards to maintain, if I am to become the ear of the emperor.

'As the dawn rises, you will be king and before the end of tomorrow you will have declared your fealty to our Emperor.'

'It will be so. Now I must return to my father's side.'

Tigranous watched Prince Asylaion head down the passageway, disappearing from view. *With a son like that,* thought Tigranous, *who needs enemies?*

The Seleucid general unsheathed his hefty broadsword, felt the weight in his hand, smiled. *Yes, there will be plenty of blood tonight.*

****

Overhead, thunder rumbled, and a cool resonant wind tinged with a foul odour blew in from the north as Zaim sprinted out of the royal palace. The Falcons formed up behind him. In the principal square where the king would meet the people once a week, silence reigned, but a quick glance towards the eastern and northern routes told a different story. Fires raged and as he drew closer he heard cries and screams echoing through the night. Twilight had not long passed, and a bank of dense clouds covered the city. As the wind whipped around him he knew rain was on its way.

Crossing the courtyard were Nabataean residents, screaming in fear, several women clutching babes to their chests.

'To the palace,' Zaim instructed them.

How can this be? The walls are well guarded, the passes into the city narrow, Petra cannot be breached. A dark thought took hold in the prince's mind. *Could it be the traitor? If so, it would mean one of my brothers was such a person. No!* He pushed the idea away. Despite their defects, he loved his brothers; they would not be so callous.

Lightning flashed. Zaim made out the shapes of Bedouin making their way up the eastern street, past the great temple.

'Aiee,' a scream sounded, as a clutch of men, robes whipping around them, charged at the Falcons.

'Step in,' Zaim ordered. Steel flashed from leather sheaths as the Falcons formed a tight formation around their prince. The first droplets of rain landed on his cheeks as Zaim tried to focus his attention on the approaching Bedouin.

'Drive them back to the desert!' a Falcon shouted close behind Zaim.

Rows upon rows of Bedouin sprinted at the heavily outnumbered Falcons. Zaim cleared his mind but for one thought – *protect my family*.

Zaim ducked under the first Bedouin blade, slashing open the man's stomach with this sword, then plunging the dagger in his left hand into the neck of a second man, before rolling under a spear thrust. Spinning behind, he slashed the back of the man's knees, dropping him to the ground, before opening his windpipe with his blade. Up on his feet again, he fell upon the Bedouin surrounding him – slashing, swinging, slicing through bodies. They had greater numbers but less skill than the Falcons.

Around Zaim the soldiers drove a wedge between the oncoming body of Bedouin and the second flank.

Then, the sound of shields hammering on stone caught Zaim's attention, as he noted a regiment of fully-armoured Seleucid soldiers come up behind the Bedouin. The men formed up a line and advanced into the melee.

Zaim leapt forward, his men following his lead as his sword rose and fell in a furious set of lethal strikes. The Bedouin poured in, surrounding him, cutting him off from his men. Soon he realised he had pushed on too far and had left the Falcons behind unable to support him. A Bedouin drove a spear tip at his foot, making him leap aside, but as he landed, he saw a sword coming at him. Avoiding it, he tripped and was on the ground.

Instinctively he rolled away, as a sword plunged into the earth where he had lain only moments earlier. Looking up, he saw a

Bedouin silhouetted against a flash of lightning. The Bedouin aimed his sword at the prince. Zaim was unable to bring his own weapon up in time to defend himself.

Is this it?

Just then, a sword pierced the Bedouin's chest from back to front and the man toppled forwards. Zaim rolled away, as three more Bedouin fell in quick succession to the flashing sword strikes, whilst two more were kicked to the ground.

'Fall back,' Chao shouted.

The Han explorer hauled Zaim up, deflecting a sword strike as he did so, before kicking the man's knees away and smacking his hilt against the Bedouin's temple.

'There are too many; you are surrounded,' Chao cried.

The heavens opened and rain pelted down. Thunder boomed around the mountain city, shaking the rock. Momentarily the fighters on both sides stopped and looked up at the darkened sky.

'Retreat!' Zaim shouted as the stinging rain pinged on their armour.

Sprinting back towards the royal residence, Zaim came in after the other Falcons had entered the gates. With Fahad and Taimur's help he lowered a giant crossbeam to hold the door in place.

'My thanks once more,' Zaim said to Chao.

The Han explorer waved it away, adding, 'I went to the watchtower after you left. I saw at least five hundred Bedouin crossing the city. There may be more outside. As for the Seleucids, they match them in numbers and there may be more waiting to enter.'

'More than a thousand?' Fahad asked.

'Assume more,' Chao replied.

'How many men do we have within the royal residence?' Zaim asked.

'Fighting men, not more than two hundred,' Fahad declared. 'The others are stationed around the city. But if the Bedouin and Seleucid forces have already taken control of Petra, then the soldiers we have within the city may already have been slaughtered or scattered.'

General Ghassan made his way through the throng of men gathered at the eastern gates of the palace.

Slam. Bodies rammed into the gate. *They will hold for now,* thought Zaim, *but if our enemies have battering rams, then these doors will soon crack.*

'What is happening out there, your Highness?' Ghassan asked.

'A combined force of Bedouin and Seleucids is within the city, possibly one thousand strong, maybe more, we cannot be certain,' Zaim replied.

'Get a message to the western garrison by sending a runner over Jebel Ad-Deir. There are at least one hundred men there who can lend their swords to this fight,' Ghassan said.

Zaim issued instructions to one of his Falcon's, placing his arm on the man's shoulders and whispering some comforting words before ordering him out on his dangerous mission.

'I will have the king and the royal family retreat back to the first floor of the throne room,' Ghassan declared. 'There is only one staircase in and out of that room. If the worst comes to the worst, we will defend it to our last man.'

'These walls will be scaled as soon as they have enough men, and if they have brought ladders, then it will not be long before they are coming over this wall. To slow them, have archers positioned here and here,' the Han explorer said, pointing to two locations. 'Pepper the enemy with arrows, buy time for us. If no reinforcements arrive the situation looks grim.'

'You are?' Ghassan asked.

Zaim interjected. 'This is Chao Zhang, special envoy of the Han Emperor from the east. He is an adept martial artist.'

'Defending a city is a different matter to fighting hand-to-hand,' Ghassan said.

'I do not mean to trespass on anyone's authority, General, but I am from the ancient city of Chang'an, and we have defended it against marauding tribes on several occasions. I have some *experience* in such situations,' Chao said.

'And you will fight for us when this is not your kingdom?' Ghassan asked.

'I will,' Chao replied.

'Good, then I leave these outer defences in Prince Zaim's hands, with you as his counsellor,' Ghassan declared. 'Prepare the men and then report back to me. I will be in the throne room.'

Chapter 24
A FORGOTTEN ROYAL

Pandemonium and fear gripped Petra. Before departing, General Ghassan ushered the royals from the banqueting hall deeper into the recesses of the palace, leaving them safely within the well protected throne room. Apollonia anxiously watched Zaim and the Falcons stream out of the great banqueting hall, whilst the other princes retreated to safer positions. Fastiq, like a terrified reptile, stuck close to his father and mother, ensuring he was always the first through any doorway. Stylian tried his best to keep up, whilst the cold-eyed Asylaion exuded a surprising calm.

Then it struck her – Luja.

The young princess had not been invited to the banquet and would be in the Great Temple. Yet if she was, how was she going to be protected, if no one went to her? *This invasion of Petra is most likely my fault,* thought Apollonia. *At the very least my arrival was the catalyst for it all. Luja is an innocent child, and I cannot let anything happen to her.*

As the soldiers were guiding them towards the throne room Apollonia saw fit to slip away in all the commotion. She wrapped herself in a well-worn riding cloak, covering her head, and picked up a bow and arrows – being familiar with these weapons. Every royal of Alexandria was trained in the use of at least one weapon, should the need arise for them to defend themselves, and she had kept up regular practice. The bow was of a comfortable weight, its bowstring slack enough for her to pull back.

Surprisingly no one paid her any attention, thinking she was a servant running for their life. Apollonia kept the bow hidden within the

folds of the old cloak, as she made her way back out of the banqueting hall and out towards the central courtyard. The rain drenched
her. Apollonia stuck to the edges of the open spaces, keeping to the
shadows. She saw General Ghassan march back towards the royal
residence, soldiers trailing in his wake. Leaving the courtyard, she
set off down a narrow city lane, which was surrounded by dwellings
for the ordinary citizens of the city. All of the doors and windows
were tightly shut and she could not tell whether anyone was inside.

Cries and screams echoed somewhere in the distance, so Apollonia
quickened her pace. Lightning flashed overhead, followed by a deep
rumble of thunder which shook the walls around her. She heard a
gasp from close by and realised someone must have been hiding
behind one of the doors she passed. As Apollonia continued towards
the great temple, a shadow crossed the path up ahead. She froze.
Apollonia slid up against the wall, trying to blend into it. Silence
pressed down around her, before she decided to continue, crossing
the path without incident. The road ahead curved downwards, then
followed a slight gradient coming up towards the gate of the great
temple.

She slipped through the central gate, bow at her side. Raindrops fell
from the edge of her cloak leaving a trail of water on the stonework.
She crossed the central hall, noting the idols she had seen on previous
visits. Candles flickered around them, illuminating their shapes. She
took the corridor she knew would lead her to the apartment where
she had first encountered Luja.

Apollonia knocked. No answer. She opened the door. Gloom filled
the interior and Apollonia was about to leave when she heard a moan.

'Luja?' Apollonia said.

'Sister,' Luja replied.

Apollonia rushed forward, realising the young girl was curled up
on her bedroll. Touching her, she found she was burning with fever.

'You are ill!' Apollonia exclaimed.

'It is nothing,' Luja croaked. 'It will pass.'

Taking a cloth from within the folds of her dress, Apollonia sprin-
kled it with water from a beaker before placing it on Luja's forehead.

'Here, here, drink,' Apollonia said, pressing a cup to the princess' lips. Luja sipped a small amount, then sank back onto her bedroll.

'What is happening, sister? Why are you here?' Luja asked.

'I came to fetch you. Petra has been invaded and there are bad men inside the city walls. I want to get you to the safety of the royal palace.'

The girl shivered. Apollonia held her in a tight embrace. 'You will be fine.'

'I will not live out this year,' Luja said. 'But you and Zaim will.'

'Hush, don't say such a thing. You are young, you have a long life ahead of you.'

'I do not.'

Apollonia was taken aback by her earnest tone. 'Why?' she asked, pulling away a little from the girl so she could see her face.

'I have been dying for years; this is why I am kept in the temple. It is so I can pray to the gods for forgiveness, but these idols cannot do anything. There is only the one true God, the God of Abraham and Ishmael and Ishaq who is worthy of being praised. If it is His will for me to die, then I am at peace, for He is the one who gave me this blessing of life and He is the one who can take it from me.'

Her young sister-in-law was dying!

'Sister,' Luja gripped Apollonia's hand. 'You must not marry Fastiq, for though he is my brother, he is a bad man. You will marry Zaim.'

'I am betrothed to Fastiq,' Apollonia replied.

The girl shivered, teeth chattering. Apollonia held her close, wiping her brow with the cloth. Thunder rumbled outside.

Just then there were shouts from inside the temple, as Apollonia heard the sound of men running through the building.

'Come, we must go now. Is there a back entrance?' Apollonia asked.

'Yes, but leave me here,' Luja said.

'I cannot. if the men find you ...' Apollonia shuddered at the thought.

She lifted the girl into her arms and made for the door. The child was heavier than she expected, and suddenly she doubted she could carry her all the way back to the palace. Within a few paces, Apollonia was feeling the strain on her arms, but she gritted her teeth and kept going.

The voices grew louder behind her.

'Hey, you!' a man's voice shouted behind her.

They had seen them.

Apollonia started running, the weight of the girl slowing her progress. Luja's feverish head flopped around in her arms, the whites of her eyes showing. For a moment Apollonia thought Luja had lost consciousness, before she blinked.

'Stop!' The voice sounded closer.

Turning a corner, Apollonia entered an open courtyard. With Luja drifting in and out of consciousness she was not sure where to turn. She ran towards the back, where she was brought to a sudden standstill, as a group of armoured Seleucid soldiers burst through a side door and were just as stunned to see her carrying a child.

Then the voice pursuing them shouted from behind. 'Stop them!'

The seven Seleucid soldiers now cut off her route. There was a scream from another corridor and the grizzled High Priestess leapt out, swinging a sword at the men. Looking at her frail features, Apollonia was amazed the woman possessed enough strength to wield it. Unfortunately, it was only a show; the nearest soldier caught hold of the High Priestess' wrist, before her sword strike could come down, then he punched her in the stomach. She crumpled to the ground. The glittering steel sword was yanked from her hand and the Seleucid soldier tucked the jewelled weapon into his sword belt.

The Seleucid smiled. The High Priestess clawed out with her nails, scratching the man's ankle, and drawing blood. The man was furious and drove his blade into her chest. The old woman screamed and went silent. The soldier did not look too happy with what he had done, but shrugged and rejoined his fellows who were now making their way toward Apollonia. The men closed in. Apollonia's arms ached with Luja's weight, and she began to feel faint. She gently placed the girl on the ground and whipped out her bow. Notching an arrow, she drew and fired before the Seleucids could register she had a weapon. The brown feathered arrow caught the nearest soldier flush in the neck. The man fell to his knees, before keeling over onto his face.

A Seleucid lunged at her with a spear, but she had already fired off another arrow which caught the man square in the chest, propelling him backwards. She went to nock another shaft, but in her panic dropped it. As she reached for a fresh arrow, she felt a hand on her shoulder, ripping at her cloak. She rammed her bow backwards into the man's gut, but then another hand took hold of the hood of her cloak, yanking her back hard so she fell to the ground. The bow dropped from her hand, as she saw Luja's eyes go white.

'Luja!' Apollonia screamed at the top of her voice.

The Seleucid soldiers surrounded her, lecherous sneers on their faces as their eyes registered her from head to toe.

'Me first,' a soldier said.

Suddenly, Apollonia realised what was about to happen. How could she have been so stupid as to come to the temple to save Luja, when she could not even protect herself? Now, she was about to be dishonoured by these vile men and who knows what they might do to the sick child.

The soldier who had spoken stood over her, his eyes fixed on her with excitement, Apollonia tried to push back on the floor, but her arms merely bumped into another soldier who was behind her. He made a lip-smacking sound at her.

Everything was lost. *God, please, I need your help.* Tears filled Apollonia's eyes.

Then a spear burst through the back and out of the chest of the soldier who had spoken. His face contorted in agony, as he fell to his knees before her. The other Seleucids swivelled around.

Zaim and a troop of Falcons had poured into the courtyard, piling straight into the Seleucid soldiers.

Apollonia scrambled across the ground to Luja, collecting the crumpled child into her arms, cradling her feverish head.

'Stay with me,' Apollonia cried.

Around her the Falcons made short work of the Seleucid soldiers, who now sprawled lifeless on the ground.

'Apollonia, Luja!' Zaim scrambled over to them. He took his sister in his arms, feeling her burning up. 'We must get her to the healer.'

He stood with the child in his arms. Turning to Apollonia he asked, 'How is it that I find you here when the others have fled?'

Apollonia looked at Luja. 'I could not leave her alone in the temple.'

Zaim smiled. 'Nor could I.'

Thank God! she thought.

More shouts came from further down the corridor, as it seemed additional Seleucid soldiers were now entering the building.

'Come on, we must get you both out of here. This way,' Zaim said, leading them all out of the great temple.

Chapter 25

DEPLETED ARSENAL

Bedouin forces continued to rattle the palace gates, but they would hold for now. Chao stood, arms crossed, listening to the jangling of weapons and clanking of armour. Zaim had gone to fetch his sister from the great temple and had left him to prepare the defensive positions. Chao had briefed the men, and archers were in position along the upper ramparts, overlooking the wall. The attackers continued to pound the wooden and brass doors with their solitary weapons and were yet to bring anything more substantial to the attack like a battering ram. Perhaps, it struck him, they did not know of such a weapon. It would be a fine thing if they did not, he mused.

Above, along the palace walls, two dozen Nabataean archers held their positions, firing off occasional arrows. *They should preserve their shafts,* thought Chao. He realised many of them felt uncomfortable taking orders from him and he did not blame them, but he did not want to die this evening, so had placed the men where they needed to be and not where they wanted to be. The courtyard behind him led to the banqueting hall, then the throne room. General Ghassan was at the base of the building issuing orders to the defenders, before going inside.

How is it that I find myself in the heat of this battle, when I came as an explorer to these western lands? Did my revered grandfather, Zhang Qian, also become embroiled in such encounters, but choose not to write about it? If I live through this night, I will ask him.

In many ways he was not so concerned with his own personal safety, for his own wife and child were dead, but he knew that the companions he had set off with had families. Where was his small band now? Captain Zhu Di, his jovial officer who loved his food and his half-moon axe? Lieutenant Fu Youde, his hawk-eyed friend who fought with the grace of a court dancer and used his jade-encrusted sword as a painter would a brush? Where was Cartographer Ganfu, a stocky, adept fighting man who swung his staff with grace? And where was Scribe Jin Guliang, the most accomplished bowman of the party?

The four of them would have been equivalent to forty soldiers. With those men beside him he would have felt bolder, but as it was, he felt an impending sense of peril. The Nabataeans were divided. There was a traitor amongst their ranks; how else could the Seleucid and Bedouin have gained such easy entry into the city?

Having told the men to take up certain positions, he decided to take another look over the palace walls to assess what the attackers were planning. Moving across the courtyard he took the wooden stairs to the wall, where Luay, Zaim's quartermaster, crouched behind the stone parapet. In the flicker of the cresset light, the red scar across Luay's right eye was more pronounced. Zaim peeked over the wall, assessing what was out there. Beyond the few Bedouin attempting to kick and shoulder-charge the gates, it was quiet. Yet shadows did move about the city. Were they looting Petra first before attacking the palace? Was this simply a distraction, so that the invaders could empty the city of its wealth?

'Where is Prince Asylaion's Scorpion regiment? I do not see them,' Chao asked.

Luay rubbed the scar over his eye, his gravelly voice coming out steady and low. 'Scorpions like to hide, bury themselves in the desert – then when you least expect it, they bite you.'

'Are you saying …'

'I am observing.'

'I see,' Chao pondered. *Is Prince Asylaion the traitor?* Chao shook the thought from his head: it was not his concern.

Glancing down at the Bedouin by the gate Chao assessed the height of the walls to be equivalent to three tall men. Not high enough for an invading army equipped with ladders.

'How many ladders are there in Petra?' Chao asked.

'Many, for every building has high roofs requiring constant clean-ing from within. It will not be long before they come with ladders to scale these walls and we do not have enough men in the palace to defend the length of these ramparts,' Luay said.

Chao looked up and down the length of the fortifications. Even if all two hundred fighting men presently in the palace grounds were stationed along these battlements, there would still be gaps through which the enemy could gain entry. Once over the walls the Seleucids and Bedouin would get into the courtyard, go through the banquet-ing hall and head for the throne room. They simply did not have enough soldiers to defend the palace.

'Do you have an armoury within the palace?' Chao asked.

Luay nodded.

'What does your supply of arrows look like?'

'Meagre,' replied Luay.

'How so?'

'Two days ago, Captain Jahm of the Scorpions asked me to move most of the shafts, as well as other weapons, to the outer armoury beside the eastern city gates, where he said they were undertaking a military drill. He promised me they would replenish the stock before the end of the month.'

'And you did it?'

'It struck me as odd, but he is the right hand of Prince Asylaion and told me it was under direct orders of the prince. I did not question it, for men such as I take care to avoid royalty. Of course, Prince Zaim is an exception, a fine lad, but he was not free for me to check, so I complied with the request. Now, I wish I had not.'

Bows left, arrows moved – the timing could not be a coincidence.

'Hey, you,' Luay hissed at a soldier wasting an arrow on one of the Bedouin running around outside. 'Save your shafts till the real fighting begins.'

'If we cannot hold this wall,' said Chao. 'Then I would like to see where we can fall back to. I will go to the throne room and speak with General Ghassan. If they bring ladders, then ensure they are not placed against the walls. Send word and we will have more archers come forward.'

'Chao Zhang,' Luay said.

'Yes.'

'I have heard you recite uplifting words. Others have mentioned this to me. Do you have any words for me now?'

Chao nodded, considering for a moment.

'The words are not my own, but they are from the *Way*. I will recite some of it to you. The old master Lao Tsu says: He who knows others is clever; He who knows himself has discernment. He who overcomes others has force; He who overcomes himself is strong. He who knows contentment is rich; He who perseveres is a man of purpose; He who does not lose his station will endure; He who lives out his days has had a long life.'

'Good words,' said Luay softly. The grizzled old quartermaster reached out and gripped Chao's forearm. 'Thank you, my friend.'

Chao gripped Luay back, nodding silently. Then the Han explorer, crouching low, shuffled back to the stairs. Skipping down them he made his way towards the banqueting hall and on into the throne room. The bulk of the Nabataean soldiers and the Falcons were in this room, armour stretching and creaking. Some of it old and well-used, others, such as that worn by King Obodos and Prince Asylaion, shiny and new. Every man was armed, as a nervous energy took hold.

Prince Asylaion was making a point in a three-way conversation with King Obodos and General Ghassan. Asylaion made Chao uncomfortable, but despite this he approached, as General Ghassan had asked him to report back.

Ghassan noticed him but before he could say anything the king asked. 'Where is Zaim? Why is he not here?'

Zaim had told Chao not to tell anyone where he was going, so he replied, 'He will be here soon, your Highness. He is preparing the men.'

'So, he sends you instead!' Asylaion snapped.

'It is I,' Ghassan interjected, 'who asked Chao Zhang to report to me, as he has some past experience of defending a city.'

'You do?' Obodos asked.

Chao nodded, as Asylaion scoffed.

'Then we will listen to your advice,' Obodos said.

Chao looked at Ghassan who nodded before the Han explorer continued. 'We do not have enough men within the palace to defend the entire length of the walls,' he said, 'so it will be only a question of time till the invaders bring ladders and men to scale it. The walls will fall.'

'That is rubbish,' Asylaion interjected.

Obodos gave his son a solemn stare. 'Let him continue.'

Asylaion shot a murderous glance at Chao but fell silent.

'For now, we have fifty archers on the outer walls. As the ladders are placed along the walls they should shoot and kill as many as they can. But with so many ladders across the city and the low height of the wall …'

'You call my walls low?' Obodos laughed.

'Forgive me your Highness, but by Han standards they are low. We are a people used to being invaded by nomadic tribes, so we build walls three times as high.'

'I see,' Obodos replied. 'Go on.'

'A point will come in the battle when we will not be able to hold the walls. We should retreat across the courtyard and enter the inner palace, stationing ourselves along the barricades, where the bulk of the archers will remain and they can fire at will in the open space of the courtyard.'

'It will be an easy kill,' Obodos said.

'Your Highness, the Seleucids have armoured shields, so they will most likely approach in formation. In addition, Quartermaster Luay has confirmed there are not enough arrows in the palace armoury to sustain a long fight.'

'Not enough!' Obodos grimaced.

'Apparently the bulk of the stores of arrows and other weapons were moved to the outer armoury two days ago.'

'By whom?' Ghassan asked.

Chao knew the answer, as did Asylaion, but the Han explorer thought it best to feign ignorance of such a matter. 'I would ask Quartermaster Luay.'

Asylaion's eyes burned with rage. The prince clenched and unclenched his fists.

'I will,' Ghassan said. 'Please continue, Chao.'

'Once the outer courtyard has fallen, it is not wise to defend the banqueting hall, as it is porous with many entrances. Rather we should immediately fall back to this throne room. The challenge we have with so few arrows in the palace and the throne room doors not being reinforced, is that the attackers, if they have battering rams, will get through this door behind me. As there is only one door, we can hold them, but their numbers will eventually turn the tide in their favour.'

'Gods help us,' Obodos mumbled. 'What do you suggest, Chao?'

Chao cast his gaze around the room, spotting a heavily reinforced doorway. 'What is beyond that door?' he asked.

'None of your business,' Asylaion snapped.

'Don't be so tetchy, boy,' Obodos said. 'It is the entry to the king and queen's private chambers, which can be reached by a single staircase. It is where the women of the royal household are currently taking shelter.'

'And that balcony,' Chao pointed. 'Is attached to the private chamber.'

'Yes,' Obodos said.

The balcony was lower than the outer wall and could easily be scaled by a set of ladders.

'Then if we have to fall back to the apartments, that balcony will become the last line of defence.'

'How dare you speak of entering my parents' apartment?' Asylaion said, taking a step toward the Han explorer.

Obodos raised his hand, ordering his son to be silent.

'May I see the staircase?' Chao asked.

The four men strode over to the armoured door, as Ghassan opened it.

Just then, Zaim returned, along with a few of the Falcons. He was carrying Luja in his arms and Apollonia was beside him. The young girl looked terribly ill.

'My child!' Obodos cried, crouching over her as Zaim held her in his arms.

The girl did not move.

'She needs a healer, Father,' Zaim said.

'Up in the apartments,' Obodos said. 'Asylaion, relieve your brother of his burden and take your sister up to the healer. Apollonia, I do not know why you are not in the apartments already but go with him now.'

Asylaion did not look pleased at being sent away but took his sister from Zaim and with Apollonia beside him ascended the stairs.

Chao watched them walk up the twenty or so steps. It was wide enough for three. In his mind he could see the fight unfolding on this staircase. It was going to be bloody and messy.

The king turned to Zaim. 'Chao Zhang thinks we cannot hold the outer palace walls, courtyard, banqueting hall and throne room for long, as there are insufficient men in the palace, and the armoury does not have enough weapons. He suggests we retreat to the private apartments. What do you say, son?'

'Chao is the only man amongst us who has lived through a siege and defended a wall. I will listen to his advice.'

'So, it will be then,' Obodos said to Ghassan. 'We take the advice of a visitor from the east who came to the aid of the Arabs of Petra in their most dire need. It will indeed be a story to tell future generations – if we live to tell it, that is.'

Having contemplated the staircase, Chao addressed the prince. 'When the attackers reach this point and if they get through this door, you and I will be on the other side of it. We must not fail.'

'God willing, we will not,' Zaim replied.

Chapter 26

THE BATTLE CRIES

———————

Quartermaster Luay silently fumed at the lack of weapons in the palace armoury. He blamed himself for giving in to Captain Jahm's order. In fact, he had intended to replenish the palace armoury the next day from the southern perimeter wall's stock, but one thing or another seemed more important at the time. How was he going to show his face to the king after this? It might all be immaterial if they didn't survive the night. Movement on the stair caught his attention.

Chao climbed up the slippery staircase, now drenched by the downpour, and joined Luay. 'What is it like out there?'

'Silent for now,' Luay replied. 'But there is movement in the shadows. Something is coming but with this rain it's difficult to tell.'

'It will not be long,' Chao said, pulling his cloak around him as the wind whipped along the battlements. *Sieges are never a rushed affair,* thought Chao. *The attacking army rarely arrives with everything they need and they spend the first few hours stripping assets from the town and bolstering their own arsenal. They would have taken what they needed by now.*

'What did the king decide?'

'We hold here, killing as many enemies as possible with our arrows. Then when the wall is breached we fall back across the courtyard to the inner palace, hold those gates, and when they are breached we retreat to the throne room, and if required we will secure ourselves in the apartments of the king and queen.'

'Their apartments! Why, few have set foot in there.'

'Today is not a day to be picky,' Chao replied.

'Indeed, it is not, friend Chao.'

Chao heard bow strings being pulled back. 'When death approaches, all you can do is pray you have lived a life of virtue,' he said.

A young soldier posted further down the ramparts grew animated. 'I see them. They're coming.' In his excitement, the young man stood up, pointing at the attackers. *Whoosh*! An arrow pierced his eyeball, entering his skull. The soldier screamed, toppling back off the rampart.

'Stupid boy!' Luay exclaimed. Turning to the other soldiers, he shouted. 'Keep low, follow my lead, don't waste arrows.'

Chao glanced back down at the crumpled form of the young man, the rain pounding his body. *Such a waste. But I have seen this before, many times and if I live beyond this night, I will see it again. For the young are brash, thinking themselves invincible, yet death does not swerve out of the way for a foolish young man.*

'Aiee!' A cry went up outside the walls.

Luay raised his bow, notching an arrow to the string, pulling it back and taking aim. The defenders to his right and left followed suit.

Thunder boomed somewhere on the horizon. Bedouin charged at the wall. The Nabataeans assembled and fired.

Chao watched as half the arrows missed their targets in the darkness, but at least two men carrying the dozen or so ladders were shot. Other Bedouin picked up the fallen ladders, each one carried by a set of four men. The Nabataeans fired once more. More Bedouin fell, but others took their place. Lightning lit up the night sky and Chao's heart sank when he saw the hundreds of Bedouin waiting to join the battle, as well as the hundreds of Seleucid soldiers, fully armoured with reinforced shields, lined up behind them. His assessment of a thousand was about right, then.

'God help us,' Luay exclaimed as he too assessed the size of the enemy force.

Ladders rattled against the walls. An arrow flew past Luay's head, followed by others. Chao noted the Seleucid archers had taken up an advanced position to give the Bedouin cover. Men were now ascending the ladders.

'Draw your swords,' Chao commanded.

The Bedouin were coming over the wall and onto the rampart. Chao skimmed past two defenders and thrust his sword into the first Bedouin's gut, before kicking a second man off the wall. He swung and took out a third who had just set foot on the rampart. Everywhere along the battlements, Nabataean soldiers were now engaged in hand-to-hand combat with Bedouin. Chao noted a group of Bedouin overwhelming some of the younger soldiers and he leapt into the fight, slashing high and low, cutting through muscle and vein, shattering bone with his pommel and clearing the path for the Nabataean soldiers to regroup around him. 'Work together,' he said, as he moved down the fortifications to assist others.

More Bedouin poured over the walls. Glancing up and down the ramparts he could see that half the Nabataeans were down. Twenty men lost so quickly. He grimly reminded himself there were only two hundred defenders within the walls at this time and to lose a tenth in the first wave was a bad sign.

Just then, behind him he heard a familiar voice shout. 'Hold firm!'

Zaim and a troop of twenty Falcons had scaled the stairs to join the defence. These experienced fighters laid into the Bedouin, cutting through them, throwing some off the wall. Other attackers died where they stood. The tide began turning as Bedouin bodies fell or were thrown back over the palace wall. Men stopped coming over the parapet and the Falcons pushed the remaining ladders free of the ramparts.

Through the pelting rain, Chao peered back across the barricades. Dead Bedouin and some Nabataean soldiers lay strewn outside the palace, ladders lying on the ground. Lightning flared and again he could see the mass of Bedouin and Seleucid forces lined up just beyond the range of their arrows.

It was going to be a long night.

Zaim approached him and was joined by Luay.

'We cannot defend this wall, even with three hundred men,' Chao said. 'It is too long, and they are too many of them.'

'Yet we beat them back?' Luay asked.

'And we lost half our men. Next time we will be overrun,' Chao said.

'What do you suggest?' Zaim asked.

'Throw any enemy bodies back over the wall, carry our dead down, remove any armour or weapons we can use later and withdraw to the inner palace. We must act quickly before the next wave of attack.'

'We abandon our position?' Luay asked.

'It will be done,' Zaim replied, issuing instructions to his Falcons. 'Go to General Ghassan, inform him to expect us soon. He should have archers on the stockades for when the enemy enters the palace courtyard. It is open ground, and we should use it as an opportunity to whittle down their numbers.'

And Zaim thought, *of course the problem remains that we do not have enough arrows to last the night. How could such an error be made?*

Throwing off the thought, Zaim strode along the fortifications, amongst the men who had just led the first defence of the outer palace wall. There were smiles on some faces; men puffed out their chests when they saw him approach. Their confidence was up and a good thing too, he thought, for worse was to come.

Where are Asylaion's Scorpions, he wondered. Have they been immobilised by the invaders? Is this why they do not come to our aid? Petra was an unbreachable city and so the Nabataean forces had never been large: they had preferred to deploy soldiers across several of northern coastal ports and towns, such as Gaza, as well as deeper south in Hegra, to keep the Bedouin from overrunning the southern kingdom. Now that Petra had been invaded, that seemed a poor strategy. *How could this be? The walls were secure, well-guarded and there was nowhere an army could mobilise without being picked off by archers. But the walls were breached and there was a shortage of weapons in the palace.*

Then a terrible thought struck him.

The prince sat back on his haunches, back pressed against a stone parapet, chin cupped in his hands, elbows resting on his knees, staring at the ground before him, lost in thought. Rain poured, puddles forming in the stone by his feet. But for the raging storm everything else was silent, as the Nabataean soldiers withdrew deeper into the palace. Eventually, none were left on the battlements bar the prince. Still, he did not move. Lightning flashed overhead, followed by claps of thunder, but Zaim ignored it, probing his mind for all the excuses he could make to avoid the conclusion – *one of my brothers is a traitor.*

'Prince Zaim.'

It was Chao. The Han explorer had made his way along the battlements wrapped in a cloak, the wind whipping at the edges of it. Peering down at the forlorn prince, he said, 'We must retreat to the inner tower, your Highness, for they are coming.'

Zaim was on his feet, glancing over the edge of the battlements. The area on the other side swarmed with Bedouin and Seleucid and for the first time he could make out an exceptionally tall Seleucid amongst their ranks. It was General Tigranous; his thoughts went to his friend Pelagios. *I will slay the beast for my dear uncle, for such an opportunity will not present itself again.* Units of men carried a dozen fresh ladders, as they advanced towards the fortifications. *Not long now*, Zaim considered.

'Let us go,' Zaim said, following Chao back across the rampart and down the staircase.

'Your Highness, there is a matter I wish to make known to you,' Chao said in guarded tones.

'Please, go ahead.'

The shouts of men's voices grew louder behind them as they started to cross the courtyard.

'In Sela, I remained for a time at the foot of the mountain. I saw a man there, meeting with Seleucid soldiers. Of course, I did not know him, nor did I see him again, until this evening.'

'This evening?'

'Yes, he was by the side of Prince Asylaion as they left the banquet. He had a scar on his face and the insignia of a Scorpion on his breastplate.'

'Jahm!' said Zaim. 'He is a Captain of the Scorpions.'

The terrible notion surged through him, poisoning his mind with wretched thoughts. It felt as though a scorpion had pinched the insides of his stomach.

Could the traitor be my own flesh and blood, Asylaion? Jahm would not bat an eyelid without his master's say so. His head felt light and the prince had to grip the hilt of his sword to steady himself as he and Chao marched across the courtyard.

The rainfall intensified, hammering their leather breastplates. He found it hard to think as turmoil gripped him with feverish intent. *Do I tell father? Yet what evidence do I have, for it could be said that Chao was mistaken.*

For now, all he could do was watch for the knife that strikes from within.

Chapter 27

A BLOODY COURTYARD

General Tigranous watched the hardy Bedouin scaling the walls. They were nimble and fast. The ambush in the wadi had proven so, but they were not an organised fighting force, preferring to loot and quickly disappear. They would never make a regiment, let alone an army. Still, they had a purpose to fulfil. Their chief, Sakhr, lived true to his word. He had amassed what was for them their single largest fighting force and he was here on time.

The spoils from Petra would last them a lifetime, and any chief who had this much booty would be remembered in poems recited by the Bedouin for generations to come. To live immortally through heroic tales was what every chief wanted. These unrefined desert Arabs, motivated by the booty of Petra, were making a decent fist of it, as far as Tigranous could see. Their efforts had forced the defenders to abandon the outer palace wall.

It was odd, thought Tigranous.

He had expected to be kept here for some time, but now as the Bedouin leapt onto the upper ramparts, it was clear the palace gates were going to be opened shortly. Did the Nabataeans have a nasty surprise waiting on the other side of the gates? If so, let the Bedouin take the brunt of it; he would keep his elite Seleucid troops back from the initial fighting. The emperor would not be pleased if they suffered unnecessary casualties against these measly Nabataeans.

I will draw my sword, but it will be to kill Prince Zaim and the Dragon from the East, Tigranous thought. The pair of them were proving to be quite resourceful and he would not underestimate their martial abilities, yet when the time was right, he would put them to the sword. Of that there was no doubt in his mind. *Whatever the Nabataeans call Hades, I will send their young prince and the rest of his family there.*

The gates opened.

A roar went up amongst the Bedouin, who now lost all sense of place and rank and tore through the gates. Suddenly Sakhr was beside him, his eyes squinting through the pummelling rain to see what lay beyond the gate.

'What devilry is this?' Sakhr said. 'Where is the royal booty we were promised?'

Tigranous looked at the Bedouin. He had to remind himself Sakhr and his people were unfamiliar with cities and palaces. The thought of a gate opening into a courtyard was alien to them and it was little wonder they were left bemused.

'How many doors must we open to find the gold?' Sakhr asked.

'It will not be long now,' Tigranous replied. 'I am told beyond the next courtyard is the inner palace and the throne room. The Nabataeans will not be able to hide all their treasures, there will be plenty for you to take.'

'The throne room, yes, it sounds like a place of wealth,' Sakhr said. 'I will see you there.' The Bedouin chief wrapped his cloak about him and straight as an arrow he set off after the large contingent of Bedouin who had already stormed through the gates.

Tigranous raised his arm to chest height, indicating that the Seleucids should wait a moment. Screams and shouts erupted from the courtyard. So, there was still some fight left in the Nabataeans.

****

The inner palace was not a fortified building. It had one long ceremonial balcony upon which the king and queen would sometimes stand and wave at those assembled in the courtyard. The wooden doorway below it was not reinforced and with sufficient bodies it could be smashed open. Upon the long balcony stood fifty Nabataean bowmen. Each nocked an arrow and fired at a moving target in the courtyard below. There was no cover, so either the defenders kept up the onslaught or they would be picked off by invading archers.

The Bedouin below scattered to the corners of the courtyard, their lack of armour proving a hindrance. Bodies of the desert Arabs littered the area, at least some thirty killed. Chao stood behind a set of Nabataean defenders to the left side of the balcony, observing the fight unfold. The courtyard was quiet now, the Bedouin taking to the shadows. Thunder roared overhead and the rain continued to fall.

From the other end of the courtyard, coming into the range of Nabataean archers, was a phalanx of Seleucids advancing in formation. Slow and steady, their steps measured, their bodies kept hidden behind a wall of shields. The emblem of an elephant was emblazoned on their armour. After the first hundred, another hundred came through, then another. Three hundred soldiers advancing, shields up.

'Fire!' Taimur shouted. The lieutenant of the Falcons and the most accomplished bowman amongst the Arabs was placed in the centre of the archers and his bowstring hummed with the sound of arrows.

Chao could see this was the last stand of the Nabataean archers. Despite their skill, they did not have many arrows left. It would not be long before they would have to abandon this balcony and take the men back through the banqueting hall and into the throne room, where they would meet the Seleucid and Bedouin forces in hand-to-hand combat.

Arrows pinged off shields or became lodged in them. Some advancing Seleucids were caught on ankles or wrists, momentarily dropping the protections of those around them, before they were replaced. The first hundred men were now halfway across the courtyard.

Chao moved to stand behind Taimur, placing a hand on his shoulder. 'Do not use up all the arrows,' Chao said. 'Keep some in reserve. The enemy should not know we have no ammunition. Keep them guessing.'

'We will, friend Chao,' Taimur replied, before notching another shaft and firing into the exposed foot of a Seleucid.

Chao skipped down the stairs, making his way past a set of Falcons who were standing ready to replace any bowmen hit. He swiftly made his way through the banqueting hall and entered the throne room.

He saw Zaim surrounded by Falcons and approached him. 'Not many arrows left and the Seleucids have shield walls, to help them advance to these gates,' Chao pointed at the wooden doors which they had tried to reinforce with some additional bars. 'This gate will not hold long.'

'The fighting will be brutal in the throne room. What do you suggest?' Zaim asked.

Chao studied the area. The chamber, with the throne at one end, was about fifty yards wide and was just as long if not longer. To the rear was the staircase leading up to the private apartments of the king and queen. A quick glance back there showed the balcony was packed with women, watching to see what was going to happen.

'Have bowmen placed on that balcony,' he said pointing towards the private apartments of the royal couple. 'Equip them with long spears, as the balcony is not particularly high.' Turning back to the gate, Chao said. 'Whatever happens at these gates, do not break formation, remain in the throne room. If we spill out into the banqueting hall, we will be surrounded sooner than we would be here.'

'We will hold,' Zaim replied. 'What formation do you suggest?'

'How many men do you estimate we have left?' Chao asked.

'Not more than one hundred and fifty in the entire palace,' Zaim replied.

'There are at least six hundred, if not seven hundred waiting to come through those doors. The advantage we have is that no more than twenty can come through at a time. We will form a triangle. I will take this frontal position, with fifty men, in rows of two. Zaim, you will command forty on the right flank, so that when they come through the doorway and see us before them, you will hit them hard from the right. Fahad will command the left flank and do the same with his forty.'

'How long do you think we can hold out, friend Chao?' one of the Falcons asked.

'I do not know, but I do know this, if we stand together we have a fighting chance, and your names will go into the stories told by future generations as the soldiers who held the last line at Petra, who did not break when the odds were against them, who did not wince in the face of uncertain odds, but who remained resolute and firm.'

The doors of the banqueting hall, which they could see from the throne room, rattled, as the first shields of the Seleucid forces clattered into it.

Chao drew his Dragon Blade, the red-tinged sword catching the light of the cressets. 'The Dragon will taste blood this night and will soar with the Arabian Falcon.' He raised the blade aloft. The men around him drew their weapons and copied his rallying call.

'Positions!' Zaim ordered.

A group of Nabataean soldiers shut the doors to the throne room, placing a set of crossbeams and bolts in place. They then barricaded it with other furniture.

As the men dispersed to the right and left flanks and Chao settled into formation with his fifty Falcons, he calmed his Chi, drawing on seven parts of his breath, circulating the life force around his body, strengthening each muscle and fibre, relaxing his inner being.

Smash! They heard the doors to the banqueting hall splitting. Then the rushing of boots and feet across the banqueting hall, whoops of joy going up, before bodies slammed into the doors of the throne room.

A battering ram smashed against the throne room door. Then again. It cracked. Once more, and it split. Chao heard screams from the women gathered in the royal apartments behind them. A final onslaught and the two doors were smashed off their hinges, landing before the oncoming horde.

'Kill them all!'

A cry went up amongst the Seleucid soldiers. They were coming through the door screaming and shouting at the top of their voices.

Chao raised the Dragon Blade. 'With me!' he urged the Falcons around him. They stepped forward, into the Seleucid onslaught. The Elephant warriors had abandoned their shields for close combat, hacking at the Nabataeans with their steel blades. Chao picked out the tallest most brutish looking attacker and went straight for him.

Ducking under his sword strike, he sliced through the man's belly, bringing him to his knees, before leaping at the next two. opening their windpipes and cutting off a man's ear. The Falcons were only a few steps behind him, keeping formation. The Seleucids backed off a few paces, as the Han warrior swept through them like a scythe at harvest. High and low his blade cut, swift as the lightning overhead, imperious as the rumbling thunder, roaring like a whirlwind, a maelstrom of destruction.

****

In the royal apartments, Apollonia peered through the line of Nabataean archers who had appeared moments earlier, taking up positions along the balcony. Bowstrings at the ready, along with long spears, they formed a welcome defensive line, but then to her horror she realised they did not possess enough arrows. *Surely, these will run out after a few rounds? Where is the rest of their supply?*

The fighting was fierce in the throne room and she could see the defenders had formed into three groups. Her eyes kept darting to Zaim on the right of the hall. He was in the thick of the melee. The Han explorer Chao Zhang commanded the unit facing the doorway; he himself was a skilled warrior but the Nabataean soldiers beside him were not. They were dying around him and there was a painful certainty about what was going to happen next. As she watched with fear-filled eyes, two Falcons met their death, and another gap opened up in the defence. Additional battle-weary Nabataean warriors stepped forward to close ranks, but there were not enough of them.

The Seleucid numbers were vast and now she noticed Bedouin appearing at the fringes of the melee. They kept neither formation nor positions and seemed simply to want to peer inside the throne room. *It must be a mystery to them. What would the glorious marvel of her father's palace in Alexandria look like to these thirsty Arabs? I will never know, for I am now of the desert and the desert does not give back what it takes.*

She could bear to watch no longer. As the defenders fell with an inevitable certainty she turned away, to enter the apartments. The king stood a few paces back from the balcony, hand on the hilt of his sword. Behind him, Prince Asylaion watched his father intently. Was that a smile she detected on his face? Surely not.

Elsewhere in the apartment Prince Stylian lay sprawling on a bed, maidens by his side, placing food into this mouth, as he sweated profusely. How bizarre, Apollonia thought, but then he is doing the one thing he knows how to do well: eat. Then there was Fastiq, her betrothed, who marched back and forth beside the only doorway out of the apartments, anxious and pensive, with the look of a man who craved the intoxication of wine at a time like this.

Most of the women, including her aunt and handmaiden, huddled close to the queen who was dabbing a wet cloth to Luja's head, speaking softly to her daughter. To think the child had been forgotten amongst the mayhem! If it had not been for Zaim, they would both have met a terrible end.

Zaim!

At every opportunity Zaim had demonstrated his courage and valour, his commitment to his family and loyalty to his kingdom. In their present situation her convictions were all but pointless as they were not going to live through the night.

Thump!

A few of the women screamed as one of the Falcons who had been standing upon the balcony was knocked back into the apartment, an arrow piercing his skull. The man lay motionless. No one in the room moved, waiting to see what else was going to happen. The man still clutched his bow and a pack of his arrows was tied to his back.

Apollonia stepped forward, kneeling beside the man, removing the shaft from his dead hands and unstrapping the quiver of arrows.

'What are you doing, child?' Obodos asked.

'My aim is true; I am needed on the balcony.'

Obodos looked stunned for a moment, then smiled, his admiration plain to see. He glanced over at his three sons, none of whom moved. 'Then I will also be by your side, daughter. Asylaion, fetch my bow.'

The prince stood uncertainly for a moment, before collecting his father's bow and handing it to the King.

'Come, daughter,' he said. 'Let us show these Seleucids what Nabataean royalty can do when provoked.'

Chapter 28

ABANDONING A THRONE

Seleucid soldiers pressed into the throne room, even as bodies piled up at the entrance. The Bedouin desperately tried to get around the back of the defenders, but Zaim's and Fahad's men kept their attacks swift and cut any down. The dead soon created a wall which could be used by the Nabataeans as a defence-barrier.

Zaim swung his blade, cutting a Bedouin down, before slicing the fingers off a Seleucid soldier's right hand and driving his blade into the man's belly. As he leapt forward, thrusting his blade into another soldier, he caught sight of Chao, now separated from the Nabataean soldiers, as he charged like an arrow piercing the front Seleucid line. He had lost half his men and was in danger of being left without any support. Surely, even a man of his calibre and fighting skill could not overcome a hundred opponents by himself, let alone a few hundred who were now coming through the door.

'Pull back!' he heard a voice roar above the din, as the Seleucids suddenly retreated, leaving the Bedouin looking confused and un- sure. The defenders used it as a chance to cut down any Bedouin who remained.

The throne room was left with defenders only, and a pile of bodies beside the doorway.

'What's happening?' Fahad asked.

Zaim looked back towards the balcony of the private apartments and saw two soldiers he had stationed there, and beside them the king with his bow, and Apollonia with another bow. She looked incredibly beautiful amongst the bloody carnage. He shook himself clear of her image and focused on the gates.

'Son, they come once more!' Obodos cried, his position offering a view over the pile of bodies.

The Seleucids raised their shields, maintaining a tight formation, advancing step by step over the bodies. Other soldiers behind them began to pull the bodies back through the door into the courtyard, so clearing the human wall. It was a slow laborious process, but it would allow the attackers access to launch a fresh wave of attacks against the defenders.

'Chao?' Zaim called across to the Han warrior.

The prince watched as the easterner surveyed the numbers of men around them. Defending this doorway had led to the loss of half of their men, leaving them with about seventy who now stood with weapons drawn. The attackers had lost closer to two hundred, but with so many more still to come, the Nabataeans could not hold this position.

Chao strode across to Zaim. 'We must pull back to the private apartments, your Highness.'

Zaim did not like the idea of giving up the precious throne room, with its elaborate fixtures, jewelled armour and valuable royal possessions. The Bedouin would strip this area clear as soon as they gained access to it. Yet, what other choice did they have but to retreat to the apartments to make their last stand? *The lives of men are more precious than the things of this world.*

The advance line of Seleucid began striking the bottom of their shields on the stone ground, sending a reverberation around the throne room. It was a scare tactic, but it was having its effect, as many of the defenders cast nervous glances around them. There was nothing else they could do.

'Back to the apartments,' Zaim shouted, above the sound of the clattering shields.

The defenders of Petra funnelled back through the throne room to the rear and the only door leading up to the apartments. Once the men were through it, Zaim and Chao bolted it firmly from the inside and took up positions upon the first few steps. Behind them were stationed Fahad and Luay, then two more warriors every two steps upwards. If the Seleucids were going to get through, they would need to cut them all down. Zaim sent Taimur to the balcony to command its defence, along with thirty other soldiers. There were only two ways in now: the stairs or the balcony. Both needed defending to the death.

****

Apollonia watched the men stream into the private apartments. Many were taken aback by the plush surroundings, but recovered their composure and took up positions along the balcony edge.

Taimur approached the king. 'Your Highness, may we take charge of the balcony?'

'Of course, but there are few shafts left and we have no shields.'

'We will hold with whatever we have, your Highness,' Taimur said.

'Where is Zaim?' the king asked.

At the sound of the prince's name, Apollonia's heart missed a beat. *Surely, he has made it safely back to the apartments?*

'He is at the bottom of the stairwell, with Chao and the bravest men we have left in Petra,' Taimur replied, casting a quick glance across at the other three princes.

Obodos strode to the entry to the stairwell, Apollonia and Ghassan a few steps behind him. He peered down the steps. It was dark, but for two cressets burning, illuminating the warriors lined up on each step. Apollonia could just about make out Zaim's features, along with Chao's. They had fought like heroes in the stories of old. *Death tonight will be too cruel a fate after such gallantry. Oh God we are in need, please help us.*

'Brave men,' Obodos whispered quietly to himself. 'If only others were such.'

Apollonia noted the king's frown as he glanced at his other sons. Stylian sprawled on cushions, surrounded by maidens; Fastiq sat quietly brooding in a corner, biting his fingernails, and Asylaion was unnecessarily ordering Taimur about.

'He will survive,' Apollonia said.

Obodos looked at her questioningly. 'How can you be so sure?'

'My heart tells me that *the* Prince of Petra will not die tonight at the hands of the Seleucids. He is destined for greater things.'

The king smiled, then turned his anxious gaze towards the stairwell. 'I pray your heart speaks the truth,' he said.

Ladders were brought into the throne room by the invading force, then propped against the balcony to the private apartments. Taimur and two other men pushed one ladder away before any man could ascend it, only to have another ladder appear, which others shoved away. More ladders smacked against the stone balcony. Too many to keep pushing away.

'Fire!' a voice called, as a volley of arrows flew from Seleucid archers' bows, at the Nabataeans on the balcony. Two Nabataeans toppled to their deaths, as Taimur and the other men managed to duck out of the way behind the balcony. More ladders appeared and now the Seleucids began ascending in earnest.

The Bedouin, having lost momentum, scattered across the throne room, collecting up any booty they could find, tucking it into the folds of their clothing, or carrying it away before disappearing. They had got what they wanted and were content with these spoils.

The Seleucids were not.

'We need more men on the balcony!' Taimur shouted back into the apartment.

Obodos heard the cry for help and went to assist.

'Your Highness, please send another, we cannot lose you,' Ghassan appealed.

Obodos looked at her then around the room at the other men. There were only the three princes remaining, and none seemed fit nor worthy enough to take up sword and shield to defend his kingdom.

'Fastiq,' Obodos said. The eldest prince looked up, surprised that his father should call to him now. 'They need reinforcements on the balcony. Tell Zaim to send more men this way.'

'I will do it, Father,' Asylaion said, striding through the door and into the stairwell, disappearing from view.

'I am done with this madness,' Fastiq hissed.

'Fastiq!' Queen Fazluna cried out.

The eldest prince darted towards the stairwell, then froze when he saw it was full of bodies brawling at close bloody quarters. He spun around, anxious, scanning the room in confusion.

'I need a drink,' he kept saying. The prince made for the balcony. Obodos stepped in his way to block him, but he darted around him. 'Tell them to bring me a drink …' Fastiq shouted as he ran out onto the balcony.

Whack! An arrow pierced the eldest prince's throat, and he toppled over the balcony to his death below.

'Fastiq, my son!' Fazluna cried out, running towards the balcony.

'No,' Obodos stopped his wife, holding her back.

Fastiq, my betrothed!

Apollonia watched Seleucid forces reach the top of the ladders, and Taimur and the men around him started to hack at them with their swords, knocking them away, before other Seleucids swarmed around them.

Where are the reinforcements Taimur asked for? Why hasn't Zaim sent them?

****

The door to the staircase smashed open before it was ripped back and taken off its hinges. Chao took a step back, along with Zaim. A moment later, the first Seleucid showed his face. Chao rammed his blade into the man's neck. The fellow fell to the ground, as others took his place. Four men crammed through the tight space, shields up. Chao searched for a gap, then stabbed his blade through it, felling a man. As the Seleucid's knee buckled, his shield dropped, Zaim sliced through the man's neck, sending a gushing wave of blood into the face of the man beside him, before stabbing the other man in the neck with his short blade. Chao kicked at the remaining Seleucid's shield, sending the soldier flying back into the other men behind him. More Seleucids took their places.

Chao and Zaim were pushed back by the weight of the onslaught, having to regain their footing as more Seleucids squeezed into the stairwell. Chao drove his blade into an enormous soldier who filled up half the width of the stairwell; the man toppled backwards taking down a few others behind him. Zaim used the opening to thrust with a spear which Fahad had given him, sending another attacker to his death.

So, the fight continued, Chao and Zaim holding out against the onslaught, but being pushed back a step at a time. The attackers continued to fall, but there was no end to them. Chao wondered how the defence of the balcony was going. If they lost that position, then they would be overrun.

A spear thrust almost penetrated his guard and Chao quickly brought his focus back to the fight. Losing focus was a sure sign of imminent death. He had to live, to complete this mission for his emperor, to journey to the Middle Sea and return. If he died now, none would know of the people he had met on his journey.

Chao's sword shattered the breastplate of a Seleucid, after which Zaim plunged his spear into the man. The injured soldier yanked the spear, and in an effort to hold onto the weapon, Zaim gripped it, but the weight of the falling man made the prince topple forward. Slipping on blood-soaked steps, he fell amongst the Seleucid soldiers.

Chao saw Zaim fall forwards in a sickening slow motion, out of his reach. The prince was grabbed by Seleucid hands as blades went up to slay him. Moments later, someone further up the stairwell called out.

'Zaim is dead.'

Chapter 29

A KING'S REVENGE

In the royal apartment a voice rang out loud and clear. 'Zaim is dead.'

It was Prince Asylaion who shouted the news. Apollonia rushed across to the stairwell, Obodos beside her, Ghassan behind him.

'Out of the way,' Obodos pushed past Asylaion, descending a couple of steps as he peered down into the gloom of the shaft. The brutal ruckus had moved further up the stairwell. It was in this moment of confusion that Apollonia witnessed Asylaion draw a blade from his belt and drive it towards his father's back.

'*No!*' Apollonia leapt forward, pushing Asylaion's arm aside.

The dagger's blow shifted from its original target, the king's heart, instead slicing the top right of his shoulder.

Obodos toppled forward. Asylaion drew the knife back for a second attack, but Apollonia threw herself at him, knocking him into the stairwell. The soldiers at the top of the stairs spun around to catch their king and see the prince with the bloody dagger in his hand. In his fury, Asylaion swiped at Apollonia, the dagger aimed at her face. She saw it coming, but her balance was off and she could not deflect the blow. She tried to turn her face away.

Clang!

A soldier parried Asylaion's strike with his sword.

'How dare,' Asylaion spat out, kicking the soldier in the chest, sending him back into the pile of bodies, before rounding on Apollonia once more. His eyes blazed with hatred and his white teeth shone with the hunger of a tiger about to strike its prey.

'Stop him,' Obodos said, through clenched teeth.

Ghassan leapt to restrain the treacherous prince, who thrashed as other soldiers grabbed him. Apollonia was pushed against the wall in the melee, the back of her head striking the stone, sending a numbing pain down her neck. Three soldiers held the prince in an arm lock, the dagger removed from his hand.

Obodos was on his knees, his hand propping him against the wall. Blood soaked his back. Apollonia caught him by the arm. 'Your Highness.' Within moments, two other soldiers were by the king's side, taking his weight, dragging him back up the stairs.

Apollonia glanced down the stairwell. The fighting was now past the mid-point and she could now see Chao the easterner in the thick of the brawl, his red tinged Dragon Blade thrusting skilfully to and fro. *Where is Zaim? Where is my prince? Where?*

Then she saw Zaim leap up amongst a crowd of Seleucid soldiers. He elbowed one man in the neck, punched another, stabbed another with his fingertips in the windpipe, before leaping away from them. A soldier who had taken his place handed the Nabataean prince a sword and he thrust it backwards into the neck of an oncoming Seleucid.

Apollonia felt relief flood through her. *Thank God.*

Nonetheless, it did not look good. A stream of Seleucids waited to come through the entry to the stairwell. She knew there were hundreds of Seleucids and an equal number of Bedouin but had no idea how many more were to come. The defenders were down to only a few dozen. Whatever heroics took place in the stairwell, the result would be inevitable.

With a heavy heart she helped the two soldiers carry the king back into the apartment, to be met by wailing from the women when they saw him, before even louder screaming at the appearance of Seleucid soldiers on the balcony, overpowering Taimur and the few men he had.

It would not be long before the Seleucids were in the apartment, where only a few royals and the women of the household remained. *I will die this day, before I have even been married. How will this news reach my parents and will they even care, since I was never their favourite?*

Father may just regard this as a poor choice of ally and start again.

****

Tigranous had lost more men than he thought possible against these mangy desert Arabs, but it would not be long now till his men entered the private apartments and slewed the king and his family. It was a respectable night's work. It would enhance his reputation as the sacker of cities and raise his status amongst the Seleucids. Had it not been for the easterner, whom Tigranous had to admit was an adept martial artist, and the young Arab prince, the fighting would have already been over.

Such a shame, thought Tigranous. *To kill an able warrior in a brawl. I would rather have slain them in single combat. Yet I cannot afford such luxuries: the emperor is looking for a quick result. Petra is after all a mere distraction, keeping the Nabataeans occupied while Antiochus brings his main force south and occupies Gaza. By the time the Arabs know what is happening, the Seleucid army will be firmly entrenched in Gaza, along with our Elephant Legions.*

Tigranous spotted his troops flooding onto the balcony of the private apartments. *Not long now,* he thought. With the balcony taken, the stairs would fall soon. With any luck that fool of a prince, Asylaion, should have killed his father by now.

Bodies were constantly being dragged out of the stairwell. He had lost plenty of seasoned fighters, but the weight of numbers was on his side and more than three hundred Seleucids still waited to enter the fray. He estimated the defenders were down to twenty or thirty men. *There is no way they will last much longer. We can complete the killing and depart before reinforcements arrive. The appointment of Asylaion as king will provide us with a compliant monarch who will keep his throne but bow to my emperor.*

Tigranous chuckled to himself and gripped the hilt of his broadsword. He had not had to use his weapon the whole evening. The general liked to be amongst the blood; he found it helped him relax. Maybe he would save his weapon to decapitate the king if the old fool had not already been killed by his son. He was sure Antiochus would not mind this indulgence – for how many generals could claim to be king-slayers? Tigranous smiled. *Yes, it will not be long.*

****

From what Pelagios observed, the outer defences to the city were non-existent, with no guards to be seen along either the northern or southern walls. Reports came to him that the Scorpion regiment loyal to Prince Asylaion had been stationed away from the city. Frustration turned to anger, then all he could see was the face of the one man he wanted to kill – Tigranous. The presence of Tigranous galvanised Pelagios to mobilise all Nabataean forces from neighbouring areas. Together they now made up three hundred armed men.

Pelagios led the small army past the great temple towards the royal palace. As the palace came into view his heart sank. Fires raged, Bedouin were carrying away spoils and dead Nabataean soldiers and citizens littered the way.

'Faster!' he shouted.

The outer palace gates were open. He ran through. The courtyard was strewn with hundreds of bodies. He saw the emblem of the elephant on some helmets; there were Bedouin who lay dying, as well as Nabataeans who were either dead or close to it. The doorway to the inner palace leading to the throne room was piled with bodies. Pelagios made straight for it.

He ran through the banqueting hall and entered the throne room, to see the fighting massed around two epicentres. One was the balcony attached to the private royal apartments, where half a dozen ladders were propped up. Men fought upon the balcony and Pelagios thought he saw Taimur swinging his sword amongst the defenders. It was a worse sight by the doorway to the stairwell, where bodies were pressed on top of one another, and heaps of dead blocked the entry. Outside the stairwell was a blond-haired soldier, who stood a head taller than most.

'Tigranous!' Pelagios screamed the name across the throne room.

The Seleucid general heard his name, as did others present.

Pelagios' blade twirled gently around his wrist. He only had eyes for one man. Behind him the few hundred Nabataeans soldiers roared and charged into the Seleucid soldiers occupying the floor outside the private royal apartment, as well as the area outside the stairwell.

'My, it is a surprise to see you, Pelagios,' Tigranous said, a wide smile on his face.

'I wouldn't want to miss this evening,' Pelagios replied.

'Like you missed your sister's death,' Tigranous chided.

Pelagios winced at the memory of his sister's death and what this beast had subjected her to before it.

Tigranous smiled. 'Her children squealed like swine, and your sister was most satisfying before I stabbed her through the heart.'

Seething, Pelagios strode toward the Seleucid general. Tigranous levelled his blade, the muscles on his forearms rippling. He sneered as Pelagios raised his weapon and ran at him. Tigranous stepped into the blow, blocking with his weapon, before catching Pelagios with a back-handed swipe which knocked the Aegean king forward. Pelagios skidded to a halt, slicing through the tendon of a Seleucid soldier close to him, before spinning around and relaunching himself at Tigranous. The younger man blocked with his blade, then kicked out at the older man, sending him tumbling back. Pelagios had only a moment to roll away before the giant Seleucid's sword cracked the ground where his head had been moments earlier.

He's fast, for a big brute, thought Pelagios, rolling back onto his haunches, then jumping to one side as his enemy's sword whistled past him.

'I'm disappointed, Pelagios,' said Tigranous. 'Your sister deserves better than this messy effort at revenge.'

The fighting raged around the two of them. The newly arrived Nabataean soldiers cut into Seleucid ranks. One Nabataean, seeing Pelagios single-handedly take on Tigranous, launched himself at the Seleucid, but the general was too quick and cut the man down with ease, his steel slicing open the Nabataean's throat.

'You are not worth my time. Let me end this now,' Tigranous declared, striding toward Pelagios.

Swinging his weapon, he swept it at the king, who ducked, then parried. The impact of the two swords smashing together sent a painful vibration up Pelagios' arm, rattling his skull. Tigranous shoulder-barged Pelagios, knocking him back, before leaping wildly at him with his sword. Pelagios rolled under the blade but before he could react Tigranous had already spun around and smashed him in the back with his forearm, knocking Pelagios to the ground and sending his sword sliding across the stone floor. The Aegean ruler was hunched on all fours, breathing heavily, the fight knocked out of him.

The colossal Seleucid warrior strode across to finish the fight. Just as Tigranous confidently raised his weapon, Pelagios rolled forward, producing two short blades from his side belts, and drove these knives into the lower section of Tigranous' stomach, where there was no armour.

Tigranous froze mid-step, incredulous. He grabbed Pelagios by the neck, lifting him clear of the ground. Pelagios, a knife in each hand, plunged them into either side of Tigranous' neck, then yanked them out. Still the behemoth of a man did not loosen his grip. Shock and surprise were etched on his face, his brow furrowed, his mouth gaping, eyes wide in shock. He squeezed Pelagios' neck in one final effort to slay the older man, before his strength gave way. His fingers loosened from around the king's neck, and he collapsed on his knees. Blood poured out of his neck wounds. The general made a last feeble attempt to grab Pelagios, but his arm did not rise.

Pelagios stared at the mammoth man before him, twirled the knife in his hand, then slit the general's throat. Blood gushed out. Tigranous, eyes wide open, fell on his face.

'It's definitely been worth *my* time,' said Pelagios.

Pelagios sheathed his knives, collected up his sword and turned to assess the fight around him. The Nabataean reinforcements and his men had taken the Seleucids by surprise, ramming into the back of them with a flurry of arrows, then following up with swords and spears. Though the fighting still raged, the tide had turned and it was not long before the final Seleucids were put to the blade, the Bedouin having long since fled the city with their booty.

Pelagios made his way towards the stairwell that was clogged with dead bodies.

'Get these out of the way,' he ordered.

Some of the Nabataean soldiers dragged the bloodied corpses clear, throwing them into the throne room. Soon the way up the stair was clear.

Pelagios, along with the barrel-chested Andreas and the eagle-faced Theron, ascended the steps slippery with blood and vomit. The stench was unbearable, and Pelagios took two steps at a time, before exiting at the upper end into the royal apartments.

What he saw next shocked him.

Chapter 30

BROKEN PIECES

The king was down, soaked in blood. Several women crowded around him. For a moment Pelagios thought Obodos was slain, then he was told he was badly hurt; a stab wound in the shoulder. He learned that Fastiq the Grim had taken an arrow in the neck and toppled off the balcony. *Grim in life and grim in death*, thought Pelagios. What troubled him most was the sight of two Nabataean soldiers standing guard over Asylaion, whose hands were tied behind his back. *Is he the traitor who Zaim feared, the older brother?* It was a terrible thought, but alas, a dreadful situation which monarchs and sons sometimes had to contend with. *I pray my own children are loyal to me throughout our lives.*

Seeing Pelagios enter, Zaim came over.

'Thank God, uncle, you returned!' he declared, wrapping the older man in a bear hug.

Once he let him go, Pelagios whispered to Zaim. 'And when were you going to tell me about Tigranous?'

'Uncle, I …wanted you to safely return home ….' Zaim replied.

'Then it is a good thing I did not want what you wanted,' Pelagios said, placing a hand on the younger man's shoulder.

Apollonia sat on a chair, close to the women surrounding the king, her gaze every so often flicking towards Obodos. *Poor child*, thought Pelagios. *She must be wondering what is to become of her now that her betrothed is no more. It is simple in my mind: she should marry Zaim. But then if life were so easy, it would not throw up so many problems.* The Ptolemaic princess had streaks of blood across her forehead and along her bare arms. It looked to Pelagios as if she had been involved in the fighting.

'Pelagios!' The king had noticed him speaking with Zaim and now waved the women away, leaving his wife Fazluna, who pressed the dressing around his wound, to restrict the blood flow.

'The healer will be here soon, dear husband,' Fazluna said.

'Bah! This is just a flesh wound, it looks worse than it is,' Obodos declared. 'Had it not been for our … for Apollonia, I would have been killed by my jealous son. Damn misfortune, to have sired such a child.'

Fazluna remained quiet, glancing with the sympathetic eye of a mother at Asylaion, before taking in Stylian, finally turning to Zaim. The young prince brought a smile to her face.

'We came as fast as we could,' Pelagios said.

'For which I will be eternally grateful, Pelagios. I will someday return this great debt,' Obodos said.

'I am at your service,' Pelagios replied. *The Romans wanted me to provide them an intricate design of Petra. News will soon spread of my returning with Nabataean reinforcements, and this information will reach Roman ears. There will be no way to deny I have been in the city and privy to what lies within the walls. Yet how can I betray these fiercely loyal Arabs?* Then he remembered his beautiful island of Mithymna and what the Romans would do to it if he did not comply with their demands. Melancholy filled him.

'Zaim,' Obodos said. 'Fetch Chao Zhang.'

Throughout the time Pelagios had been in the private apartments he had failed to see the Han explorer, who stood serenely by the balcony, observing events out in the throne room. His clothing was stained with blood.

Zaim returned with Chao, who despite his appearance exuded an infectious calm.

'Your Highness,' Chao said, crouching before the king.

Pelagios smiled at the decorum of the easterner.

'Zaim tells me that without your efforts this night, Petra would have fallen to the Seleucids,' Obodos said.

'I played my part in defending the city,' Chao said.

'Marshalling the defences of an entire city, leading the fight from the front and slaying more enemies than all the others put together? I would say that is a significant part, for which I thank you. Ask of me whatever you wish and if it is in my power, I will grant it to you.'

Chao nodded, placing a palm over his heart. 'I am honoured by your kindness, King Obodos, and if there is anything, I will mention it.'

The healer arrived, ushering others away so he could get to work.

****

Elated at having survived the night, Apollonia now felt an awful isolation take hold of her. Petra was to be her home as wife of Fastiq the Grim, but the hideous prince had perished. What was to become of her?

Will my parents take me back? Or will I be abandoned to live with the Arabs? I am at the mercy of King Obodos and Queen Fazluna, but they have more important matters to attend to. Their kingdom must be defended, their people rallied, their armies supplied. I am a burden upon them now. Or am I? If my father sends reinforcements to the Nabataeans, oh then it would be a wondrous thing. But will he? Apollonia was not filled with confidence.

Looking up, she saw Zaim in conversation with Pelagios, the easterner Chao close beside them. Asylaion was tied up, head lowered in shame. Stylian was being pampered by two maidens. *Fastiq's broken body lies somewhere outside.* She did not want to see it. Whatever manner of prince he was, he was still the son of Fazluna, and observing the queen now, Apollonia's heart went out to her.

Only one son to truly be proud of – Zaim.

At that moment Zaim turned to look at her. Their eyes met. He crossed the apartment to take a seat beside her. They sat in silence, before both spoke at the same time.

'How are you?'

They smiled and Zaim signalled for her to speak first.

'I thought you had been killed in the stairwell ... I ...' Her eyes welled up, tears trickling down her cheeks.

'I thought so too,' Zaim replied softly.

'Then I saw you rise, and joy filled my heart.'

He smiled.

'In that moment, with the crush of bodies, arms and legs flailing, there was something I saw that gave me cause to rise,' Zaim said.

'What was it?' Apollonia asked.

'I could see Chao fighting his way towards me but knew he would not reach me in time. Then I saw you appear at the top of the stairwell. Your face, it flickered momentarily in the light of the cresset, but it was enough to ignite one last effort on my part to rise, to ascend through the throng of bodies. If you had not appeared on the stairwell I would not have risen.'

Apollonia blushed. *Thank God, thank the Creator.*

Silence descended once more, each unsure what to say next.

Just then, her Aunt Corrina appeared at the doorway along with her handmaiden Zoe.

'Apollonia, dear child!' Corrina cried, rushing over to embrace her.

Zaim immediately gave his seat up to her.

'I'm so glad to see you, where were you?' Apollonia said.

'When the fighting broke out, we took refuge with one of the merchant families in their home on one of the higher mountain passes behind the great temple. From there we could see all the soldiers coming and going, but none ventured up, so we managed to avoid the trouble. When I saw that Pelagios was leading reinforcements into the city and the fighting had ended, I decided to come out of hiding and find you. I am so glad you are alive.' Corrina crushed her niece in an embrace. Then she let out a small scream, when she saw Asylaion tied up and bundled into a corner.

'A lot has happened, Auntie,' Apollonia said.

'Where is Fastiq, where is your betrothed?' Corrina asked.

Apollonia did not say anything. It was left to Zaim who said. 'My brother Fastiq's soul has returned to the Creator.'

'Oh my,' Corrina declared, taking Apollonia's hands in hers.

'The betrothal … oh … we will need to talk to the queen,' Corrina motioned in the direction of Fazluna. 'Oh!'

'In the morning, Auntie,' Apollonia said.

Chapter 31

MARCHING OUT

The days following the failed siege of Petra were filled with ceremonies for the dead. Prince Fastiq was given an austere burial, his body placed in the Royal Tombs with his ancestors. Other Nabataeans were buried further down Jabal Umm al-'Amr. The soldiers who fell were given an honorary position with their bodies laid to rest close to the Silk Tombs. The bodies of the Seleucids were piled up outside the eastern entry to Petra and when a breezy westerly wind blew, their corpses were set on fire. Vultures and crows circled for days and wolves were heard. Messengers were dispatched by Obodos to all neighbouring kingdoms, rulers and tribal chiefs, notifying them of the Seleucid attack on Petra. The Nabataean monarch knew that without unity amongst the Arabs they would be open to another attack. Obodos even sent a messenger to Jerusalem to reach out to the Jewish Hasmonean monarch Alexander Jannaeus.

On the third day after the attack a messenger arrived from Gaza, sent by Dorian, the helmsman of the *Chloe*. The communiqué changed the mood of the city.

A Seleucid fleet under the command of Emperor Antiochus and accompanied by several Elephant Legions had landed in Gaza and taken control of the port from the Nabataeans. It was a well-known fact that Gaza provided the Nabataean spice-trade access to wider markets and losing the port was going to affect the treasury. It soon dawned upon the inhabitants of Petra that the attack on their mountain stronghold had merely been a distraction to keep them occupied whilst the Seleucids landed their primary forces at Gaza.

Obodos convened a meeting of his advisors in the annex to the great temple.

Pelagios was invited to attend this council of advisors and took his seat at the stone table. In between his fingers he twirled a silver coin depicting the head of Antiochus. Dorian, his helmsman, had sent the currency as evidence of Seleucid designs on the trade route. They were introducing their own currency and forcing the merchants to trade with it. This would devalue the Nabataean means of exchange. *Damn Seleucids, always interfering where they aren't wanted,* thought Pelagios. *If it's not the Romans, it's the Seleucids. One of these imperial powers will take this region one day. When I do not know, nor do I want to be alive when it happens, but happen it will, for the east is the prize all westerners crave. It is what drove Alexander eastward, what spurred the expansion plans of his generals, Ptolemy and Seleucius, the latter even going to the borders of the Indus and signing a treaty with the Mauryan Emperor, Chandragupta. Without him the Seleucids would have no elephants in their army. I am a westerner, yet all I crave is to return home to my small island of Mithymna and live out my days with my family.*

Zaim entered the annex, taking a seat beside his father.

The easterner, Chao Zhang, was invited for the skill he had shown in military tactics and arrived with Zaim, taking a seat at the far end of the table. He nodded to Pelagios, who returned the gesture. *I would like to sail to the lands of the Han one day,* thought Pelagios.

The grizzled General Ghassan took up a position on the other side of the king. He was seething at the way Prince Asylaion had manipulated troop movements behind his back, ensuring there were insufficient soldiers in Petra other than his Scorpion regiment at the time of the attack, and that days before the attack most of their weapons had been moved to armouries on the edge of each of the walls. *And for what?* thought Pelagios. *So that a scheming prince can ascend the throne and replace his father before Obodos made his youngest and most competent son, Zaim, his successor?*

The strategos Hesham had survived the siege by running to one of the surrounding mountains and watching the battle unfold, only returning when he was sure the enemy was vanquished. He was not a fighting man and Pelagios could forgive him for fleeing the scene. It seemed to Pelagios the king was less impressed, giving the strategos an icy glare when he entered the annex, causing Hesham to take a seat beside Chao Zhang. The easterner politely greeted Hesham.

The final person in the room was the elegant Queen Fazluna, who had the ear of her husband and as far as Pelagios was concerned always provided wise counsel. She reminded him of the wife of Ptolemy and mother of Apollonia – Queen Cleopatra, regal and beautiful even at her age. Pelagios had heard the two women – Fazluna and Cleopatra – were distant cousins, and looking at these mature beauties he could well believe it. Fazluna's white silk dress was matched by a stunning pearl necklace nestling against her collar bone.

Prince Stylian, still recovering from his exertions during the siege, was excused from attending. For his part Pelagios considered the obese prince was a liability. He wondered whether the siege and the banishment of Asylaion would make him change his ways. If anything now happened to Zaim, it would be Stylian who inherited the throne. *A dire outcome and one that would surely mark the end of the Nabataeans.*

The treacherous Prince Asylaion had been sent under guard south to the Nabataean stronghold of Hegra, to a stone prison in the desert. Obodos had said he would deal with him when he ventured south and till then the out-of-favour prince could subsist on rations provided to him by his guards. Pelagios had advised Obodos to ensure the guards were well paid and abundant provisions made available for their families. This very act would make them immune to any bribes that Asylaion offered.

Wincing, as he stiffly turned in his seat, his back and shoulder were strapped up, Obodos addressed his general. 'Ghassan, with the replies from allies, how many soldiers can we muster to march on Gaza?'

'We can assemble ten thousand Nabataean infantry and one thousand cavalry. Along the way the tribes loyal to us have committed a further ten thousand fighters. If the Hasmonean Jewish king lends his support, then it is likely he can deploy a further ten thousand men in the field.'

'What are the Seleucid numbers?' Obodos asked.

'Reports estimate there are fifty thousand infantry, as well as a few hundred elephants. There are also Seleucid vessels moored off the coast, possibly with additional soldiers.'

Shifting his position Obodos grimaced, placing a hand on the stone table to steady himself.

'Twenty thousand men short and facing elephants,' Obodos said, turning to Pelagios.

'You have my support, but my men come to less than fifty and by all accounts my ship has been impounded by the Seleucids,' said Pelagios.

'Any other allies you can arm-twist, Pelagios?' Obodos asked.

Pelagios shook his head. The notion of asking the Romans would not go down well as they had not yet played their hand, and the safety of his own home was tied up in the mess he was already in, thanks to them.

The strategos Hesham cleared his throat.

'Yes,' the king said in an icy tone.

'Your Highness,' Hesham began. 'I understand we have not heard back from Ptolemy after you sent messengers.'

'No, we have not,' Obodos sighed.

'Yet, we do have a princess of the Ptolemaic empire with us,' Hesham continued.

'Yes,' Obodos said, sudden interest on his face.

Pelagios saw Zaim give Hesham a hard stare.

'And I understand that it was Seleucid mercenaries who tried to abduct Princess Apollonia at Bozrah,' Hesham said, eyeing Zaim with an equally cold stare.

'It was,' Obodos said.

'Then it would seem Antiochus seeks the princess,' Hesham said.

'Perhaps,' mused Obodos. 'Where are you taking this, Hesham?'

'We cannot read the mind of Antiochus nor his court, but if he sought to abduct the girl, then it would be to either hold her to ransom or marry her. Either of those two scenarios works in our favour.'

Zaim had now leant forward, a hand on the table, and Pelagios could see the prince was holding his anger back.

'I can see your line of logic,' Obodos replied. 'What do you propose?'

Hesham relaxed, leaning back on his chair. 'If she is such a valuable, um ... asset to the Seleucids, then it would do well for us to take her on the march to Gaza. Of course, she would remain in your camp at all times. Yet, if the moment presented itself and we needed to negotiate directly with Antiochus, we could offer the girl as part of a settlement. After all, her betrothal to ... what I mean is that she is not part of your family, but to all intents and purposes is presently a visitor.'

'No,' Zaim snapped.

Obodos looked surprised at his son's outburst and studied him for a moment, before asking, 'You object, Zaim?'

'Father, it would be dishonourable. She is as good as family – we cannot hand her over to the Seleucids.'

'I am afraid son, she is a slave of her imperial destiny,' Obodos said. The comment did not quell the frustration on Zaim's face.

Pelagios recognised the lover's bond between Zaim and Apollonia. He had convinced himself that their union was only a question of time, now that Fastiq was dead. Yet, here was another hurdle being placed before these two young people. *Why am I surprised when such a thing happens, for I have seen many seasons and witnessed much in life that would cause me to doubt the right things happen to good people.*

Obodos exchanged looks with his wife, who did not appear pleased at Hesham's suggestion. Fazluna had clearly recognised the bond between Zaim and Apollonia, thought Pelagios. Obodos was oblivious to it.

'I sense there is a matter here which cannot be discussed at this gathering, but we will talk about it as a family. As for the decision we must make now, Apollonia is a lovely child, and she saved my life, but as you indicate, Hesham, after the death of Fastiq she is not tied to us through any formal bond of marriage. This means we can send her and her aunt home. To return to Ptolemy we will need to take them to Gaza anyway. As we are all venturing there now, it would make sense they accompany us. If, before or during the battle, the matter comes up, then having her in our tent will make it easier for us to hand her over to the Seleucids. If it saves Nabataean lives, and our negotiations see a return of all or some of our trade routes from Gaza, then despite the fact that she played a part in saving me from my wayward son's attempt at assassination, I am willing to consider this option.'

Chapter 32
A FATE SEALED

———

Apollonia observed relatives and friends of the dead saying prayers by graves scattered across Jabal Umm al-'Amr. On this fifth day after the siege the mountainside was awash with ceremonial activities honouring the recently deceased. As she peered across to the Royal Tombs to where Fastiq the Grim was buried, Apollonia felt empty. The late prince had appalled her with his behaviour and now in death he was a fading memory. Yet, she pondered, *I would not be amongst these Arabs, were it not for my betrothal to Fastiq. I would not have seen the world beyond Alexandria, and I would have continued to live within my cocoon and the gossip of the palace. I am glad I ventured out, but what does the future hold for me? In fact, what use do I have, if not to become a bride for a Nabataean prince?*

The princess lingered for a time before making her way down the mountain and heading west in the direction of the damaged royal palace, where she intended to visit the sick Luja. Wrapped in a simple woollen riding cloak, the princess was not recognisable as she made her way along the central street of the city. People were too busy clearing up the mess the Seleucids and Bedouin had made, to pay any heed to her.

Arriving at the palace, she found Luja being watched over by her handmaiden and court healer, who told Apollonia that the young royal was in a state of fitful sleep. Her fever raged and she often spoke in her sleep, the words unintelligible. Apollonia sat for a time beside Luja, stroking her hand but she did not get a response. After a while she left, telling the handmaiden to fetch her should Luja wake.

Apollonia made her way through the upper floors of the palace and emerged onto the terrace overlooking the southern side of the city. Debris from the recent battle littered every corner. As she sat on a recliner, a familiar miaowing sound greeted her and Javairea whisked through her ankles, before leaping onto her lap. The cat's smooth fur felt calming to her fingers and Apollonia sat back, closing her eyes as she stroked the creature, which purred with pleasure.

She must have dozed off, for when she opened her eyes, Prince Zaim was seated beside her, a faraway look upon his face as he stared out at the mountains on the horizon.

'Oh ...' Apollonia said.

'How are you?' Zaim asked.

'Well, and you?'

He nodded, but by the look in his eyes she could tell there was something weighing on him.

'What is the matter?' she asked.

He looked at her then stared back at the horizon.

'Come on, tell me,' she pressed.

Javairea stretched her paws, before leaping into Zaim's lap. He caressed the cat under the ears and neck, which pleased the animal, which curled up tighter, shutting her eyes and napping.

'You know we march for Gaza tomorrow,' Zaim said.

'Yes, and I am to accompany the king's party as he intends to send me back home to Alexandria,' said Apollonia.

'He does,' Zaim replied quickly.

'And how does that make you feel?'

The prince cleared his throat. 'I ... will obey the instructions of my father and see you safely to Alexandria.'

'Yes, but how do you feel about it, Zaim?' Apollonia reached out and took his hand. He let her. For a moment they held hands, before Zaim let go, as did she.

'You were to marry my brother Fastiq, and though I know he was a man of many faults, he was still my brother, and it was the wish of my parents. Now that he is dead, I am not sure what to feel. We are marching into battle with the mighty Seleucid army with their elephant legions and I cannot be sure I will live through it. I do not want to offer any false hope of what might be ...'

'What *might* be?' Apollonia gently probed.

Zaim flushed red. 'Between ... us.'

Apollonia smiled. *He feels the same way I do. That's all I wanted to know. His dignity does not allow him to express what he feels at this time. For this I am more drawn to him, for his character is noble and his deeds are honourable. If I am to marry any man, it will be Zaim.*

Zaim glanced sheepishly at her, but she was now the one staring distantly at the horizon.

'Apollonia,' Zaim said.

'Yes.'

'If we live through the battle, we can talk again, and I would like to tell you what I feel, but at this moment in time, I cannot.'

'I understand,' she replied.

Looking at her now, Zaim thought she was more beautiful than ever and he wanted to tell her that he had strong feelings for her, and had done since they met, and that every moment they spent together only reinforced this bond. In fact, he was adamant that if he were to marry any woman, it would be Apollonia. *Yet my father is willing to sacrifice her for the sake of our kingdom, and there is nothing I can do about it. I cannot abandon my family at this time, nor can I abandon Apollonia to the ignoble Seleucid Emperor Antiochus, if he plans to marry her. What can I do?*

He desperately wanted to say something to her. It was better that she did not know that his father was willing to hand her over to the Seleucids.

****

Establishing a military camp at the port city of Gaza proved trickier than Emperor Antiochus of Seleucia had expected. His army had arrived with ample supplies and munitions, the elephant legions led by the ruthless Commander Spitamenes were out in full force, and his elite fighting squadron, the *Hetairoi* or royal companions had travelled across from the military colony of Jebel Khalid. All in all, the right pieces were on the board, yet Antiochus kept thinking something was missing as he stood on a hill looking down at his army. *It's all there: the munitions, the men, the war elephants. It is quite a sight,* thought Antiochus. *We successfully distracted the Nabataeans at Petra, and whether Tigranous takes the city or not is neither here nor there in the grand scheme of things. I hope he makes it back as the beast does have his uses.*

Then it struck him.

General Pharnuches, the old rascal, had remained behind with the fleet and was going to be positioned off the coast of Gaza with ten ships, each with a crew of three hundred. *Undoubtably he will be spending the extra days in the comforting embrace of my mother, damn the two of them. I should have insisted on him riding with me.* Without the general at his side, he was missing an experienced battle-planner. Of course, there were younger men and perhaps they would be more able in the years to come, yet without seasoned battlefield commanders like Pharnuches, or the legendary Achaeus, his army lacked strategic thinking honed by years of experience in the field. Then he remembered that it had been his idea to keep Pharnuches away from the battlefield. What was he thinking when he issued that order?

He felt a twitch below his left eye. All the legions assembled in Gaza were now looking to him to make the key decisions in the upcoming battle. It was not a role he had performed before; his only experiences of leading the army had been with men such as Achaeus by his side. It dawned on Antiochus that perhaps these generals had shouldered more responsibility than he gave them credit for. *I can do without them,* he reassured himself.

Antiochus noticed the scribe Mithradates scurrying through the camp. He hailed him to join him on the hill. The young scribe, a close confidant of Minister Milesius, was often in a daze and Antiochus was not sure the fellow fully had his wits about him. Antiochus remembered Mithradates originated from the eastern corner of the empire, from the town of Aï-Khanoum in Bactria. *Well, I've brought him a little closer to his home, I hope he appreciates it.*

'My Emperor,' Mithradates bowed deeply.

'What is the tally of our soldiers presently at Gaza?'

The scribe furrowed his brow. 'I believe it is fifty thousand on land and a further three thousand reserves at sea.'

'What breakdown have you documented?

'Ten thousand silver shields. Twenty thousand bronze shields. Three thousand archers and slingers. Fifteen thousand mercenaries. Two thousand *Hetairoi*.'

'And how many elephants do we have?'

Mithradates glanced behind him and replied, 'The total Commander Spitamenes gave me was one hundred.'

Antiochus waved the scribe away and considered how the world was primed for conquer by a leader with a vision. Alexander the Great had demonstrated this. *I will be the next Alexander. Expand my borders east and west.* However, he reminded himself, he had a truce with Maurya in the east and the Romans were an intimidating presence in the west. For now, expansion north and south would have to do. *Secure trade routes in the south, raid the north.* Clasping his hands behind his back, he made for his command tent in the centre of his camp. Of course he had known the numbers, but wanted to ensure they were being recorded correctly in the journals, for posterity.

The *Hetairoi*, his royal companions, were the most fanatical of his followers, trained as they were to love the emperor from early childhood, through harsh indoctrination and training at the military camp of Jebel Khalid. Perhaps he should have brought more of these elite soldiers? Mercenaries were unreliable, but he expected his well-trained bronze and silver shields to keep them in order.

Inside his command tent, younger officers whom he had promoted to senior positions rushed about with missives and information. He barely knew the names of any of them, but he noted their gleaming armour, the emblem of the elephant shining on their breastplates, their bright sword hilts and fine leather scabbards. Everything looked new – unused even. When he entered, they stopped and stared in his direction, like well-trained dogs awaiting their master's bidding.

One of the younger officers, whose name he thought was Cosmas, approached.

'My Emperor,' Cosmas bowed reverentially.

'Yes,' Antiochus replied with a haughty air.

'A messenger has just arrived from north Africa. The Romans and Ptolemy made a truce two weeks ago. They did not engage in battle but settled without going to war.'

This was interesting news, for if Ptolemy was no longer engaged in fighting Rome, his attention would shift once more to what the Seleucids were doing. Antiochus clenched his fist. *Damn bloody Romans, why couldn't they have engaged Ptolemy in a protracted war in Africa? Now, the old rascal Ptolemy may actually turn his attention eastwards, and with his daughter in these lands ... no, I don't want to think about it.*

Antiochus maintained his composure before Cosmas and the other young men. 'Any other messages of importance?'

Cosmas shook his head, as though expecting Antiochus to say something profound. *What does he take me for? Some Oracle? No, I don't want to remember that old witch and her words about Falcons and Dragons.*

'Yes, my Emperor. Our scouts reported that the Nabataeans left Petra five days ago and we should expect the arrival of their army in the next four to five days.'

'Do we know the size of their force?'

'Yes, my Emperor, it is estimated at twenty thousand. Much smaller than our own numbers.'

'I know our numbers!' Antiochus snapped, waving the young man away.

So, they come to war with a lesser force than ours. This is good but is also a sign that Tigranous failed. No matter, one of the young fanatics from the Hetairoi can be groomed to become the next Tigranous – they possess the required zeal and drive for violence. Ptolemy is currently not in the picture, and so long as he remains out of it, this should be an easy victory. As the Hasmonean Jews have not allied with us, they are likely to join the Arabs, but they cannot field more than ten thousand men. I will punish the Jews for not joining us. I will march on Jerusalem after we have defeated the Arabs, and like my predecessor Antiochus Epiphanes I will destroy their Temple.

Chapter 33

PLEDGES UNDONE

———————

The arrival of Seleucid forces in Gaza brought King Alexander Jannaeus and his army out of Jerusalem, forcing them to make camp in Gaza. Pelagios was on an errand to the Jewish King from the Nabataean Arabs to shore up an alliance against the Seleucids. Pelagios left Petra with little prospect of success but now as he waited for Jannaeus in his command tent, he felt a sprinkling of hope. *He has agreed to meet me, after all. Knowing his temperament, he could have kept me waiting for days.*

Sitting on a wooden chair, he took in the sparse furnishings of the command tent. But for a large table in the centre, with several stones on it to mark troop positions, there was little else there. Jannaeus had a reputation as a busy ruler, so he probably paid little attention to the finer things in life. And Pelagios thought, *I have become entangled in this conflict. Even though I have tried to avoid it, fate has thrust me into situations where the Romans will know who I have been meeting with and will interrogate me about what I learned from whom. All I want to do is go home, but with the Chloe impounded by the Seleucids at Gaza, even that is impossible.*

The tent-flap parted and Jannaeus strode in. Without greeting Pelagios, the Hasmonean monarch came and sat opposite him.

'Your reputation is mud, Pelagios, for you have built it on not taking sides and here you are, allying with the Arabs. What do you have to say for yourself?' Jannaeus asked.

Pelagios smiled.

Personalities like the Jewish King liked to start a conversation with an accusation, forcing the other party onto the defensive. The Aegean was well past this form of intimidation and rubbed his chin with his fingers before replying. 'The Seleucids have my ship. I merely want it back. If ending hostilities will do that, so be it; if going to war will do that, so be it. I just want my ship to sail home.'

'Your ship! You are not interested in the spoils of war, the income from the spice routes, the acquisition of lands? Tell me this is not true.'

'I just want my ship.'

Jannaeus scoffed at his response. 'You are a ruler and expansion of your borders is part of what makes you a king.'

'I already have more than I need, and my people are content living in Mithymna. Why should I seek more?' Pelagios replied.

'We always want more: it keeps the masses at bay, content that their king is ruling in their interest. If you don't expand your borders, your neighbours will, which means unhappy people living under your rule and before long they will start to have funny ideas about who the next ruler should be. Bah! I will not entertain such notions in my kingdom.'

'You make it sound as though there are only two approaches.'

'Of course,' Jannaeus replied. 'Expand or contract. Live or die.'

'I would rather have a friendly neighbour, where I trade with my neighbours, and we benefit from our mutual cooperation, so there is no need for one of us to invade the other.'

'Rubbish!' Jannaeus waved his hand in the air. 'Sentimental claptrap. Surely you do not believe such nonsense?'

'I do. At least these are these ideals I aspire to,' Pelagios replied, uncertain where the Hasmonean ruler was taking the conversation.

'And the imperial powers around the Aegean, allow you to *aspire* to these ideals?' Jannaeus asked.

Unexpected, thought Pelagios. *I will need to choose my words carefully.* 'We have always been surrounded by empires and they have always impressed their needs upon us. At times we can work with these, other times we cannot. We are a sovereign people after all, but we try and maintain relationships with all around us. This is a well-known fact.'

'What of the Romans?' Jannaeus asked.

'Yes, what about them?'

'Are they not a thorn in your belly, Pelagios of Mithymna?'

'The Romans have many interests in the Aegean,' Pelagios replied.

'Yes, but do you not fear Rome's legions invading your beloved island and reducing it to ashes? Their legions march where Rome sends them and if you upset them, they will come to your home, will they not?'

'They have their ways,' Pelagios replied, feeling uncomfortable under the stony stare Jannaeus was giving him. *Does the Jewish King know I am a slave to my Roman masters? If he does, I may not even leave this camp alive.*

'And you would know their ways better than most men, would you not, Pelagios?'

'What makes the King of the Jews so sure about my relationship with the Romans and why does he bring it up at such a time, when I am on an errand for Obodos, King of the Nabataean Arabs?'

Jannaeus rested his elbow on the armrest and drummed his fingers against his forehead. 'Pelagios, let me speak frankly. Your reputation as a trader is but a cover for your real role, is it not?'

'Which is?' Pelagios asked.

'You are a Roman spy.'

It was the truth, but when another said it so openly it hurt. He wanted to lash out and silence the Hasmonean King. Pelagios remained silent, eyes locked on Jannaeus.

Jannaeus continued, 'They ask you to report on your travels, the people you meet, their military strength, the commercial trade routes and who controls what. In return they offer you protection, or to put it more crudely, they do not invade your lands, so long as you comply with their demands. This is the nature of the relationship, is it not?'

'The Romans are quite persuasive in their demands, and it is true we have conversations, as I do with other empires. There is nothing to hide there.'

'No, there isn't but your dialogue with the Romans goes to another level, for they see you as their man, whose sole use is to give their spies information, is it not?'

'What prompts King Jannaeus to say this?' Pelagios asked.

Jannaeus stared hard at him. 'A king must choose his allies carefully, for if he bets on the wrong side, he loses everything, does he not?'

The Romans have him under their thumb as well, thought Pelagios. *He knows so much about my arrangement with the Romans, because they have him in a similar trap! Damn bloody Romans. They must have told him to come out and meet the Seleucid army, to help the Nabataeans and push them back. The Romans are using these lesser powers to fight a proxy war with the Seleucids.*

'Allies can make or break a kingdom,' Pelagios said.

'Then tell Obodos the Arab King that I will lend my support to him on this one occasion, for we have a common enemy in the Seleucid. I do not want them coming anywhere near Jerusalem, not an inch closer.'

'He will be pleased to hear this,' Pelagios replied.

'And on the matter of your special relationship with the Romans, we will keep this matter to ourselves, on one condition.'

And what about your relationship with the Romans, Jannaeus? wondered Pelagios. 'What is the condition?'

'Not long ago, it was brought to my attention that a Seleucid legend, Achaeus, was in Jerusalem, visiting a local rabbi.'

'*The* Achaeus?' Pelagios asked, remembering the Seleucid warrior with some fondness.

'Yes,' Jannaeus said. 'Hearing of his presence in my city I invited him to stay with me so that I could learn a little more of Seleucid tactics and battleplans, for who better to share this information than a distinguished general from their ranks? Unfortunately, despite my generous hospitality, he has to date been unwilling to share anything with me or my military planners.'

'I see,' said Pelagios, thinking, *I would not share anything with you either.*

'I would ask you, Pelagios of Mithymna, to visit Achaeus, who has travelled here with my army. Convince him to comply with my wishes and share what he knows about Seleucid military strategy. If you can do that, then I promise that the nature of your special relationship with the Romans will remain between us only. This is fair, is it not?'

****

'May I enter?'

The voice was familiar, but Achaeus of Seleucid could not place it. He checked that his sword rested against the bedroll he sat upon.

'You may,' Achaeus replied.

The flaps to his tent parted and Pelagios King of Mithymna came in. The man had saved his life and immediately Achaeus rose to his feet and stretched out his hand in welcome. Pelagios grasped it with a firm grip before the two men sat back down on the ground.

'May I offer you some tea?' Achaeus said, motioning to the kettle on the stove.

'That would be nice,' Pelagios replied.

Achaeus poured the mint tea for Pelagios and took a cup himself before settling back, crossing his legs on the ground. Pelagios was a decent man who had shown him respect and honour when he did not need to.

'I thought you'd have been halfway to the Aegean by now,' Achaeus said.

'Aye, so did I, but matters took a turn for the worse after we parted. My young Nabataean friend, Prince Zaim, needed some assistance with transporting his sister-in-law to Petra.'

'You went to Petra?'

'I did.'

'I hear it is an impenetrable mountain fortress,' Achaeus said, excitement in his voice.

'The city is a marvel of engineering and architecture and the Nabataeans have learned to cultivate a barren environment through ingenious ways such as capturing and storing water in underground cisterns.'

'You tarried there for long?'

'I stayed for a short while then left, but went back once more.'

Achaeus was confused at his comment and waited for the Aegean to continue.

'Sela had fallen to Seleucid forces– '

Achaeus cut him off. 'Seleucids, so far south!'

Pelagios nodded. 'I left Petra on the insistence of King Obodos and Zaim who said that the approaching Seleucid army was not my concern and that I should return safely home. My men and I took the high pass out of the city, but something made me return to the city during the siege.'

'What?' Achaeus asked.

Pelagios sucked in the air between his teeth. 'Tigranous.'

Achaeus leant forward speaking softly, for he knew the history between Pelagios and Tigranous. 'The Beast led the siege on Petra?'

'Yes, he brought Seleucid soldiers aided by the Bedouin and the Scorpion regiment of Prince Asylaion who betrayed his father and intended to take the kingdom for himself. The defenders were pushed back into the palace, as far as the royal apartments. The battle was finally concentrated in one stairwell, where Prince Zaim and a skilled martial artist from Eastern lands by the name of Chao Zhang held the Seleucids at bay. I was fortunate to be able to amass enough Nabataean soldiers from Bozrah and other towns to take the Seleucids by surprise, before slaying every single one of them.'

'The beast as well?'

Pelagios nodded, his expression grim.

'Then you have your revenge and I am pleased for you, Pelagios of Mithymna, but I am upset to hear of the loss of my countrymen. However, it seems the siege of Petra was merely a distraction to keep the Nabataeans busy whilst my people arrived in Gaza. I understand a sizeable force is here. Elephant Legions and even the Emperor.'

'Antiochus is here?' Pelagios asked.

'So I am told by the Jews,' Achaeus said.

'What of General Pharnuches? Is he in attendance?' asked Pelagios.

'I do not know, but without Pharnuches, the young emperor will be relying on his less experienced officers, none of whom strike me as particularly skilled in warfare.'

'Yet they have overwhelming numbers, at least twenty thousand more,' Pelagios said.

'If Antiochus becomes overconfident then I would give the Arabs and the Jews a chance, otherwise it will be difficult,' Achaeus said, sipping his tea.

'I know,' Pelagios said, also taking a sip from his cup. 'Yet there is someone with knowledge that could turn the tables on the Seleucids.'

Achaeus froze, cup at his lips, and slowly shook his head. 'Pelagios of Mithymna, I am a Seleucid. How can I advise an opposing army against my own people?'

'It is a difficult request, but Antiochus has sent several assassins after you; why, there were even a few on the *Chloe* when we set sail from Alexandria. You have no loyalty to the Seleucids, but you do have a loyalty to your people and nation. And so, you must ask yourself the question – is the leadership of Antiochus and men such as Pharnuches going to help your empire, or should you play your part in removing them?'

'Replacing them with whom? The entire royal family is as bad as Antiochus. In their hubris they will destroy the empire and we will become but a relic, a tomb of empires, which future generations will not even remember.'

'Antiochus' rule is a low point, a very low point, but if by removing him you could bring about the necessary change, then you must be hopeful that things can improve.'

Achaeus shook his head.

'You do not think there is any prospect of a more benevolent rule?'

'No,' said Achaeus.

Pelagios took a letter from within his cloak, looking at it with sadness before handing it over to Achaeus.

'What is this?' the Seleucid asked.

'After you departed from Gaza the previous time we were here, we did not know where you went. We intercepted a Seleucid messenger who had been sent to one of the local Seleucid spy networks. He was carrying this official communiqué from Antiochus.'

'You know what it says?' Achaeus said, unrolling it. He immediately recognised the imperial seal of Antiochus himself.

'I have read it,' Pelagios replied, lowering his eyes.

Achaeus read through the scroll, the colour leaving his face, as tears welled up. His head felt light and he put his cup of tea down, resting his palm on the ground to steady himself.

'I am sorry,' Pelagios spoke softly. 'Remember Achaeus of Seleucid, the future will only seem disturbing to you, if you let it.'

The Aegean king rose and left, leaving Achaeus to stare at the words through tear-filled eyes.

Chapter 34

UNCERTAIN TERMS

On the plains north of Rafah, close to the coast and south of Gaza, sea gusts swept across the flat land. The few olive trees leant eastward, buffeted by the strong westerly wind. A raven flying overhead would have seen masses of men lined up in ranks, elephants and horses amongst them. The Indian elephants brought by the Seleucids were trained for warfare, their long white tusks sharpened to points, their gleaming battle armour adorned with armoured spikes.

For Chao Zhang, the sight of the Seleucid army, fifty thousand strong, reminded him of battles he'd fought earlier in life when he was an officer in the Han army. He hadn't expected to live through any of the wars he fought, yet somehow he had, and had even been promoted to the rank of general. Chao gripped the hilt of the Dragon Blade.

The sight of the Middle Sea to his far left gave him some confidence. It was the final goal of his mission, to reach it and return. He had now achieved this purpose, and this knowledge soothed any turmoil he felt. *Despite the difficulties I have faced, the journey has made me see the world and its people differently. Does this make me a better servant to my emperor?*

Yet the Middle Sea was for the moment filled with Seleucid vessels, at least ten, each carrying three hundred soldiers. The emperor, it seemed, was confident he would not need to call upon them. By occupying the coastline the Seleucids had also ensured the Nabataeans could not land any vessels with reinforcements.

'Friend Chao!' he heard a familiar voice call. He turned: coming up the slope was the left-handed swordsman, Fahad, his long brown hair tied back in a bun. The captain was accompanied by four other men.

'Lord Chao!' exclaimed a rotund, healthy looking fellow.

Captain Zhu Di!

'Zhu!' Chao exclaimed, running down the incline to embrace him.

Beside him was the hawk-eyed graceful Lieutenant Fu Youde with his jade-encrusted sword, as well as the short stocky cartographer Ganfu, gripping his trusty fighting staff, and finally wiry scribe Jin Guliang, his bow strapped across his shoulder.

Chao grabbed each man, squeezing him in a tight hug, grateful to be reunited with his men, finding it hard to believe it had happened.

'They said they knew you *Lord* Chao, and clearly they did,' Fahad said, a smile on his face. Chao had not disclosed his rank to any of the Nabataeans, but there would be questions now about it.

'My travelling companions,' Chao said, introducing each one to Fahad.

'I have heard great things about you all,' Fahad said. 'If you can fight as well as Lord Chao, then you've arrived at just the right time.'

'Lord Chao was one of the greatest generals of the Han army,' added Captain Zhu eagerly. 'We do not possess his ability, but we have some skill with weapons and will make up for our shortcomings through hard work.'

'General?' Fahad smiled ruefully.

Chao shook his head, trying not to make much of it, but realised the news that he was a general would soon spread across the camp. Fahad turned to him, bowing respectfully. 'Lord Chao,' he said, before heading for the king's command tent.

'I thought you had all perished,' Chao said.

'We thought the same about you, Lord Chao,' Zhu said. 'But it is so good to see you.'

'What happened after we separated?' Chao asked.

'We searched for days and weeks, venturing in all directions to see where the slave traders had taken you,' said Zhu. 'If you lived, we knew they would not be able to keep you long and sooner or later you would escape and make your way to the Middle Sea. But we did not expect you to bring your army with you.'

'It is not my army!' Chao replied.

'Why would anybody else be leading this army, when Lord Chao, the only Han general never to have lost a battle, is present.'

'I am merely assisting these people. I am not leading,' Chao replied.

'Oh, I see,' Zhu said, scratching his pot belly.

'Lord Chao,' Lieutenant Fu said. 'There is a sizeable force waiting to engage you on the other side.' He motioned in the direction of the Seleucid encampment.

'It is a long story for another day, but I was taken far further south than you may have gone and came upon the Arab kingdoms, where I was welcomed and rested. I have been travelling with them and have become involved in their struggle against the Seleucids.'

'But Lord Chao, were we not told to observe only?' asked Jin the scribe.

'You are right, my friend,' said Chao. 'But I have committed myself to helping these people in this battle. If I live to see its end, I will journey on to the Middle Sea with each of you before we head for home.'

'We are with you, Lord Chao,' said Zhu, glancing at the others, who nodded their approval.

'I cannot ask you to take part in this battle and risk your lives,' Chao said.

'We are your men; we have always fought alongside you and we will fight alongside you today,' said Captain Zhu.

Chao gave each man a look and nodded. 'All right, but tell me, how long have you been here?'

'After we lost you,' said Ganfu the cartographer. 'We continued as planned, noting map coordinates, elevations, land contours, waterways and other details, then decided to continue west till we reached the Middle Sea. We had some difficulties along the way, but none that could not be overcome, and we have been waiting here for three weeks now. We have learned much about the ways of these people. In the brief time we have been here, we have come to believe we can trade with them.'

'Quite frankly, Lord Chao, we have been growing fat enjoying the local food,' Captain Zhu added, patting his stomach.

Lieutenant Fu poked him in the belly. 'It takes a lot to fill that, and Zhu has been busy.'

'Ah, you jest,' Captain Zhu replied. 'But honestly speaking, Lord Chao, we need a good fight to shake off the rust of the past few weeks.'

Chao laughed and thought, *I am so pleased to see these men again. My spirits have been lifted before battle.*

'There is just one thing,' Captain Zhu continued, frowning.

'Which is?' Chao asked.

'You will need to tell us who we are fighting *for* and who we are fighting *against!*'

'Come,' Chao chuckled, 'let us get some food and I will fill you in on everything you should know. I would not want you attacking your own side.'

****

Three kings took to the field of battle the next morning against one emperor who possessed superior numbers, animals, weapons and an abundance of confidence. As Emperor Antiochus approached the assigned meeting point, with the sea to his right, he noted with amusement that it needed three monarchs to contend with one emperor. *So it should do,* he maintained.

On his horse before Antiochus was King Obodos the Arab Nabataean ruler, who was clearly in some pain. *Perhaps,* thought Antiochus, *Tigranous got closer to killing Obodos than I thought.* Seated behind Obodos on a silver charger was his most accomplished son, Prince Zaim. The powerfully-built leader of the Falcons looked about the same age as Antiochus and sat confidently on his mount, calmly studying Antiochus. *A dangerous enemy. Let me put an end to the prince today,* thought Antiochus.

On a black stallion to the left of Obodos was King Alexander Jannaeus, who was as the reports declared – sullen, brooding, his iron helmet high on his head, gripping a long spear. His spies told him Jannaeus had come very close to siding with the Seleucids against the Arabs but had been met by an internal rebellion of rabbis who vociferously reminded him what Antiochus' predecessor had done in Jerusalem. *Once I've defeated the Jewish king today, I too will sack Jerusalem, so that my name is also immortalised by the scribes.*

To the left of Jannaeus was King Pelagios, apparently friend to all, and enemy to none, but here he was lining up against Antiochus and surely his reputation for impartiality would not survive the day. Then Antiochus remembered he had ordered Pelagios' ship, the *Chloe*, to be impounded and his men arrested. *Perhaps this stirs his ire. No matter – defeat today may see Pelagios survive as he is wise and has his uses. I will let him live, so long as he pledges allegiance to me. The others, I have no use for.*

Antiochus drew his steed to a halt, some metres from the three kings.

Behind Antiochus, Spitamendes, the head of the Elephant Legion, was on horseback, surrounded by some of the junior officers. The irritable scribe Mithradates had also been asked to accompany them, as Antiochus wanted his victory documented from the moment the leaders met before the battle, to the humiliating terms he would offer to the defeated parties at the end of hostilities.

They will reject my terms, but once I have them on their knees they will accept them.

A soft gust blew in from the sea, and Antiochus turned his gaze to the horizon to see his ten vessels waiting for his signal. General Pharnuches would be aboard the lead vessel. He regretted not having the old rascal by his side now: Pharnuches had a reputation as a strategist which his opponents would know about.

'What are your terms?' Obodos asked.

So, the Arab King is willing to talk terms already. He must be quaking at the sight of my army. Good.

Antiochus looked at Mithradates who hurriedly unfolded a parchment and read. 'Emperor Antiochus, ruler of the lands of the east and the west, defender of the people, champion of the oppressed, restorer of goodwill and unifier of the western world, offers the following terms.

'All Nabataean trade routes will henceforth be under the control of the Seleucid empire. The Nabataeans will renounce ownership of all ports including Gaza, Aden, Alia, Leuce Come, Mokha, Myos Homos and the land routes connecting them. They will also hand over the cities of Bozrah, Sela, and stop all trading in Palmyra and Sumhuram. In return, Emperor Antiochus in his beneficence, will remunerate King Obodos with an administrative percentage of five per cent of any profits made. King Obodos will declare his unqualified fealty to Emperor Antiochus and place all his armies at the disposal of the great Seleucid empire, to deploy at will. King Obodos and his family will be allowed to keep all royal privileges as well as the cities of Petra and Hegra. King Obodos also agrees to hand over the daughter of Ptolemy and Cleopatra, the Princess Apollonia, whom Emperor Antiochus will take as his bride.

'To the Hasmonean King, Alexander Jannaeus, similar terms are offered. The Hasmonean kingdom will become part of the Seleucid empire and for his efforts King Jannaeus will be given a five per cent administration fee based on annual profits generated from his territory. In return he will maintain all rights and privileges. The Jewish people will continue to worship their God, but the gods of the Seleucid empire will be given equal prominence in Jewish temples and it is expected that over time the Jews will abandon their one God for the pantheon of gods of the Seleucids who will bring peace and prosperity to their lands.

'These are the terms. Do you accept?'

The scribe hurriedly put the paper away and pulled his mount back, as though he were expecting an immediate reaction.

Obodos puffed out his cheeks, grimly replying. 'Five per cent for administration! These terms are unacceptable.'

'Your people will benefit from being part of the Seleucid economy. I am informed you are an enterprising people and I see this as an opportunity for you to enter new markets. It is too good an offer to reject,' Antiochus declared, knowing full well that the terms were unacceptable.

'We cannot accept,' Obodos announced, turning sideways to look at the Jewish king.

'I too reject such folly,' Jannaeus replied. 'We will barely survive and how can I be sure you will not do what your ancestor did?'

'Are you sure you want to reject and see your people suffer my wrath?' Antiochus asked.

He could see the Jewish king hesitate, before he shrugged. 'These are unacceptable terms. We reject them.'

'Then we are done talking,' Antiochus said with a smirk. He was about to turn his horse around.

'Antiochus,' Pelagios spoke up.

The young emperor turned to the Aegean ruler. 'Yes, what is it, Pelagios?'

'I am told your defeat to Ptolemy was a result of you not heeding the advice of your most senior generals, namely Pharnuches and Achaeus. Instead, you relied on younger officers with no battlefield experience. Is this not so?'

'You offer an interpretation of events,' Antiochus replied.

'It looks to me like you have once more sacrificed experience to youth,' Pelagios said, waving his hand in the direction of the younger officers behind Antiochus and Spitamendes.

'You speak like a man past his prime, Pelagios. We have over-whelming numbers, fifty thousand to your thirty thousand. Enough of this talk.' The emperor was about to spur his horse away, when Pelagios spoke up once more.

'One last thing, Antiochus. I should let you know, that within our ranks, there is a Seleucid legend, who was betrayed by you. You sent assassins to kill him on several occasions, but he survived, for legends do not die so easily. And today on this battlefield, he lends his support to the three kings. There is no greater Seleucid general of his generation. He fights for the people of the Seleucid empire, for he knows the defeat of Antiochus will improve the situation of the populace.'

'Achaeus!' whispered Antiochus. *I was told it was a sure thing the man was dead. How is it that he still lives?*

A frosty shiver went down Antiochus' spine. He gave Pelagios a cold stare, before leading his mount away, a little less certain about the outcome of events, despite his superior numbers.

Chapter 35

BINDING AN ARMY

———————

From a hill outside the royal tent of the Nabataean king, Apollonia observed the two armies below. The Seleucid force was said to be fifty thousand strong, and the one opposing it a mere thirty thousand. The Seleucids were reinforced by a daunting Elephant Legion trumpeting aggressive overtures towards the opposing army. Some of the ominous beasts were marched around in a large circle behind the primary infantry named the bronze shields. It was an impressive formation of men and beasts to add to the reserves on board the Seleucid galleys out at sea.

Accompanied by only her aunt and handmaiden, Apollonia was certain of her fate. Should the Nabataeans lose, then as part of the negotiations she was to be offered to the Seleucids. Perhaps Emperor Antiochus would marry her, or simply imprison her and ransom her back to her father. Either option did not bode well for her. *I am but a pawn in this imperial game. The one Nabataean dear to me, is the one who I cannot marry. Why does fate cast up such situations?*

Her thoughts soon turned back to the battlefield below. She was informed that after a visit from Pelagios, the Seleucid legend Achaeus had agreed to join the Nabataean and Hasmonaean camp. The Aegean king did have a way with words. *I wonder what he told him,* she thought. *Had Pelagios not been asked to take me to Petra, he would be on his way back to his wife and family on Mithymna. I do pray that he survives what is to come and returns safely. Too many men are embroiled in the imperial wars of my father and his enemies. Too many.*

Her aunt came to stand beside her, linking her arm with Apollonia's.

'My child,' she said. 'You know what will happen to you should the Nabataeans lose.'

My dear aunt is always direct.

'I do, Auntie.'

'You will need to be strong, should you … we be taken by Emperor Antiochus. I have some distant relationship with his mother, Tryphanea, a quite striking woman rather like your own mother. He will not do anything to you without first discussing it with her, and I will be with you, when we meet her. If all goes well, we can be ransomed back to Ptolemy.'

'And if it doesn't?'

'Then you will either end up in a prison for the rest of your life in a remote corner of the empire, or married to Antiochus, or one of his lackeys. I do not know which of these is worse.'

'Could it be as bad as being married to Fastiq?'

Corrina gave her a sideways look. 'On a par, maybe, but we all know who your heart is really taken by.'

'What do you mean, Auntie?'

'I was not born yesterday, child. It was perfectly obvious from the first moment you met in Bozrah, that he was attracted to you and you to him. Of course, being an honourable man, he did not pursue his feelings, but now that his brother is dead, well, there is no reason for the two of you not to think about marriage. Apart from this battle standing in the way, of course, but other than that!'

'You really think it possible that Zaim and I could …'

'Why not? He is quite a catch, as are you and it would fulfil your father's purpose in sending you.'

'But King Obodos has brought me here to be handed over to the Seleucids should they lose.'

Corrina nodded. 'Without a doubt this is true, but before we left Petra, I spoke with Queen Fazluna, and she likes you, likes you a lot. You have made a very good impression on the Nabataean royal family. She thinks you would be an excellent match for Zaim. She even tried to persuade her husband to leave you in Petra, but he said he could not, as the fate of the empire was at stake.'

Suddenly, Apollonia felt some of that weight leaving her. *I should be pleased but with what is about to unfold how can I be anything but terrified of what the future will bring?*

A horn sounded across the battlefield and in the Seleucid phalanx the soldiers smashed their spear tips against their round bronze shields, then started marching towards the Nabataean infantry.

'I pray God brings victory to these brave men,' Apollonia said.

****

At the head of the Nabataean infantry, Achaeus surveyed the soldiers. He had lined them up in three rows, trying to reflect what he knew would be the formation of the Seleucid infantry. Achaeus knew the Nabataeans had little chance against the professional fighting men of the bronze shields, let alone the better trained silver shields. However, it was a question of buying time and waiting for the inexperienced emperor to make a fatal mistake – at least this is what he told the three kings before battle. It was not a war he'd expected to be present at, but after the letter which Pelagios brought him, he did not have a choice.

He had issued specific instructions to each of the regiments and the men leading them. Zaim, Pelagios, Chao Zhang, and the two kings were under firm orders as to when and how they should engage the enemy after the initial coming together of the infantry divisions. *If I die today with my sword swinging, so be it. But if the gods decree, I will have my revenge, and may my steel pierce Antiochus' miserable heart.*

'Your orders?' Luay the Nabataean quartermaster asked, keeping a watchful eye on the Seleucid bronze shields.

Achaeus took a few steps ahead of the Nabataean infantry then turned to face them so that every man could see him.

'Match their formation. Do not lose shape. They are a well-drilled army fighting for their emperor. You may not match them in skill, but you are fighting for something far greater than they are. You are fighting for your land, for your family and for your livelihoods,' he said, pointing his sword at them. 'Know this, there are many amongst their ranks who hate their emperor, who detest his actions, but they are forced to fight. If you survive this first onslaught of the bronze shields you will surprise them. If you survive the second offensive, they will begin to doubt themselves. Will you do this for me?'

'Yes!' a roar went up along the lines of Nabataean infantry. 'We will!'

'Good, for when the bronze shields doubt themselves, that is when Prince Zaim will lead the Falcons and hit the silver shields. Ready yourselves.'

Achaeus took his place back on the front line, thinking, *we will need a divine miracle if we are to survive the day. Whatever Zaim can do against the silver shields, whatever mischief the Han explorer can wreak on the Elephant Legions, however sharp Pelagios' mind is on the battlefield, and however good the combined force of Obodos and Jannaeus is, we are still destined to die today. But let us perish with our heads held high, our chests out, as our souls are released from our bodies to journey to the fields of Elysium and sit in the halls of our forefathers.*

The approaching Seleucid bronze shields picked up speed; the formation of ten thousand men was four to five deep. By sending half the bronze shields in the first assault the Seleucids were looking to deliver a hammer blow at the start of the battle.

'Brace yourselves,' Achaeus shouted.

The spike-wielding Seleucid bronze shields kicked up dust as they accelerated. The two armies came together. Pikes and spears smashed against shields. Swords flew from hands, lances snapped, helmets cracked, armoured greaves ripped, body armour split – and the bones of men cracked, flesh tore, ankles buckled, wrists twisted, blood vessels burst, eyes were gouged, fingers snapped, thumbs twisted and knees bowed. Around Achaeus' men was a confused melee of movements, cries, cuts and thrusts, glances, thrusts, parries and feints.

Achaeus' sword ripped through two Seleucid infantrymen, as he spun and took off the fingers of the next man, before stabbing his knife through a soldier's neck. Pulling his weapon clear, he plunged the blade into the eye of an attacker, then whipped his sword upwards, leaving a soldier on his backside. Luay the quartermaster remained by his side and finished the fallen soldier off.

'Hold!' Achaeus screamed above the din of battle, desperate to keep the Nabataean front line together, as the Seleucids' fourth and fifth row smashed into them.

'Achaeus, you traitor!' a large Seleucid infantryman thrust a pole straight at Achaeus. The former general twisted out of the way, then ducked under the strike, and came up against the shoulder of his attacker. Achaeus swung his sword, but the soldier blocked it with an oval shield. The vibration sent a shock up Achaeus' arm, but he ignored it, and jabbed down with his knife at the exposed thigh of the big man, causing him to stumble, before Achaeus smashed his shield away with the pommel of his blade. But before he could finish his opponent off, the infantryman leapt at Achaeus, taking him down and landing on top of him. Achaeus fell to the ground, the back of his head slamming into the earth. His eyes watered and through the blur he watched the Seleucid soldier lift a helmet from the ground and aim its spike straight at his head.

Swish! A clean sword strike took off the Seleucid's head, the helmet falling from his hand. In the next moment, Luay kicked the decapitated body away and pulled the general up.

'Thanks, that was close,' Achaeus said.

Around him swords and shields rose and fell, like the waves of an ocean, and he felt like a piece of driftwood on a stormy sea. His head spun and he lost all sense of which way was forward, heading off in the wrong direction, before Luay grabbed him by the elbow and pointed him the right way.

'You weren't about to leave, were you?' Luay jested.

Achaeus shook himself, clearing the fog in his head. 'Far from it. The fighting is just beginning, my friend; this is only the first wave. Quick, strip five dead Seleucid soldiers of their uniforms and weapons and have these sent by runner back to King Pelagios. He has urgent need of these.'

****

The hill position on which the Falcons assembled, gave Prince Zaim and his troop a clear view of the first onslaught by the Seleucid bronze shields. Achaeus had told Zaim to wait for the second wave to hit them, before launching his cavalry attack against the silver shields, who numbered ten thousand compared to the twenty thousand bronze shields. The militia looked to be about fifteen thousand strong and was, for the time being, kept back by the emperor. *Militia are always less reliable in a pitched battle,* thought Zaim. *Achaeus believes most do not want to fight and have been strong-armed into turning up. If we can deliver a blow to the professional infantry corps it will rock the confidence of the militia and perhaps some may turn and leave.*

'Our men held the first wave. Achaeus' plan is working,' said Fahad on his horse.

'Thank God,' said Zaim.

Though the Nabataean line had initially buckled under the impact of the bronze shields, it seemed to Zaim that Achaeus snapped the soldiers back into formation, and less than a hundred Seleucid infantry broke through. Those that did were picked off by a set of Nabataean archers Achaeus had placed behind the Nabataean infantry. *It was a smart move,* thought Zaim, *archers paired with infantrymen.*

'Proclaim our deeds,' Fahad announced loudly, so the men either side could hear, before continuing:

'We stand primed for battle. Our nerves like steel.

Is there a fight we have ever feared?

Our bravery comes from our fathers. Descendants of prophets.

In the maelstrom of swords, our fates are sealed.

The enemy's breastplates will be dyed red, as we bring upon them the hammer of death.'

There was a murmur of acknowledgement from the men who had overheard Fahad. Zaim noticed some sit higher in their saddles.

'Here comes the second wave,' Fahad observed.

Another ten thousand bronze shields were sent forwards by the Seleucids and sprinted towards the Nabataean front line, long poles in their hands, screaming in battle fury.

'May God help our men,' Zaim whispered.

Achaeus had told Zaim to hold till the last possible moment: the former general wanted the Nabataeans to prove they could hold the line against the Seleucid bronze shields. It would give Antiochus much to think about. *Yet can they hold?* pondered Zaim. The ten thousand strong Hasmonean Jewish army under King Alexander Jannaeus stood ready to the rear of the Nabataeans, should the Arab line need reinforcing. Once more Achaeus had told Jannaeus not to send any soldiers, unless it looked like the Nabataean line was about to break. It was a mind game the former Seleucid general was playing with the young emperor: throw your best punch and watch how we take it. Achaeus wanted Antiochus to panic after seeing the failure of his infantry. He wanted him to make a mistake, for this was the only way the battle was going to be won against such overwhelming odds.

The second wave broke against the Nabataean line.

This time the Nabataean infantry buckled, snapped in places, allowing hundreds of Seleucid bronze shields through. Some were stopped in their tracks by the archers, but too many were coming through. Zaim saw Jannaeus raise his sword and the Hasmonean infantry charged to shore up the Nabataean back line. Soon the Jews were fighting alongside the Arabs, to drive the Seleucid army back. Time passed; the Nabataean infantry swayed – it was like watching a wave hit the shore, sometimes overwhelming it, other times going back out to sea.

Zaim could wait no longer. 'Give the order,' he told Fahad.

'Attack!' Fahad screamed at the top of his voice.

The one thousand Nabataean cavalrymen dug their heels into the sides of their horses and descended the hill. A thousand hooves shook the ground and as the Nabataean cavalry quickly made up ground, the silver shields realised they were being attacked from their left flank. The Seleucid infantrymen began to turn their positions around, lances and poles out to face the riders.

The steeds bolted across the sloping ground, picking up speed. Zaim observed the armoured faces of the silver shields as his one thousand horsemen streamed in their direction. As the two lines met, Zaim's horse vaulted over the poles. Zaim's sword swung out, splitting a man's skull. Other Nabataean cavalrymen followed the prince's lead. Zaim turned to see that most of his horsemen had broken through the silver shields. He whirled his horse around and began to hack at the Seleucid soldiers near him. Zaim charged at a pair of soldiers; sword swinging, he cut them in a single swipe, wheeling his horse again and sweeping through a line of three soldiers. Around him Nabataean cavalrymen were decimating the silver shields, who began to scatter, losing formation and the ability to defend themselves.

Fahad ploughed through a group of soldiers, cutting them down with ease.

Suddenly, the ground shook and an enormous trumpeting sound erupted around them. Zaim looked up to see the silver shields parting and a group of at least a hundred elephants with their mahouts onboard stampeding in their direction. The elephants' enormous glistening sharpened tusks swung from side to side. One strike from those would impale a horse and throw a man twenty feet in the air.

'Prince Zaim,' Fahad called out, sword over his head, pointing at the oncoming elephants.

Zaim had no idea how to fight these monsters. He noticed that the beasts left plenty of space between them. The mahouts must be guiding them to stay apart, spreading them across the field of battle. The earth below his horses' hooves was shaking. The Nabataean steeds started to panic, wanting to flee.

'Two riders to each elephant, stay either side. Cut the saddle-straps of the mahout,' Zaim shouted. 'Fahad with me. Rest of you pair up now. Go!'

Zaim and Fahad directed their terrified mounts straight at an oncoming elephant, charging as one. As they drew closer to the beast, they directed their steeds to either side of it. Ducking to avoid the tusks, they sliced the straps fastening the mahout's saddle with their swords, drawing blood from the elephant at the same time. The beast screamed in fury, throwing the saddleless mahout from its back. The mahout down, Zaim fired an arrow into the elephant's head. The riderless elephant now ran sideways, knocking into other elephants, sending them off course.

The other Nabataean cavalry now began to repeat the manoeuvre.

Mahouts fell from unbuckled saddles; elephants lost all sense of direction and ran crazed with wounds on their backs. Zaim saw several silver shields impaled on their tusks.

Whoosh!

Nabataean riders fell from their horses. Arrows fired from those seated on a fresh batch of elephants found their marks, throwing riders to the ground. An arrow skimmed past Zaim's ear. He turned to see more elephants, each with two archers riding either side of the mahout, approaching them. There was no way the archers would let them get close to the elephants.

'Retreat!' Zaim shouted above the din.

With arrows raining down on them, the Nabataean cavalry spun around and started to ride back up the hill. As they crested the hill, out of arrow range, Zaim turned to make a quick assessment of his cavalry. He scolded himself when he realised that only half his men had made it back.

Chapter 36

SPLITTING A MILITIA

Pelagios had wanted to see with his own eyes the Jewish army deploy its strength alongside the Arab army. It had done so. He had worried that King Alexander Jannaeus would not stay true to his promise to fight with the Nabataeans, but the Hasmonean ruler kept his word. Both King Jannaeus and King Obodos sat on their steeds, their royal guards surrounding them on horseback, as they observed the battle unfold in the valley below.

Remarkably, Pelagios noted from his vantage point above the battle, Achaeus had rallied the Nabataean infantry, who, with the support of the Hasmonean cavalry, had held back the momentum of the Seleucid bronze shields, now twenty thousand strong. Emperor Antiochus had thrown many men into the attack but had yet to achieve a breakthrough. It looked to Pelagios as if Zaim had achieved some success in disrupting the entry of the silver shields into battle, but how many prized horsemen had it cost the Nabataeans? Some of his sailors from the *Chloe* were also part of that attack.

Having seen others ride into battle, it was now his turn.

Turing to Jannaeus and Obodos, Pelagios declared, 'I will see this land made bloody today, or I will see you in the halls of my fathers.'

'Honour and glory,' Obodos replied, raising his gauntleted arm, grimacing as he did so. The Jewish King nodded.

Pelagios rode down to join the rest of the cavalry, which was made up of five hundred horsemen, primarily Hasmoneans with some Nabataeans. There were also the five Han explorers dressed as Seleucid infantrymen. He had been quietly amused to learn that

Chao was in fact a general who had led armies far larger than anything that was present today in Gaza. *I will need to speak with that one after this battle; perhaps he can help me with my Roman problem.*

Veering his cavalry towards the right flank of the Seleucid army, Pelagios led them at the fifteen thousand-strong assembled militia. It was an unpredictable stratagem. riding at such a large body of men, but when the opposition had the advantage in numbers, confusion and trickery on the battlefield were tactics a general needed to employ, Achaeus had told him.

The horses gathered speed, Andreas and Theron, his closest comrades riding either side of him. He prayed all his men would come through the battle, as relaying the news of their deaths to loved ones on Mithymna would not be something he relished. Noting the approach of the Nabataean cavalry, the Seleucid militia mobilised.

Slice through their ranks, killing as many as you can, drop the Han explorers and then get out as fast as you can, causing as much confusion as possible, Achaeus had told him at the planning meeting. The attack would leave the Seleucids perplexed, whilst the main reason would remain hidden.

The horses hurtled across the ground as Pelagios maintained the gallop. The other riders formed the tip of the spear shape around him. The militia men had raised their oval *thyreos* shields and they carried a mixture of short swords and spears. They were not as well equipped as the bronze or silver shields and were not used to facing a cavalry attack. Every Seleucid emperor had used a well-equipped militia as part of his regular infantry, but Achaeus had rightly predicted that in his supreme arrogance Antiochus preferred not to use them at all. If they were not deployed, then Antiochus would argue that he would not need to pay them the full wage promised.

The horses ripped through the badly-organised militia, who barely resisted the charge of Pelagios' five hundred riders, allowing them to cut through with ease. Pelagios swung his weapon right and left, hacking at the heads of militiamen, the men around him following suit, as they charged through the ranks. Over the heads of the massed militia he could see the Elephant Legions, now turning in their direction. *I do not fancy riding against one of those beasts. I will simply drop the Han, as planned, then swing around and get out as fast as possible.*

The horses surged forward, far too easily. The militiamen were appalling fighters, either running away or being felled on the spot. Soon, Pelagios and an initial group of riders had pierced the entire militia and come out on the other side, where a group of elephants trumpeted their fury.

Pelagios turned to see five riderless steeds behind him. *Good, the Han explorers have mingled with the opposing army. We have done what we set out to do.*

'Ride!' he shouted, waving his sword in the air and pulling his beast away to the left of the Elephant Legions. As he led his men out of the pocket between the militia and the elephants, the clearing ahead of them was closed by a well-armoured Seleucid cavalry regiment, at least five hundred strong, matching the number of the riders he had. Pelagios yanked on the reins of his horse. Now they were blocked in on all four sides.

'Your Highness,' Andreas called out, bringing his horse up alongside Pelagios.

No wonder the militia allowed us to pass through with such ease: they wanted to box us in, blocking off the escape route.

'What will it be? Ride against the cavalry or back out through the militia?' Andreas asked.

The militia were now closing ranks and suddenly looking more aggressive and well-organised. The elephant riders were advancing slowly in their direction and an ominous Seleucid cavalry was lined up before them. Behind them lay the main bulk of the Seleucid army, including as yet undeployed bronze and silver shields, another Elephant Legion and another set of infantry.

****

Chao Zhang and his small troop of Han men whisked by unnoticed, gliding between the legs of the elephants, who were not bothered by them. The other Seleucids ignored them, for they wore the uniform with the elephant symbol and carried bronze shields on their persons.

Chao sensed a momentary pause in the mayhem caused by Pelagios' wild cavalry charge. From his low position below and between the elephants he could not see what was happening, but he and his men steadily made their way to the back of the Elephant Legion to do what they had planned. Almost at the rear of the legion, he noted in the distance what looked to be the emperor's tent up on a ridge, surrounded by royal companions and a troop of five hundred guards. *Let us give the emperor a show he will remember,* he thought.

He motioned for his four companions to split up. Each chose an elephant and withdrew a blade. They silently cut the drawstrings holding the mahout on top of the saddle, then tied a rope with a knot around the leg of the first elephant. Uncoiling the rope behind them, each man continued forward to the next stationary elephant and repeated the step. Silently gliding between the mighty tree trunk legs of the beasts they continued to cut the saddle bonds and tie their ropes around the legs of the beasts, so soon enough each man had threaded the same rope around the leg of five elephants, securing knots as he went. They uncoiled the next set of ropes they carried looped around their arms and shoulders and worked their way towards the middle of the legion. Finally, Chao chose an elephant to mount, whose saddle drawstrings he left intact. His companions, he knew, would have done the same.

Chao put his foot in the stirrup then leaped up, hauling himself onto the boxed saddle inside of which sat the mahout. A quick chop at the man's pressure points put the rider to sleep. He looped the rope he was carrying around the elephant's neck and secured it firmly with a knot. As the boxes were closed from the rear, the act went unnoticed. By now he guessed his companions would also be in control of one elephant each. From this vantage point Chao saw the blue waters of the Middle Sea. Upon it were the reserve vessels the Seleucids had brought with them.

A quick glance to his right and left told him that Zhu, Fu, Ganfu and Jin were now each in charge of an elephant. He patted the elephant behind the head and said to the beast. 'I am sorry, mighty one, this will hurt, but it will save you from worse battle wounds.'

Chao lifted his dagger and plunged it into the side of the elephant's shoulder blade at the point where it joined its neck. The animal squealed. Chao's companions repeated the procedure on their mounts, and soon five elephants had risen up in fury on their hind legs before bolting forwards in terror. Chao choose this moment to leap from his mount, as did the other Han men.

As he had tied the rope firmly around the neck of his elephant and this then wound its way around the legs of the elephants behind him, the charge of the wounded beast yanked the animals behind them, some of whom tripped and fell on ropes, dragging other beasts down with them too, whilst others toppled sideways. A mahout was thrown from each elephant.

'Like a pack of cards,' Chao said, watching the elephants and mahouts go down.

Those elephants not secured by ropes were now tripping on them, sending their riders tumbling. The beasts began to run in all directions. As Chao watched, half the Elephant Legion was taken out.

Chao glanced sideways at his men, who signalled with their hands they were ready: in unison they ran forwards behind the stampeding herd.

****

The mayhem caused by the charging elephants was absolute. Pelagios ordered his riders to one side, as the beasts roared by, heading straight for the Seleucid cavalry who had been blocking the way out for his men. He and his men galloped behind the stampeding elephants. Sensibly, the Seleucid horsemen moved out of the way of the elephants, only to find Pelagios and his men approaching from behind, picking them off with arrows as they went past. The surprise did not last long, and soon the Seleucid cavalry gave chase to Pelagios and his horsemen, as they veered back towards the Nabataean army.

Arrows whizzed past Pelagios' ear, as he rode hard and low. A quick glance behind him told him he had lost half the men he led into battle. *More than I expected, but each one we lost, had a family, a parent, a lover, a child.*

****

High up on secure ground the imperial tent flapped in the sea breeze, as Emperor Antiochus observed the carnage of the elephant stampede. *How can this be? The beasts should be under control.*

Elephants on the right flank of his army ran loose, piling into Seleucid cavalry and militia. On the left, after a surprise foray by Nabataean horsemen, his elephant legions had taken back control. He had not expected Nabataean and Hasmonean forces to be so bold against his far greater numbers. The enemy was like a swarm of irritating hornets, biting and darting away. *This is the work of that traitor Achaeus,* he thought. *If he survives, I will have his mutilated body displayed for all to see in Damascus, then take it to Antioch. I will keep him alive till we reach the capital, and he will wish for death a million times, but I will not give it to him. I will make him rot to death in this world before he rots in Hades.*

Spitamandes, the portly commander of the elephant legions, came running up the incline. Out of breath, he bowed before the emperor.

'What do you call this?' Antiochus waved his hand at the stampede.

'It was a small group of enemy soldiers who infiltrated our ranks. They tied ropes around the legs of the elephants and cut the mahouts from their saddles. They were skilled and have slipped away.'

'Bah!' Antiochus said, backhanding Spitamandes around the cheek. 'Get back control of your elephants, now!' he shouted.

The young emperor's gaze turned to the coast once more. Ten ships, three hundred soldiers in each vessel: making an extra three thousand men. He could have them on shore soon. He looked back at the balance of power on the battlefield. Despite the annoyance with the elephant legions on either flank, the Nabataean cavalry had retreated with sizeable losses. Ahead of him, the bronze shields were being held by the Nabataean and Hasmonean infantry. He had still to deploy the bulk of his ten thousand silver shields, who were fresh and eager for battle, and his two thousand *Hetairoi*, a fanatic corps of fighters, willing to die for him in an instant.

'Timon,' Antiochus addressed the lieutenant closest to him.

'My Emperor,' Timon was before him, head lowered.

'This battle has gone on long enough. I want to deliver a fatal blow to these Arabs and Jews. Send out all of the royal companions, all two thousand of them, and send out all of the remaining silver shields, for a direct assault on the Nabataean and Hasmonean front line.'

'*All* of the remaining soldiers?' Timon asked.

Antiochus turned indignantly to stare at him.

'Yes, my Emperor, I will arrange it,' Timon stuttered, before rushing away to execute the instructions.

'I will break their front line and then we will execute their rulers. Today is not a day to show mercy,' said Antiochus.

Chapter 37
WEIGHING THE ODDS

———————

They implemented the plan as Achaeus had devised, causing chaos amongst Seleucid ranks. It bought them time, and served to annoy Antiochus, but as Zaim stood beside his father and surveyed the battle below, he could see that despite their best efforts the sheer volume of Seleucid numbers meant the enemy still had many men in reserve. Now these fresh fighters were being unleashed against the Nabataean and Hasmonean front line.

He heard footsteps running towards him; breathless, Pelagios returned from his foray. 'Those Han know a thing or two about how to create mischief,' he said with a wry smile.

'Did Chao and his men make it back?' Zaim asked.

'I have not seen them, but don't worry. I think General Chao and his men can handle themselves,' Pelagios replied.

'General,' Zaim smiled. 'He never once mentioned it.'

'The battle turns,' Obodos said, keenly observing the fighting below. 'Antiochus has deployed his fanatical *Hetairoi*, his two thousand elite fighters, as well as the remaining silver shields. They enter the field now, charging at our men.'

The king's morose tone surprised Zaim. He said, 'As long as we live, we will fight them to the end. Father, there is still hope..'

'Is there?' Obodos said, looking at his son.

'Always,' Zaim replied. 'If not today, then in the future, but we cannot go down without a fight.'

'Ah, the invincibility of youth,' Obodos smiled. 'But how many more lives will we lose?' He addressed the Hasmonean King. 'What do you say, Jannaeus?'

The Jewish King rubbed his chin. 'If we lose here, then Jerusalem will fall to the Seleucids. I will give my life rather than see such an eventuality. I say we fight to the death.'

Obodos raised an eyebrow. 'So be it,' he said. 'When swords clash and the mighty fall, I give my life to the cause of my men. I give everything to avert disaster.'

'Father?' Zaim said, looking at his father.

'We stand and fight till the last man,' Obodos said.

Down on the front line the eager *Hetairoi* slammed into the Nabataean infantry.

Zaim turned to his father, taking his hand, kissing it, then pressing it against his own head. 'May God protect us.' Then the Nabataean prince was gone, sprinting down the slope, leading his Falcons towards the front line.

Obodos had tears in his eyes. He looked across at Pelagios, who shrugged, saying, 'Nothing for it then. I'd better go and see he makes it out alive.' Pelagios saluted the two kings and ran after the prince.

****

The unrelenting intensity of battle was wearing Achaeus down. He was not the man he was ten years ago, and his arms and legs ached as his body implored him to stop. The infantry force he commanded had thinned to less than a third of its original size, but then so had the bronze shields. He felt a glimmer of hope as reports came back that the Elephant Legions were rampaging, and that the cavalry led by Zaim and Pelagios on either flank had managed to cut through the Seleucid ranks.

Then his heart sank.

As he looked up from striking a man down, he saw the *Hetairoi* smash into the Nabataean and Hasmonean infantry, merely a single row deep in places. Behind the *Hetairoi* there were waves of silver shields coming.

This is where it ends, then, thought Achaeus. *Killed by my own people. I hope none recognise me before they thrust a sword through my heart.* He tilted his visor a little lower to hide his face, then the Seleucid legend stepped towards the enemy, kicking away the knee of a *Hetairoi*, before driving his blade at the man, who blocked the strike. Achaeus used his elbow to slam into the man's chin, before swinging his blade to open the man's belly.

More *Hetairoi* swarmed around Achaeus. These were young men, with vigour and energy in their movements, zeal in their eyes and an uncompromising loyalty to the emperor. Achaeus was joined by Luay and together they stood, back-to-back as the *Hetairoi* jabbed at them with their short swords and round shields. Achaeus swiped away a sword strike, then felt the thud of a shield against his shoulder blade, sending a numbing pain down his back. He instinctively ducked as a sword went over his head, before spinning and plunging his sword into the belly of an attacker. A blade whisked past his head, and he felt the steel cut part of his ear. He pulled back, swinging his sword behind him to clear the way and then leapt, coming down on a *Hetairoi* with a raised shield.

The quartermaster Luay cried out. The old fighter was on his knees, as Achaeus saw a sword burst through his chest. As Luay fell, their eyes met momentarily before life left the quartermaster's body.

Achaeus looked up to see more Seleucid silver shields arriving. The fighting had become concentrated around him, as he realised that other parts of the Nabataean infantry had caved in, and there were barely any Nabataean or Hasmonean soldiers remaining. The line was collapsing in on itself and he would be one of the last men standing.

He heard a voice behind him.

'Fall back!'

He spun around to see Prince Zaim and his Falcons fighting their way towards him. These men were as relentless as the *Hetairoi* and they matched their zeal. The exchange of swords and shields was furious, as the *Hetairoi* turned their attention to the Falcons. Achaeus took a deep breath. His ribcage hurt from where he had taken a blow earlier in the battle. He felt something in his mouth and spat it out. Two broken teeth fell to the ground.

Then Pelagios was by his side, taking him by the elbow, his fighting corps around them, creating cover for them to retreat.

'Come, Achaeus,' Pelagios said.

Achaeus' head was spinning from the noise and fury around him. He stumbled as Pelagios supported him back up the slope. He suddenly realised how tired he was. He had been fighting non-stop since the battle commenced, a thing he had not done for years. To his surprise he was still alive, but for how much longer? It would be better to die in battle than be captured alive by the emperor.

Pelagios' men fell in around the two of them, providing a safe retreat. Soon they were climbing up the mound, upon which the two kings stood watching the battle below. For the first time Achaeus was able to see the devastation clearly.

The infantry had collapsed around a single point, where the *Hetairoi* and silver shields now focussed. The Nabataeans and Hasmoneans were heavily outnumbered, even with the arrival of the Falcons. On the flanks, Nabataean and Hasmonean cavalry tried to stop the oncoming silver shields from reaching the mound upon which the kings stood. Far on the other side, the Elephant Legions rampaged. He could imagine Commander Spitamendes' fury at his elite beasts. The Han fighters had fulfilled their part of the battle and were still causing mayhem amongst the Seleucids. *If they are wise, those Han will slip away from battle and head home.*

'You have done what no other man could, Achaeus,' Obodos said, placing a hand on his shoulder. 'You gave us hope that maybe we could halt the Seleucid onslaught. And for a time, with our cavalry causing havoc amongst their ranks and our Han friends disrupting their Elephant Legions, I too believed we would survive the day, but now I see all hope is lost. We will die today, and Antiochus will triumph.'

Achaeus wanted to say something, but he was too tired to speak.

'Jannaeus?' Obodos asked.

The Hasmonean King also wore a resigned look. 'I will join you in the fray, Obodos. Perhaps we will die at the same time, perhaps we will be spared, but let it be known that today the Arabs and Jews fought alongside one another against the western Seleucid aggressor and though we lost, we formed a friendship that will last through time.'

The two kings clasped hands before ordering their armour to be tightened. Men set about doing this as Achaeus panted heavily. Perhaps he had broken a rib: he was in pain and he found it difficult to stand straight. A skin of water was brought, and he drank from it greedily. He could feel the space in his mouth left by the two teeth he'd lost. He was already beginning to miss those teeth.

****

Moving swiftly from beast to beast, Chao evaded the Seleucid soldiers who sought him and his men. The commotion they caused amongst the elephants served to distract the entire regiment, who were taken out of the fighting, thus buying the Nabataean and Hasmonean forces some breathing space. He glanced back towards where the Arabs and Jews defended the hill upon which the kings stood and could see they were now heavily outnumbered. It would not be long now, till the Seleucid infantry snapped its jaws around the remaining defenders, extinguishing all resistance.

Whatever happened next, the Nabataeans and Hasmoneans had put up a respectable defence and were it not for the overwhelming numbers against them, would have succeeded, for their tactics disrupted the stronger army and removed its most lethal weapon, the Elephant Legion, from the face of battle. The Seleucid army might have started at fifty thousand, but it was less than a third of that now – the Seleucids had sustained heavy casualties, but their superior numbers were going to crush the remaining Nabataeans and Hasmoneans.

Is now the time to disappear from the battlefield? Chao asked himself. He remembered Zaim telling him very clearly: 'If the fighting turns against us and it is inevitable that we will lose, I do not want to see you and your men again. I want you to leave the battlefield and make it safely back to your lands. You must promise me this.' Now it looked like the moment had arrived.

Scanning the elephants stampeding around him, he spotted his four companions, who seemed to be enjoying themselves riding these magnificent beasts. He decided to hail them. As he was about to, something caught his eye on the horizon.

Out at sea, a new fleet of vessels had heaved into view. At least fifty by the looks of it; they filled the entire horizon and were drawing closer to shore. *Now we are definitely done for*, thought Chao. *If these are additional Seleucid reinforcements, each vessel will have three hundred soldiers on board, which will mean an army of fifteen thousand, fresh and ready for battle.*

He signalled to his men. With a heavy heart, he realised now was the time to leave.

****

Apollonia watched the chamberlains fasten the straps on the armour of the two kings who had collected up their weapons and were about to head down the slope to make the final stand with their bloody and beaten troops. She could not take her eyes off Zaim who fought with such grace, but he was one man, facing hundreds. Even with his skills he would not last much longer. Her heart was heavy with what might have been and the desert family she had almost been part of.

Soon she would be the captive of Emperor Antiochus and he would do with her as he pleased.

Then, as light-headedness was about to overwhelm her, she glanced out to sea and her mouth went completely dry. There were fifty new vessels on the horizon. As she watched them approach, she saw the Seleucid vessels which had been stationed with reinforcements, now leaving.

The Seleucids ships were leaving?

Wait! The new vessels, what flag do they fly?

Apollonia peered out to sea. At first she thought her eyes were deceiving her. Then she saw clearly the golden eagle standing on a thunderbolt.

The emblem of the Ptolemaic empire.

'Father has sent reinforcements!' Apollonia screamed.

Corrina rushed to her side, grabbing her arm.

'Look, Auntie,' Apollonia cried. 'It's our fleet, from Alexandria! Father got the message. He came!'

****

The sudden appearance of fifty vessels of the Ptolemaic empire, carrying what Emperor Antiochus estimated to be fifteen thousand soldiers, fresh and battle-hardened, had one effect on him.

He froze.

Antiochus was so close to victory he could smell it, yet the power of the Ptolemaic army could not be countered by the tired soldiers he had left on the battlefield.

As he watched, the Seleucid fleet departed. He realised that General Pharnuches, on board the lead vessel, must have ordered the retreat, for fear of being captured by Ptolemy. *Damn the General. I knew he could not be trusted on the battlefield, yet he even betrays me at sea.*

Antiochus then did the one thing he knew would save his life: he fled from the battle, turning north with a small group of *Hetairoi.*

Antiochus did not look back to see that his army had almost broken through the Nabataean and Hasmonean lines, nor that the kings of both armies were about to enter the fray. He only saw the road north, filled as he was with the desire to return to his southern capital, Damascus, a well-fortified city.

Yet if Ptolemy has come to Gaza, he may venture north to Damascus, thought Antiochus. *I will head straight for my heartlands and not rest till I reach Antioch. Surely Ptolemy will not take his army so deep into my territory.*

The emperor galloped away with a small cadre, his imperial tent and possessions left behind. *I will have Pharnuches beheaded. Let's see what Mother has to say about that.*

Chapter 38

FINAL CHOICES

———

Zaim was unaware of Antiochus' departure from the field, as were the Seleucids he was fighting, so the battle raged on, with more Falcons falling. Up on the hill, the Nabataeans and Hasmoneans could see the approaching Ptolemaic ships, so they joined the Falcons for a last stand against the Seleucids. It was only when a rumour spread across the battlefield that the emperor's standard was no longer present, that the silver shields and the *Hetairoi* began to look uncertainly around for instructions. The appearance of fifteen thousand Ptolemaic troops carrying their eagle and thunderbolt banners on the horizon finally put an end to the conflict. Some silver shields escaped, but the *Hetairoi* fought to the last man.

Zaim sank to his knees along with his closest Falcons, before Pelagios helped him away. Without their final efforts, the Seleucids would have broken through and massacred the royals assembled on the hill. The reinforcements from Ptolemy would have been too late.

Zaim now sat in an exhausted heap beside Achaeus, the older man looking worse for wear, as food and water were brought to them. Zaim watched the Ptolemaic forces massacre the remaining Seleucid soldiers.

Such terrible death and suffering. And for what? Spice and commerce, power and influence? These are not the things the Creator will ask about when I return to Him. Rather He will ask me about my character, my virtuous behaviour, my generosity particularly towards the poor, my clemency, especially for those with no support. How much of that did I achieve today? Yet if we had not fought, the Seleucids would have inflicted a worse future on our people and the Hasmoneans.

'Impressive army,' Achaeus said, his voice hoarse, as he pointed to the Ptolemaic soldiers, whose breastplates and greaves glittered, whose weapons were clean and sharp and whose mood was victorious. 'Twice have they defeated Antiochus. Yet I believe today will not be remembered as a day for Ptolemy but a day in which the Nabataean Arabs and the Hasmonean Jews faced down the might of the superior Seleucid army and came out alive.'

Zaim nodded, adding, 'With the aid of a Seleucid general, without whose tactics we would not have survived long enough to be saved by a Ptolemaic army.'

Achaeus shrugged, coughing, as he sipped from a water skin. 'I would rather this Seleucid general's name be left out of the stories told about today.'

Zaim looked across at him. 'For the victors, Achaeus, your name can never be forgotten. Your reputation will live long in our collective memory, and we will pray for you, for without your wise counsel, we would be corpses on the battlefield.'

Achaeus smiled. 'Oh, I would rather you remember the Han explorers, for they caused as much damage as anyone. Removing the entire elephant cavalry from deployment in battle is quite a feat. Where is Chao? I hope he made it.'

'Of that there is little doubt. We will honour the Han through tales of valour and their names will be remembered by generations to come.'

Down on the battlefield a lone glittering chariot made its way through the piles of dead bodies. On it was a rider in shining armour, and beside him a man wearing a crown over his helmet. His gold and silver armour caught the rays of the sun, as he made his way through the Ptolemaic men, who saluted him with enthusiasm.

'Emperor Ptolemy,' Achaeus said. 'I did not think I would see him again.'

'He is Apollonia's father,' Zaim said.

'Indeed, lad.'

'What sort of man is he?'

Leaning back against a rock, Achaeus replied. 'Like every emperor I have met, vain and full of himself. Yet, he does have a softer side which Antiochus does not, and his love of the good life makes him more amenable to discussion. But have no doubt, to be emperor and survive you must be implacable and when the need arises, ruthless. He is all those things as well.'

Zaim was not sure what he expected Apollonia's father to be like. *What are his intentions? With fifteen thousand soldiers in Gaza, does he come to conquer us, or to twist our arm to sign new treaties and offer him more favourable terms? What will he do?*

The emperor's chariot reached the foot of the hill, where King Obodos, King Alexander Jannaeus and King Pelagios awaited.

Ptolemy dismounted before greeting each King, starting with Obodos and ending with Pelagios, who guided him up the hill, Ptolemy's own royal guards close behind. At the crest, Zaim watched Apollonia emerge from the royal tent and run over to embrace her father, who held her tight, patting her on the head and comforting her. Corrina was a few paces behind and the emperor acknowledged her. Ptolemy said some words to his daughter, wiped tears from her eyes and ushered her back to the royal tent, before continuing with the other kings to the tent used as headquarters during the battle.

The emperor and the three kings disappeared through the flaps.

'I wonder what they will discuss?' Zaim asked.

'I'm too tired to even think about it,' Achaeus said, slumping into a supine position. 'Wake me when you know more.' Within moments the Seleucid legend was asleep.

Zaim tried to sit up, but the tiredness was overwhelming. He looked around him; he was surrounded by Falcons and his father's soldiers. He too decided to sleep.

****

Later in the day Apollonia sat with her father Emperor Ptolemy and described everything that had happened since she left Alexandria. For the most part he listened attentively. Ptolemy said he and her mother Cleopatra had missed her deeply, a fact of which she was unconvinced, and that her siblings asked about her regularly, which she could not believe, and told her that she should have written more regularly to them, which she had.

Having listened to his youngest daughter for some time, Ptolemy said, 'My child, if you wish to return to Alexandria, then we will set sail in two days and you can return with me. You are, after all, an emperor's daughter, and there are plenty of suitors for your hand in marriage. What do you say?'

I long to return to my home in Alexandria, to see the blue waters of the sea with my own eyes. This is my opportunity to do so and I will never have one like this again, thought Apollonia. *Yet, I must also be true to the voice of my heart.*

'I ...' Apollonia fell silent, unsure how to express her feelings.

Ptolemy, noticing the doubt on his daughter's face, said, 'I have also been informed by Obodos and Corrina, that you and Obodos' youngest son, Zaim, have feelings for one another. Is this so?'

'Oh,' Apollonia gasped, her cheeks flushing red.

'Well, is it?'

Sheepishly Apollonia nodded, her gaze lowered, adding. 'It is, Father.'

'Well then, if you could not marry Obodos' oldest son, then you will marry his youngest one.'

'I will? I can?'

'I am here for two days, so the wedding will be tomorrow. I have already asked Pelagios and Janneus to be witnesses and they have agreed.'

I am to wed Zaim tomorrow!

'Oh Father!' Apollonia leapt across and embraced him. 'Thank you!'

'Dear, dear child. You have had a harrowing time, and this is the least I can do, whilst I am here. Now, you must promise me, that once you are comfortably settled in your desert home, you will return to Alexandria with your husband and pay us a visit.'

'I will! Of course I will, Father.'

****

That evening, the day before the royal wedding, many cooking fires burned along the coast of Gaza. Merriment was made and stories told, songs sung and dances performed. Around one such anonymous fire sat four men, the youngest, Zaim, stirring a pot of lamb stew, before serving it to his companions. The steamy broth was eaten with much relish by Zaim's companions, Pelagios, Achaeus and Chao Zhang.

The Nabataean prince felt both excited and nervous. The thrill of battle had ebbed slowly and tiredness weighed heavy on his limbs, but the anticipation of marrying Apollonia the next day filled him with zestful enthusiasm.

The four companions sipped the broth silently, staring into the fire, each lost in his thoughts, before the silence was broken.

'I am pleased for you, Zaim,' said Pelagios. 'Now you will be the son-in-law of an emperor but don't expect me to be calling you "your Highness".'

'Not at all, Uncle.'

'And "uncle" was for just when it's the two of us. In front of others,' motioning to Achaeus and Chao, 'it makes me sound old.'

The four men chuckled.

'Though I feel it too, Pelagios. We are getting old,' said Achaeus. 'You at least have your family to return to.'

Pelagios was thoughtful for a moment, before saying. 'Come with me to the Aegean. Cassandra and I will find you a good woman, a homemaker, who will settle your heart and restless spirit, Achaeus. Settle down, build a home, farm a field, have children, they will be a coolness to your eyes.'

The Seleucid warrior let out a deep breath. 'Though it is an enticing thought, King Pelagios, there is a matter I must take care of before I consider settling down for good.'

'What can be so important as your happiness? You are a legend, Achaeus, even before today. Surely there is nothing else you can achieve with your heroic deeds that you have not done already? Put your feet up and let the younger lads here take some of the strain,' Pelagios waved towards Zaim.

Achaeus smiled. 'Soon, but not just yet.' The Seleucid turned towards Chao Zhang. 'What of your plans, Lord Chao?'

'We have completed our mission to the Middle Sea. We will stay in these lands for a few weeks longer, exploring and documenting, before heading back east.'

'And what happens when you return home, General?' Pelagios asked, winking at Zaim.

'I will take your advice, King Pelagios, I will find a good wife, build a home, farm a field, have children,' Chao said, to the men's laughter.

'See, Achaeus?' Pelagios said. 'Lord Chao here has his priorities right.'

'Indeed he does,' Achaeus said.

'There, I rest my case,' Pelagios declared.

Achaeus turned towards the Han explorer. 'Lord Chao, I can show you much of the country you wish to see, but I do have one request. I have something I need to take care of and I need some men, trusted men such as yourself who can move silently like shadows and disappear before they are detected. Will you help me with this task?'

'We will,' Chao replied.

'*Then* will you come to the Aegean for me to settle you down with a good wife?' Pelagios asked.

'I may do,' Achaeus replied with a wry smile.

Chapter 39

DRAGON ENTERS THE FALCON

———

Avoiding Damascus, Emperor Antiochus headed straight to the seat of his power, Antioch. In his opinion there was no chance Ptolemy would bring his forces so far north. Travelling by day and resting at night, the emperor and a group of twelve *hetairoi* travelled discreetly under the guise of a nobleman and his retinue.

Four days had passed since the battle and Antiochus still cursed his bad luck. He had been so close to defeating the Nabataean and Hasmonean forces, *so* close, yet they had prevailed, and it was he who suffered loss and humiliation.

Who can I blame this defeat on, was the thought clouding his mind. *In the absence of my senior generals, I was the commander, yet it will do me no good to take responsibility for what happened. I will have to pin it onto one of the younger officers in the official account of the battle.*

Antiochus dismounted from his horse, throwing the reins to one of the *hetairoi* before marching towards the inn where his men had arranged accommodation for the evening. *Filthy places, these inns – you don't know who has stayed in the rooms, and no matter how many times you ask these innkeepers to ensure the rooms are spotless, there is always some grime left by previous guests.*

Antiochus strode through the main door, avoided the hall where other guests sat and made his way up the stairs.

Two *hetairoi* stood guard outside his room. He knew the other men were stationed at key points around the inn. He was perfectly safe, but still had a nagging concern at the back of his mind. In fact, it had been plaguing him ever since he went to see the Oracle on Falika

Island. The old hag predicted many things, but it was the one about him being undone by the *Falcon* and a *Dragon* that still rankled. The Nabataean unit under Prince Zaim was called the Falcons, so that must have been related to him, but they had not caused his death, so the Oracle was only partly right.

Entering his room, he threw off his riding cloak and went to the clean bowl of water on a stand, where he washed his face and dried it. He collapsed into a chair by a window, which looked out onto an ordinary square in this mediocre town where no one important lived, where nothing important would ever happen. His empire was full of such nondescript places and people, all living out their miserable little lives with no purpose. Bah! *I am the Emperor of the Seleucid realm, I command armies and wield power – why am I running in such a manner?*

Then he remembered the recent battle and sank deeper into the chair, a melancholic mood having taken hold of him.

****

It had taken Achaeus and the Han explorers a day to trace and follow the imperial trail, gaining ground as they did. Emperor Antiochus had not covered his tracks as he fled the battle. Achaeus soon learned that Antiochus was travelling as a wealthy nobleman with his retinue. Once picked up, the scent was easy to follow and told Achaeus that Antiochus was heading for Antioch, not Damascus.

Good thing too, considered Achaeus, *as entering Damascus might have been a problem for me. My face is too well known there.*

Finally, Achaeus and the Han explorers caught up with Antiochus in an ordinary town, where it looked like nothing important ever happened. But Achaeus knew something very important was about to.

The *Hetairoi* stationed at the stable were the first to be knocked unconscious by Captain Zhu and Lieutenant Fu. Lord Chao took care of the royal companions outside the inn. As Achaeus was about to head towards the inn, he realised he had left his sword and scabbard on his horse.

'Take mine,' said Chao, drawing the Dragon Blade and handing it to him.

'So light,' said Achaeus, feeling the weapon's heft. He continued towards the inn.

Cartographer Ganfu and scribe Jin scaled the outside of the building and were soon in position on the upper floor where Antiochus' room lay.

Nothing remained but for Achaeus to walk through the front door of the inn, which he noted was called the *Falcon*.

Once inside, he paid the innkeeper a small bag of coins and made his way towards the stairs, keeping the Dragon Blade hidden within his riding robes. At the foot of the stairs there was a tired looking *Hetairoi* resting with his back to the wall. A swift pommel strike from his sword knocked the man out cold and Achaeus ascended the stairs. At the top he found two *Hetairoi* lying unconscious and noted Ganfu and Jin, both perched on a windowsill at the other end of the corridor. They nodded at him as he approached the room in which the emperor slept.

He knocked.

'How dare…? Who is it…?' he heard Antiochus say as he entered.

In the light of the candle, Achaeus saw Antiochus half-rise from a chair by the window. He saw Antiochus' face shrivel in horror.

'Achaeus!' Antiochus whispered harshly, scrambling for his weapon.

Achaeus kicked the sword and sheath away, drawing his own sword and placing it against Antiochus' chest. The emperor was pushed back into the chair, trying to escape the point of the blade.

'General,' Antiochus said more formally, his eyes darting towards the corridor.

'Don't worry, all your precious *Hetairoi* will be sleeping till morning, when they'll wake with a terrible headache. At least in their case they *will* wake, which cannot be said for you.'

'You … you dare to …'

'Yes,' Achaeus hissed.

It was then Achaeus saw Antiochus staring intently at the emblem on the sword.

'It's a dragon!' Antiochus voice trembled with realisation.

'Yes, it belongs to a friend of mine.'

Antiochus gulped, sweat forming in beads upon his brow. 'What is the name of this inn?' he asked, his voice trembling.

'The *Falcon*,' Achaeus said, recalling the sign on the door.

'*Beware the day the Dragon enters the Falcon ...*' whispered Antiochus.

'What?' Achaeus asked.

Regaining some composure, Antiochus beseeched him, 'Achaeus, General, legend of the Seleucid empire, I have done so much for you. There must be a misunderstanding. I am sure we can clear this up.'

'No misunderstanding, not from the moment you sent me to Alexandria to take the blame for your mistakes, to the day you sent assassins to slay me on the *Chloe*, or in Gaza, or ...' Achaeus swallowed hard before continuing, 'when you ordered the execution of all my family and relatives.'

He threw the letter which King Pelagios had given him before the battle in Antiochus' face.

Antiochus' eyes widened. He knew now that he was not going to be able to talk his way out of this situation.

'It is your seal and signature ordering the deaths of my entire family.'

'I ..."' Antiochus stuttered.

Achaeus observed Antiochus' right-hand edge towards the knife on his belt.

'I can explain ...' Antiochus was saying as Achaeus pushed the tip of the Dragon Blade into the emperor's chest, puncturing his heart. Antiochus' body spasmed, blood coating his tunic as a trickle of blood fell from his mouth. His eyes were open but lifeless.

Achaeus withdrew the Dragon Blade, wiping it against the emperor's clothes, then sheathed the weapon, before heading out of the *Falcon*.

Joining Chao Zhang outside, he returned the sword. 'That's a fine weapon, Lord Chao,' he said.

'Forged in the imperial city of Chang'an. Best steel in the world.'

'Really? So where can I get a blade like that?' Achaeus asked.

'There is only one place,' Chao said, as they rejoined the others and mounted their steeds.

'Only one place, this Chang'an, you say?'

Chao Zhang nodded.

'I think' mulled Achaeus. 'I need to get a good weapon, before I get a good wife.'

Chao smiled and the Han explorers, accompanied by a Seleucid legend, headed east.

EPILOGUE

Returning home to Mithymna was a welcome relief for Pelagios, King of the Aegean Island. His men disembarked eagerly, making their way to their homes and families. The *Chloe* docked in a private harbour, away from the port used by visitors and other vessels. From this point the walk home to his modest palace was a short one.

Usually, the route was filled with conversation, his subjects approaching him and eager to hear his stories of the east, his adventures on the high seas and the commercial benefits brought by his travels to their small kingdom. Surprisingly, today few conversations took place and those that did were with subjects who appeared guarded and unsure.

An unusual welcome thought Pelagios. *Perhaps I have been gone too long and they have forgotten their king.*

Shaking off the uncomfortable feeling, he trekked up the hill to his home, from where he had a panoramic view of the island. As he drew closer, he saw his beautiful wife, Cassandra, on the porch. She waved and came out to embrace him. She held him tight, but there was something unusual. As though she were frightened.

'What is the matter, my love?' Pelagios whispered into her ear.

'The Romans are here,' Cassandra whispered back, tightening her grip even more.

'Hush!' Pelagios whispered. 'It will be fine. I will speak with them. Where are they?'

Cassandra pulled away from him and motioned with her eyes that they were in their house.

'When did they arrive?'

'A few hours ago. They said they knew you were on your way

home. Why are they here, my love? What have we done to incur their wrath?'

Was it the Roman spy in Alexandria who called in the legions? If I see him again, I will slit his throat.

'The Romans do not need provocation. They serve Rome and her interests,' he said, taking her hand as they started to walk back towards their home.

'Where are the children?' Pelagios asked.

'When I saw the Romans coming up the hill, I sent them to the other side of the island with Jacintha, to the secret hiding place, and told her not to return until I sent word or came myself. Is this not what we said we'd do, if ever such a thing happened?'

'You did the right thing, my love,' Pelagios said.

The couple entered their home, coming through the corridor into the inner courtyard, where a heavyset Roman official sat in one of their chairs. To either side of the courtyard were a pair of Roman legionnaires, fully armed. *They have more soldiers nearby, probably on ships in the main port, waiting to disembark, depending on how this conversation goes*, thought Pelagios.

'Pelagios, King,' the Roman stood, holding out his hand.

Pelagios shook it, then turned to his wife. 'Cassandra, can you please give us some time alone?'

'What we speak about are not pleasant matters, why trouble the hearts of women with politics, eh,' said the Roman, once Cassandra had left.

'You are?' Pelagios asked.

'Lucius Caesar, Consul.'

They have sent a statesman, perhaps that's a good sign. They could have sent a military dictator who would have torched the island by now. Perhaps they simply want to talk.

'Welcome,' Pelagios said. 'May I get you anything?'

'No, not at all. You have only just returned from your travels in the east, and I am already rested. Please let us sit and we can talk. We have much to discuss.'

Wincing at the suggestion, Pelagios took a seat opposite the consul.

'Let me be direct, as I do not want to keep you long from your dear wife, and two children, though I do not see them anywhere. Pelagios, you have been quite a busy fellow these past few months, visiting many places Rome has interests in. As you know we are developing an eastern strategy, one to combat Ptolemy and the Seleucids, as well as neutralise the Nabataeans and Hasmoneans. I think you have a lot to share with us.'

Lucius Caesar smiled, sitting back in his chair. 'Shall we begin?'

And Pelagios thought, not for the first time: *Damn bloody Romans!*

****

Apollonia shut the gate to the royal tomb which held Luja's body. She and Zaim, now husband and wife, trekked hand in hand back down Jabal Umm al-'Amr. Winter was cold in Petra and she wore a fur-lined cloak and a hood to keep the biting wind from her neck and ears. Some goats grazing on the mountain bleated as the couple walked by.

They rejoined the thoroughfare by the theatre, which was bustling with people who greeted the royal couple as they walked past. Apollonia still marvelled at the way these desert dwellers had used these mountains as a base, against which they built their homes, which stood in front of the mountains, in some cases two and three storeys high. Walking through Petra took some time because of the constant interruptions from well-wishers and requests from the poor.

Her husband never refused a person asking for money or help. He always gave them something and when he had nothing material, he would offer them a smile and promise he would have something for them the following day. His generosity was infectious, and she now found herself adopting the same approach. They passed the place where the entrance to the royal palace began and she spotted her Javairea, sitting by the gate, looking out at the passers-by. *We are both of the desert now, Javairea,* thought Apollonia.

Before they reached the spot where the ascent started, leading to the great temple, Zaim stopped her.

'There is something I must tell you, Apollonia,' he said, his voice reflective and solemn.

'What is it, my dear?'

'The Nabataean gods are not God. What I mean is that they are not *the* God worshipped by Nabjot, father of the Nabataeans.'

'They are not?' she asked.

'Once in the desert I met a religious mendicant who told me that Nabjot was the second son of Ishmael, who in turn was the son of Abraham.'

'I have heard of Abraham,' Apollonia said.

'This spiritual wayfarer enlightened me about the God of Abraham. He said that whatever you can imagine Him to be, He is not, yet He is immanent and transcendent, close and far. This God is everywhere, he said, at all times and is involved in the affairs of the world and when His people call upon Him, He listens to their prayers.'

Apollonia listened attentively. 'Whatever I can imagine Him to be He is not. Then the idols in the Temple …?'

'Precisely, they are not God nor do they deserve our worship. Today, I will take you to a place where we can sit together and worship the God of Abraham.'

He took her by the hand and together they walked towards the southern defence wall and beyond it into the open desert. Eventually they stopped. Apollonia watched him closely.

Staring out at the horizon Zaim said: 'Everything that exists, this desert, the falcon that flies over it, the date palm, you and I, all manifest the divine names of God but in different degrees of preference.' He placed her hand on his heart and looking deeply into her eyes said: 'Yet it is only the human heart when it is in a state of obedience to God and in the presence of his divine Majesty that has the capacity to manifest all His attributes. And that is how we get closer to God, that is how we know Him.'

She smiled, leaning into him so her head was placed on his chest and his arms wrapped her in a soothing embrace. *I know,* and it dawned on her that she always knew.

HISTORICAL NOTE

There is some artistic license I have taken to recorded history for the purposes of writing *Tomb of Empires*. Firstly, the Nabataeans rarely lived within the walls of Petra. They were a nomadic people and visited Petra when there was something specific to do, such as a burial, or a festivity. I took the liberty of organising a royal wedding in Petra for the purposes of the story.

Secondly, the Han Chinese had been exploring the lands to the west of their sphere of influence. Most famously the well-known explorer Zhang Qian visited the Yuezhi people around 138 BC, who lived in lands in what is today Tajikistan and Afghanistan. There is no documentary evidence that his grandson visited the Mediterranean, or the lands of the Arabs, so that part of the novel involving Zhang Chao's mission to the Middle Sea is entirely fictionalised.

Finally, the plot line involving the Seleucids wanting to seize the Nabataean's spice routes up from Aden and Mocha is a construction for the purposes of the novel. Though, of course both the Seleucid Empire and the Nabataeans Kingdom did famously go to war in 312 BC when the Seleucids attacked Petra. The loot they took from the city was so great that their return north was slowed down, allowing the Nabataeans to launch a counter offensive and reclaim the treasures taken by the Seleucids. The Nabataean Kingdom was finally annexed by the Romans around 106 AD when they also brought troops down to Petra.

Rehan Khan
www.rehankhan.com

ACKNOWLEDGEMENTS

Having written three novels set in the Ottoman Empire and Tudor England in the sixteenth century, I was challenged by a friend who said you have lived in the Middle East for two decades, why don't you write a novel about this region. For that comment, I will be eternally grateful to Fadi Ismail, without whom I don't think I would have written *Tomb of Empires*.

One of the most exciting aspects of being a historical fiction novelist is that you can visit many of the sites your story takes place in. Fortunately, for this novel, thanks to my son Yusuf, who was studying Arabic in Jordan at the time, I got to visit Petra, as well as Bozrah and Sela, both important Nabataean sites. Bozrah and Sela today are mere ruins, and our driver asked us a couple of times why we wanted to visit them – according to him there was nothing to see. He was pleasantly surprised when we got there, as were we all.

Thanks once again to my wonderful editor, Lorna Fergusson, who I always learn so much from. Her deft touch improves every manuscript. For the beautifully drawn map I would like to thank the talented illustrator Asya Leztizia, as well as Peter Gould for introducing me to her. Special thanks to Fatima Mejbil for the amazing cover design which I feel really captures the tone of the characters. I am really thrilled that my publishers Sadia Anwar and Mehnaz Anshah at Uhibbook have shown so much enthusiasm for this novel and have provided me the opportunity to work with them. A deep heartfelt thanks goes out to them, as well as all the team at Uhibbook.

For helping me better understand Han Chinese history and culture I would like to thank Dr Shaojin Chai, and for helping me with

Chinese naming conventions I am indebted to Xiang Cheow. For providing me with scholarly insight of the Nabataean civilisation I would like to thank Dr Umar Faruq Abd-Allah.

My mother, Shahida, has always been a huge enthusiast of history and a special thanks to the dynamic energy she provided as we toured obscure ruins on remote Jordanian plateaus and mountainsides. Finally, as always, a special thanks to my wife, Faiza and our two children Yusuf and Imaan.

Rehan Khan has always been intrigued by the way in which legends and chronicles from all over the world have the power to cross time and space to delight and unite us centuries later – whoever and wherever we may be. A lover of history, he has read extensively about past civilisations and the role virtue has played in the lives of people. His exciting descriptions of swordplay, weaponry and close combat in battle are the result of these studies, although in real life, Rehan prefers to wield a tennis racquet rather than a scimitar.

When not writing, Rehan helps executives improve their focus, and teaches management topics. Born and educated in London, he now lives in Dubai with his family.

Website: www.rehankhan.com

You can follow Rehan on social feeds: @rehankhanauthor

By the same author

Fiction:

Last of the Tasburai (2014)

Scream of the Tasburai (2016)

Legends of the Tasburai (2021)

A Tudor Turk (2019)

A King's Armour (2020)

A Demon's Touch (2022)

Non-Fiction:

Distracting Ourselves to Death (2021)